Praise for the novels of T. R. Hendricks

"A brilliant debut by an author who obviously knows his stuff! Derek Harrington is a terrific new hero, a former Marine and wilderness survival expert who finds himself in a battle of wits against both a determined enemy and nature itself. Packed with action, tension, and humanity, *The Instructor* delivers."

—Mark Greaney, #1 *New York Times* bestselling author of *Burner,* a Gray Man novel, on *The Instructor*

"*The Instructor* is an unexpected pleasure, crackling with intensity, vivid with authenticity and emotion. T. R. Hendricks writes like a knife fight on a moonless night—fast, brutal, and bloody."

—Nick Petrie, bestselling author of *The Breaker* and other Peter Ash novels

"Gritty, timely, and packed with action, *The Instructor* is a pulse-pounding thriller and a fabulous start to the Derek Harrington series. T. R. Hendricks delivers on all cylinders!"

—Simon Gervais, former RCMP counterterrorism officer and bestselling author of *The Last Protector*

"Thrumming with action and authenticity, Hendricks knocks it out of the park with his debut. *The Instructor* is not to be missed!"

—Connor Sullivan, author of *Sleeping Bear*

THE DEREK HARRINGTON SERIES

The Instructor

The Infiltrator

THE
INSTRUCTOR

T. R. HENDRICKS

Tor Publishing Group
New York

This is a work of fiction. All of the characters, organizations, and events portrayed in this novel are either products of the author's imagination or are used fictitiously.

THE INSTRUCTOR

A Forge Book
Published by Tom Doherty Associates/Tor Publishing Group
120 Broadway
New York, NY 10271

www.tor-forge.com

Forge® is a registered trademark of Macmillan Publishing Group, LLC.

ISBN 978-1-250-83296-2

Our books may be purchased in bulk for promotional, educational, or business use. Please contact your local bookseller or the Macmillan Corporate and Premium Sales Department at 1-800-221-7945, extension 5442, or by email at MacmillanSpecialMarkets@macmillan.com.

First Edition: April 2023
First Mass Market Edition: February 2024

Printed in the United States of America

8 7 6 5 4 3 2 1

FOR DAD
My Hero
Semper Fidelis

THE INSTRUCTOR

1

Everything capable of combustion has an ignition point.

The key to survival is knowing when and how to produce that flame, and then, once it's burning, to keep it fed. Even if a fire dwindles down to a few embers, it can always be revived. A single glowing coal can be stoked into a raging inferno.

Derek drills this into his students as much as he does the other survival mantras. The rule of threes. The four priorities. He doesn't like parsing the first three priorities out. They're all critically important. Without shelter, you freeze, but the same can be said for fire. What good is water if you can't boil it? You'll either die of thirst by not finding it or giardiasis if you do nothing to remove the parasites. Three weeks is a hell of a long time in the survival world, and you can go without food for most of that stretch. Without the others, you're in deep shit in short order.

His latest class stands in a loose semicircle around him as he crouches and demonstrates the proper construction of a tinder bundle. They're the typical weekend mix. Three guys on a bachelor party. A couple of people on a corporate team-building outing. Two seasoned hikers preparing for a multimonth trek across the Appalachian Trail. Another small group of overzealous, doomsday-prepper types.

"So you have to be able to identify the different types of trees and from them select a medium wood." As he lectures, Derek rubs a piece carved from a nearby cedar between two rocks, grating the material down. "Hardwoods like oak will take too long to ignite. You'll burn through calories that can be better spent elsewhere. Softwoods like pine might seem like a good option, but they're not. True, the sap is flammable, but the wood itself is so resinous and full of moisture that it'll take you forever to get a flame to catch."

He takes the piece of wood from between the rocks and holds it up. It resembles a cotton ball that has been stretched thin. "So medium woods are the perfect balance. Cedar trees. Weeping willows. Those are the ones you go for. Then you work it over mechanically until you get it processed to this point. You want it nice and fluffy."

"Light enough to wipe your ass with, I reckon!" This comes from Gil, a gangly hayseed with a mess of blond hair. Since arriving at the class, he hasn't shut up. The others give him a look. No shortage of eye rolls. Gil doesn't seem to notice.

Derek plays it off. "Yeah . . . well, whatever helps you remember." He adds the newly processed tinder to a larger bundle of dried leaves, grass, and shredded bark formed like a bird's nest. He walks the class through the rest of the operation. With a single stroke of his ferro rod, a shower of sparks lands on the cedar tinder, and slowly, the bundle ignites. He places it under a tepee of kindling he had prearranged and, when the flames catch, adds larger pieces of fuel.

With his fire going, the demonstration is complete. Derek breaks out the groups to begin practicing their own bundles. They all work in unison to exclude Gil, so Derek teams up with the redneck. He bites the inside of his mouth as he watches the man floundering the process Derek just painstakingly walked them through, much in the same way he had the night before when Gil was constructing his hasty lean-to shelter. The man was more concerned with chatting than he was getting the skills right.

"And then I told that fat bitch—"

"Wait. Gil. I thought you were just talking about your wife."

The man turns to look at Derek and furrows his eyebrows. "I was. Guess I left that detail out, eh, D?"

Derek grinds his teeth. The degradation of the woman aside for a moment, he isn't sure when he started letting this country bumpkin call him "D." Sheer necessity forces the modicum of customer service he had developed to tolerate the abbreviation. The disparaging remark, however, was putting Gil on thin ice, prepaid or not.

"Yeah, my old lady is a real pig. Fuckin' two sixty that bitch is pulling down. Easy." The man cackles with a laugh as he turns back to his bundle.

One of the women with the corporate group clicks her tongue while another's mouth drops open. Several of the students look over at Derek. He raises his hand and gives a small nod. They turn back to their bundles with shakes of their heads.

It comes upon him so quickly that for a moment

Derek has trouble wrestling it under control. His teeth clench while a muscle throbs in his jaw. His pulse quickens, his heart thundering in his chest. Derek exhales forcefully out of his nostrils. He feels his limbs tingling with the onset of a fight-or-flight blood rush.

With effort, he tamps the anger down, slowly unclenching his fists. What remains is a simmering undertone of tension. It was bad enough that after twenty-two years of service he had to scratch a living this way. A military pension only went so far, especially with circumstances being what they were. To look a man in the face and smile while his ignorance threatens the bread crumbs Derek is bringing in is more than enough to set him off.

Thankfully, logic takes over. Logic, and the guidance of his counselor at the VA clinic, her words echoing through his mind. *Deep breaths. Remain grounded.* As bad as Gil might be for business, it would be far worse if Derek broke his nose. He can't allow the anger that comes with his PTSD to dictate his actions. Still, Derek sighs. In another time and place, he would have called Gil into his office for some wall-to-wall counseling.

But this isn't the infantry anymore, and while banter like this was common in the barracks, civilian life is something else entirely, and Derek is always just one bad online review from going out of business, something that absolutely cannot happen. That said, he can't let the remarks go without some sort of redress. Derek squats down on his haunches and lowers his voice so only Gil can hear. "Hey, partner, I know you're having fun and all, but let's keep that kind of language quiet for the rest of the weekend."

Gil turns his head from his bundle, a broad smile

on his face until he sees the look on Derek's. The grin vanishes as the man's eyebrows arch up. His Adam's apple gives a bob as he swallows. "You serious, aintcha, D?"

Derek affirms with a nod. "Dead. You're not the only one in this class, and I won't tolerate you ruining it for the others. You speak out like that again and I'm going to have to ask you to leave."

Staring at Derek for a moment, Gil breaks out into another wide smile. "Shit, no problem, boss. Won't hear nothin' like that no more from me." As he finishes speaking, Gil slaps at his ferro rod repeatedly.

"Whoa, whoa. Ease up, Gil. I told you. You're not peeling a carrot here. One deliberate strike is all it should take."

"Oh yeah. You did. Right." The man makes an exaggerated swipe. As his striker comes off the rod, his right hand flies forward, knocking over his tepee of kindling.

"Easy, Gil. Remember, slow is smooth. Smooth is fast. Your striker hand should be stationary over the tinder bundle. Pull your rod across the striker toward you, so you're moving it away from the tepee and avoiding what you just did."

"I got it, boss, I got it." Gil sets up his kindling again and immediately goes back to striking his ferro rod as fast as he can.

Derek stands up. "Keep at it. I gotta check on the others." He doesn't wait for a reply. Not getting the material is one thing. He never expects people to master this stuff in a weekend. It is his basic class, after all. Some of these guys come out and he can tell they've never roughed it a day in their lives. Nothing but picking up the phone for whatever they need, whether it be takeout or a plumber.

Disregarding everything he teaches. Not listening to a word he'd just said. That's another thing altogether. It angers him to no end, but Derek can't afford to tear into any of his students. If he laid into every attendee who pissed him off, he'd be screaming from dawn to dusk.

Instead, he steps a few feet away, closes his eyes, and lifts his head to the sky. A light breeze rattles some of the branches above the group. Remembering one of the recent discussions with his counselor, Derek takes a deep, cleansing breath. The scent of the fresh pine lifts to his nose. The remnant of the early-morning rain that hit their camp. The richness of the soil.

Ignoring the chatter of his students, he listens to the symphony of the songbirds and buzzing insects. Beyond that, silence. The constant buzz of the Long Island parkways is notably absent in this place.

Derek revels in it. No matter how insane life can get, nature is his sanctuary. His redeemer. The one place he can be himself and forget everything that has happened. That is happening. That will happen. The dread of all that is waiting for him back home. In this place, he can just . . . be. No one, not even this rube, can take that from him.

The tract of land Derek conducts his classes on is just north of the city and belongs to his father, a future investment for the retirement cabin he had planned on building. His father was the latest in a long line of Harringtons that fell short of the family dream. The way Derek's postmilitary life is turning out, he won't be achieving the dream either.

He takes the class through the rest of Saturday,

showing them some basic snares for trapping, and then has them improve their shelters before nightfall. The attendees boil stream water on their newly made fires while Derek passes out rations of beef jerky for dinner. Another point driving the survival process home. You're not going to be comfortable. Or full. This is about staying alive. Nothing more.

In the morning, before they hike back out, Derek gives them a quick lesson from his advanced class. He shows them primitive fire-making techniques using the hand drill and bow drill. The difference between a shower of sparks from a rod and nurturing a single ember into a flame isn't lost on the group. Even the hikers have trouble with it, but after a few hours and his help, everyone has fires going.

Everyone except Gil.

The man is a shit show. First, he builds his bundle wrong, putting hunks of pine so thick and resinous that they'll never catch. He doesn't work the hand drill consistently. The bow drill too slowly. When Derek finally gets an ember into a corrected tinder bundle for him, the yokel blows on it like he's trying to put out forty birthday candles. The coal instantly winks out of existence.

It takes three more tries before Derek can get the man to blow gently enough to get his tinder smoking. Gil turns his face to take another breath but fails to keep his hands moving in a figure eight pattern, threatening to extinguish the ember from lack of air. Derek pops in and moves the man's arms for him. When Gil breathes back into the bundle, even more smoke pours out. The redneck somehow manages to suck it in like a bong hit and immediately doubles over coughing and choking.

"All right, everyone," says Derek as he stands, stamping out the smoky bundle. "That'll do it for this class. Let's put out the fires and break camp. I want to get you all back to your vehicles in time."

As the group hits the trail, Gil lingers behind, still coughing. Derek grabs the man's rucksack. If he doesn't take it now, the entire group will lose ground, and he has to get them back in time. He spares a moment to glance at his watch again—12:15. Forty-five minutes to his promised 1:00 p.m. conclusion. If he can gain some ground, they should still make it.

The redneck drones on and on about God knows what as they fall farther behind the rest of the group. "One hour, baby. One hour to go. Then it's some pushin' on that hog tonight! Know what I'm sayin', D? You know it, baby! Balls-deep!"

He throws a sideways glance.

Gil catches the look and shrugs. "What? Come on, D! Ain't no one back here but us. They can't hear me. Besides, can't kick me out when the class is over, amirite?"

Derek focuses on tuning him out, especially since he has to haul the man's bag. Readjusting the shoulder straps, he hefts the ruck onto his upper back and tightens them down without breaking stride. The bag has to weigh forty-five, maybe even fifty pounds. Add to that the ten pounds that he carries in his own bag, now tied to the top of the other man's pack.

Who knows how much crap this rube packed? Ninety percent of it is probably unnecessary. The whole point of Derek's class is to learn how to survive without all this gear. Hauling it the last three days defeated the purpose of what the guy signed up for, but hey, Derek wasn't about to tell a paying customer he couldn't bring what he wanted. Of course, now he wishes he had. He makes a mental note to update his website with some guidelines on packing before his next class.

When it becomes clear that Gil can't move any faster than a straggle, Derek asks the two hikers to take the rest of the class ahead. Ninety minutes later, he and the hayseed trudge into the clearing where they left their cars on Friday evening. The rest of the group already has their gear off and stowed in their vehicles. The hikers and corporates talk quietly with one another. The bachelor party laughs and passes a bottle of scotch between them. The preppers congratulate themselves for "accomplishing" the weekend. Derek drops the man's ruck and quickly undoes the straps to free his own bag. Gil collapses to the ground next to his backpack while trying to catch his breath.

Small victories. In the last half mile, Derek had picked up the pace on him, forcing the man's cardio to the point that Gil couldn't talk if he wanted to keep up. That, at least, saved Derek from the inane babbling. He pulls the front of his sweat-soaked shirt free from clinging to his chest, mops his face with one hand, and adjusts his ball cap. Ignoring the gasps for air behind him, Derek steps into the center of the clearing.

"Hey, folks, if we can gather around one last time," he announces to the group.

The participants make their way over and form a semicircle in front of him. Derek starts his conclusion speech even though Gil is still sitting down and hasn't joined the rest of them.

"I want to thank you all again for coming out this weekend. You've made remarkable progress in just a

few days. Normally, I like to get back here a little earlier so that we can do a final review and some Q and
A, but unfortunately, we didn't make the best time
today. Which is okay. It happens sometimes. Still, I
know a bunch of you had a hard out of one o'clock,
so I don't want to hold you any longer. At the same
time, I don't want to rob you of the final class, so for
the next week, if you have any questions or want to
do any reviews of the things we covered, feel free to
shoot me an email or give me a call. No extra charge."

The preppers and corporates nod appreciatively
while the hikers throw a grimace Gil's way.

"Just remember your priorities," Derek continues.

"Shelter, water, fire, food," the group responds in
unison, echoing the mantra a final time. Their collective tone is filled with monotonous exacerbation.

Derek smiles. "Right. You guys got it. But above all
else, the number one priority is a positive attitude. No
matter the problem. No matter the challenge, keep
hold of that and you'll make it out alive. Thanks
again for coming. Make sure you tell your friends
and family. If they mention that you referred them, I'll
give them a ten percent discount."

The group smiles and breaks up. Derek shakes
hands with the corporates, who then quickly retreat
to their vehicles to make their way back to NYC. He
circles back to Gil, who at this point is at least on his
feet and hunched over with his hands on his knees.

Derek places a hand on his back, and the man looks
up. "You feel all right, Gil? You're not light-headed
or anything, are you?"

Sweat pours down Gil's face into his blond mustache and goatee. "Nah. Just ain't walked so far so
fast in a bit. I'll be fine in a minute."

Derek nods. "Okay. You gonna be all right to drive back upstate? I don't want to hear about you passing out behind the wheel and ending up in a ditch on the news tonight."

Gil smiles in return. "Fit as a fiddle. Yes, sir," the man replies and then immediately begins coughing.

"All right, then. Be safe. Thanks for coming." Derek pats him on the back one more time and walks off. He shakes his head as he approaches the rest of his attendees. Saying his final goodbyes, Derek watches as the cliques get in their respective vehicles. He spins and makes his way back to his pickup, noting the familiar rust around the wheel wells.

Really need to do something about that. Maybe after the next class. As he gets closer, Derek sees Gil approaching from the corner of his eye. Quickening his pace, he throws his bag into the bed and opens the door to the cab.

"Hey, D! D!" Gil yells after him.

Derek sighs. Silently setting a goal to end the conversation as quickly as possible, he turns. Gil ambles over the rest of the way. Despite Derek's waiting, the hayseed makes no effort to close the distance any faster. The thin ice is about to crack.

When Gil is within a few feet, he starts speaking in his slow drawl. "I just wanted to apologize for slowin' you down back there."

Derek flashes him a smile and waves him off. "No worries, Gil. We didn't get back too late. It happens. Take care now."

"No, no. I mean it. I feel terrible that you didn't get to do your final class on account of me."

Behind Gil, the last car drives out of the clearing. The bachelor party honks and waves as they speed away. Derek waves back, smiling at the thought of whatever strip club they're about to frequent. They had privately shared the plans for their anticipated "stink and drink" with him over the weekend, bringing back memories of him and his buddies spending their paychecks as young, single, and stupid Marines.

Gil watches the car as it goes farther down the gravel path, still talking but eyes fixated on the vehicle. "You see, I ain't never had to do something like this before. Heck, I guess you can say I was a little in over my head. That damn Bear Grylls makes it look so easy and all, and I . . ." The car disappears from sight as he trails off. "All right. Enough horseshit."

Derek snaps his head back to Gil. The last four words came out as if spoken by a completely different person. The drawl vanished. The statement was sharp and exacting. Even as he looks the man over, Derek can see Gil change. His posture goes from stooped to standing erect. His gangly frame now seems to ripple with wiry strength. The man's features tighten from a slack-jawed idiot to someone with a hardened disposition. Gil's eyes alight with a fiery intelligence that hadn't been present the last three days.

It's enough to set off internal alarms.

2

erek takes the smallest of side steps, a nonchalant move in perception that accomplishes getting him away from the open cab of his truck, lest Gil should try to rush him. At the same time, he squares to the man and sets his feet. Derek thinks of the Stat-Gear survival knife on his belt and the Sig Sauer .40 caliber he keeps in the glove box. "I'm sorry? What was that, Gil?"

"I said we can stop playing around now." The voice is the same, clear of any country drawl and lethargy.

"Playing? Gil . . . what . . ."

The man shakes his head and waves a hand. "Don't get all worried, D. There's no cause for panic. Let me cut to the chase."

Derek squints and inclines his head. "Umm, all right, I guess."

Gil's lip twitches upward in the slightest of smirks. "I represent a certain . . . group. One that wishes to remain anonymous and is in the market for some advanced training. I came here to check you out, and after this weekend, I think you're the right man for the job."

Derek regards the man a moment. "What kind of advanced training are we talking about?"

"Nothing outside of what you did here, but we don't want the broad strokes. We need someone that can get into the details. Teach us true survival. Natural medicine. Wild edibles. Trapping. Primitive tools. Real off-the-grid skill sets, you know? And I need someone who can stick around and teach it until we've gotten it down pat. You game?"

Another pause. Derek eyes the man. It's not the first time he's been asked for specialized training from groups looking to remain hidden. Between all the TV shows about prepping and the zombie apocalypse, the way the country seemed ready to tear itself apart—hell, the state of the world in general—there was no shortage of survival extremists out there. Mostly, they were harmless. People who believed that the next civil war or world-ending event was right around the corner and they wanted to get a leg up on the competition for the ensuing aftermath. At the same time, they could barely run their normal day-to-day lives, much less have hope for defeating the undead in an atomic aftermath. Even with that reality, they were paying customers . . .

"I mean . . . I can teach all that, sure. That and some stuff you didn't mention. How long of a time frame are we talking here?"

"Two weeks minimum with the possibility for longer."

Derek sighs. "It'll be tough to schedule, but I might be able to arrange that with enough notice. When are you looking to do this?"

"We leave right now."

Derek laughs, shaking his head. "No way. I gotta get home, Gil. I've got other classes scheduled that I need to prep for. I'd have to cancel them. Issue refunds. Not to mention my other commitments." He turns and starts to get into the cab.

"Not even going to entertain the idea?" Gil asks.

"I couldn't even if I wanted to," Derek replies, turning the truck over. He goes to pull his door shut.

Gil grabs the frame and leans in. "Will ten grand change your mind?"

Derek freezes. The two men stare at each other. Derek searches his eyes for dishonesty and finds no trace of it. That doesn't mean he has to clue Gil in to that fact. "Horseshit. I don't know what kind of a charade you're trying to pull here, but if you think I'm gonna believe you've got ten grand to spend, you're crazy."

Gil frowns and takes a step back from the door. He digs into a cargo pocket and produces a plastic bag with a stack of bills in it. The man takes out the stack, pulls off a rubber band, and fans out the money. Benjamins. Every last one.

Derek looks at the money. Looks at the man. Looks back at the money. Even if he could guarantee a class every weekend, which he couldn't, it would take two and a half months to make that much money. Times were tough, and Derek had to keep lowering his rates just to attract customers. He cuts off the truck. "Other than the time frame, what's the catch?"

"No catch, D. Just what I told you. You come. You teach. You get paid. You go home. Simple."

Derek slides out of the cab. "This group I'd be teaching? Your group. You're not mixed up in something that's gonna get me thrown in jail, are you? Because I'm telling you right now, I sense even the slightest bit of impropriety, I'm gone. Not only am I gone, I'll expect to be paid full freight for my trouble."

Gil's smirk returns, a little wider than before. "No impropriety, D. Just a bunch of concerned citizens looking to safeguard their future. That's all. But we've got conditions too. The pay isn't just for the training, it's for your discretion as well. I wasn't kidding before about our anonymity. We're expecting that our identities and anything else you learn about us will remain confidential. Indefinitely."

"I can keep a secret."

"Yeah. Something about you tells me that you can. That's why I made the offer. You in?"

Derek rubs his beard. "Two weeks?"

Gil nods. "Starting tomorrow. It'll take us most of today to travel up."

A long pause passes between them. After a few moments, Gil smiles.

Derek gives in. "Let me make a call."

Gil steps back and gestures to the clearing. "Of course."

Derek walks out and thumbs open his home screen.

She picks up on the third ring. Her voice is stressed, like she's been running late for most of the day. It's also tinged with sadness. Nothing deep or even alarming. Just a sliver of it underneath the surface. A perpetual drip coming from a leaky faucet. "Hey. You on the road yet?"

"Hey. No. Not yet."

The rustling of grocery bags comes through the other end of the phone. "You'd better get a move on.

The game is in two hours. You don't want to be late. He's the starting pitcher today."

A twinge tightens the muscles in his stomach. Derek searches for the words, but they don't come. The rustling stops on the other end.

"Derek?"

"Yeah, I'm here, Kim. Listen, about today . . ." Dead silence greets his lead-in. He knows that she's steeling herself. Bracing for yet another disappointment. "I've got an opportunity developing here. Something pretty substantial, otherwise I wouldn't even entertain the idea, but it means taking the job now."

The silence lingers on. She sniffles into the receiver before speaking again. "Derek, he's been talking about having you there all week. You know how much this is going to hurt?"

Looking back over his shoulder, he sees Gil leaning against the tailgate of his truck, that same devious smirk locked on his face. Derek turns back and walks farther into the clearing, lowering his voice at the same time. "You know that's the last thing I would ever want to cause, but you also know how far back I am with the support payments. I'm trying to do the right thing here. This job will let me square things away."

"I told you that we're doing okay. I'm making it work."

"And I appreciate that, but I still need to be able to support my family. Whether we're together or not. Please. I'm asking you not to take that away from me or make this any harder than it already is."

More sniffles. "All right. Okay," Kim replies. "How long will you be gone?"

"Two weeks."

"Okay. I can rearrange things for next weekend. Could you at least take him for a little bit the Sunday that you get back? He has a game then too. Four o'clock."

Derek swallows. His legs suddenly feel shaky. "Yes. I'll make sure to be back in time."

"Do you have a few minutes? Could you at least talk to him quickly?"

"Would that be all right? I'd like to explain it to him myself if I could," Derek says, looking up into the trees. A pair of squirrels scurry after each other, their tails twitching.

"Sure. Hang on." The phone jumbles as Kim walks across the house.

A thought jumps into the forefront of Derek's mind while he waits. He was out grabbing beers with some of the guys after work, back when he was trying to make a post-military career sitting behind a desk. It wasn't anything crazy, two or three beers each, and then they all split off to go their separate ways. He stopped in a KFC drive-through to pick up dinner.

Right at that instant, Michael, barely two years old at the time, was choking on a penny he'd ingested and turning blue. To this day, he'll never forget the panicked hysterics in Kim's voice as he walked in the door with a sack of fried chicken and sides. She'd gotten the coin out and calmed Michael down, but was still reeling from the adrenaline and shock from seeing their son that way.

Derek hadn't been there. He hadn't been there because he was out drinking with the guys. Beers and fried chicken, and he'd almost lost his son as a result. How many more of those instances would come up that he wouldn't be there for?

How many more beyond not being there today?

"Michael, your father is on the phone," Kim calls.

Derek can hear the pounding of feet down the stairs. The phone jostles a little before his son's voice comes over the line.

"Daddy?"

His own voice immediately softens. "Hey, buddy! How's everything going?"

"Good. Why are you calling? Will I see you before the game?"

"Well . . ."

Disappointment seeps through the line. "You're not coming, are you?"

The pit in Derek's stomach grows. He swallows before going on. "No, buddy, I'm not. I have to work. I'm sorry."

"It's okay. I understand." His son tries to be resilient despite the heartache Derek knows he just caused.

"There's my good boy. And listen, Mike, I'm going to make this up to you. I promise. How about we finally go to that Yankee game together?"

The voice on the other end brightens. "Really? We can go?"

"Sure can, bud. Once I finish this job, I can get us tickets."

"And hot dogs? And ice cream too?"

Derek chuckles a little. "Sure, bud. Whatever you want."

"Can the seats be behind home plate?"

"Almost anything you want. But I have to work first before I can buy them. Is that okay with you?"

Michael's exuberance can hardly be contained. "Sure, Dad. No problem."

"There's a good boy. Good luck today. Use that

split-finger grip I showed you, and don't forget to choke up on your bat."

"I know, Dad," Michael returns in an exaggerated voice.

Derek laughs. "All right, champ. Now put your mom back on for me. Okay?"

"Okay, Daddy."

"Love you, buddy."

"Love you too, Dad." And then a second later, "Mom! Dad wants to talk to you again!"

The phone jostles, and Kim's voice returns. "So, I guess I'll see you in two weeks, then. You need me to call the VA for you and change your appointment?"

Derek resists going down that road with her and pivots the conversation. "Listen, Kim. I also need a favor."

She hesitates, seemingly reading his mind. "Derek, I don't know. It's hard enough getting everything accomplished between Michael and work."

"I know it is, and I'm sorry to even have to ask, but he'll just be sitting in the apartment the whole time without me there. Just look in on him. Two or three times tops, if only to make sure he's eating and showering."

A deep sigh comes through the phone. "What happened to that nurse's aide you were going to hire?"

"I did. Three of them so far. He hated two of them, and I found out the third was stealing his shit." He moves into a tried-and-true methodology. "Come on. You know he still adores you. He blames me every day for our splitting up. And you know you love your talks with him. No one else gets him to respond like that. Stock the fridge. Have a cup of coffee with him.

I'll reimburse you whatever you spend and throw a hundred on top of it."

"Yeah, okay," she says, resignation intertwined in her voice. There's a brief hesitation, almost as if Kim didn't want to ask but couldn't help herself. "Are you okay? I don't like that you'll be going so long between appointments."

The issue of his counseling, or lack thereof, had long been contested in the house before their divorce. It was always a sore subject for him, one that he felt she leveraged in every argument as a force multiplier. The resistance to talking to someone undoubtedly contributed to their eventual parting. It wasn't until the anger got to be so bad that he was being triggered by his son that Derek finally started going to counseling. Even with having accepted the need, it still rubbed him the wrong way acknowledging it.

"I'll be all right. I'm going to be outdoors the whole time. You know that's sanctuary to me. I'll go when I get back."

A final pause. A final sniffle. "Okay, then. Safe driving. See you in two weeks."

"Yeah. Two weeks. Thanks, Kim. I mean it."

"Goodbye, Derek."

"Bye."

He takes a moment to gather himself before stuffing his phone in his pocket and spinning around. As he crosses back to his pickup, Gil stands up from his lean.

"So, we good?"

"I'll do it," Derek says, "on one condition."

"That being?"

"Ten grand for the two weeks, but that's it. I won't

do it with the whole extension parameter tacked on to the end. We go tomorrow through next Saturday. If at the end of that time you think you need more training, we'll make a new arrangement, but Sunday morning, I drive back."

Gil considers the man for a moment. "That it?"

"The money you just showed me. I hold on to that starting now. Consider it a security deposit. Just in case."

The man's eyebrows furrow. Gil stares at Derek as he runs his tongue over his front teeth, the motion ending in a click. "I suppose I can live with that too," Gil says as he hands over the bundle. "It's only half, anyhow. The rest I'll get you after we're done. Anything else?"

"That's it."

The man breaks into a wide smile. "Well, let's get movin', then. Got a long drive ahead. Follow me."

Gil crosses over to his Suburban, and Derek climbs into his truck. Twenty minutes later, they pull onto Interstate 87 and head north. Derek sags into his seat, wrestling with fatigue and wondering if he's made the right decision. The miles and hours tick by. Derek cranks the radio to help stay awake. Gil's Suburban ambles on, not driving slowly but not exactly opening it up either. They maintain a steady sixty-five to seventy-five the entire ride. Most cars whip past them on their left. They stop quickly along the way to fuel up, use the bathroom, and grab some snacks, but then they're back on the road.

It's another several hours before they pull off onto Route 73 and then later connect to Route 86 heading northwest past Lake Placid. Exiting onto roads less and less traveled, large stretches of open farmland

and dense woods greet them. Even the towns they pass through barely qualify as such. Maybe a post office. A few traffic lights. A VFW. That's about it. Derek soaks it all in. People don't realize, but there's just as much country life going on in upstate New York as there is in rural Oklahoma.

He zones out, following through the twisting roads until he realizes a lot of time is drifting by. Sitting up, Derek starts taking closer stock of their movements. It only takes a few minutes to notice they are winding around in circles. The lead vehicle doubles back in the direction they just came and overlaps routes with no discernable rhyme or reason.

Too late, he realizes that Gil is purposely trying to disorient him. Derek curses himself for not paying closer attention. His anger boils to the surface as new reservations put him on guard. What reason could the man have for taking such a deliberate action? Derek remembers the emphasis Gil had placed on the group remaining anonymous, but was that it, or something more?

He focuses on getting his bearings and searches for a terrain feature that he can fixate on. The vehicle ahead of him pulls off into thick woods and drives down a gravel path deep into the forest. Derek has no choice but to follow. As they ascend higher and higher into the hills, the roads diminish even further, from packed gravel to dirt trails, some barely wide enough for the vehicles to fit through. His side-view mirrors scrape against branches and bushes.

Gil weaves them through a network of changing directions, which, when combined with the dense forest and the setting sun, compounds Derek's confusion. Even if he wanted to bail, he would be hard-pressed to find his way out of the woods on his own. Taking stock of everything, Derek decides to press on, the needs of the job outweighing his concerns for the moment. For the second time that day, his mind drifts to the pistol in his glove compartment.

3

A little before seven o'clock, they pull onto the crest of a hill. Amid a dense stand of trees is a small clearing with a cluster of buildings. Four look identical and resemble cabins from a sleepaway camp. The fifth, at the far left end of the space, is an elongated cinder block building with a corrugated tin roof. Two pickups sit to the right of the buildings, a group of men milling about them. A dozen hiking backpacks are strewn about in a few different piles. Gil parks and jumps out.

"What's up, you fuckin' hogs?" he screams.

The men laugh and yell back. Derek slides out of his cab, surveying his surroundings. Gil roughhouses and jokes with the other men and then calls him over.

One look at the group is enough to assuage his apprehension from the ride in. They're a ragtag bunch, dressed in a kaleidoscope of John Deere and *Duck Dynasty*. To a man, they're wearing one pattern of hunting camouflage or another. Moreover, they're not hardened individuals looking to spring an ambush. Men of the land, to be sure, conditioned from years of manual labor on a farm, job site, or both, but more suited to barbecue and cornhole than lobbing hand grenades.

"Anyway, y'all," Gil says as he walks up, "this here is Derek, or 'D' for short. His class is the best I've taken yet. I managed to convince him to come back and show y'all some shit, so you'd best listen to what he has to say." The men crowd around. Gil starts introducing them. "This is Brian."

Brian makes no move to shake hands. Decently built with cropped black hair, the man stares at Derek with a skeptical glint in his eyes.

"And this bastard here is Gerry." By comparison, Gerry doesn't seem to have a care in the world. The oldest among the men, he has dark gray and silver hair pulled back into a tight ponytail, with a beard nearly as long to match. Both are bound with a rubber band halfway down their lengths.

The introductions continue. Sebastian. Thin and oily, face like a rat. Jimmy. Tall and built like a brick shithouse. Thomas. Baby-faced with dusty blond hair that makes him look like he ought to be surfing somewhere. A name Derek doesn't catch but that Gil amends by saying everyone calls the man "Beets" anyway. Dillon. Parker. Henry. Tired and realizing he's in redneck hell, Derek loses interest. The last three are named Brandon, Billy, and Bo, but for all he cares, they might as well be Bibbidi, Bobbidi, and Boo.

I gave up my son's game for this lot? And then he quickly admonishes himself. *Idiot. You gave up your son's game for your son.* "Yeah. Great. Nice to meet you," Derek tosses out after Gil is done, the thought still leaving a sour taste in his mind. "Ready to get started?"

The men exchange glances, most of them directed at Gil. He speaks up on their behalf. "You don't want to rack out for a night, D? Start fresh in the morning?"

"You only got me for two weeks. I figured you'd want to get your money's worth. There's still an hour or so of daylight to get to a good campsite."

"Yeah, well . . ." Gil hesitates. "Yeah, I guess so."

"Great," Derek says and then turns to the group. "I see you all have your packs ready to go. That's good. Now go ahead and ground them inside the cabins. You won't be taking anything with you."

"What?" Brian responds, indignant. "We've got all our gear and rations in those!"

"Which is exactly why you're leaving it behind. This isn't a glorified camping trip, fellas. I was hired to teach you how to survive with nothing but the clothes on your back, which is exactly what I intend to do."

"Gil," Sebastian fires back. The man's hand starts to twitch, and he suddenly appears jittery. "This is crazy. I mean, in what scenario wouldn't we have our packs?"

Gil looks to Derek, to which Derek stares flatly back. Finally, the man turns to the group. "D's right. Ain't no way we're gonna learn if we have all our stuff to rely on. Do as he says."

Before they can move off, Derek adds, "Oh, and if you have any knives or firearms on your person, go ahead and ground those too. When I say just the clothes on your back, that's what I mean. Now hustle up. We're burning daylight."

While the men move off, Derek grabs his pack out of the flatbed, sticking his .40-caliber pistol from the glove compartment into it when no one is looking.

They may appear harmless, but the extra effort Gil put into masking his route still leaves Derek suspicious, and he learned long ago to always trust his intuition. He isn't about to start taking chances going into the woods with a dozen men he just met.

As he comes back, Brian chirps again. "Do as I say, not as I do, huh?"

"Maybe, but I've found that my classes really don't amount to much if my students end up dying during training. That's why I haul a pack of emergency gear and medical supplies. Rare as it might be, I bet you wouldn't be too happy if you got bit by a timber rattler. Of course, if you'd rather I leave the antivenom along with everything else I got in here, that's fine by me. Won't be any skin off my ass." The men fall silent, even Gil. "No more objections? Okay, then. Let's go."

He leads them out into the woods at a decent clip. Some of the men start to joke around again, but that dies off after a few hundred yards, replaced instead with grumbles and ragged breath. Derek takes them into the forest until the sun has all but disappeared, and then stops. He spins around in a small saddle between two hills. It's level and dry, but it could hardly be called a clearing.

"All right, we'll stop here. Gather what you can and start making your shelters for the night. Someone get a fire started."

"We ain't got nothing to use," Gerry says. Not confrontational, just merely stating facts.

"You've got your heads. Use those."

Grumbles of "Bullshit" and "Nonsense" rise, but the men scramble about anyway, not wanting to be caught out in the open with the approaching dark falling upon them. After fifteen minutes, Gil comes over while the rest of the group works.

"Hey, uh, D. You ain't doing much training, you know?"

"I'm assessing their knowledge, adaptability, and ingenuity. That'll give me a gauge of what I need to focus on."

Gil nods. "Oh yeah. Okay. That makes sense."

Derek looks the man in the eyes. "This is what you hired me to teach, Gil, and let's not forget, you're a part of this group. The same rules apply to you as it does to them. Don't question me or second-guess my methods. I suggest you get started on your own shelter."

A flash of anger streaks across Gil's face. The man stalks away without another word. There's some truth to Derek wanting to assess the men, but in reality, he's setting them up for failure. With the limited light, lack of resources, and no way to strike a fire, they will be in for a hard night. He wants them uncomfortable, to shake free any perceptions and expectations. Living out in the wild is hard. Derek isn't about to make it any easier for them.

For his part, he's able to lash together a hasty lean-to in what seems like a matter of minutes to the men. In the final moments before shadow closes to dark, he scrapes a bed of pine needles under his shelter, lays his head down on his pack, and waits for the men to drift off. When enough snores are coming from the group, Derek allows himself to sleep as well, but still jolts awake every time one of the men grumbles about a rock in his back, or not having had dinner, or being thirsty. It's a night of broken rest, but long ago, he had become accustomed to sleeping anywhere and at any time, and sleeping under the stars was better than his bedroom. For these men, those conditions probably couldn't be further from the truth.

* * * * *

In the morning, he begins their training in earnest. Derek moves them through the forest, pointing out the resources available to them. Driving points home. He finds a rocky patch and sets up a class while standing over it.

"Okay, so you've got nothing on you. Your first priority is shelter. You don't necessarily have to have a tool to make one. As you saw last night, you can throw together hasty shelters." This is met by more than a few groans for those that spent the night exposed to the elements. "However, you should always be looking to improve that shelter, and doing so will be made infinitely easier if you have a tool. That means a stone knife. Which means flint knapping." He holds up a couple of dark gray rocks.

"This is Onondaga chert. When you strike it, it flakes apart. You can sharpen the edges easily, making it one of the best rocks in the area to use to form a knife or arrowheads. You'll find it in or near riverbeds this far north—which, coincidentally, is your second-highest priority. So, by working toward your knife, you'll also be working toward your water. Sometimes you'll find them in groups like this one, which is where a river used to flow. Chances are it wasn't diverted too far from its origin, so looking out for these collections is another way to tell you're near water."

Derek has them select stones to work with and walks them through the procedure. He shows them how to use percussion flaking to break the stone into smaller sections, then precision flaking to give it an edge.

"You'll want to keep an eye out for a shed set of antlers as you move. They're great for all-around tools, but they're especially useful at the precision step. If you end up making arrow- or spearheads, an antler is perfect for creating notches at the attachment point for lashing to the shafts."

They spend hours working the rocks, cracking and shattering them. Each time one of them breaks their knife, he forces them to start over. The men whine and complain about their empty stomachs. Their fingers bleed with dozens of tiny cuts from the flaking shards. Derek berates them as morning turns to afternoon.

"Suck it up, ladies. Cavemen did this shit. You're telling me you can't do more than they did? Get it done, unless you want to spend another night out in the open."

When each man has a halfway serviceable knife, they move on. Derek stops along the way, pointing out roots that can be dug up and eaten using their new tool. He halts the group next to a stand of plants.

"Anyone tell me what this is?"

"Dogbane, ain't it?" one of the Bobbidis says in reply.

"Good. Now what is it used for?" Blank stares come back at him. "It's a fibrous plant. You can pull apart the stem and get these long strands." Derek demonstrates and holds them up for the group to see. "Gather enough and then weave them together and you'll have strong cordage that can be used for lashings."

They move off again. He points at leaves growing out of the side of a tree, shaped like the head of a cat.

"Tulip poplar. The bark and wood underneath shred apart nicely. You can use these trees to build a tinder bundle. A couple of scrapes with the knife. Stuff a few handfuls down your shirt. This will help dry out the material with your body heat as you keep moving to your next objective."

Derek sets them to work in another campsite before dark, this time giving them more daylight to construct simple shelters. As the skies open on them, he demonstrates building and insulating lean-tos against the rain. He shows them how to improvise catches using their clothing and large leaves, giving the men their first drink of water that day.

They walk the woods for hours at a time, learning which plants and berries are edible. Drinking the rainwater from puddles. Derek kicks a hole in a rotted log and starts popping the fat grubs inside like they're candy. Sebastian throws up. Others, green in the face though they may be, choose the insects rather than their increasing hunger.

They scrounge, picking up anything that can be useful. Discarded litter. Broken bottles. He shows them how to find purpose in everything. To think beyond the standard usage of an item. They work on primitive tools, mastering the bow drill. Creating bone gorge hooks and attaching them to their woven cordage for fishing.

As they settle into a permanent site, the days begin to blend together. Although hungry and tired, the men take to the training. Their shelters improve daily. Fires start quicker. They complain less. The group creates its own routines of drawing and boiling water in the refuse they discovered. Foraging for bugs and berries. He teaches them about different snares and deadfalls for trapping small game. To this, the men respond eagerly—not only to the construction, of which several already know the basics, but the placement.

Derck isn't surprised at the outcome. Men such as these spent their lifetimes hunting. They knew how to spot rabbit holes and game trails. Days of hunger washing over them, they fan out from camp just before dark. In these woods, high in the mountains and relatively untouched by human presence, the results are plentiful. The next morning, more than a few hollers come from the forest, and minutes later, three squirrels and a rabbit are roasting over a spit. The group laughs and jokes for the first time in a week as they pass the carcasses around to get a few mouthfuls each.

Derek seizes on the theme and introduces primitive hunting. They create bows and arrows and spears from scratch. While the men affix their arrowheads, he walks among them, inspecting and commenting on the implements.

"Good work, fellas. Stuff is coming along nicely. Just keep in mind the amount of time and energy that's getting put into this. Something as simple as having a bag of fishhooks or a slingshot with some ball bearings on your person could have you hunting or fishing right away."

A couple of the men laugh.

"I'm serious. Fishhooks weigh next to nothing, so you can carry a ton of them, and they come in all different sizes. You can catch any living animal with a baited hook. You're not just limited to the water. A bit of meat or entrails can land a squirrel or a bird just as much as it could a fish."

Brian sniffs from across the campsite. "Yeah, okay, I get the fishhooks, but a slingshot? You can't hit shit in these woods with a fucking slingshot."

Derek turns, arching an eyebrow. "Oh, really?"

The man looks up at him. "In your backyard shooting beer cans at ten feet? Sure. But out here? Good luck with that shit."

Reaching into his left cargo pocket, Derek pulls out a small pouch. He quickly assembles the pieces of a slingshot and strings rubber hoses holding a leather pad. Putting a ball bearing in the pad, Derek calls out to the group. "Everyone drop what they're doing and follow me."

The group gets up, sharing questioning looks and turning to Brian, who just shrugs in response. Derek leads them a ways out, the land turning soft and soggy as they get farther and farther from camp. They crest a small ridge that looks down on a pond, easily a hundred yards away. A dam of limbs and branches cuts a third of the pond off from the rest. A large beaver lodge sits at the end of the dam.

Derek looks over his shoulder. "Stay here and don't make a sound."

Easing himself down the hillside, Derek moves with a speed and stealth that they've never witnessed before. As he reaches level ground, he drops into the marsh, crawling his way closer and closer toward the dam. A beaver appears out of the hovel, scurries about some, and heads back inside. Derek continues his steady progress, moving painstakingly slowly as he closes the distance. The man remains unseen and unheard as he does so.

"No way in hell he kills that thing," Jimmy says to the group.

"Ten bucks," Parker replies.

"Done," Jimmy returns.

"Shut the fuck up, you two," Gil admonishes with a harsh whisper.

Their patience is tested as they wait and watch. For his part, Derek appears to be content biding his time in the mud. It's close to an hour later when the beaver shows himself again. It inches along the dam, a few hops at a time. A *thwip* sounds out, barely heard over the din of the forest. As the beaver lurches and topples over, Derek is up and sprinting, leaping over logs as his survival knife appears in his hand. He jumps onto the dam and seizes the beaver, lancing his blade into its neck.

"Holy shit."

"That had to be twenty yards out."

"Closer to thirty."

"Where'd you find this guy, Gil?"

Derek hoists his fresh kill into the air. "Dinner's on me tonight, boys!"

The men laugh and cheer, and as they head back to camp, Derek dispatches them to check their traps and lines. A few return with fish and squirrels. Others come back with roots and berries. With the beaver added to the bounty, it is a veritable Thanksgiving Day feast.

Sitting around the fire and eating, they continue with their banter. At a certain point, Sebastian starts laughing for no discernible reason. If Derek didn't know any better, he would think the man had a buzz on.

"I gotta know, Derek. Where in the hell you learn all this shit anyhow?"

He smiles in response, tossing wood chips into

the flames. "My dad started teaching me when I was pretty young. Been in the woods most of my life, like you fellas."

Henry laughs. "Don't know 'bout that. I've been hunting a long time, but I ain't never seen anybody bag a beaver like that. And then the way you ran him through!" He laughs, and more join in.

"Go ahead, D. Tell them," Gil says.

He exchanges glances with the mullet-haired man. In the moment before he responds, something passes between them. Derek can't quite place it, but it brings back his suspicion nonetheless. "Nothing really to tell."

"Pfft. Stop being modest." Gil turns to the group. "D's a retired Marine. Service-disabled, veteran-owned business. Says so right on his website."

A few cheers and obligatory "Thank you for your service" are thrown his way. "Yeah, but they teach this shit in the Marines?" Bo asks.

Derek nods. "Some of the basics, yeah. If you get to go to the schools, that is. The rest I picked up on my own over the years."

"What'd you do in the military? Like what was your job?" This comes from Beets.

"Instructor, mostly."

"You ever deploy?" Dillon asks.

"Twice," Derek replies, downplaying the actual number. "Kinda hard to avoid that in this day and age."

Gil chuckles. "You know what I think, D? I think that's a lame attempt at a cover story. You know, like all them spy movies and shit. Guy's always a radio repairman, and then we see that he's really Charles Bronson."

Derek laughs in response. "Nothing like that, I'm afraid. That's why the movies are the movies. I was just your run-of-the-mill jarhead, and a schoolhouse one at that."

"Come on. Level with us," Gil presses. "We're all friends here. Tell us the truth. You don't pull that shit off by being in a schoolhouse your whole career. What were you? Raiders? Force Recon? Some crazy Delta Force shit we never heard of?"

A bunch of the men stare at him, hanging on Gil's words and adding their own anticipation. The mere prospect of him being one of the military's elite is enough to put stars in their eyes. Derek doesn't show any emotion, but internally, he's annoyed at the line of questioning. "Not this guy. Besides, if I were Delta Force, wouldn't that make me Chuck Norris?" The men erupt in laughter. Derek waits until it dies a little and then redirects. "What about you fellas? What'd you do in your past lives?"

Sebastian is all too happy to chime in. As he spills, Derek throws a glance at Gil across the fire. He stares back at Derek, a smirk on his face that seems to convey he knows more than he's letting on. Lifting his wrist, Derek looks at the date on his watch.

A few more days to go.

4

At first light on their last day together, Derek has them up and moving. Hastening their trek back to the vehicles, he looks to cash out and bug out. If he can be on the road by eight, there's a good chance he can make Michael's baseball game.

The men groggily follow along despite their grumbling mouths and stomachs. He doesn't provide much in the way of training. Instead, Derek points out when and where the group misses a bush containing some berries or a plant with edible roots. As day breaks in earnest, their eyes rise with the sun. The men incorporate his tutelage with less and less prodding. Derek smiles with a self-satisfied grin. It's always redeeming to see students putting his lessons into practice.

With the pace he sets, Derek catches sight of the cluster of buildings a little before 7:00 a.m. The men see the shacks through the trees a few moments later, and their talk immediately turns cheerful. He had pushed them hard the last two weeks. Sleeping on a bed of pine needles and pebbles could never be as comfortable as a mattress after a nice shower. As visions of burgers and beer likely course through their heads, the joking that had been ever present in the beginning of their training now returns.

The group enters the clearing amid raised pulses, sweaty brows, and heavy breathing, but the relief at having completed their training is enough to keep the smiles going. A few of them move off to the shacks to gather equipment. The rest start dropping it into the trucks, some shaking hands with Derek first, offering their thanks. He responds in kind, but quickly moves to his own truck. Throwing his bag in the flatbed, he searches out Gil and makes his way to the man.

Gil finishes chatting with Thomas and turns to face Derek. He hooks his thumbs in his belt and smirks with the left side of his face. "Not bad, D," he says as Derek approaches. "Not bad at all. The fellas are impressed. That's no easy thing to do with this lot."

"Thanks," he returns. "Always great to teach when you have guys so willing to learn. They're a good group."

"The best, D. The best." Gil regards him for a moment that carries on a little longer than it probably should. "Anyway, I suppose you'll be wanting to get paid, then?"

Derek smiles and resists the urge to look at his watch. "If you wouldn't mind. I gotta get on the road."

"Of course I don't mind, D. It's what you came up for, ain't it? We just have to head down into camp proper first," he says with a nod toward one of the trucks. Gil starts to walk off.

Derek doesn't follow. "Wait. What do you mean, go into camp?"

Turning back, Gil stares at him with furrowed eyebrows, his face a picture of confusion. "What? When did I ever have a chance to go down there and get the rest of your money? Besides, even if I did have it on me, you think I'm gonna walk around the woods for two weeks with thousands of dollars on me? It was bad enough when I did that our first weekend together, and that was five grand."

Clenching his teeth, Derek feels a surge of anger shooting up. He takes a breath and hesitates a moment before responding. "This is nonsense. We agreed on Sunday morning, and I met my obligation. It's time to pay up, so whatever you need to do to make that happen, you'd better get on it."

"You're gonna get paid, D. But I gotta take you to see the boss first. Only thing holding up your money is you."

A few of the others glance in their direction before going back to stowing their gear in the flatbeds. Gil smirks and closes the distance between them. He stares up into Derek's eyes, suddenly smug and satisfied.

"Guess you're gonna have to adapt and overcome, huh, Marine instructor? Out there, you might have been the commander, but back here, the only one with more rank than me is Marshal, and I say you got to go see him."

Clenching his fists, Derek takes a step closer. The two are practically nose to nose, but Gil doesn't retreat. Instead, his smirk grows into a full-blown smile. Jimmy and Brian turn their attention completely to Derek. They do a crap job of pretending to mind their own business. It's clear what they're there for. Derek doesn't give a shit.

"Listen, you redneck bastard. I'm tired of your little games. You understand? Get me my money or I'm gonna beat your ass."

An even wider smile. "What? You gonna take us all on? How about getting out of here? Think you can navigate these trails before we'd catch up to you? No, D, your turn to listen. I say you're not getting paid until you've met the boss. It's not like he ain't gonna give you the cash. I talked with the fellas, and we all agree that the training was top-notch. Worth every penny. No one's reneging here."

Gil playfully claps him on the arm. Derek looks at the appendage and then back at the smaller man, his mouth forced slightly open by indignation. *He touches me again, it's on.*

"Not at all. Still don't change nothing. Now if you want to get in your truck and drive outta here, be my guest. No one's gonna stop you. Of course, you'll be out the rest of your money. You want to get paid, you'll come down to the camp. I promise it won't take more than an hour."

They stare at each other. Derek looks over at the men standing nearby, the others climbing into the flatbeds beyond. He glances down at his watch. Gil had taken his time on the drive up. Derek could make up the hour delay on the road. All the practical reasons for going to the camp add up to him doing so, but the principle of the thing fuels a simmering rage bubbling just under the surface.

In the end, ten grand is ten grand. He was in no position to walk out on five thousand dollars that he had rightfully earned.

"An hour. That's it. I'll follow you down."

Gil slaps him on the arm again. "That's the spirit, Marine!"

Derek resists the urge to punch him in the base of his neck. Storming off to his own truck, he grabs his bag out of the back and brings it into the cab with him. As the trucks pull away, Derek reaches into the top of the pack. He takes out the .40 caliber, digs a little deeper to find his concealed carry holster, and then straps the weapon to his belt.

Heading north, the trio of trucks descends a steep and bumpy hill. The men in the flatbed in front of him cling on for dear life and laugh like they're on a carnival ride. Derek's frustration grows with how slowly the vehicles progress down the track. Eventually, the road levels out and banks off to the east, winding and weaving its way through thick woods.

Curving back around to the north, the vehicles enter a wide clearing where several other trucks, work vans, and ATVs are parked. Beyond the improvised lot, the road continues into the woods heading north. An opening in the tree line to the west denotes a smaller trail.

The engines killed, his students spill out and shoulder their bags. Derek does the same. If this ended up being some sort of trap and he couldn't make it back to his truck, he wanted to at least have his gear with him.

"Come on, D," Gil says, waving him over to a side-by-side ATV. "There ain't much room for full-size vehicles in camp. If we stay on the road, it'll take a bit longer to get there too. The trail is more direct, but it's still another two klicks at least. This baby will save some time."

He and Derek ride in silence the rest of the way to the camp. The track terminates at the edge of a moderate clearing. Climbing out, Derek spots another cinder block building off to his right. A quick scan of the perimeter reveals various wooden shacks set back into the tree line. He can hear the running water of a nearby river even though he can't see it. Saws and hammers ring out over the steady rush. A dozen people are moving about from one building to the next. They throw glances at the newcomer but quickly go about their business.

"I'll set you up in the mess tent. Most everybody should be out of there by this hour. We start things early 'round here. Darryl can hook you up with a hot meal while I grab Marshal. Be better than those grubs, right?"

"I don't give a shit about your food, Gil. Or about your Marshal. I want to get my money and get out of here. So whatever you have to do to make that happen, do it."

The man glares at him, one nostril ticking up in a brief snarl, and then Gil's face smooths over. "Whatever you say, D. Over here."

They cut across the clearing, a massive military tent wedged into the space between the trees coming into view as they draw closer. The olive-drab canvas walls wave lightly in a warm breeze. Two smokestacks stick out of the roof on the left side, vacating gray smoke along with the smells of cooking meat and baking bread.

Instincts kick in. After two plus decades of practice, intelligence gathering is as second nature to him as breathing. Derek makes small talk all the while cataloging the responses, indexing them next to the sights and sounds of the camp. "How long were you in?"

There's a long pause, so long that Derek isn't sure the man will respond. A few paces past his doubt, Gil clears his throat. "How'd you know?"

Derek shrugs. "Little things, really. Referring to me

as 'commander.' Ticking off distance in klicks instead of miles. Your knowledge of Special Operations units. Then there's the way you carry yourself. The way you move. You may be a redneck, but you're a trained one. That's for certain."

Another long pause passes between them. "Eleven years. Plus or minus."

"You forget how to count?" Derek grumbles.

"Nah, nothing like that, D. Just the last few years I wouldn't exactly classify as service time."

"Oh yeah? What would you classify it as?"

"A waste, D. And we'll leave it at that for now."

Reaching the tent, Gil makes a mock flourish of bowing as he steps aside and pulls a flap back. Derek ducks through the entranceway and notices a crew of three working at wood-burning stoves and ovens arranged behind the chow line to his left. A beady, balding, greasy skeleton of a man looks up as Gil steps in behind him.

"Hey, Darryl. You got any breakfast still?"

Darryl wipes at his nose with the back of his hand. "Gave the rest to the kids to bait with. I can finish up some of this quick. Take a seat."

"You heard the man," Gil quips. "Take a seat, D."

Derek moves over to one of the many picnic benches inside and eases himself down. As he does so, the remaining few people still eating clear their dishes and exit out the back, Gil following close behind. Derek watches as Darryl lifts what appears to be a steak skewered on a fork and throws it onto another part of the grill. Flames shoot up, and Derek can hear the meat sizzling.

He looks around. The tent. The tables. It's all eerily familiar. Like the chow tents he used to take meals in on deployment. Even down to the arrangement of the napkin holders and Tabasco bottles in the center of the tables. Except they aren't in some foreign hellhole. They're in upstate New York. The tent is trying to mimic the military in a place where you don't need to.

Darryl walks over, steaming plate in one hand, a pitcher of water and a glass in another. A cigarette dangles from his mouth, a quarter inch of ash holding precariously to the edge of it. The man drops the plate in front of him and sets down the pitcher and glass. Reaching into the pocket of his stain-covered apron, he pulls out a set of silverware. Derek looks at the plate. It holds a slab of meat burned to a crisp, still-bubbling beans ladled next to it, and a heel of crusty bread. He looks back at Darryl.

The man stares right back at him. After a few moments, Darryl's eyes go wide. "Well, boy? Don't just stare at it."

"The hell is it?"

"Venison. What else?" Darryl replies, smoke pouring from his mouth as he does so.

"Can you put it back on the grill for me? I don't think it's done yet."

Darryl's eyes narrow. He reaches up and takes another long drag of his cigarette. The cook lowers his hand and flicks the ash into the pitcher of water. Darryl blows the smoke out while mumbling, "Smartass," as he walks away.

Derek's tolerance for this place wanes ever closer to him losing his shit. Still, beyond the anger of his delay, there is the necessity of fueling the body. A plate of hot food sits in front of him. Another lesson he learned long ago. Eat when you have the opportunity to do so.

Despite the meat being charred, the smells ignite a deep, voracious hunger. The hunger of not having eaten anything substantial in nearly two and a half weeks. Derek grabs the fork and knife and tears into the venison. After a few bites, he starts shoveling in beans, barely noticing how hot they still are.

Pouring a glass of water, Derek downs it in a few gulps, regardless of the ash floating on the surface. It's flat and tastes like it's been purified or at least boiled, but it's cool as it rushes down his throat. Venison finished, he's still mopping up beans into his mouth with the remainder of his bread when a figure steps in front of him on the other side of the table.

"Yeah. Darryl can cook, can't he now?"

Derek looks up.

For a guy that must be in his late seventies or early eighties, the man is built like an ox. He wears Realtree camouflage pants tucked into a pair of hunting boots. His tan T-shirt stretches over a broad chest and shoulders and is tucked in around a narrow waist. A shock of closely cropped white hair rests atop a deeply lined face. Heavy bags sit under the man's eyes, but the eyes themselves are alive with all the faculties of a man half his age.

A fleeting image of Derek's father passes through his mind, recognized for what it is and dismissed immediately in favor of the matter at hand.

"Name's Marshal," the old man says, extending a hand.

Leaning back, Derek crosses his arms in front of him.

Marshal awkwardly leaves his hand hanging over the table before pulling it back. The old man holds his gaze a bit but then gets antsy. Marshal looks around some, scratches his head, and then looks back. "How about some coffee? I could use a cup. You?"

Derek swallows his last piece of bread. He could not care less about the man's manners and hospitality. "How about you just explain why you're holding out on me."

The cooks behind the chow line pick up their heads and look at the table. Their faces are frozen in astonishment, one of them in outright fear. Marshal's face remains stoic while a long moment passes between them.

"Afraid we don't have much to offer in the way of milk and sugar. Plenty of that artificial creamer, though. So how do you take it? Black or full of powder?"

The old man hadn't flinched at his abruptness, but the reactions of the chow crew were telling. It spikes Derek's curiosity. "Black."

The old man smiles and raps his knuckles on the table. "Coming right up."

Retreating to a small folding table set on the far side of the chow line, Marshal returns a minute later and pushes a steaming mug across the table. He sits opposite Derek and sips on his own cup. Derek takes a swig and then shakes from the bitterness. The shit tastes like roofing tar.

"Jesus. I've had some foulness before, but . . . fuck."

Marshal grimaces, apparently not pleased with his profanity. Or is it the blasphemy? Or insulting his cook's coffee? Whatever the reason, the old man keeps it to himself. Derek catalogs the reaction, storing it for later analysis.

Marshal takes another long drink and then leans forward, puts his elbows on the table, and looks him square in the eye. "First things first, son. I'm sorry for delaying you. Truly, I am. I just thought it prudent we meet."

Derek furrows his eyebrows. "That's great and all, but we had an agreement, and I have other responsibilities. I don't have time for this amateur-hour nonsense."

"You're upset. I get it. I would be too. Please understand there's a purpose to all this. Gil is a scary judge of talent and all, but . . . we don't bring outsiders into our group too often. Even with his recommendation, before we extend an invite, I . . . need to be certain about a person."

"So this was all some kind of test?"

"I suppose you could look at it that way." The old man scratches his head again, then glances off to the side, looking perturbed. When he looks back, there is some sorrow behind his eyes. "Would you mind taking a walk? I think it might make more sense if I show you what we're trying to do here."

The question gets under his skin. He can't help thinking of the time being wasted. Of the promise he made. Of how late he's going to be as a result. "Do I even have a choice? I'm not gonna get my goddamn money if I refuse, right?"

The old man looks over his shoulder quickly and then leans in. When he speaks, there is an edge to his voice. It's still respectful just . . . harder. "I'm asking, not telling you, son. Fifteen more minutes. Twenty, tops. But if you're gonna come along, you will stop taking the Lord's name in vain and hear me out. Do those things and I'll see you on your way with your money. You decide to keep pushing it, and you can drive out of here with empty pockets."

Anger still sets fire to his blood. Impatience along

with it, urging him to get on the road. But the old man's insistence and assertiveness is unexpected, and it drives the intelligence-collection side of his training to the forefront. It's something Derek can't resist even if he wanted to. He needs to know where this is heading.

Rather than forcing further confrontation, he decides to play along. "All right, then. Lead the way."

5

Marshal smiles and turns for the entrance. Leaving the mess, the old man walks to his right and starts along the tree line that forms the perimeter of the clearing. They pass a pair of deer carcasses hanging from a railroad tie suspended between two trees just outside the mess tent. A little ways beyond them are four wooden shower stalls, with large cisterns behind them and hoses running along the ground off to the west.

Derek's gaze follows the lengths, seeing them stretch toward the sound of the river. He spots flickers of light through the trees, presumably the reflection of the summer sun off the breaks of the running water. It's some distance, but he can just make out the edges of a long, rectangular structure.

Taking notice of the direction Derek is looking, Marshal glances that way before turning back over his shoulder. "That's the old sawmill. My grandfather, God rest his soul, put his last bit of money into this land after the Great Depression cleaned him out. He thought the Adirondacks would be the next big logging territory. That tributary showed promise for getting timber downstate, but then . . . let's just say progress got impeded."

They cross through a thick stand of trees. Marshal halts them on the other side. A man with a massive beard and equally large gut sits on a camp stool. A group of boys and girls dressed in hunting camo cluster around him. The youngest is around eight, the oldest no more than twelve, yet each of them carries a brand-new bolt-action rifle. One by one, they step before the man and clear their firearm, ejecting a single cartridge before handing it over. The man places each bullet in his shirt pocket before inspecting the breach. Once he's deemed it empty, he hands the rifle back and sends the kids across the clearing toward the cinder block building.

Marshal watches the whole process unfold with a satisfied smile on his face. Derek notices that two of the kids are already empty when they pull their bolts back. They also have a fair amount of blood on their hands and sleeves. Marshal pats them each on the shoulder as he passes them by.

"Good work, Janie. Easton. We eat again tonight because of you."

"Thank you, Marshal." The young girl beams.

"Thank you, sir," Easton adds with a starstruck look.

A younger boy steps up behind them and also reveals an empty breach. His eyes, shimmering with tears, dart to Marshal before looking back at his rifle. Unlike the predecessors, he's devoid of any blood on his person. The old man's smile fades.

"And thank God that Janie's and Easton's shots were true," Marshal says to the remaining children still waiting in line. They all stare at him save for the boy having his rifle inspected. "Still, think of how many more bellies might be full if everyone did their part. If all of you fulfilled your duty to this family. Wouldn't that be a moment of true rejoicing? One that celebrates bounty instead of failure."

The watching gazes all shift back to the boy. Hands trembling, he accepts his inspected rifle from the man on the stool. The boy rushes toward the clearing with his head bowed, not daring to lift his eyes and meet those boring into him. When he gets beyond the old man, the kid can no longer keep his composure and breaks down crying.

Derek holds back on his comment, a scathing remark about beating up on a kid who should have his nose in a coloring book, not a rifle in his hands. His mind immediately goes to Michael. How many times had he unreasonably expected more from his own boy? Derek tamps down the guilt before it can distract him from his observations.

As quickly as it vanished, Marshal's smile returns. "Shall we?" The old man moves on, talking over his shoulder again as he weaves his way through the trees. "Hunting party. Just coming in from their morning shift."

Walking by the inspection line, Derek gets a closer look at the rifles. Remington 700 SPS. Tactical versions. Matte black. Bull barrels. Each one is equipped with a high-powered scope. The kind of rifles police departments, even some military units, favored giving their snipers. Not cheap setups either, and there were at least ten kids in the group.

"Everyone has a job to do around here, even the

little ones," Marshal continues. "Heck, they're the luckiest of us all. They only have one job to do. Now they'll be off to their studies."

"You send them out there to hunt with one bullet?"

"Well, resources aren't infinite up here, but also, there's no better way to learn than by limiting them to a single round."

"I suppose," Derek responds. "Although if you're banking on kids keeping the pantry full, I would think you'd want to hedge your bets a bit more."

"Perhaps," the man replies without turning his head. "Maybe think of it this way, then. When they know they only have one round, they learn to hit their target in such a way that it doesn't get back up." The sharpness is there again. A voice teetering on the edge of violent outburst. And just like that, it's gone.

When he speaks again, Marshal's voice is warm and inviting. "This, Derek," the man says, lifting his arms to the canopy above, "is what we have built here. What we are building. This is refuge. This is what we call Sanctuary. The people you see around you. These are the downtrodden. The castaways of a vitriolic society so consumed by itself that it no longer has the capacity for common human decency, much less compassion.

"We have recognized that to truly live as God's people, we must leave the grid behind. Not just the grid, mind you, but society as we know it. We've emancipated ourselves. No more being subject to the corruption of politicians. No more pissing away our money into taxes that get spent overseas versus at home. We refuse to be a part of a country where queers are celebrated. Where criminals are lauded and cops are made to be the villains. 'Ah, sinful nation, a people laden with iniquity, offspring of evildoers, children who deal corruptly.' Isaiah, chapter one, verse four."

The perimeter tree line bends around the rough circle of the clearing. Off to their right, an open-front structure shows men working at a forge and anvils, while just next to it, others use the saws and hammers Derek heard earlier. Marshal waves. One man waves back before dressing down a sixteenish-year-old boy. Derek makes note of the religious zealotry. From watching, he records a disciplined and organized camp.

"No more, Derek. Here in this solitude, we are committed to returning society into what makes sense. Into what God intended. No government will hold sway over us any longer. We are accountable to Him, one another, and that's all."

They pass by cabins set back in the woods, near enough to the same style Derek saw at the outbuildings when he first arrived two weeks ago. To his left, in the clearing, a different group of men from the ones he trained move toward the cinder block building. Each one carries an AR-style assault rifle slung across plate carriers laden with magazines and other gear pouches. All four also sport a sidearm holstered in a thigh rig.

The Remingtons are one thing. These are another altogether. No way the weapons and gear could be justified by hunting.

"Nice sermon. I fail to see what it has to do with my getting paid. And what's with the hardware?"

Marshal looks past him to the clearing, the remnants of a grimace vanishing from his face. "They,

Derek, are what this has to do with you. If you'll indulge me a few minutes longer."

Derek shrugs, and Marshal turns back to the trees, losing himself in the foliage and songbirds. Slowly, they make their turn toward the north, the trail back to Derek's truck just ahead of them.

"We mean to live in peace here. Truly, we do. I want nothing more than that for my flock. But in these trying times, it seems we are still to be tested. There are those whose wickedness will not relent so easily. That finds us even now.

"These hills. There is a certain . . . lawlessness to them," Marshal continues. "The remoteness of these mountains means there is virtually no presence from the police up here. Perhaps the occasional DEC patrol will go through the nearby state park, but that's it. Those conditions attract a certain element. Groups with ill intentions. Groups that are the epitome of the evil that has consumed the rest of this country. We are surrounded by wolves, Derek, and when a pack of wolves sees easy prey, they pounce."

"I take it you've already had a couple of run-ins with these groups, then?" As they walk by the cinder block building, the armed men step up to a steel dutch door, the top portion swung open. A large woman fills the space, taking the rifles one by one and placing them inside. Between her, the men, and the darkness of the interior, Derek can't see what else is behind her.

Marshal nods and continues, oblivious to Derek's line of sight. "We have. A couple of goons cornered some of my kids. Took their rifles at gunpoint. Terrified them in the process. Others were spotted sneaking around our vehicles. Some in camp have told me they hear voices around our perimeter at night. Those men there are coming off a lookout shift. I started putting them out at night after the incident with the rifles."

They reach a cabin with a covered porch. Marshal steps up and into the building. As Derek follows, he notices a shack to the left of the cabin. No bigger than a shed, it's adorned with several satellite dishes and antennas. Cables run from the roof and connect to gasoline-powered generators placed next to the building.

When he steps inside, he finds a simple enough room, dimly lit and musty. A closed door is set in the left wall, a large stone fireplace set into the back one. The center of the room is dominated by a large desk hewn from oak. It's covered in intricate scrollwork and polished to a high shine. Two chairs are set before it, a grand recliner behind. On the wall to his right, a grandfather clock ticks softly, the long pendulum swinging behind a glass door. It's also polished and in immaculate condition.

Marshal walks around the desk, running his hand along the wood as he does so. "How about something a little stronger than coffee?" he says, opening one of the desk drawers. Glasses clink together in the process.

"I don't think there's anything on earth stronger than that shit."

The old man laughs. "Yeah. Darryl is pretty brutal. I just thank God he cooks the stuff to the point we're not dying from salmonella." He puts two glasses onto coasters on the desktop and pours from a bottle of Johnnie Walker Red. Marshal picks up both glasses and hands one over. He smells the scotch before taking a long sip.

Derek takes a sip of his own. "What happened to him being a great cook?"

Marshal's eyebrows perk up. "In your career, did you ever find it beneficial to tear up a subordinate in front of a complete stranger?"

So a subordinate is off-limits, but a kid is okay? "All the time."

"Well, I'll have to disagree on your leadership style there. Besides, despite the man being my second cousin, he's the only cook we got up here." Marshal gestures to the chairs, and they sit. Silence lingers between them. "What do you think of the desk?"

Derek looks at it again. "Yeah . . . it's nice."

"Belonged to my grandfather. The clock too. All I have left of him. Of my whole family, really, Darryl notwithstanding. When he knew the bank was coming for his factory, he got these out the night before and brought them here." The man stares at the desk longingly.

Derek sips the scotch sparingly, knowing full well that he has a long drive still. The contradictions of the old man begin adding up. His sudden flips of aggression. The adoration for the furniture. The Bible quotes. A profile begins building of a man not completely grounded in reality. Perhaps it's the age. Perhaps something more.

Eventually, the old man looks up. "Let me lay it all out, Derek. The good Lord was called on to be a shepherd, and it seems that I have received a similar call. Every good shepherd must not only tend to his flock but protect them from the wolves.

"When we first started out here, it was just my kin and me. Our numbers have swelled as of late. Unfortunate, in that it means more are becoming despondent, but a blessing in that they are turning to our ways. I finally have the numbers I need to put together a security team. A group of men beyond the lookouts. Men who can patrol our land and, if necessary, interdict on our behalf for the safety of all who are here."

"You want a QRF," Derek says. "A quick reaction force."

"Yes," the old man replies, his face breaking into a wide smile. "Exactly. I have the men picked out, but I need someone to assess them for me. To ensure that they are trustworthy. That they will be able to perform under fire and then, once I have approved them for it, to train them how to do so." He pauses and stares flatly.

Derek stares back. After a moment, he sets the scotch down on the desk. "Yeah. Not interested."

"You haven't heard what I'm willing to pay yet."

"Listen, Marshal. You want to secede from the Union, be my guest. I won't stop you. I couldn't care less what you and your flock does, but don't ask me to join in. I didn't spend the better part of my life defending this country just so I could come home and teach a bunch of inbred assholes how to play soldier while they turn their backs on it."

The man's eyebrows furrow, his face becoming even more creased. Marshal works his jaw around before responding. "I'm only going to say this once, son—"

"And you can cut out the calling me 'son' shit while you're at it."

Another long pause. "All right. Derek. Don't assume that your service somehow elevates you above the rest of us. There are those in this camp, including myself, who have worn the uniform and spilled blood for this country. The difference is that we realize we were hung out to dry by the same country we signed up to protect."

"Great. Good for you. You don't need me, then. Hell, you've got Gil. He looks like he spent some time in the sandbox. Have him teach your boys."

Leaning back in his chair, Marshal folds his hands over his chest. "Gil. Gil is a good man. You're right. He was an MP in Iraq. Had a run-in with his company commander that . . . Well, let's just say he's sacrificed a lot more than most here.

"The thing that makes Gil so great is his humility. He knows that riding up and down roads laden with IEDs isn't the same as patrolling a forest in northern New York. He freely admitted he was unequal to the task of training the team. He suggested we find someone more qualified. He truly puts the good of this camp ahead of everything, most of all his pride."

"This is real touching and all, but I'm not the guy you're looking for. All I did was teach survival."

Another frown. Marshal leans over to pull out a drawer to his left. When he comes back up, he's holding a manila folder in his hand. The old man flips it open and starts reading out loud. "Derek A. Harrington, USMC. Chief Warrant Officer Four. Military intelligence with specializations in human and counterintelligence. Infantry school in 1994. Embassy duty after that. Accepted into Force Recon, then served with dev group."

"Where the fuck did you get that?"

Ignoring him, Marshal continues, "Warrant school and then the intel teams. Deployments to Iraq and Afghanistan. Libya, Syria, Saudi Arabia, the Horn of Africa. Airborne qualified. Air assault. HALO. Medic as your primary designation. Cross-trained in demo-litions. Scuba certified."

On the surface, his face is placid, but underneath, Derek is seething. He feels his teeth grinding together. His grip tightening on the armrests of the chair. It takes all he has not to leap over the desk. *How the hell did this guy get my file?*

"Seems like after your last deployment, you made the transition to the schoolhouse side. Instructor, small arms and crew-served weapons. Black belt and in-structor in Marine Corps martial arts. Edged weap-ons instructor. This, though. This right here is what I found particularly interesting. SERE school level C graduate and instructor. Spent the remainder of your time in the Corps there."

Marshal flips the folder closed and looks at Derek again. "So you see, son. You're exactly the kind of person I need. A Special Forces operator proficient in teaching woodland survival. One that can give my men a fighting chance against these gangs and drug runners."

It takes him a moment to gather himself. When he does speak, Derek's voice is barely contained from breaking out into full-fledged beratement. "I'd like to get paid, and then I'd like to put you and the rest of this collection of crazy in my rearview."

Frowning, Marshal scoops the folder from the desk. "Very well." He bends down again. Metal on metal scraping sounds out, followed by a click. The old man starts piling stacks of money onto the desktop.

At first, he puts two stacks together and then pushes them aside. After that, Marshal starts pulling out more money. Four stacks. Seven. Ten. When he's done, he looks back over at Derek and gestures to the smaller pile.

"That's ten thousand dollars, on top of the five you already have, on account of this inconvenience. You can take it now and head back to your truck. So long as you remember our agreement about anonymity, that will be the end of our dealings."

His hand hovers over the ten stacks. "But if you agree to train my men, I'll pay you fifty thousand dollars. It's mid-June now, so let's say by early autumn. Ten weeks to get them up to speed. That's five thousand a week, Derek. When we get to the fall, if you tell me they need more training, I'll pay you more money."

Although he doesn't look at it, Derek feels a pang in his heart over the cash. Visions of finally meeting his obligations, of an end to broken promises to his boy, briefly streak through his mind. The money could be life-changing.

But so would the baggage it would come with.

He shakes his head. "I won't sell out, Marshal. Not for you. Not for anyone. What am I supposed to do, huh? You already told me you're breaking off. That your numbers are growing. Eventually, those missing people are gonna get noticed.

"It may not be for a while, but eventually, the government, like them or not, is going to come looking for you. What then, Marshal? Men that I've trained for their own protection gunning it out with the poor cops they send in to round you all up? I won't be a part of that. I've already got too much blood on my hands. I won't be responsible for the next Waco or Ruby Ridge."

Derek stands, scoops up a stack of cash, and turns for the door. Marshal jumps up out of his chair.

"Derek, please. It's not like that, I can assure you. I'm merely a father looking out for his children. We need you. Don't leave us out here at the mercy of these . . . these . . . savages."

He pivots and looks at the old man. "I'm sorry, Marshal. Never gonna happen."

"Will you at least take this?" He digs in another drawer and comes out from around the desk, holding out a cell phone and charger. "There isn't any reception up here. This phone has a preprogrammed number to a sympathetic place in St. Regis Falls. If you call there and ask for me, they'll get a message up to us. As soon as I receive it, I'll head into town and call you back."

Derek stares at the phone and then meets the old man's eyes. They shine with the brimming of tears.

"Please. Only God deals in absolutes. Take it, son. At least consider my offer and have a way to get back to us if you change your mind."

He can't be certain what his reason is. Maybe the old man's apparent sincerity wore him down. Maybe it's the stacks of money on the desk. Perhaps it's nothing more than those ingrained instincts, pieces of intelligence that can be put to use later on. Whatever it may be, Derek grabs the phone and charger and sticks them in his cargo pocket as he strides out the door.

6

The ping of a baseball getting slapped by an aluminum bat rings through Derek's open window, followed immediately by the cheers of parents sitting in the bleachers. He eases his truck into the parking lot of the ball field just as the batter reaches second base and the families settle back onto their seats. Hopping out of the truck, he checks his watch and silently curses. Late again.

Derek does his best to breathe, his anger from earlier still sitting at a slow boil, to clear his mind. He's home now. Time to see his boy. To enjoy a summer Sunday. As much as he tries to acknowledge the mantra, the words fall short of their intended purpose.

Outside of Marshal's cabin, Gil had met him, extending an empty palm while also holding up a strip of black cloth. "Keys. Then blindfold up, Marine."

Derek looked the man up and down. "Not a chance."

The slender man laughed and shook his head. "Then you ain't going anywhere anytime soon, broseph. You see, we're willing to bet that you didn't

pay nearly enough attention on your way in here, but
now that you've seen the place, we're not gonna take
any chances getting you out of here. No need to give
an intelligence officer free rein at mapping out our avenues of approach. This way, we drive you out while
one of my guys follows in your truck."

All things compounding, Derek felt the muscles
pulsing in his jaw from clenching his teeth so tightly.
His eyes burrowed into the other man.

For his part, Gil had his amused smirk plastered
across his face the entire time. "I know. Decisions, decisions. Take as long as you like, D. It's your daylight
burning."

In the end, Derek relented, agreeing to the ride and
allowing his truck to be driven out of the woods. Despite the blindfold, he did his best to memorize the
twists and turns, timing how long between each and
the directions made, but eventually, he lost track. The
group spent so much time wheeling him around the
woods that Derek couldn't keep up. He'd have barely
a notion as to where the camp was beyond the turn-
off from the street.

By the time he'd gotten onto actual roads, he was
two hours behind schedule. Hitting the interstate, Derek's anger had finally broken. He'd ranted into the
empty space of his truck as it barreled down I-87.
With no one to witness, he was free to scream, and
he did so until the veins bulged from his neck, his face
went red, and sweat streaked down his face. Everything from the group withholding payment to the
delay to the insinuation that he would sell out his
country. He shouted until his voice went hoarse, railing against everything from the traffic to his divorce
and to civilian life in general.

Somewhere around Saratoga Springs, he finally stopped yelling.

Now crossing behind the backstop, he walks over to the bleachers on the third base line. Kim notices him and pushes up from her bench. Her lips are compressed into a thin line, and although her eyes are hidden by her Ray-Bans, he's certain they're alight with annoyance.

Shorter than he is by a foot and a half, she's wearing tight jeans, a pair of low-top Converse All Stars, and an untucked baseball shirt, the blue sleeves matching the color of Michael's uniform. Her dirty-blond hair is pulled back into a ponytail save for a wisp that she has to push back over her ear.

Kim stops a little ways from the bleachers, crossing her arms and grabbing them at the elbows. Not as defiant a posture as folding them but defensive nonetheless.

"Hey, Derek," one of the moms in the bleachers says.

"Hi, Shari," he returns with a small wave as he closes the final few feet to Kim. "How are we doing?" he says to his ex.

"Hey there, big guy!" a dad calls out.

"Yeah, hi, Carl" Derek returns less cordially than the last.

Kim pauses a moment before answering. When she does, her voice is level, but tinged with the effort to make it so. "We're getting crushed. Ten to two, I think, although I lost count."

"Dang," he replies, searching over the field. "How about Michael?"

"Strikeout, base hit, and a walk so far. He's out in center." She pauses a moment. "It's really late, Derek."

"I know. I had to stop at the apartment first to shower and check on Dad. He was none too pleased with me."

A smile attempts to break past the corners of her mouth. "Silver linings, I suppose. Better than you showing up here straight out of the field. I remember what those days smelled like."

"Yeah, well, two and a half weeks in the woods will do that to you." Straining his neck to see, Derek waves to his son. When he looks back, Kim is staring at him. "Sorry I'm late."

"It's not me, Derek. I know what to expect. It's Michael that you keep disappointing. You said you'd be home in time to take him."

"I know. I was upstate and hit traffic at the Tappan Zee. Crawled the rest of the way. You know how this damn—how this island is." He doesn't want to get into the real reason for his delay.

A deep sigh. "I should. You point it out every chance you get."

"Yeah, well. It's true." He reaches into his back pocket and produces the stacks of cash, wrapped in a plastic Target bag he found on the floor of his truck. "Here you go."

Kim feels the piles through the plastic and holds it back out to him. "Do me a favor and get a bank check for this. Then give it to me." He makes no move to take it. "We talked about this. The court needs to see records." She hesitates and then adds, "It's for your own good."

The umpire yells toward their side of the field. "I told you, Coach, you gotta get back by the dugout. You can't keep walking up the line."

"Did you reschedule the appointment with your counselor that you missed?"

Suppressing a grimace, he looks past her. The other parents are focused on the field, but the PTA grapevine was always straining to hear another juicy tidbit they could pass around. He lowers his voice.

"Not yet, but I will. I've been going, Kim. Every other week for the last four months. This was the first session I missed since I started."

She doesn't lower her voice. "Is it helping?"

Now it's his turn to sigh. "I don't know. Don't look at me like that; I'm being honest with you. I've just started. There's . . . a lot to sift through."

"And the medication? When are you going on it?"

A few of the ladies lean into one another and whisper.

"Can we talk about this later maybe?" he says. "After the game perhaps? I'll take you guys for pizza."

Kim's jaw shifts, and she has to look away. "I don't think that's the best idea, Derek. My coming along. It'll just confuse him. We need to keep things clear for the time being."

"How long are we going to do this, Kim? He's my son. You're my wife."

"Ex-wife."

Derek swallows. "Right, but even so. I still have hope for us. I want to be with my family. I want us back together."

A quick wipe of her cheek erases the tear that emerged from under her sunglasses. "If that's what you want, get the help that you need."

"Coach, I'm not gonna tell you again!"

"I'm just trying to adjust my batter's stance, ump."

"I don't care what—"

"How about you lay the fuck off, ump!" a man roars from the dugout.

The umpire pulls off his mask and starts walking up the line. "Excuse me?"

The man comes stalking out. He's bald and tan, a graying goatee and mustache on his face. Thick arms stick out of a sleeveless blaze-orange shirt stretched over a beer belly. The logo of whatever trade union he belongs to sits over his left breast. "You heard me! You been riding our coach the whole game. You let them do whatever the hell they feel like over there, but we can't even talk to our kids? What the hell is that?"

"You'd better settle down, buddy, or you'll be out of here."

"You're gonna throw me out? I'd like to see you try."

"Okay, okay, Larry," the coach says, stepping in between the two men. "We got it, ump. I'll stay back."

Derek raises an eyebrow. "What was that all about?"

"Oh, that's Jeremy's dad. Gets a little hotheaded sometimes. One of our kids got hurt earlier, and the dad coaching first base carried the boy back to the dugout. The ump didn't even wait for the guy to get back before he went on with the game. Seems to have ruffled Larry's feathers, I guess."

"Got it. So about later?"

"I'll think about it," she says, but from the tone of her voice, he can tell her mind is already made up. As she retreats to the stands, the inning ends, and the sides return to their dugouts. Michael's coach and the umpire have an animated yet quiet conversation while the other team takes the field. Derek walks up to the fence and waves again.

"Dad!" Michael yells, his face beaming.

"Hey, slugger, how's it going?"

"We're losing."

"That's okay. You need to learn what it feels like to win and lose. And when you're losing, you keep fighting, right?"

"Right."

"Because we don't do what?"

"Give up!"

"That's my boy," Derek says with a smile.

"Are you coming over tonight, Dad? I miss you."

A twinge of heartache ripples across his chest. Derek bites the inside of his check. "Probably not tonight, pal, but I'll talk to your mom. Maybe we can hang out a bit after the game is over."

Michael beams again. "Okay, great!"

"Now get in there with the rest of your team. Remember to choke up on the bat like I showed you. And wait for your pitch."

Not wanting to hold on to the cash, Derek goes back to the truck and locks it in his glove compartment. The game goes on for another few innings. Larry and the ump go at it again in between the eighth. Threats of getting tossed with the "Come try it" response get lobbed at each other. A few of the parents on both sets of bleachers add their subdued grumbles to the increasing banter.

When the game ends, the kids line up on their respective sides and then march across home plate to shake hands.

Larry brings up the rear of the line and launches another salvo. "Nice job, guys. Imagine how good of a game it would've been if the ump called it fair for both teams."

"All right, I've had about enough of you," the umpire replies.

"Fellas, maybe not here in front of the kids," the opposing coach says, but the words don't gain any traction.

"I'm putting a call in to the league. You're done coming to any games, pal." The umpire strides through the gate leading out of the field.

Larry shoves his way through the kids and follows the umpire closely. The two meet behind the backstop, where parents are trying to gather up their children for the ride home. More than a few cell phones come out and start recording.

"Who the hell do you think you are? You're gonna say I can't see my kid play ball?"

"You'd better back off, buddy!" the umpire says, pointing a finger.

"Or what? What the fuck are you gonna do?"

"I'll kick your ass," the ump replies, but there's no conviction in his voice. Maybe back in the day he would have been a match, but the man is well into his sixties.

Conversely, Larry looks to be twenty years his junior and used to throwing his weight around. The remark lights him up like a powder keg. "Come kick my ass, then!" he hollers as he balls up his fists. "Come on, try it!"

A bunch of the parents on both sides start shouting at the two men and then at one another. Larry approaches the umpire, who retreats against the backstop, his eyes uncertain. He searches around for any ally he can find.

Derek steps forward, afraid the older guy is about to get knocked out. "Gents, gents," he says, stepping in between them.

The umpire extricates himself and uses the interruption to back several feet away from the aggressor.

"Come on, not in front of the boys. It's just a game, right?"

Larry furrows his eyebrows and looks Derek up and down. "I don't recall asking you anything, friend. How about you just mind your own fucking business?"

"Come on, man. You really want to tune up a guy over a Little League game? This ain't worth it."

"How about you get outta my face before I mess your ass up too?"

Derek holds his hands up in front of him. "I don't want any trouble, partner. I just want everyone to calm down, all right?"

Larry stops searching for the umpire and fixates his attention on Derek. "I get it. You think because you're big I won't throw down with you, that it? Well you ain't that big, motherfucker. I've taken down plenty of assholes like you before."

Derek feels his anger welling back up. The surge of heat that makes him incapable of dealing with the benign nonsense civilians let upset them. Wrong orders at Starbucks. Cars speeding up to prevent them from merging onto the parkway. Parents incredulous over a kid's game. The trivialness of it frays his already stretched edges, threatening to snap his rope. So much is taken for granted here. So much energy spent on bullshit.

He catches a glimpse of Kim standing with Michael. Her arm is around his shoulders while his thumbnail is in his teeth, his eyes watching frantically. For their sakes and that of his tenuous relationship, he works to tamp the rage back down. "I don't doubt it. Tell you what. How about you and I go and grab a beer? I'm buying. Maybe we can both settle down a bit?"

"A beer? How about I shove your beer bottle up your ass?"

It's there. Derek can read the man's body language. His muscles tensed, eyes flaring. Larry is primed for a fight. He's never had to back down before. Never had cause to, and he's not about to start now.

Derek squares himself. Sets his feet. He's had enough. With everything. "Listen, you loudmouth. I've tried to be reasonable, but you're being an asshole. Last chance to back off."

"Man, fuck you!" Larry hauls back with his right and launches a massive paw at him.

The punch can't be more telegraphed. Larry is clearly capable of laying people out with one-punch haymakers. He never expects anyone to still be standing afterward, which is why he winds up like a big-league reliever fresh from the bull pen.

Conversely, Derek's movements are sharp and exacting. Fierce. Bordering on involuntary. The precognitive leap of a mongoose avoiding the fangs of a cobra.

His hands shoot up. His left arm shields his head while he steps in and twists his hips. Derek's right elbow catches Larry flush on his jaw, staggering him. He rotates back in the other direction just as fast, lowering his level into a squat version of his stance and delivering a short left into the man's gut. As Larry doubles over, Derek springs up, the two blows landing in the space of a second.

Derek can picture what will happen next. He'll drive his knee into the man's face. Larry's head will snap back. Blood and teeth flinging into the air as the large man topples over onto his side. He will stick a defensive arm up in the air while turning his broken face away. Seeing the exposed limb, Derek will pounce, pinning him with his knees as he laces his left arm around Larry's. Grabbing the man's wrist with his right hand, Derek will bend it over his own at the elbow joint, and then grasp his right forearm with his left hand. The figure-four lock complete, he'll torque to the point of dislocation, incapacitating his enemy for the rest of the engagement, with Derek and everyone else out of harm's way.

Instead, Derek catches himself. He's not in Fallujah, and this man isn't his enemy. He gives Larry a halfhearted shove that topples the man to the ground. Derek looks up as his fists slowly lower. Everyone is staring, many with their hands to their mouths. A couple of the kids are crying, Michael among them.

"Please," one of the boys begs between shuddering cries. "Please don't hurt my daddy anymore."

A low groan comes from Larry as he lies on the ground. Derek looks down and feels the knot in his stomach tighten. He didn't think he'd hit him all that hard.

Kim drags Michael away toward the parking lot. "What the hell is wrong with you?" she says as she walks by, her words laced with venom.

A couple of the other parents help roll Larry over onto his back. Already, the left side of his face is swelling up, and a cut above his eyebrow bleeds profusely from where he hit his head. Sirens are getting closer.

Derek backs away. The people standing around

shrink from him like he's the dangerous one and not the guy he protected them all from. Turning, he walks to the curb of the parking lot, sits down, and waits for the cops to arrive.

7

It's too late in the day for his arraignment, so Derek spends the rest of the weekend in jail. Sitting in a cell while trapped in the prison of his mind, he endlessly berates himself for what he did. For what his boy witnessed him doing. Every time the memory of Michael's face, contorted with terror, flashes in front of him, Derek drives the whip of guilt with even more force. By nightfall, he's already laid himself bare several times over.

Compounding his failure is the knowledge of how much more this is going to confuse his father. He finds some relief from his trust in Kim. Even as furious as she would be with him, she wouldn't leave the old man alone. At least not without checking on him first.

It takes until late in the afternoon on Monday, but when Derek's appearance occurs, his public defender does right by him. Citing Derek's home on the island, being the primary caregiver for his father, and his self-defense in the altercation, the lawyer gets a reasonable bail set. He posts, and within a half hour of stepping before the judge, Derek is released.

When he gets his phone back, there are three missed calls and two voice mails on it. Derek recognizes the number. It belongs to the Northport VA. He ignores the messages for the moment. More than likely, his counselor had learned of his arrest and wanted to connect, but he was in no frame of mind to start addressing what had happened. Instead, Derek orders an Uber back to the ballpark to pick up his truck.

Desperately wanting to drive straight to their house—her house, as it were, for the time being—Derek fights off the urge. Some of Larry's blood had dried on his clothes. He has to change first, lest he further traumatize his kid, and he needs to be sure his dad is taken care of before heading over.

Pulling in front of the house where he rents his apartment, Derek heads around back and down a flight of concrete stairs. The familiar hint of mold somewhere in the basement wafts up as he opens the door. Crossing through the kitchenette, he knocks on the door to the left-hand bedroom.

"Dad. Hey, Dad, you awake?" When there's no response, he opens the door. The bedroom is empty. The bed precisely made. Four inches of folded sheet and blanket. Eighteen inches from the head of the mattress to the fold. Four inches from pillow to fold. Crisp hospital corners. Despite everything happening with him, his father still bounces a quarter off his rack every day.

Derek checks the bathroom and his own bedroom, but the apartment is empty. He calls Kim twice in quick succession, but she doesn't pick up on either attempt. Derek showers quickly and checks for any missed calls or voice mails as soon as he's out. Nothing. He calls her again while putting on fresh clothes, but she doesn't answer. Frustration and worry competing for a hold over him, Derek grabs his keys and heads back out.

It only takes him ten minutes to get from his place in Calverton up to hers in Wading River. The property sits on a small knoll, surrounded by a wrought iron fence. Derek bottoms his truck out as he pulls into the long, winding paver driveway. Knee-high stone pedestals adorned with electric lanterns line the way up to a two-car garage. The house itself is two stories. All peaks and windows. Beautiful clapboard shingles and baby-blue decorative shutters. White pillars support a porch that runs the entire length of the front of the house and disappears as it wraps around to the right of it.

The place was much too large for just the three of them, but when they'd bought it, they had visions of expanding their family to fill in some of the rooms. Kim worked as a registered nurse out at the Peconic Bay Medical Center. Between her salary, his pension, and the assumption he would have a lucrative post-military career, they decided to go for their dream house, even if it was larger than they needed. Go big or go home, right? They earned it. They deserved it.

Little did they know they would be split up five years later. The needs of maintaining a separate place to live, his father's mounting medical expenses, and the fledgling survival school business had strained his finances to the point of asphyxiation. Kim wouldn't admit it, but he knew from their past mortgage statements that she wouldn't be able to keep the place, even with pulling in overtime the nights he had Michael. Not without him keeping up with the child support.

The front door to the house opens before he is completely out of the cab of his truck. Kim stands on the porch, closing the door behind her and wrapping her arms across her body. Even from this distance, he can tell she's upset. Her eyes are red and puffy from crying. Her hair a mess of tangles thrown up in a hasty ponytail pulled over her right shoulder. A bundle of folded papers sit in the back pocket of her jeans.

When he's within ten feet of the porch, she holds a hand up to him. "I think that's far enough, Derek." Her voice trembles, but her delivery is firm. The push and pull of fear combined with assertiveness. "You've got a lot of nerve showing up here after what you did."

Frowning, he lowers his head. "I'm sorry that happened. I wanted to come and talk to Michael about it. To both of you."

"Larry's in the hospital. Did you know that? The man's going to be in a neck brace for weeks."

"Kim, he swung at me."

"Are you kidding me right now?" she says, coming down the steps. "You know what you're capable of." Kim jabs a finger at him. "No way Larry could match up to that."

Derek spreads his hands in defense. "What was I supposed to do? Just let him knock out a guy twenty years older than he is? You saw the whole thing. I tried to stop it from happening."

Tears run down her cheeks. Her mouth opens slightly as she takes in a shuddering breath. "Always the defender. Right, Derek? The protector? No one else could have prevented it. And in no other way, right? Violence is always the answer. Is that it?"

"I didn't exactly see anyone else leaping into action, did you? They were more concerned with recording it on their cell phones than doing anything to stop him." The anger rises. A flitting notion courses through his head that he should probably clip off his words here, but they spill out nonetheless. "If I'm being honest, I held back on him, but I wish I hadn't. That bastard more than likely got what he deserved. Maybe he'll think twice next time before hauling off on someone."

Her lips compress into a thin line. Derek can practically hear her teeth grinding. Fresh tears quiver on the ledges of her eyes, just waiting to fall free. Jumpers in the door. She shakes. When her mouth opens to speak, no sound comes out at first.

"You know what I think? I think you wanted him to swing at you," she finally says.

"What? That's crazy."

"No, Derek. It's not." Her voice is even. The tears fall. Others streak behind them. "Ever since you got out. It's been building to this. Incrementally, but here we are. You didn't step in because you were afraid for the umpire or because it was the right thing to do. You were hoping Larry would do what he did."

"Kim. Please. That's—"

She shakes her head. "It's the truth. You know it, and I know it. I saw your face. You were smiling the whole time. You enjoyed taking that man apart the way you did."

The silence stretches between them. A pit gathers in his stomach. Bile rises in his throat. Derek swallows it back down. A buzz starts to build in the back of his head. His peripheral vision clouds at the edges. His early-warning senses kicking in and telling him that something is impending.

Turning her head, she wipes her eyes. "How long,

Derek? How long until that suppression gives way for good? How long until your 'holding it back' snaps and we're the ones directly in your path?"

"Kim, I would never hurt you. Either of you. You two are my everything." He's vaguely aware of his own trembling voice, even as disassociated as it appears to be.

"I'm sorry," she replies, finally breaking into a full-out cry. "I can't take that chance." She takes the bundle from her back pocket and hands it to him but can't meet his eyes.

He takes the papers gingerly from her grasp and opens the trifolded packet. *Suffolk County Family Court* is emblazoned across the top of the first page. Derek scans the documents quickly, clammy sweat breaking out on his neck and under his arms as he does so. Words and phrases leap out at him. *Hearing. Full custody. Temporary restraining order. No visitation.* She had to have filed for them at the same time he was being processed through the system.

"Got your scumbag lawyer friend Carl to push these through pretty fast, huh? How many favors did he have to call in to make that happen? That snake always had his eye on you, and now he sees his chance."

She flinches as if each word were physically striking her.

He instantly knows it was the wrong thing to say. Derek takes a deep breath, softens his tone. "Kim. Please. I'm begging you. Don't do this."

"I have to," she says, forcing herself to meet his eyes again. "I don't want it to be this way, but you scare our son, Derek. Hell, you scare me half the time. I have to do what's right for him. For us."

Derek shakes. "Kim . . . I can't. You two are the only thing I have left. The only thing that has any meaning for me. Please." He chokes down the crackle in his voice. When he speaks again, his words come out in barely a whisper. "Please don't take my boy from me."

Her crying is finished. Even though tears still run down her face, her resolve has solidified.

His hand twitches, involuntarily rising to wipe the water from her smooth cheeks. She takes a step back. As she does so, Derek can momentarily see behind her. The front door is cracked open, and his son's eyes peek through.

Derek waves. "Hey, buddy, Daddy's here!"

The door quickly shuts.

When his hand falls back to his side, it brings on a wave of resignation. He looks back to Kim. "What's the matter with Michael? Can I see him, please? Before I go."

A shake of her head. Another whimper. "He's terrified, Derek. He knows that you didn't start it, but seeing you do what you did has traumatized him all the same."

"Please, Kim," he says, pointing to the papers. "No visitations. Full custody. The hearing date is months away. You're telling me the next time I get to see my boy will be in a courtroom in October? That it could be the last time I ever see him?"

"Derek . . . I think it's best if you just go. For all of us."

His features slacken. Derek straightens, even as tears run from his eyes. He makes no move to wipe them away. Instead of anger, calmness washes over him.

When overseas, you couldn't let emotions get in the way. A raid gone wrong. Learning of yet another friend's death. One of the too many close calls. They couldn't be allowed to affect you. There was always another mission, and your brothers were depending on you to be at your best.

So he walled them off. An invisible barrier that allowed Derek to get the job his country, the Corps, and his unit needed him to get done. It was only after getting out that the wall was removed and the anger came flooding in.

His wall is returning, brick by insulating brick, stacking atop one another in quick succession to lock him away from what was happening. From what needs to be done. In the space of an instant, the emotional connection is severed, his defenses put in place. His guard up.

"Goodbye, Kim."

She shudders with a cry again, but he is unfeeling. Unmoved. Derek turns and walks to his truck. It barely registers when she says goodbye over his shoulder. A thought occurs to him just before he is about to climb back in the cab. When he turns to look at her, he is all business.

"Kim."

She wipes at her eyes. "Yes?"

"Where's my dad?"

8

Derek shows his Veterans Affairs ID card to the security guard posted at the entrance to the Northport VA parking lot. The man gives the card a cursory once-over and then hands it back, waving him in. Easing his truck into the lot, Derek goes through the hospital's main entrance and quickly finds the patient information desk.

"Stanley Harrington, please."

The receptionist directs him to the appropriate floor. Derek makes his way to the elevator through the whitewashed halls. The entire place smells of disinfectant and sterile plastic. Eyes downcast, he moves past the veterans of multiple generations. Korean War vets in hospital gowns and walkers being helped by nurses to the same waiting rooms that hold Global War on Terror twentysomething-year-old double amputees.

The collection of pain and sacrifice is a strong reminder of his contributions to both categories. Memories of lost brothers in arms. IEDs going off on the sides of roads. Blistering firefights. Men and women screaming in agony as they bled out. Limbs severed by hot, jagged metal.

Stepping into an elevator and pushing the button to the third floor, Derek stares at the faux wood paneling as the doors close. Fatigue washes over him. He absentmindedly traces the lines of the wood grain pattern with his fingers.

When he steps out into the hall, his vision blurs with that of a Baghdad street. The sand-colored two-story structures. Spiderwebs of ad hoc power cables crisscrossed overhead. Piles of trash strewn about. Standing puddles of foul wretchedness secreted from humans and spilled out onto the pavement due to the crumbling sewage infrastructure.

Two Abrams tanks idled at either end of the T intersection they were covering, their seventy tons formed the teeth of an outer cordon. The heat put out from their engines added to the sweltering 130-degree temperature. The scent of the exhaust blended with that of the perpetual blanket covering the city. A mix of air pollution, excrement, and decomposition.

The scene was always the same. His team standing outside their target building in the aftermath of the mission. The raid had been a bust. There was a flicker of orange from the corner of his eye. He twisted, rifle coming up in one smooth motion. The acquisition and engagement were second nature. Practiced precision of a seasoned professional. The combatant was down before his shell casings hit the deck.

And then the eyes. Those blood-spattered, frightened eyes.

Followed by the fire.

Stumbling, Derek braces himself with one arm

against the hospital wall, the other clutching his chest. He shakes his head and blinks the image from his vision. *Breathe. Deep, cleansing breaths. It's not real. You're not there. You're home.*

After a few exhales, he stands, grateful that the area around the elevator bank has remained empty. He doesn't want to deal with prying doctors—or to explain what is happening to anyone else, for that matter. There are larger concerns at hand.

Derek rounds the corner of the hall and comes up to a nurse's station. "Excuse me," he says to the woman seated there typing. "What room is Stanley Harrington in?"

The nurse looks at him over the rim of her glasses. "I'm sorry. You are?"

"I'm his son."

"Oh. We've been trying to reach you."

Derek stares down at the sign-in sheet as he scribbles his name. "Yeah, sorry about that. I was out of town and lost my phone. I only got back this morning." It is an amalgamation of several half-truths, but he seriously doubts that the nurse wants to hear the full explanation. It's just easier to forge ahead with the plausible.

Her eyes narrow. Apparently, his idea of plausible sounds like horseshit to her anyway, but his assessment of her level of interest is spot-on. She looks down at the computer again. After a few mouse clicks, she looks back up. "Your father's in room 312."

"Is he awake? Can I go see him?"

A tray of food comes flying out of a door down the hall and crashes against the far wall. "You call this dinner? What blind fuck do you have down there cooking this slop?"

The nurse looks at him with a grimace on her face. "That answer your question?"

Derek rounds the station. "Sorry about that too."

"Mmm-hmm," the nurse replies while picking up the phone. "I'll call his case manager. She'll want to speak with you now that you're here."

Derek walks toward the ranting coming from the room. An orderly works to gather up the food while another nurse stands in the door.

"Mr. Harrington, this is unacceptable. We have other patients on this floor." She ducks as a cup flies by her head.

"I don't give a damn! I want out of this slaughterhouse! Now!" his father screams.

Derek places a hand on the nurse's shoulder. "I'm sorry. I'm his son. I'll get him calmed down."

The young woman looks at him. "Better late than never, I suppose. Please do. A man recovering from a heart attack shouldn't have such an elevated pulse."

Derek nods and steps into the doorway. His father stands with his back to him, peering out the room's windows. The opening in his gown shows skin ashy and pulled taut against the knobs of his spine like the leathery scales of a dying dragon. Conversely, the skin bunches and sags at the lower end of his buttocks. His frail limbs jut out of the oversize gown like twigs.

Just like every time Derek bathes him or cleans him up after he's used the toilet, it's a callous reminder that the physical presence of the man standing before him is a pale comparison to what he once was.

"Hey, Dad."

Stanley spins around. "Well, look who decided to

show up! My good-for-nothing asshole son! Leaves for three weeks without telling nobody nothing!"

Unfortunately for Derek, when the man speaks, he is still every bit of the bastard he's always been. "Come on, Dad. Why don't you sit down a bit?"

"I will sit down. In my own goddamn chair in that shithole apartment you have us living in. Been trying to tell these people that I don't want to stay here, but they insist I can't leave! In a VA hospital! The very freedoms I defended, and they hold me prisoner here! Yeah, I'm talking to you out there!"

Derek flinches after seeing the orderly still cleaning up the food in the hall. He steps in and closes the door. "Dad. Come on. Just take it easy. Have a seat and tell me what happened."

"I won't take it easy! Don't you talk back to me! You want another spanking? The irony of it. The gall! They run this country into the ground, and then they're gonna use a place like this? Like this! To keep us here. To lock us up! After everything we've done!"

Derek puts his hands up and walks forward. "All right, Dad. All right. Come on. Just talk to me a bit." He gets closer and manages to put his hands on his dad's shoulders.

His face afire, chest heaving, Stanley suddenly looks around the room. His features soften as his eyes vacate. He works his mouth open and closed several times, but no sound comes out. Stanley's eyes settle on his son. They glisten with moisture.

"Son? Oh, son. What's wrong? What's going on?"

Derek guides his father over to the bed and sits him on the edge. "It's all right, Dad. Don't worry about it. You gotta stay calm, okay?"

His father looks around. "Where's Beth? Bethany? Beth!"

Derek swallows. "Mom isn't here, Dad, remember? She died a long time ago."

Stanley's face whips up, eyes alert, lip trembling. "My— She died? Bethany? Gone?" He lowers his face into his hands and begins sobbing uncontrollably. Derek puts an arm across his dad's shoulders and rocks him gently. His own eyes well up.

After a while, he manages to get his father to lie down. It isn't long before he falls asleep. Derek stands at the foot of the bed, one arm across his chest while the other strokes his beard. His eyes fall on to the wisps of his dad's hair, still flowing over his scalp from left to right despite how few of them remain.

Memory of wind by the river, lifting a full head of that hair, comes barreling forward. It was the only time the man could be patient. The only time that they saw eye to eye. The hours spent learning how to fish. How to hunt and trap.

At one moment, his hands could be soft and gentle. His father expertly demonstrating to Derek how to secure his fly to his line. Then an instant later, those same hands could be lashing Derek's knuckles with a fly rod. Punishment for not executing the task that had been so clearly articulated. It didn't matter that Derek was only seven or eight. Under Stanley's tutelage, you either did things right the first time or you reaped the whirlwind.

He banishes the sting of the rod and instead remembers the look on his father's face when he pulled his first rainbow trout from the stream on their land. Bagged his first eight-pointer. The look of pride after the parade on Parris Island when he graduated basic.

Those were the memories that Derek clung to the most. The ones that overruled his father throwing furniture around or tripping on empty beer cans strewn about the kitchen floor. That banished his recollection of the violent rages he and his mother had to endure. It was his father who'd introduced him to the wilderness, and in many ways beyond his training, pushed Derek to seek solace there again and again.

Marshal pops into his mind in that instant. He's younger than his father by a few years, but still. Each of them are in their eighties. It's inexplicable to him that two men roughly the same age could be so acutely opposite to each other at this stage in their lives.

A gentle knock comes from the door. It opens a crack, and a woman in her late forties pokes her head in. Derek signals for quiet and then makes his way out into the hall. She wears brown pants and a tan long-sleeve shirt. Her chestnut hair is pulled back into a tight bun, and thick eyeglasses adorn her face. A hospital badge on a retractable lanyard dangles from her right hip while a large clipboard clutched in one hand sits perched on her left.

"Mr. Harrington. I'm Darlene Miercevski, your father's caseworker."

Derek takes her outstretched hand. "Nice to meet you."

"It's nice to meet you as well. And speak with you. We've been trying to reach you for several days now."

"Yeah. I told the nurse at the station. I'm sorry. I work out of town, and I lost my phone during this last trip."

"Yes. That notwithstanding, I recommend you find us another emergency contact for your father. Your ex-wife, she was lovely and helpful in getting him here, but she no longer has power of attorney. With the situation being what it was, we had little choice but to hold your father, even though it was against his wishes. It's put us in quite the bind, what with our not being able to get in contact with you."

The explanation hollows him out in more ways than one. Even with everything that had happened at the ball field, Kim had still looked in on his father. While he sat in jail. Then he spoke to her the way that he did earlier. The guilt settles onto his shoulders like a yoke.

"I'm sorry, but can you just back up a little, please? My . . . ex. She said that he had a heart attack but that it had something to do with his medication?"

"Oh, yes. Of course." She looks at her clipboard. "He was brought in on Sunday with severe chest pains. Your ex-wife said he had been manic during her visit with him. She called an ambulance, which brought him here. After we had him sedated and got a proper read on his medications, it turned out that he hadn't been taking many doses, and others he was mixing up. It all led to a dangerous state of flux that ultimately induced a minor heart attack."

Derek feels his skin prickle and the hairs stand on end. Another member of his family that he had failed. "How is he now? His heart, I mean?"

The woman glances at the board. "Surprisingly, his heart has bounced back to normal since the incident. Once his medication was regulated at least. Physically, he seems fine. There is the larger issue at hand, however."

"You're talking about the outbursts, aren't you?"

She gives him a solemn nod. "Mr. Harrington, this is never easy to say to a loved one. Your father is showing the symptoms of progressive dementia. The ranting. Vacancy. Confusion. It's all there and appears to have been there for some time."

Derek grits his teeth. "He was doing better for a while. The meds, they were helping to keep things . . . stable."

"That may well have been the case, but at this point, your father is going to need round-the-clock care. I understand that you travel for work, but he just cannot be left alone any longer. Not after this episode. He came dangerously close to inadvertently causing his own death. The best thing for him now is to get him into a veterans' home. We tried explaining this to him in his periods of lucidity, but he refuses any such transfer."

"He won't go to one," Derek says, shaking his head. "He thinks the VA system is a political dog and pony show."

"Whatever he thinks, Mr. Harrington, it's in his best interest to convince him otherwise. Unfortunately, we can't keep him here in the hospital. This is a matter for outpatient care at this point, especially now that you as his primary caretaker are back."

What else? Why now? The thoughts ricochet around his head. He immediately chastises himself for even thinking of them. No matter his condition now, no matter what he had done in the past, the man was still his father.

The caseworker must've read something in his demeanor because her face softens. "In any case, Mr. Harrington, I'm sorry to have to deliver all of this to you. We're here to assist, but the staff has had quite a hard time dealing with the outbursts. We really do need to get him into a long-term care facility that's better equipped for patients with his condition. I can assist with the paperwork and placement, if you like." She starts pulling out a stack of papers from the board.

Derek holds a hand up. "I appreciate it. The offer and what everybody here has done for him. But I told you, he won't do it. He won't go into a vets' home. I'll just have to find a private place nearby."

"But . . . that could be thousands of dollars, Mr. Harrington. Really. He's earned the access to these facilities, just like you have. You shouldn't have to pay out of pocket."

He lets out a deep sigh. "It is what it is, ma'am. I made a promise to my mom when she was passing that I would look after him. If this is what it takes to make him comfortable until . . . well, then, that's what will have to happen."

Darlene gives one final nod with a small smile at the end of it. "I understand, Mr. Harrington. Here, take this." She hands over a business card. "Give me a call in a few days. I'll put together a list of places for you. Maybe that will help get things started a bit."

He takes the card and puts it in his pocket and then shakes her hand. "Yes. That would be a big help. Thank you."

"It was nice meeting you."

"And you as well."

As she heads down the hall, Derek slips back inside. He will keep his promise; he just has to figure out how to do so. Derek rounds the bed, his leg brushing against the metal frame. A clink sounds out.

He reaches down and grabs the cargo pocket. His jaw tightens as he feels the phone Marshal had given him. In his haste to get cleaned up, he had emptied his pockets onto his bed and then filled them back up when he'd put on a fresh pair of pants.

The thought crosses his mind, and he dismisses it outright, but like the smell of smoke long after the house has finished burning, it lingers on. Derek watches his father, but his mind wanders upstate. Sitting in one of the chairs, he leans forward, interlacing his fingers in front of his mouth. More so than ever, he feels himself being pulled apart.

9

Kelly Scarsboro stares at the giant inkblot embedded in the twenty-year-old carpet. At least once a day, he delves into its murky depths. The morning drags on, even more so than usual, and as Kelly stares at the spot, a revelation dawns on him. After so many contemplations, it's finally become clear. The ink spot is synonymous with his career.

They both aren't going anywhere.

And if the ink spot is a symbol of his stagnant progression through the ranks of the FBI, then the archaic 1980s-era copy machine the size of a taxi is clearly the metaphor that applies to the agents he works with in the organized crime division. His partner, Caleb, had joined the Bureau the year Kelly entered junior high.

After a stint in the Navy, Kelly had used the GI Bill to attend college and law school. While completing his last semester and preparing for the bar, he had applied to the Bureau. The timing couldn't have worked out any better. Shortly after passing the exam, he received his academy date. Kelly was promptly assigned to the

New York field office upon graduation from Quantico.

From there, the good fortune continued. Kelly's Special Agent in Charge said his intelligence background and deployments overseas had "breathed new life" into the division. That, combined with a bunch of low-level mobsters infatuated with being the next godfather, had resulted in several significant arrests in a relatively short amount of time. Kelly's rise through the ranks was meteoric. A SAC slot of his own was definitely in his future.

Then everything came to a screeching halt. The young goons went underground, probably as much from the old guard's intervention as the FBI's prowess. Interbureau politics reared its ugly head, with superiors jostling for position while utilizing their all-star subordinates as pawns on the board.

After several years of building successful cases, as well as a stellar reputation, Kelly found himself painted into a corner. He tried for transfers into other divisions, but his SAC was holding on to him. No way was the man going to give up his stud pony while the race was still being run.

Standing and stretching, he looks over his cubicle wall, one of four grouped together. Multiple iterations of the clustered desks run the entire length of the floor, like fossilized British squares from the battle of Waterloo. Most of them are empty. Many of them are piled high with boxes of old paper files. Notebooks. Outdated tech like VCRs and cassette recorders that the Bureau doesn't use any longer but refuses to get rid of.

Caleb walks by with his friend Frank. They tell him they're going to lunch but don't invite him along. Kelly looks at his watch—1:30 p.m. By the time they get to where they're going, it'll be 2:00, which is right about the time the afternoon cocktails start flowing. It's unlikely he'll see them again until tomorrow.

A few minutes later, he's trying to decide whether he should eat or hit the gym two floors up when his phone buzzes on the desk. A text message lights up his home screen.

**Hey Kel it's Derek. How've
you been?**

Kelly hesitates a moment. It had been years since he'd heard from him. **Holy shit! DH! What's up man?**

**All good. Listen, you
available later? I need to
talk.**

The message piques his interest. Derek was good people, a bit of a recluse since getting out, but that's just how some guys were. It didn't change the fact that he was as solid as they came, and when it came to professionalism, there was no one better. If Derek needed to talk about something, chances were it was legit.

**Sure man. I can get away.
When and where?**

Fraunces Tavern at 4?

**Sounds like a plan. See you
there.**

The colonial-style brick building located on the corner of Pearl Street is nestled near the southern tip of Manhattan. The room upstairs famously hosted

George Washington's farewell dinner with his officers at the end of the revolution. The bill from the group's meal is still on display, including a bar tab that tallied enough alcohol to put a small elephant in a coma.

When Kelly walks in, he sees a smattering of businesspeople at tables in the bar section, just to the left of the entrance. At the far corner of the bar is a patron by himself. Even from where he stands, Kelly can see the hulking shoulders and muscular arms. Derek's tan T-shirt stretches to its limit at the sleeves and chest. Looking out from under the brim of his baseball cap, Derek smiles and stands up.

Crossing the floor, Kelly notices that Derek looks a little thinner than he remembers. Besides that, the only thing different about him is the dark beard, the first signs of silver creeping into it.

They shake hands and pull each other into a quick, backslapping hug.

"I almost didn't think you'd be here," Kelly says. "Like this was some sort of old-school readiness drill flashback or some shit."

A glint of something passes over Derek's face, and then it's gone just as fast as it arrived. He smiles, but the gesture doesn't meet his eyes. "It's good to see you, man. How long has it been?"

"Hell," Kelly says as they sit down on the stools. "Five years, right? Last time we got together was your retirement party."

Derek flushes with embarrassment. "You're right. I'm sorry, man. I can't believe it's been that long."

Waving his hand in dismissal, Kelly smiles back. "No worries. That's the military lifestyle anyway, right? There one day, gone the next. We always pick up right where we left off."

The bartender comes over. "What are you having?"

Kelly notices the empty rocks glass next to Derek's pint glass. "Lemme see. Let's go with . . . you know what? Let me get an Allagash White."

"Another Yuengling here," Derek says, raising the pint glass up even though it's still half-full. He turns back to Kelly. "Thanks for meeting me on such short notice."

"Are you kidding? I mean you're DH. The designated hitter himself, here in the flesh. How do I not meet up with you?"

Smirking at the old nickname, Derek takes a sip of his beer. "I appreciate it all the same. I know it must be hard to get away."

"It's easier than you might think. Things are so slow I may start committing the crimes just to spur an investigation. It's not like the old days when I was attached to you guys."

"I wouldn't think things would be slow in the FBI."

After the bartender delivers his drink Kelly takes a long pull. "They're not. Just in the organized crime unit—which, coincidentally is where I landed. There isn't much to do these days in that area of the criminal justice system. Time is on our side with the old mobsters. We just wait the bastards out until they die."

The big man laughs into the rim of his glass. "Organized crime? I would've thought that with your background you'd be with counterterrorism."

"That is the golden calf, my friend. You should see their floors. Multiple, mind you. Not just one. Newly renovated. State-of-the-art computers. Even those fancy ergonomic chairs. I swear, ever since Bush 2.0 opened up the register drawer, those guys have been living the high life."

"So . . . how come you didn't end up there?" Derek asks, rubbing his beard.

Kelly looks off to the right, gritting his teeth through a mouthful of beer. "The counterterrorism division? A Navy guy being attached as support to an intel team wasn't enough boots-on-the-ground experience for them."

Derek's face suddenly gets very sullen. He calls the bartender over and orders another Bulleit for his empty rocks glass. They continue to sip on their drinks without speaking until the new one arrives and the bartender retreats.

"So what's up, man? You said you had something you wanted to run by me?"

Twisting on his stool, Derek looks around the interior of the bar. His body tenses up. "I had a run-in with a group upstate. Thought the Bureau should be aware of them, but I didn't want to go through any tip line bullshit."

"Shit. Sounds serious. Hit me with it."

The man relays the story of Gil's recruitment, the two weeks spent in the field with the group, and Marshal's offer. In true military intelligence fashion, Derek relays the equipment and armament that he observed. The number of people. Their names. Vehicles. Pertinent facts like Marshal and Gil having served. He reveals that they had his file, a point that Derek gets particularly concerned about.

"I don't buy the whole utopian-society shit, at least not for everyone," he says at the bottom of his bourbon. "Some of the families are probably in the dark about what is actually going on up there, but best as I can put together, the cash on hand and the firepower lead to two possibilities—they're either running guns across the border or they're running drugs. Not much that I observed on the latter, but the money would support that theory, no?"

"Sure," Kelly says, nodding. "I doubt they're a Humboldt County weed empire, but that doesn't mean that they're not cooking something. Probably meth. Maybe their labs are separate from the main camp somewhere. More discreet that way. They might want the training to help better protect those."

"Or eliminate their rivals."

"Dog-eat-dog world when you're in that kind of business," Kelly replies, taking another sip of his beer. He watches as Derek throws back the bourbon and chases it with the remainder of his second pint. "Everything all right with you, DH?"

A sideward glance. "Yeah. Why?"

"I mean, it's just this whole thing seems a little disjointed."

Derek looks away as he replies, "How do you figure?"

"Well, there's the texting and meeting up after five years, for starters. Don't get me wrong, I love seeing you. But you know from your experience that there's not much to this. Whatever these guys are up to, it doesn't rise to the level of the FBI. Hell, most groups don't unless they're chanting, 'Death to America' in Arabic and burning the president in effigy. This is something for local law, maybe the state police at best."

"What about them having my file?"

"Who knows?" Kelly says, shrugging. "Probably some farmer's kid they have on the payroll playing hacker. After that VA data breach a few years back, it's not as hard as you might think to get access to someone's DD214. Those shits are practically auctioned off on the dark web."

"What are you getting at?" Derek grumbles.

Kelly sighs. "Is there something else going on with you? Are you okay?"

Derek tenses again. So much so that Kelly can see a muscle pulsing in his jaw, but then he visibly deflates. "Nah, man. I'm pretty far from okay."

Keeping his eyes averted and his voice low, Derek relates his split from Kim and everything in between, all leading up to the fight with Larry and having to put his dad in a home. "I don't know, Kel. It wasn't supposed to be like this. Everything is so goddamn . . . hard. I get set off at every little thing. A person cutting the line at the movies. My USB cord not connecting to the computer. A few months before the split, I slammed my fist onto the tabletop because Michael wouldn't chew with his mouth closed. I scared the kid half to death."

Rotating away from him on his stool, Kelly watches as Derek wipes at his eyes with the back of his hand. "It's a clusterfuck, man. I'm sorry. Try not to be so hard on yourself. All those years spent fighting. The aggression and adrenaline. You can't just throw the switch on that."

"Yeah. I guess."

"And it's understandable why you're lashing out. Ninety-nine percent of people out there couldn't care less about the war on terror. They couldn't pick Afghanistan out on a map. Being thrust smack-dab into the middle of it? You really think you can just be a house dad and a survival teacher overnight after all you've done?"

Derek swirls the ice in his empty glass and stares into it. "I just . . . I feel like a shadow."

His heart aches for his friend. Kelly had experienced his own difficulty with reintegration. He called it *navigating the minefield.* If his level of misery was any indication after just four years of service, he could only imagine how compounded that would be for someone who served twenty-two years in today's operational tempo. It would be . . . exponential.

The two men sit in silence. After a minute, a smile creases Kelly's lips. "You know what you need, DH? A mission."

"What? Like start running marathons or take up ice sculpting? No thanks."

"No," Kelly says with a small chuckle. "I mean a mission. A real one."

Derek's head slowly turns. There's a hint of fire in his eyes.

"Why don't you head back up there?" He's met with a dismissive frown.

"Yeah, okay. I'll just jump back into *Buckmasters.* Sure, Kel."

"No, listen. Hear me out on this. We send you back in. Let's just say for a second that there is a legit concern with these guys. It would take the Bureau months to find someone with your unique skill set. Months more to get them established to a point that they're invited in. You've already met that criteria for both.

"So we leverage that. I have enough leeway with my ops, and my SAC will bless off on basically whatever I present to him. As it stands now, there's strong circumstantial evidence for money laundering and drugs, both of which fall under my purview. You could be like . . . an unofficial confidential informant."

Derek stares at him.

Kelly can tell the wheels are churning.

"You can't be serious, Kel."

"I am. Look, you go in there and collect intel on these guys while teaching them what they want to know. Best-case scenario, there's nothing to them, and you collect your payday. Worst case, they're a bunch of assholes. If that ends up happening, we go in and clean them out. You will have helped rid the country of one more threat."

"Doesn't work," Derek says, shaking his head. "With everything I got going on? I can't just up and leave my life for three months."

"So don't," Kelly replies with a shrug. "Obviously, they want you. Otherwise, why would they go through the trouble of checking you out? You know better than I that's leverage you can exploit. Turn it to your advantage and strike a deal. Maybe you just head up there for a month to see what's what?"

Derek takes another swig. His features soften somewhat. "Even if I wanted to, which I'm not saying I do, I couldn't do it. These guys want to learn how to run and gun. You can't fake that. I'd have to teach them the real thing."

"How are they gonna know what that is?" Kelly says, feeling himself getting animated. "Even the vets up there. Their knowledge of special ops is probably filled with whatever nonsense the movies have given them. I bet if you show them even the most basic shit, they'll think they're all Jason Bourne."

A smile creases Derek's face. "And you're not concerned about them getting trained? I don't want to be an accomplice to whatever bank heist or police shoot-out these idiots end up in."

Kelly upends his beer. "If it gets to the point that we know they're serious about something like that, we'll take them down well beforehand. Make that one of your objectives. Intel prep for an operation. Map out their camp. Scout the best avenues of approach and all that shit. I would put HRT, the Hostage Rescue Team, up against anyone under normal circumstances, but you arm our guys with that knowledge? They'll go in there and bust *Deliverance* up."

They both burst out laughing.

"We'd need comms. There's no signal up there," Derek offers.

"Details. Details, man," Kelly says, waving him off. "I'm sure between the two of us, we can come up with enough tradecraft to make this work."

The smile that was there just a few moments ago vanishes. Derek hangs his head. When he speaks, his voice is low. Almost . . . ashamed. "If it's the best-case scenario. If it's nothing but inheritance from an old man that wants to live in the woods. You really think it's okay that I take the money? What with their turning their back on the country and all?"

"Yeah, Derek, I do." Kelly's voice comes across full of compassion for his friend. "Listen to me. No matter what they're choosing to do, you're not betraying your oath. You and I both know that. It's not every day an opportunity for this kind of money comes around. You owe it to yourself to at least try. If it ends up being bad, I have enough rank to authorize a discretionary spend. It won't be the full freight, but it'll at least be some compensation for your time."

Derek lets out a deep exhale. "Tell me that we're not considering this just because we're getting drunk."

Kelly laughs. "No, man. Nothing like that. After

everything you've told me, you need this. Don't spend the next few months tearing yourself apart over Michael and your dad. Trying to scrounge together classes to pay for both. You have the experience to handle this situation better than anyone. If there is something to this case, you'd be doing what you do best. Serving your country.

"So we send you up there and run you like an op. In the meantime, I can reach out to one or two assistant U.S. attorneys I know. In exchange for bringing them this, I'm sure they'll reciprocate with whatever help they can lend on your criminal case and custody hearing."

Nodding at Kelly, his lips compressing into a thin line, Derek's eyes glisten. "Thank you, Kel. Truly."

"No worries, brother. This is what we do for each other. I'll make sure to help you out in any way I can." Truth be told, there was another reason why he wanted to reach out to his litigator contacts. Both of them had tried cases for the counterterrorism division and could put in a good word if he was able to serve them up some prime convictions.

Derek claps Kelly on the shoulder. "You're a good man, Kel."

Raising his glass, Kelly replies, "You too, DH. Always have been. One of the best."

Smiling, Derek upends his beer. "Another round?"

Checking his watch, Kelly reaches up and loosens his tie. "The hell with it. Why not?"

10

The apartment is dark and strangely quiet, save for the buzz of the fridge and the clock ticking on the wall. Derek sits at the small table wedged in the space between the two bedroom doors. A rocks glass of bourbon sits perspiring on the tabletop. The phone Marshal gave him and a digital recorder next to it. He stares at the empty chair across from him and takes a sip.

Darlene from the VA had provided the contact information for several facilities nearby that had room for his father. Derek had checked them out online and then made a round of calls, finally settling on one that he thought could best provide care without bankrupting him in the process. Decision made, Derek had used the time his dad was parked in front of the TV to pack his bags, feeling like he was betraying his mother's wishes with each article of clothing he folded up.

Though it wasn't a veterans' home, the old bastard had put up a fight. Derek practically had to drag him into the truck and then again to get him into the home. Stanley had promptly trashed his new room once he was inside it. The nurse reassured Derek that his father was in good hands, but Stanley was still ranting when Derek left. He silently asked for his mom's forgiveness as he climbed back into his truck.

From there, his attention had turned to upstate. After another round of convincing from Kelly, they launched into planning the op in earnest. The rough framework had come together quickly. On top of Kelly's ability to arrange resources, he surprisingly had a lot of time to dedicate toward the plan. Throughout their strategy sessions, there had been palpable excitement coming from him.

Derek can't ignore the small surge of excitement he feels. There is a familiarity to the coordination. Going through the intelligence assessment. Determining their objectives. In short order, he has fallen back into the routines that defined the operational part of his career before transitioning to work as an instructor. Even if it is only precautionary, the prospect of being part of an op again works as a slight counterbalance to the mountain of shit that has piled up in his life.

Their preparations complete after just a few days, it is now on him to make the call. Derek spins his glass. He looks at the clock. Leans back in his chair. Slowly, the momentum builds. His eyes fall on a picture taped to the fridge of him, his dad, and Michael on a charter fishing boat the previous summer. It was the last time his dad was really lucid, and just a few months before Derek and Kim split up.

Finally scooping up the phone, he scrolls to Contacts and highlights the only number in the folder. Derek's finger hovers over the Call button. He raises the glass to his lips and takes a long pull.

"Damn it," he says as he presses down. He raises the phone to his ear as it begins to ring.

On the fourth iteration, the other end picks up. People talking overshadow a song playing in the background. "Riverside Tavern," a gruff voice belches into the receiver.

"Marshal there?"

The man on the other end hesitates for a moment before answering, "Give it an hour. He'll call you back."

The line goes dead. Derek tosses down the phone and upends his bourbon. Jumping out of his seat, he flicks the ice into the sink and grabs another handful from the freezer. Pouring, he sits on the edge of the couch and turns on the TV. As much as he tries, not even his Yankees beating on the Red Sox can distract him from what he's just set in motion. As the time drags on, he wrestles with whether he should call the whole thing off.

When the phone rings, he leaps off the couch. Before answering, he switches the recorder on. Punching the Speakerphone button, the sounds of the bar come through again, albeit subdued. Maybe a back office, then, or a storeroom.

"Derek?" Marshal says.

"Yeah, I'm here."

"Hey there, young man. Good to hear your voice!" Marshal is practically dripping with anticipation. "I'd almost given up hope of ever talking to you again, but it looks like the good Lord had other plans."

Suppressing an eye roll, Derek presses on. "Right. Whatever. Listen, the offer you made? Is it still good?"

"Are you kidding? Of course it is! When can you—"

"Hang on, Marshal. There are a few things we need to discuss before I agree to anything."

The old man pauses, his voice coming through decidedly less jovially. "If this is about the money, I have to tell you I won't budge on the price. I think the compensation is more than fair."

"The rate is fine. It's the time we've got to talk about."

"I'm not sure I . . ." Marshal starts and then trails off. "What do you mean, the time?"

"Just what it sounds like. Three months is something I can't commit to. Not right now anyway. I've got classes I'd have to put off and other responsibilities beyond those. I can give you a month. That's it. At the end of it, we can evaluate where your people are and make a new arrangement, if you like."

A long pause filled with clinking glassware and muffled laughter goes by. "So I take it by rate, you mean the five grand a week I offered, then?"

It was how he finally justified it. Just like what you get charged when you need a plumber right away. You can pay top dollar for that fix, or you can let your pipes keep leaking while the plumber carries on with his life. The way Derek figured, if they really wanted him, they'd go for the twenty grand and he could make a bundle fast. If they didn't, then he could stop entertaining this whole mess. "Correct, but there's more. I want to be clear about expectations."

Seconds tick by. "All right," Marshal returns. "I haven't agreed to the altered timeline just yet, but let's hear what you have to say as if I have."

Derek sniffs. Despite the verbiage, he knows he's gotten his first concession. Now it's just a matter of rolling the snowball down the hill. "Next, I'm not waiting until the end of the month to get paid. Not after what you guys pulled the last time. I won't have you holding out on me."

"Derek," Marshal says, then coughs a few times. "I'm not about to hand you twenty thousand dollars just for showing up."

"I didn't ask for that, did I?" he snaps back. "I want my first payment up front. After that, I get paid every week when we come out of the field."

"Okay. That's acceptable."

"The day after tomorrow, have someone meet me at the Adirondack Bank in Saranac Lake at fifteen hundred. It's about an hour from you, if I recollect. Address is 67 Main Street. Have them bring the first payment. It'll be put into a safe-deposit box that I've arranged. I expect to be given the time to run the money out there every Saturday."

He and Kelly had decided that the bank would present the best opportunity for communications. The justification of wanting to receive payment in increments was plausible given how the group had withheld on him the last time. Using a safe-deposit box instead of putting the money into an account would provide an opportunity to pass messages. Kelly had already arranged for a junior agent to be placed in the bank as a teller. Derek would slip notes into the box with the cash, which the agent would then retrieve and transmit to Kelly in New York City. It would also preserve the bills should they need them for evidence later.

Marshal's leery response allows Derek to gauge how in tune the group is with their operational security. "Derek, we're already putting a lot of trust in you with what you've been shown so far. I don't know how I feel about you coming and going."

"You're gonna have to live with it, Marshal. You're paying me for my silence as well as my training. On that note, when I'm in town, I'm also going to want some time to call my boy."

Sharpness comes through the line. "Listen, Derek. I am more than willing to bend a little and accommodate things that make sense, but this is asking a lot."

"I'm not going a month without talking to my son, Marshal."

"I understand what you're saying, of course. Family is important, but you have to understand where my reluctance is coming from on this. The way we're conducting this call is evidence of the steps we've taken to avoid communications tied to our camp."

"You're a man of faith. Time for you to take a leap. You want me to train your people or not?"

After a few moments, Marshal finally speaks. "I will allow it, provided you meet me halfway and agree to have one of my people go with you into town. Your calls will be made in their presence as well."

"I can live with that." He'd already done his research. The safe-deposit boxes are in a private room that only he would be allowed to access as a holder, and he's certain that he can manage to redirect one of Marshal's inbred idiots long enough to make a call in private. If it even came to that. Phone communication to Kelly was a secondary option anyway. They had both agreed that the messages through the intermediary would be the most secure. The key was to get Marshal to agree to the bank drops. This concession assured that he did.

"Good. What else would you like to discuss?" the old man goes on.

"You've taken steps for your security. I need some put in place for mine. I don't know you or your people, and I'm not about to blindly turn over my well-being."

The knife's edge in Marshal's voice gets sharper with each passing minute. "What steps are we talking about here?"

"When I get there, I want my pick of one of those ARs I saw your men with, and it stays with me for the duration. I won't be checking it in at night like the others."

"A man of your stature, I'm surprised you don't have your own."

The snide remark gets under Derek's skin. "Yeah, well, let's just say I've had other priorities. You have any idea how expensive aluminum baseball bats are?"

Marshal sighs. "I'll grant you the rifle, but it stays in camp when you go into town. I won't have you riding around with it under the back seat of your truck."

"Fine, but that goes to my next point. I room alone. If you can manage that, I'll leave my rifle in the cabin."

"There are cabins on the north side of the camp that are unoccupied for the moment. You can have one of those. What else?"

"Ten magazines."

"Derek . . . that's three hundred rounds."

"Standard combat loadout, Marshal," Derek replies matter-of-factly. "Better get your boys started on carrying that much too. If the expectation is that they're going to operate as a QRF, then they need to get used to carrying enough ammo to do the job right. Issuing that much won't be a problem, will it?"

"No. No, it won't."

Derek had done the math before the call as well. Twelve students and himself at three hundred rounds a piece equaled out to just under four thousand. Not a terribly large number, but the fact that they're able to give out that much in one shot let's Derek know they've probably got plenty more on hand.

"All right, good."

"Is that everything, son?"

Derek runs through the punch list in his head. "I'll need a few supplies from the camp. Two of those metal buckets that I saw near the showers. Things like that. I'll pick out the rest when I get there. Won't be a lot."

"Excellent. Now it's my turn for expectations."

"I'm listening," he replies flatly, his curiosity hidden behind the tone.

"I told you earlier that I need you to assess the ones I've chosen. If I'm going to be sure they're the right men for the job, I need to know what they're made of. How they're going to act under fire. Under . . . duress. I need to know what will break them and what they will say when they do. You understand what I'm asking?"

Clenching his jaw, Derek stands up slowly and paces around the apartment. "Asking it and understanding what's involved are two different things, Marshal. You've seen my file. Where I've taught. SERE level C is no joke. It's not something you put Boots through, let alone out-of-shape forty-year-olds. You can't ever take that back once you put a man through it."

The old man's voice is matter-of-fact as it comes

back through the line. "You're just gonna have to live with it, Derek. You want your points agreed to? This is mine, and it's nonnegotiable."

"We're dealing with a condensed timeline here. You understand the shit that I'm going to have to put them through to get a good read on them this quickly?"

Another cough. "I'm not asking you to put them through shit, Derek. I'm telling you to put them through hell."

He sighs. The objective is to get Marshal to agree to the terms. "If I'm going to do what you ask, then it needs to be modified. Putting them through the full SERE course could kill some of those guys. On top of that, there's a role you have to play as well."

The old man chuckles on the other end of the line. "I'm eighty-one years old, Derek. You don't expect me to—"

"Obviously, you won't be participating, although you look like you wouldn't have a problem."

"Why, thank you."

"Yeah, whatever," Derek snaps. "What I mean is that your men need to see that you endorse my methods and that what I'm doing is not just for shits and giggles. It's because you're letting it happen. The directive comes from you, and you're condoning what I'm doing to them. If they think there's a 'get out of jail free' card with you, that they can quit whenever they want, then I'll never be able to get what you're asking for."

A long silence stretches while Marshal contemplates what Derek is saying. "I hadn't thought of watching. It won't be easy. Like I said, a lot of these people are my kin, but you have my word. I'll make sure they understand, and I won't interfere. If this is what is needed to safeguard my people, then God's will be done."

This time, there's no stopping the eye roll. "Gil goes through everything too. If you want him to be your field leader, then he has to be in it with his men."

"Agreed."

Derek sighs. "All right. Pick a bog a mile or two outside of camp. One that's a few feet deep and preferably one that's hard to get to on foot. Have your people build a cage in the water and another on shore next to it. Each one should be big enough to fit half the group, but don't make it roomy. And don't let any of the men going into training know about it. The supplies will need to be brought out there as well before I begin."

"I'll talk to the carpenters now and have them start on it first thing in the morning, and we'll be sure to get whatever you need to you."

"Make sure the cages are in place before I get there. Have the men you want trained pack all the gear and equipment they'll need for their first week in the field. I'll be taking them out shortly after arrival."

"Okay, Derek. Okay. Everything sounds fantastic! I can't wait to get started. We'll see you in two days, then?"

"In two days."

"Great!" Marshal replies. "Thank you so much! You don't know—"

Derek ends the call. Walking back to the table, Derek drops the cell and switches off the recorder. The frustration is welling up inside him, but he takes a few deep breaths and a gulp of his drink. By the time he's done with the bourbon he's calmed down. Derek fishes his personal cell out of his pocket and dials.

Kelly picks up after the third ring. "You make the call?"

"Just finished."

"How'd it go?"

"You know," Derek replies. "Amateur hour. They agreed to everything. Barely put up a fight."

"Boom! Another ribby for the designated hitter. When you heading up?"

"Day after tomorrow."

"Awesome. I'll pass the word to Emily. Tell her that we're under way."

Derek cuts off a sigh. "About her. Just how junior is this agent of yours?"

"Transferred to my unit a couple of months back from the applicant division." Derek can practically see his friend shrugging on the other end of the phone. "She's got potential, DH, and right now, she's wasting away running database searches behind a terminal. This'll be a good start for her."

"You sure she's up to the task?"

Kelly laughs. "What? You mean sitting behind a counter as a bank teller? On an op where we're pretty sure there's nothing going on anyway? Yeah, big guy, I think she'll do just fine. Besides, while I have a good amount of latitude, it's not exactly carte blanche. The only reason I was able to get her is because she doesn't have a caseload. Beggars and choosers, friend. Until something pops on this, the newbie is what we're authorized."

"Okay, then. It is what it is. You get anything yet from the phone records on the tavern? And what about the land?"

Kelly's voice comes through with a bit of resignation. "We pulled them as soon as you gave me the number, but so far, no apparent connections to anyone named Marshal or Gil. A bunch of calls that dead-end at what are probably cell phones on the other side."

"Burners."

"Exactly," Kelly replies. "That raises some eyebrows, brother. Where there are burners, there are not always the best intentions. As far as the land is concerned, officially, it belongs to the state. We're tracking down when it might have changed hands from private ownership, but they're historical records. Might take a little longer. When we get it, though, we should be able to unravel just who this Marshal really is."

"Burner phones and operating on land that needs tracing. Not exactly a bunch of yokels, Kelly."

"No, it would appear not. Keep your eyes and ears open, DH. There might be something to these guys, after all."

This time, Derek can't help the sigh. "Just remember what we discussed, Kel. Unofficial confidential informant. I don't want my name in any case notes. Whichever way this turns out, I don't want the FBI tying my information to a file, especially if this is all bullshit."

"You have my word, brother. Those requisitions I got you gonna do the trick?"

Derek grins. "Oh yeah. They're gonna do just fine."

"Outstanding. Give 'em hell."

"I plan on it." Hanging up, Derek crosses into his bedroom. Sitting on the bed, he reaches between his legs and pulls out a hardened plastic Gorilla Box footlocker. Flipping open the lid reveals his old plate carrier sitting on top, desert tan and stained with countless hours of sand and sweat. From the closet, he grabs his rucksack and assault bag and begins to pack.

* * * * *

They stare at each other across the hoods of their trucks in the bank parking lot.

"D."

"Gil."

Derek stands with his thumbs hooked into his belt. His right hand rests against the pistol tucked into its holster inside his waistband, concealed by his tan T-shirt. An older man gets out of the driver side of Gil's truck. He takes notice of Derek and Gil staring each other down but does nothing to break the silence.

Gil finally smirks. "Well, this is fun and all, but we really should be getting a move on. Don't ya think?"

Derek gestures to the bank with his free hand. "After you."

Gil smiles full on. "Watch the truck, Jasper." He strolls toward the entrance. Derek follows, throwing a glance back at Jasper along the way, who sits contently on the bumper, smoking a cigarette.

The bank manager is a puckish woman in her middle years whose wardrobe looks like it hasn't been updated in a decade. "It's nice to meet you in person, Mr. Harrington. Your box has been arranged as per your request. This way."

She shows them to the safe-deposit box room but hesitates at the door, looking at Gil. "I'm sorry, sir, this room is for box owners only."

"It's all right," Gil replies. "We're completing a transaction."

Staring at him like he owes an overdue library book, the bank manager puts on her best lecture. "Be that as it may, bank rules still stand. Unless you are an employee or a box owner, you aren't authorized in the room."

Derek smiles. "Looks like you're shit out of luck."

The manager's stare shifts to Derek, laced with indignation, but he ignores it. The sight of Gil's smirk vanishing from his face is a welcome trade-off with that of the manager's disgust. He pulls out a manila envelope that has been wrapped around itself and secured with a rubber band. Derek grabs it and turns back to the woman.

"Please proceed."

The bank manager scans her ID card on a wall-mounted keypad panel that flashes red and green. When it goes solid green, there is an audible snap as the lock unlatches. Once inside, the woman uses a key to open the corresponding locker. Pulling the box inside free, she sets it on a small table against the wall behind her and uses a second key to open the top flap of the bin. She hands both keys to Derek. "I'll be just outside while you conduct your transaction."

Derek pulls out the stack of cash from the envelope and lays out the bills in groups of ten. Counting five thousand, he re-bands the cash before putting it into the box and locking the lid. After returning the box and closing the locker door, he steps out of the room, waving the woman back over. "Ma'am?"

The bank manager returns, an inquisitive, customer-friendly look back on her face. "Yes, Mr. Harrington?"

Derek pulls out a letter-size envelope from his back pocket and hands it over along with the keys. Gil furrows his eyebrows.

"This is an authorization for the bank to retain possession of the keys for me," Derek says. "It states that other than myself, only those expressly authorized in my last will and testament can obtain the keys and the contents of the box. I took the liberty of having it notarized for you."

She gives an impressed frown as she opens the envelope. A moment after reviewing the letter, she looks up. "Very well. This is all in order. The keys will be placed in our vault key box. Just request them from any teller, and someone will bring them to you before letting you into the safe-deposit room. Is there anything else I can do for you today?"

Pulling his glare away from Gil, Derek flashes a smile at her. "No. Thank you, ma'am. You've been most helpful."

She smiles uncomfortably, her eyes shifting between the two men. "Very well, then. Good day, gentlemen."

Gil heads for the door, Derek following closely behind. He glances quickly at the teller stations. She's talking with a customer. Heart-shaped face. Pale skin. Blond hair cropped at the shoulders. Just like Kelly described her. She has a pretty but unremarkable look to her. A person that could easily have been working at the bank for years versus just starting last week.

They're a few steps outside when Gil breaks the silence. "The notary was a nice touch. Fuckin' prick."

"Just taking precautions is all. Wouldn't do much good to have a safe-deposit box if all you assholes have to do is take the keys off me, now would it?"

"Yeah. Sure." They move farther down the walkway. Jasper climbs in and turns their truck over. "I hear you're the new commander once we're in camp."

"Only during training," Derek replies. "You want to run this collection of crazy, be my guest. I don't want anything to do with the lot of you beyond what I've been hired for."

"Good. We don't need a 'too many cooks' situation here."

Derek squares to him.

Gil stops, surprised, and does the same.

"I'm not here to take your job, got it? I'm doing my part, getting paid, and going home. But when I work, I do the thing right. That means you're gonna have to fall in and toe the line like everyone else when I'm training the men. You try to undermine me, and I'll rip your balls off and stuff 'em down your throat. You got it?"

Gil's eyes narrow. "Yeah."

"Yeah, what?"

He swallows before answering. "I got it."

Wheeling around, Derek stalks back to his truck. "Let's get going, then."

After turning off the main road, Derek follows patiently as the truck in front of him drives on a crisscrossing pattern of turnarounds and double backs along the logging roads. Derek recognizes only enough to realize that they're going a different way from when he first came to the camp. After half an hour, the truck veers off toward the east, and they end up in the parking lot clearing.

Derek exits the truck with his plate carrier and assault bag in hand. He drops the bag and then throws the carrier over his head. Along the waistline, four rifle ammo pouches sit on the front of his vest. On his left breast are another two pouches holding magazines for his pistol. On his right breast is a pouch containing a clotting bandage, with a combat-action tourniquet tethered to it. Another rifle magazine pouch sits on his left oblique. On his right oblique, a larger pouch holds an assortment of gear: a compass, mini multi-tool, compact SureFire flashlight, and as always, a flint and steel fire starter.

Derek reaches back into the cab and pulls out a web belt with two leg harnesses attached to it. He clips the belt around his waist just underneath the carrier and then fastens the leg harnesses in place around his thighs. On the left leg platform, he's lashed his survival knife and two more pistol magazine pouches. On the right, he has a drop holster and a set of throwing knives.

Gil looks at him impatiently. "Done getting dressed yet?"

Reaching under the web belt, Derek pulls the Sig Sauer out of his concealed carry holster. Gil can't hide his dismay at seeing the pistol that had been there the whole time. He rams the P226 down into his leg holster. "Now I am."

"Good. Get in the side by side," Gil says, thumbing over to the ATV.

Grabbing his rucksack from his truck, Derek walks over to the vehicle. When there isn't enough room for both his ruck and his assault pack, he drops the larger of the two onto the ATV Jasper is starting up. He eyes the man flatly.

"Everything in that ruck had better make it to camp."

"I ain't no thief," the man snaps.

"You're all fucking thieves," says Derek.

It's close to five thirty by the time the Gator pulls into camp proper.

"Over there, hotshot," Gil says, pointing to Marshal, who is standing in the open. He stalks away without another word.

Gripping his pack, Derek walks across the small clearing. Already, people are stopping what they're doing to look at him and whisper to one another. He can imagine their words as plainly as if they are being shouted. *Outsider. Interloper. Not to be trusted.*

11

Marshal stands with his back to Derek. The man talking to him notices Derek approach and inclines his head in Derek's direction. Marshal turns, the surprised look on his face quickly melting away into a smile. He quickly returns his attention to the other man, who then heads off toward the perimeter of the camp a moment later.

As he draws closer, Derek notices a worn leather holster on Marshal's hip, the initials *U.S.* stamped into the cover flap. It's the exact type issued to soldiers after World War II for their 1911 .45 pistols. Marshal extends his hand as they get close enough. They shake, each with a firm grip.

"Well, you certainly look the part," Marshal says, taking a step back and eyeing him up and down.

"I like to be prepared."

"Don't we all."

"Something happen while I was gone?" Derek asks, nodding toward the weapon.

"Afraid so. There was another run-in with one of the groups nearby. A lookout spotted some of them scouting our camp. I've ordered everyone capable and comfortable with handling a gun to wear a sidearm. The ones designated for lookout and security duty have rifles. Precautionary, for sure, but I have to tell you, I feel a whole lot better now having you here."

Derek doesn't answer, and Marshal quickly changes the subject. "I trust everything at the bank went smoothly?"

Derek throws a glance toward Gil, who is standing about with some of the men from the survival training. He says something to them that Derek can't hear, and the group bursts out laughing. "As well as could be expected. How about my rifle?"

The slightest flicker of reluctance passes across Marshal's face, but then it's gone the next instant. "Of course. This way." He walks them over to the cinder block building. The big woman leans in the doorway. A rifle rack holding ten rifles is up against the outside wall.

Marshal gestures to the woman. "Derek, this is Marjorie."

Derek ignores the introduction. Between his spat with Gil earlier and Marshal already acting as if he's part of the Manson family, Derek hasn't a shred of inclination for formalities. "All right, then," he says, dropping his bag.

Moving to the rack, he grabs the first rifle, pulling the charging handle back to expose the chamber and inspecting for any rounds inside. Seeing it empty, he sets the rifle on the metal panel on the top of the rack and pops the pins connecting the upper receiver to the lower one.

His fingers move deftly with the muscle memory of something he's done thousands of times. Once the rifle is fieldstripped, Derek inspects each component before reassembling the entire weapon and performing a functions test. He places it back in the rack. "Not this one."

Over the next half hour, he performs the same task, each time refusing the weapon and placing it back in the rack. Within three rifles, the woman in the doorway gets antsy, muttering and sighing heavily with each one replaced. After seven, she starts griping.

"There ain't nothin' wrong with them. I cleaned them myself."

"I hate to see what your bathroom looks like, then," he says, not bothering to lift his head as he speaks.

The old man raises a hand before she can respond. "It's all right, Marjorie." He turns back and watches Derek, but after the tenth inspection, and Derek starting over, even Marshal begins to fidget. He looks about camp at the groups of people stopping to stare. Another three inspections and he starts picking at his fingernails.

Truth be told, Derek would have been much more comfortable bringing a rifle with him. That way, he could've had some peace of mind as to its origin and maintenance record. Maybe even get some practice with it beforehand, but ultimately, he and Kelly had decided this was the best play.

Forgetting the exceptionally remote chance that a weapon brought along could somehow be traced back to the FBI, by demanding a rifle, Derek was able to get a closer look at the group's inventory. While he feigns inspecting the cleanliness and functionality, he's also making note of the serial numbers. He can't remember all ten, but he can remember one and then if the rest are sequential. Whether the rifles belong to the same lot or not is telling-enough information, especially if trying to build a case against gun smugglers.

As he goes through each firearm, the information he memorizes becomes increasingly disconcerting. Each of the weapons has a three-round burst option on the selector switch, meaning these aren't civilian AR-style rifles but military-grade M4s. Reinforcing the fact are the attachments.

Every rifle has one of three top-of-the-line optics. ACOG magnification scopes for increased range. Holographic EOTechs for rapid target acquisition during close-quarters combat. Red-dot sights that are a blend of both attributes. The mix of optics gives the group a well-rounded range of capabilities.

In addition to the sights, each weapon is equipped with a front grip post to help with accuracy and recoil stabilization. Single-point slings so the rifle rests against your chest. A high-powered LED flashlight is mounted to the left side of the barrel. AN/PEQ-2 infrared lasers are mounted on the right side. The presence of that piece of equipment tells Derek that somewhere in the cinder block building are night vision goggles; otherwise, the PEQ-2 would be useless.

It all adds up to some very jarring conclusions. The monetary value of the ten rifles and all their accoutrements is a hefty price, and who knows how many more they have? Taking into account his own contract of twenty thousand, as well as the ten grand he made already, and Derek is further convinced that the group is funded by more than just an old man's inheritance. Beyond that, though, is the real question: How in the hell did a hundred people in the woods get access to military-grade weaponry? A few hours under way and the premise that there is no validity to the op is already fading.

Derek begins going through the rack for the third time. The woman throws her arms up. Both she and Marshal look increasingly impatient. Inspecting two more rifles, Derek finally picks up the one he made a note of during his first pass through. He completes a final review and then says, "This'll do," before throwing the sling over his head and sticking his left arm through.

"Finally!" Marjorie nearly shouts.

"Magazines?"

The woman glares, but disappears into the building. When she reappears in the doorway, she's holding five thirty-round banana clips. Derek grabs one, seats it in the magazine well, and slaps it home. He pulls back on the charging handle, putting a round into the chamber. While he's stashing the remaining four magazines into his ammo pouches, Marjorie retrieves another five. Derek secures them as well.

"You done now, Your Majesty?" she asks.

"You might want to go through those again. They're pretty gross."

As he turns away, she flips him off with both hands. Marshal waves to two men standing nearby, who help lift and carry the rack back into the building. The old man gestures to the mess tent.

"Supper's being served. Feel like grabbing something to eat with me?"

"Sure."

As they walk a short distance across the clearing, Derek notices a woman walking in the opposite direction.

"Oh, hello, Sarah. Let me introduce you two," Marshal says.

The woman picks her head up from a thick ledger-style notebook she is studying and turns, noticing them for the first time. She looks younger than Derek by five years at least, maybe even closer to ten. Chewing on a pen at the edge of her mouth, Sarah reluctantly alters her course and joins them.

She's a petite woman with auburn hair and an athletic frame, wearing a blue polo shirt and a pair of hiking pants, but with the onset of the July heat, Sarah has unzipped the bottom segments, turning them into shorts. While her arms are toned, Derek notices her legs are disproportionately muscular, denoting years of running, hiking, or both. A Glock 9 mm pistol sits on her right hip.

Long, curling locks tumble down and frame her face. Sarah stops and stares at him with green eyes behind square-rimmed glasses. After a moment, she pulls them off and hooks them between the buttons of her polo. "So this is the new meathead everyone is talking about."

Marshal grimaces, his face not pleased but not surprised either.

Derek's eyebrows perk up in amusement. "I'm sorry? What?"

"I think I was clear enough the first time. You're making a lot of people nervous around here. You'd better be worth the risk we're taking to bring you in."

Derek throws a glance at Marshal. The old man shrugs, seemingly as baffled as he is. Derek looks back at her. "Excuse me?"

"What? Isn't *meathead* the appropriate honorific

for gun-toting, dip-swallowing assholes who carry guns bigger than their dicks?"

Marshal attempts to step in. "Listen, Sarah—"

"No, it's quite all right, Marshal." She turns her attention back to Derek. "You just remember, we're investing a lot in you. Never mind the costs we're spending on overhead and matériel and the ridiculous price for this supposed 'high-level training.' I'm talking about our lives. You get it?"

"I'm here to do a job and get paid, Hermione. You don't like it, take it up with the man who hired me."

"Hermione. That's cute. You can read. Good for you, sweetheart. I'm actually impressed seeing how most of you jarheads can barely spell. Or did you just watch the movies?"

He turns to Marshal. "Are we done here?"

Sarah steps up to him, pointing her pen into his chest. "He may trust you with this, but I don't. Not so far as I can spit. Some of the others might be impressed with your résumé, but you'd better be damn certain that most of us aren't happy with your presence. So do your shit, get the hell out, and keep your mouth shut so we can go about our lives. Got it?"

Before he responds, she wheels about and stalks off. Derek looks back at Marshal. "She's an assertive one."

Marshal gives a small smile, one bordering on the edge of embarrassment. He gestures to the mess tent, and they keep walking. "I think you'll find that true of most of the women in this camp. They've dealt with their fair share and have developed a . . . forward approach as a result. I like it. There's no place for meekness here if we're going to survive. I wouldn't worry too much about repeat occurrences," he says as he holds the tent flap back for Derek to stoop inside. "Sarah wasn't embellishing when she said everyone is a little on edge with your presence. My guess is they'll be giving you a wide berth."

A few people have already gotten on the chow line, but Marshal skips it completely and walks over to an empty table near the back of the tent. Derek heads to the far side and plants himself down so that he is facing both the entrance and exit. The suddenness of his move leaves the old man staring at him for a moment before settling down on the opposite bench.

A minute later, Darryl comes over with two plates and two cups of coffee. A fatty slab of beef sits on each dish next to a mound of pale white corn. Marshal thanks the cook, who grunts and walks off.

The old man rubs his palms together and smiles broadly. "See, Derek. The good Lord is pleased with you being here. One of the farmers down the road had a milk cow die just this morning. God be praised, He sent us steak to celebrate your arrival."

Derek looks at the meat that's bloody as hell and cocks an eyebrow. "I take it you don't get beef up here that often, then?"

"Not nearly enough," Marshal says, a hunk of meat, gristle, and fat already rolling around in his mouth. Over his shoulder, Derek watches as other men from the survival training come in. Gerry and Thomas and Brian. They laugh with one another as they get on the chow line. Gil and Jimmy stand just inside the tent flap waiting for the line to progress.

Marshal gets his attention again with a dismissive wave of his hand. "Anyways, I wouldn't read into Sarah's little tirade back there. She's angrier with me than with you."

"Is that so?"

"Nothing too severe. She's merely doing her job when you break it all down. You see, Derek, I don't surround myself with yes-men. That accomplishes nothing. If we're going to thrive, then I need the best ideas from the collective group to make the most informed decision."

"But you are the one making all the decisions."

"Someone has to. Go high enough up and you'll find one person calling the shots," the old man says with his mouth still full. "In Sarah's case, she's not happy with my decision to bring you on because of what it's costing the group. She runs logistics and accounting for us, and this is forcing her to get very . . . creative with how we're going to approach the rest of the summer. Not to mention the upcoming winter. Things get pretty cold up here if you've never experienced it before." Behind Marshal, Gil and the rest of the survival trainees, more than likely the proposed QRF, make it into the tent.

Derek digs into a cargo pocket, pulling out an envelope. "Yeah, well, she's going to have to stretch things even more, then. I need your carpenters to start putting this together tomorrow," he says, sliding it across the table. "The week we're in the field should be more than enough time to get it done before we get back."

Marshal opens the paper inside and furrows his eyebrows. "What am I looking at?"

"Yeah, I'm not exactly an architect. You'll have to use a little imagination." Derek leans over the table. "This is a shoot house. Picture it seen here as a bird's-eye view. Or from the observation platform I want them to add up in the trees."

"Ahh, okay. I think I got it now."

Derek sits back. "No roof, mind you. And it doesn't have to be perfect. Log cabin–style is fine. But the walls need to be solid and the hallways tight." He grabs his coffee and sips it—instantly gags. Across the tent, the survival group sits down to their meal.

"Not to question your methods, Derek, but isn't this used for training to fight inside a building?"

Eyeing him a second, Derek thinks about chewing out the old man, but then concedes. "That's actually completely questioning my methods, but sure. You're paying the bills. Crawl, walk, run, Marshal. After the field assessment, we'll go into advanced marksmanship. From there, it's the shoot house. It'll teach the men precision and foster trust among them as a team. Once we have that, then I can teach them to patrol your woods."

Which, of course, is total horseshit. Well, not total, but it was definitely orchestrated. By teaching marksmanship and urban tactics, Derek would be wasting a good amount of time. That would leave him with a single week in the month to teach the maneuvers Marshal wanted, thus making the QRF less effective should Kelly have to come in and mop up. Presented this way, however, he hoped it sounded like he was making them all into John Rambo.

The proof is on Marshal's face as he looks up from the hand-drawn blueprint. His smile stretches from ear to ear. "Excellent, Derek. Just excellent."

"The men? They have all their gear squared away and ready to go?"

"What? Oh. Yes," Marshal says, eyes back to interpreting the schematic.

"Good. Go tell them to stand up and road march to the outbuildings. No vehicles."

Marshal's head snaps up, then turns around, seeing the survival group just now digging into their steaks. Around them, the rest of the tent is quickly filling up at other tables. The old man turns back. "Now? Can't they finish eating first? I think I told you how rare—"

"And I seem to recall you saying they would be complicit in my orders. Training time starts now. I'm ordering them out on a road march. Immediately. Blame it on me if you like. I don't really care. But they need to get moving. And no knives or firearms."

Marshal stares at him. Derek sips on his coffee. The old man finally stands up and makes his way over to the table. The men greet him cheerfully, soon followed by shouts of "What?" and "Now?" The men twist on their benches and scowl at Derek. Jimmy whines, "But it's steak night!"

The first to stand up is Gil, who stares daggers at Derek before heading to the exit. The rest of the group gets up with muttered grumbles and profanities of "Smug asshole" and "Sumbitch" as they shuffle to the door.

Derek raises his cup in salute.

After the security team has left, Marshal walks back to the table, reassuring some of the other camp patrons along the way. He sits down and sips his coffee. "They are not a happy bunch."

"Hungry men rarely are." Derek finishes his coffee. "The cabin I requested. Where's it located?"

Marshal spoons some corn into his mouth. "Out the tent and to the left. It's the first one you'll reach."

"Good."

"You know, Derek, it doesn't have to be this way. I don't want this to be adversarial. I want you to feel like you belong here. Like you're part of this group, not just some hired vendor. That's not going to happen if you antagonize and isolate yourself from everyone."

Derek sets down his cup. "I'm not here to join you, I'm here to teach you. The less I know about all of you when I walk out of here, the better it will be for everyone."

"I suppose you have a point there," Marshal replies, nodding solemnly. "Although I pray that your outlook will change over time."

"Mmm-hmm." Derek nods to his rifle. "You have a place where I can zero this thing in?"

"Yes. There's a hundred-meter lane we marked off just outside of camp to the northwest. Jasper will take you there." The old man waves to Jasper, who gives a thumbs-up in return. "Can you just give him a few more minutes to finish eating?"

"Sure thing."

"So when will the training begin in earnest?"

"Later," Derek replies as he gathers up his bag. "I'd get a few hours of z's in once you're done here. Want me to wake you when it's time or tell someone else to grab you?"

"The shack just to the left of my cabin is our communications hub. There are always two people on duty, a tech and a runner. If you go there, the runner will grab me."

"Okay," Derek says, standing up. "Make sure those men up there don't eat. I want them uncomfortable going into this."

Marshal looks up at him. "I will, but . . . aren't you gonna have yours?"

Derek stares down at the steak, then back at the old

man. "Nah. I'm good." He takes a few steps before turning back around. "Oh, and, Marshal?"

"Yes?"

Derek leans in. "No food, but I'm not opposed to you sending them a few bottles of whatever you have handy. It might help take the sting out of what you just ordered them to do, and it's going to be the last they get for a while."

Marshal's face lights up. "Okay, then. I'll see what Darryl has in the pantry."

"Great." Derek heads out of the tent, one hand on the grip of his rifle, his finger extended past the trigger guard. He feels the eyes upon him but ignores them as he walks. When he steps into the clearing, a football bounces in front of his feet.

"Little help!"

A boy, ten or maybe eleven with ashy-blond hair, waves his arms. Derek looks down at the ball and kicks it. The football tumbles over a yard but gets nowhere close to the kid. The boy tosses his hands up, jogs over, and grabs it. He looks up at Derek.

"You're fucking huge."

Derek looks down at him. "Watch your language, kid."

The boy's eyes go wide, and then he starts laughing. "You're funny. And you're as big as a linebacker. I bet you could chuck this a mile."

"All right," Derek says, holding out his hands. "I'll bite. Go long, kid."

The boy's face lights up. He tosses the ball and takes off running across the clearing. Derek heaves the football, launching it far over the kid's head.

Jasper comes out of the tent and sees the boy. He looks at Derek. "I see you met Bobby. Kid's kinda the camp mascot." He points, and they walk around the mess tent.

Across the clearing, Derek can see the security team laden with large backpacks heading up the hill to his right. Bobby comes running at them, makes a cut and a spin move, then sprints past.

"Get outta here, Waterboy!" Jasper yells at the kid. He then takes Derek a few hundred yards out into the woods. The "lane" is a clustered path in the trees that, through the center, has a somewhat clear vantage point of a large pine. Jasper walks down and staples a zeroing target to a piece of bullet-riddled plywood nailed to the tree.

Using his multitool, Derek pops off the red-dot sight on his rifle. It takes him nine rounds to zero his iron sights and then, after replacing the optic, another six to dial in the red dot. Satisfied, they head back into camp, where Derek retrieves his ruck from the ATV.

He's walking back across the clearing just as everyone else is filing out of the mess tent, ignoring their stares as he steps up into his cabin. Derek drops his gear and opens the ruck, throwing down a sleeping bag onto one of the racks and digging around until he finds a black plastic case.

Taking out a small power drill and a bolt lock, he makes a series of quick pilot holes and affixes it to the door. Derek slams the bolt home and returns the drill to its case. Acting as carefully and quietly as possible, he piles up the cots as best he can to clear some floor space. Walking back and forth slowly, he tests the wood until he hears a series of creaks in the same area. Dropping down, he pries up the floorboards with his survival knife. When he has created enough of a space to fit through easily with all his gear on, he turns each board over and painstakingly works out the nails with his fingers. He replaces the nailless planks in the floor, rearranges the rest of the cots to cover the makeshift trapdoor, and then places his so that it runs parallel to the back wall.

Taking out his cleaning kit, he lays his rucksack at his feet and sits down on his cot. He unholsters his .40 and sets it next to him. After dropping the mag and clearing his M4, Derek disassembles the weapon and gives it a proper cleaning.

12

t's close to 2:30 in the morning when he eases out
of his cabin and steps down softly on the creaking
wood stairs. A full moon illuminates the compound
in ghostly white light. Derek stands still for a few
moments, listening to the night wind rustle the tree-
tops above. Crickets sing endlessly. Across the clearing from him, he can just make out someone snoring,
the sound like a hibernating bear. He scans the entire
camp. Watching. Waiting.

Nothing. Everything is still. This late in the night,
the camp has shut down. Too late for people to be
working or drinking. Too early for the mess crew to
be up preparing the morning meal. It's the stillness he
needs to start his training regimen off right.

Derek walks along the northern edge of the compound, skirting through trees and stepping over
downed branches. He follows the loose collection of
shacks and cabins toward the east. Up ahead, a sliver
of pale yellow light spills into the darkness. He approaches the structure silently, shrugging to adjust his

plate carrier and the straps on his pack. Cradling his rifle in his hands, Derek does a slow turn every so often to check his six. A short halt comes right after the rotation to listen for anything suspicious.

As he gets closer, he can see the outlines of the antennas and satellite dishes arrayed on the roof of the comms shack. The door is cracked just a bit, the source of the sliver of light obscured behind it. He presses his muzzle against the wood and slowly pushes the door open.

Two narrow desks sit facing each other in the center of the room, each piled with various radio equipment. A shelf on the back wall holds a flickering oil lantern. The shack is small enough that there is barely any space between the desks and the walls. To his right, a person sits slumped over the desk, head resting in their arms. They wheeze softly as they sleep.

Derek steps in and around the door, rifle swinging into the left side of the hut. Sarah jumps in her seat, one hand clutching a pen and going to her chest. Her other one drops down to her pistol.

"Jesus Christ, jarhead. You almost gave me a heart attack," she says in a furious whisper.

Great. Not this one again. His eyes fall to the desktop. The large ledger he saw her with earlier lies open in front of her. A quick glance shows columns of figures and computations. She follows his eyes and hurriedly closes it.

She points at him with her pen. "What do you want?"

"It's time to get the training underway. Marshal said I should have the runner here wake him rather than do it myself."

She walks out from behind the desk and pushes

him gently out of the door, exiting the shack with him. "Fine. Follow me. The books can wait a few minutes."

He falls in next to her as they traipse the short distance from the comms shack to Marshal's cabin. "You always in the habit of letting your runner sleep through their shift?"

"When the kid's pulled double logging duty for the last eighteen days and then gets stuck on an overnight? Yeah. I do. It's called compassion."

"Huh. Didn't think you were the type."

Sarah frowns and climbs the steps up to the porch, then slips inside.

While he waits, Derek wrestles with himself yet again about his decision to return. The constant mental reinforcement is repeated, *I'm doing this for my family. I'm doing this to be with them again. I'm serving my country.*

Ten minutes later, a bleary-eyed Marshal comes out, pulling on a red-and-black checkered jacket of all things. He runs a hand through his hair and pulls on his ball cap while yawning widely. "I gotta tell you, Derek. When I saw this beauty standing over me, I thought the good Lord had called me home."

Sarah smiles as she puts an arm out, ready to help him down the steps should he need it. The man groans as he moves.

"Boy. The joints aren't what they used to be. Don't worry. They'll loosen up before long. Now. What in the hell are we doing up at three in the morning?"

"It's time to get things started. Can you make it up that hill on foot?"

Sarah's head snaps back to him, furious. "Why in the hell . . . You have any idea how old he is? We have ATVs, for crying out loud!"

"Yeah, which will wake them up and ruin the element of surprise. Not that I expect an accountant to understand anything about tactics."

She opens her mouth to reply, but Marshal raises a hand to stop her. "I'm more than capable. I've been walking these hills my whole life, and I've got a few more trips in me yet."

Derek nods and then turns to her. "You have a job in all this too."

Sarah folds her arms across her chest. "Can't wait."

"A little after we get there, you're going to hear a whole mess of noise. It's gonna wake up everyone down here and scare the shit out of them. Your job is to make sure they don't go into 'Remember the Alamo' mode and start charging the hill. I don't need a bunch of yahoos playing cavalry on four-wheelers."

"So . . . essentially you're saying I have to keep everyone from shooting you."

He smiles at her. "Exactly."

Marshal steps in. "Derek, shouldn't we be going?"

They start to walk off. When they're closer to the southern edge of the camp, the old man starts speaking again.

"She's a firecracker, ain't she?"

"She's something, all right."

Marshal chuckles. "Hey now. I wouldn't worry about it. She's that way with most newcomers. She likes to put it to them to see what they're made of before accepting someone. It's just her way."

Derek looks off as they start up the path to the outbuildings. "She's been with you since the beginning of all this, then?"

"Sarah? Sort of. Not her, exactly. I've known her family for years. Good people, her parents. Both passed on now, God rest their souls. Far too young, if you ask me. Especially if you ask me. Why God lets me walk around all this time while He takes good folk like Sarah's parents . . . well, I guess that's why He is who He is and we are who we are. We don't get to know the mysteries down here, Derek."

"What'd you mean, 'not her, exactly'?"

Marshal starts to get a little winded. "Oh, just that she was away for a long while, doing what young people do. Trying to make it in this world. Carve out their piece to hold on to while changing the rest. Unfortunately, like so many others, the world carved her up instead."

Thinking on it a moment, Derek lets the answer go without further inquiry but files it away for exploration later. The closer they get to the outbuildings, the more his focus aligns with what he is about to do. He doesn't care much for talking.

Marshal, on the other hand, seems to make a profession of it. The old man laughs a bit. "Funny. This sky. The moon. This hill. Reminds me of one exactly like it on the other side of the world, a half century ago. I didn't much care for road marching then, and I can't say the years have changed my mind in that department."

"Half century? Your math isn't adding up, Marshal."

"Well, maybe a bit more than half. A buddy of mine, Alan Sommers. He and I snuck off when we were sixteen and joined up. Had to lie on our enlistment paperwork, but the Army didn't care about those things back then. Caught the tail end of the fighting in '53."

Holy shit, Derek thinks, *this guy is a Korea vet, and he's hiking up a hill at 3:00 a.m.*

"Yeah. Old Alan and I made it out of there, thank the Lord. 'That He would grant unto us, that we being delivered out of the hand of our enemies might serve Him without fear. In holiness and righteousness before Him, all the days of our life.' Luke, chapter one, verses seventy-four and seventy-five. Still, a night like this. Memory will send a shiver down your spine. I'm sure you had similar nights? Afghanistan, maybe?"

Derek spits to the side. "I'm not much for reminiscing, Marshal. Or backstory. Why don't we just get up the hill, okay?"

The old man pauses but relents. "All right, Derek. Some other time perhaps."

Thankfully, the hill works to wind the old man even further, so conversation drops off to a minimum during their ascent. With several breaks taken, the normally ten-minute ATV ride takes them an hour to walk. It's just after 4:00 a.m. when the ground starts to level out and Derek sees the outlines of the buildings through the trees.

He holds up a finger in front of his lips, and Marshal nods once in acknowledgment. They skirt the buildings to the left side, walking into the small area where the vehicles park. Derek looks down the path running in between the four shacks leading to the cinder block building. Loud snores of men in deep sleep come from the wooden buildings.

Turning back to Marshal, he inclines his head toward the trees. "You got a call to bring down your crow?"

Marshal nods again. "Bird chirp."

"Do it."

The old man cups his hands over his mouth and chimes out a three-note melody. Moments after he is done, there is a reply call, and then a moment after that, there's rustling up in one of the trees. Derek takes his pack off and drops it to the ground. He goes to a knee and roots in the main compartment until he finds what he is looking for. Eight cylinders, four of one size and four of another. He starts hooking them to the gear loops on his plate carrier as the lookout approaches.

"Marshal? That you? What the hell are you doing out so early?" The man cradles his rifle and scowls at Derek. He's young and thin with a bushy brown beard. Derek pulls out circles of zip ties threaded through one another. He clips one bunch into a carabiner on his left side and then does the same on his right.

The old man holds up his hands. "It's all right, Brady. It's all right. We're just getting started is all."

Derek stands back up. "No other lookouts I need to worry about taking a shot at me, are there?"

Marshal shakes his head. "There's only the one here."

"Okay, good. Now listen," he says, his voice barely above a whisper. "I'm going down through the middle there. When I come back, all hell is gonna break loose." He eyes Brady. "Don't. Shoot. Me. This is all part of it."

The man looks to Marshal, who pats him on the back. Brady nods, but his knuckles are white on the grips of his rifle. Derek turns to Marshal.

"Once I have them out and secure, they'll get read the riot act. That's when I need you to step in and hammer it home."

The old man nods in affirmation.

"Okay, then." Derek moves silently down the path. He reaches the first shack on the right and gently nudges the door open. The hinges creak ever so slightly. He makes the opening wide enough to stick a basketball through without hitting the edges and then slowly pokes his head in.

Eyes just barely passing the wood, Derek can see three men splayed out on cots. The smell of cheap scotch and body odor permeates the atmosphere inside. Derek looks around and sees a glint of moonlight reflect off a glass bottle clutched in one man's hand. He smiles.

Coming back out, Derek repeats the process, going to each shack in turn and opening the door just wide enough. Reaching the clearing between the shacks and the cinder block building, he turns and faces Marshal and Brady, the two now standing at the opposite end of the path.

Derek takes a deep breath, centering himself and dialing in his focus. *Okay. Showtime.*

He reaches down and grabs a pair of cylinders off his carrier. Walking up to the first shack, Derek pulls the pin on the thicker of the two and then immediately does the same with the thinner. Gripping the cylinders on the opposite sides, he lets the spoons release from the grenades. Two metallic pings sound out as Derek rolls both into the cabin and pulls the door closed.

Moving quickly, he grabs the next set of cylinders off his carrier and pulls the pins before the first pair even go off. Derek is rolling them into the second shack when a deafening blast erupts inside the first. There are screams of terrified confusion over the echoing report. Another, lesser burst goes off in the initial shack. After the second set of grenades goes off, he hears violent coughing, and thick white smoke bellows from the first cabin.

Derek runs while priming his third set of grenades. The door to the next shack opens slightly, but when the occupant sees him charging, the man tries to shove it closed. He shoulders into the wood, keeping the door open long enough for him to throw the pair into the enclosed space. Once they are in, he pulls the door shut and holds it in place until they go off. The blast is such that it rattles the entire frame of the structure, shaking loose a century's worth of dirt and dust.

Wheeling around, the last set of pins comes out as he charges the fourth and final cabin. This time, the door is pulled completely open. Gil steps into the doorframe.

A puzzled look is plastered across his hungover face. The man's eyes go wide as Derek runs up, smiles, and kicks him square in the gut, sending him flying back into the cabin. Derek throws the grenades far into the back of the structure, the spoons popping into the air in the process. There are a few screams just before the blasts go off again.

Even out in the open, the effects of the gas can be felt. Derek's eyes stream while his nose pours snot into his mustache and beard, both of which he ignores as he walks back over to Marshal and Brady. Behind him, he can hear the men coughing and falling over themselves as they blindly search for an escape.

Brady looks nervous, like he's about to raise his rifle. Derek lashes out with a hand and grabs the barrel. Yanking hard, he pulls Brady toward him so that they are eye to eye. Brady's eyes flick back and forth as his body starts to tremble. Grabbing Brady's sling with his free hand, Derek rotates the weapon around so that the assault rifle lies against his back. He grabs the front of Brady's shirt.

"Touch that rifle again and I'll put you down," he says as he shoves Brady back. Spinning, he cradles his own weapon and stands with it at the low ready. Marshal, coughing and holding his jacket collar over his mouth, walks up next to him.

"What is that?"

"CS grenades. Riot control."

Marshal just stares at him.

"Tear gas. Now step back."

The old man does as he's told as the first men start to find their way out of the cabins. Derek shoulders his rifle and flips his safety selector switch to three-round burst. He squeezes the trigger three times in quick succession, sending a ripple of bullets down the center of the path, each impact kicking up a small geyser of earth. The staccato percussion of the shots echoes off the surrounding hills, a lesser multitude to the booming thunder that was the flash-bang grenades. The men dive back into the huts, seeking whatever cover they can find, despite the gas.

Derek adjusts his sight picture, putting his red dot on the nearest roof. He squeezes the trigger again and again, raking his rifle in an arc from right to left. The bullets rip through the old timber, showering the men inside with splintering debris. Derek drops the mag and slaps a fresh one in place. Hitting the bolt release and slamming a round into the chamber, he fires again in the opposite direction, saturating each cabin roof until the magazine runs dry.

As the report of the shots dies in the wind, all that can be heard is the men coughing inside. Derek reloads and then unslings his rifle, handing it off to Marshal without looking. The old man grabs it from him, confused. Derek strides down into the space between the four cabins and waits, eyes and nose leaking. Slowly, the yells come in choked gasps.

"He's . . . he's tryin' to kill us, man!"

"What the . . . What's going on?"

"Gil . . . Gil!"

"We're dead! We're all gonna die!"

"We gotta . . . run for it!"

Gil screams over them, or at least tries to through his strained voice. "If he wanted us dead, we'd be dead!"

"Fuck this!"

From behind him, Thomas bursts from a door and into the pathway. Derek spins and lashes out with a leg, the kick cracking Thomas in the left side of his ribs. He then pounces on him and flips him facedown. He pulls Thomas's arms back behind him and threads his hands through a pair of the zip tie handcuffs. Cinching them tightly, he leaves Thomas immobilized and lying in the dirt.

Another of the men peeks out the door to the nearest cabin just in time for Derek to grab him by the hair and yank him out. He uppercuts him in the gut and drops him to the ground, cuffing him as well. From the right side of the path, a man bursts from the cabin closer to Marshal. Derek jumps up, his sidearm in his hand in one smooth motion. He fires two rounds into the roof of the cabin the man just left.

"Next one goes in your ass!"

The man freezes, hands above his head, quivering.

"On your belly, Boot!"

The man reluctantly lowers himself to the ground.

"Hands behind your back!"

As the man complies, Derek stalks forward. He fires off the remainder of his rounds into the roofs of the cabins, eliciting more yells and scrambling back from the doors. At the end of the row, Derek drops a knee into the center of the man's back and cuffs him. He looks up at the cabin where the guy just came from. It's the one that Gil is in.

"Gil, walk your ass out the door now!" Derek shouts as he reloads his Sig.

Gil saunters out a second later, hands behind his head, fingers interlaced. His face is twisted into a scowl of pure disdain. "You and I both know this is all for show. You ain't gonna do—"

Derek flips his sidearm and delivers it across Gil's temple with the full force of his haymaker.

The scrawny man goes limp as he falls to the ground.

"Ain't gonna do what, bitch?" he says, standing over the unconscious team leader. Derek shouts into the cabin, training his pistol on the door, "Whoever the last pussy is in there had better get out here now!"

Brian comes out with his hands up. Derek tosses him a pair of zip tie cuffs. "Secure that fool. Then get your dick in the dirt next to him."

After Brian and Gil are cuffed, Derek moves down the line. He gets the next cabin to come out peacefully, all three men listening to his commands as he locks them down. The other cabin of three refuses to comply. They yell and shout, taunting him to come in and get them. Derek goes back to his bag and grabs two more grenades. Hooking the flash-bang onto his carrier, he scoops up a large branch from the ground. Derek cooks off the CS grenade in his hand so that the smoke is already billowing from the canister, then kicks in the door and hurls the grenade inside.

A chorus of shouts erupts, and a moment later, men armed with steel appendages from their cots come barreling out of the doorway. Derek throws the branch at their feet, and the man in the lead, Sebastian, gets tangled up in it. The ones following collide with him, and they all go to the ground. The presentation of his sidearm dissipates any hope for further rebellion.

The last two holed up refuse to come out, but not for the same reason.

"He's all shook up!" Gerry calls from inside. "He won't come out. I can't even get him to stand up!"

"Jimmy!" Derek yells from the path. "You get your dumb ass out here or I'm coming in after you!"

Gerry flinches at the door, poking his head in and out of the opening. "I'm telling you, he ain't coming. Just sitting here blubbering."

"All right. Enough of this shit." Derek pulls his last flash-bang and rips the pin. He is about to throw it when Marshal calls out.

"Derek. A word, please."

Derek squints over his shoulder at the old man. He turns back and hurls the grenade.

A few seconds later, the blast goes off. Gerry comes dancing out of the cabin holding his ears.

Derek looks back. "Yes?"

Marshal frowns. "Never mind."

He gets Gerry secured and then drags Jimmy out by his hair. The giant man weeps openly. The front of his pants is wet in the crotch. Derek cuffs him but keeps him on his feet and prods him down to the small clearing next to the cinder block building. He roughly seats him so that he sits crisscross, leaning forward with his cuffs behind his back. Jimmy continues to cry as Derek goes back and forth, yanking the men to their feet and dragging them to sit in the clearing two at a time. He beckons Brady to help him lift Gil, who is just beginning to stir. Once seated, he leans him back against Brady's legs.

"Gimme that water bottle," Derek says, inclining his head toward Brady's cargo pocket.

The man obliges, and Derek pours the water over Gil's head and face, slapping him firmly on the cheeks. The man finally comes to, although still groggy.

"Welcome back, Joe Dirt."

Standing up, he signals for Marshal to join them. Derek looms over the group, all of them still coughing and spitting from the effects of the gas. Their eyes water, and their nostrils run freely with snot. Sebastian doubles over and vomits, the smell distinctly reminiscent of regurgitated scotch.

Derek puts his hands on his hips. "Morning, ladies. Do I have your attention?"

13

The men won't look at Derek directly, but he hears the muttered curses under their breath. Marshal moves in behind him. Brady produces a folding chair from inside the cinder block building, and the old man sits. His face looks like someone suddenly second-guessing their decision. Or is it his men's reactions thus far that have left him concerned?

"You see, fellas, you all have home field advantage on the brain. You grew up in these woods. You can hunt and track and milk cows and bale hay. I get it. Good old country boy toughness. I bet you're all anyone can handle in a bar fight at the local watering hole."

Gil smirks. He spits out a stream of blood as if it were tobacco juice. The rest of the men keep staring at the ground. Derek paces in front of them.

"Then you get up here. You get isolated. You get filled with ideas. You walk around your camp holding assault rifles and wearing vests. You start thinking you're bad. You start saying to yourself, 'No one can touch us here. This is our place now. This is the country I belong to.'" He pauses for a long while, standing in the center of the group until a few of them pick up their heads.

"And then one man, in one night, fucked you all up."

The men that raised their eyes cast them back down.

Derek continues, "You know why? It's not just my training. Don't justify it that way. Your lack of any is part of it, sure, but it's more than that. It's the fact that you've never been in a real fight."

Gil picks his head up and stares daggers at him.

"You've never had the stakes be your life before."

Derek turns and walks behind them, moving slowly as he speaks. "You panicked. You didn't know where to go. You didn't know what to do. Some of you ran. Some of you stayed holed up. An entire cabin did exactly as I said. I'm only one man, and yet you listened to every command I gave. Only one cabin of you tried to mount any kind of defense, and even then, it was sloppy, disorganized, and easily defeated. This sniveling moose over here is still crying," he says, kicking Jimmy in the ass.

Rounding in front of the men, Derek stops pacing. He waits for their attention again. "What if it wasn't one man? What if it was those boys that have been probing your camp?"

Silence hangs in the air until one of them barks back, "Yeah, you're all big and bad when you're the one with the guns. What a complete asshole." The man, Brian, looks at him defiantly from across the group. Some of the others' faces are pictures of disbelief.

Derek strides over and grabs Brian by the cuffs and lifts his arms up. The man cries out at the posture, but Derek keeps pushing until he jumps to his feet to alleviate the pain. Drawing one of his throwing knives, Derek cuts the zip tie cuffs off.

"Stand here."

Brian looks at him as he rubs his wrists. The rest of the men are puzzled but transfixed. Derek walks over to where Marshal is sitting and grabs his M4. Holding it in his left hand, he rounds on Brian, his blade down by his side.

"So guns are the great equalizer, huh? Well, here you go."

He throws the rifle through the air. Brian bobbles the weapon as he works to get a proper grip. His eyes flicker back and forth between Derek and the group, and then to the throwing knife.

"Do it!" one of the others yells.

"Shoot his ass!" shouts Gerry.

Brian looks at Derek. Derek stares back at him. Unflinching. Unmoving. Slowly, Brian raises one hand in the air. He bends down and places the rifle on the ground. As he stands back up, Brian raises both hands over his head.

"Get on your knees, wise guy."

The man obliges, and Derek re-cuffs him. When he is done, he shoves Brian over with a boot in his back so that he lies prone in the dirt.

"Thanks for making my point for me, shithead. Having guns won't save you. Having the will to use them, that's the difference. I don't give a shit about whatever ill fortune or adversity you've had in your lives. Maybe you have what it takes, maybe you don't. We'll soon find out."

More bewildered looks, both at him and exchanged between one another.

"I'm talking about the hardened skill set and mind-set that will make you one thing and one thing only. A killer. If you're serious about defending this treasonous snake den you've got going on, that's exactly what you'll need to become.

"That's where I come in. It's my job to turn you into a cohesive fighting unit, and I only have four weeks to do it. You won't be the most proficient team. There are groups that train for years together. But if you listen, if you learn, then . . . then you'll be able to hold your own and protect this place. Before that happens, you all have to come to terms with one thing. The most important thing."

Derek squats in front of them. Slowly, they pick their heads up. He stares at each of them in turn.

"You. Are. Nothing. Right here. Right now. Get it through your heads. Any notion you have. Any past experience. Anything that you're clinging to that says, 'To hell with this guy, I can take anything.' Just toss it out now, because I promise you, we're about to find out if you can. I also promise you that if you're harboring that machismo, you're going to get seriously fucked up.

"I'm going to beat you. I'm going to test you," he says, standing back up and pacing. "I'm going to make you regret ever volunteering to become part of this sham you call a security team. And you're going to obey. You're going to accept the punishment. You're going to follow every order I say and like it, because that is exactly what this man wants."

He ends by pointing over at Marshal. The men's eyes follow.

Marshal looks to Derek and then to the men. Slowly, he stands up. "Everything he says is true, boys.

Heaven help us, but it's true. The only way we can secure ourselves is by learning what he has to teach.
I'm sorry that I have to put you through this. I really
am, but it is for our greater good. Whatever . . . methods Derek chooses to employ, you should know that
I have authorized him to do so. Every order he gives
needs to be treated as if it's coming from me. For all
intents and purposes, over the next four weeks, you
belong to him."

Several of the men's faces drop as the reality of the
order hits home. Gil in particular can't help the anguish showing through his eyes as he looks at the old
man. Derek gives Marshal an appreciative nod.

Turning back, Derek yells, "Let's get started, ladies.
The sooner we do, the sooner I'll know how many of
you are completely useless piles of shit. Get yourselves
in a straight line! Sit and face to the east! One line for
all of you! Now move!"

The men scramble to get up and follow his commands. Derek holsters his throwing knife and retrieves
his rifle. He walks over to where Marshal and Brady
are standing and leans his long gun against the wall
of the cinder block building. He inclines his head toward the lookout.

"What do you use to talk to down below?"

"We got two-ways. The little handheld ones."

Derek nods and looks at Marshal. "You can head
back down now. Ain't nothing gonna happen for the
next few hours other than a nice long walk through
the woods. After he calls you a taxi, I'll take the two-
way and radio you if I need you."

Marshal's face is stern. Concerned, even, but he
nods. "All right, then. I won't lie and say that I couldn't
go for a few more hours of sleep. Seems selfish of me,

considering what these boys are about to go through. The pens are about one and three-quarter miles north-northeast from the camp. We can draw you a map if—"

"I'll find it," Derek says. "Make the call. Leave the radio here."

In the time it takes the Gator ATV to make its way up to the top of the hill, Derek walks back and forth among the men, occasionally yelling at them to close in. The designees for the QRF oblige, scooting forward on their buttocks. Despite being submissive earlier, Brian glares at Derek every time he walks by. Gil smirks as well, his anguish dismissed, but the rest are content to let the seated posture subdue their adrenaline.

Derek moves in and out between the buildings, searching the nearby tree line for something that will suit his purpose. He stops for a moment and takes some deep breaths. The adrenaline from conducting the shock treatment he just put the men through is wearing off. As it does, other feelings surge in. A sense of familiarity—comfort, even—as he falls into his former role. With that comes the distaste for what is about to happen. Necessary, but in no way pleasant. The two responses are still wrestling with each other even as he shakes his head free and regains his focus.

By the time the engine of the ATV can be heard, Derek finds what he is looking for. A smile on his face, he walks back between two cabins and into the clearing. Marshal is leaning over Jimmy, whispering in his ear and patting him on the back. The Gator crests the hill, the headlights illuminating the outbuildings.

The driver jumps out and cradles his weapon,

searching the nearby trees. "Holy shit, Marshal! They okay? Where's the lookout?"

Marshal stands up and waves his hands. "Everything is fine, Doug. Brady is right here. This is all part of the training." Separately, he turns to the lookout. "You'd better get back in your nest, Brady. Thanks for going along with everything this morning."

The man turns and gives Derek a skeptical look. "You sure this is all right, Marshal?"

The old man glares at him.

Brady wilts under the gaze and mutters under his breath. "My apologies, Marshal. I'll be gettin' along."

Marshal smiles at him and claps him on the shoulder.

As Brady moves off, Derek accompanies the old man back to the Gator. "What was all that whispering you were doing?"

"Oh, just some words of encouragement. A few passages for each man to hold on to during this time of trial."

Derek looks him over, but Marshal doesn't return his gaze. "Fine. But that's the last of it. They can't be coddled every time they see you, and I can't have you undercutting what we're trying to do here."

"You don't have to remind me. I know what I've asked you to do, and I'm prepared to see it through," he says, climbing into the passenger side of the ATV, his eyes alight with fire. "It's just . . . these are my boys. My family. A father needs to encourage his children."

"You can do that as much as you want. After I'm finished with them."

Marshal leans out, extending his hand. Derek takes it.

"Then they're yours now," Marshal says. "Train them well, Chief Warrant Officer. We need them."

Derek watches until the Gator is out of sight and then walks back over to the tree line. Whereas before it was just an echo, the use of his official rank snaps the former role firmly into place, along with the full weight of that responsibility. To carry out the duty to which he has been assigned. To ensure the success of the operation. To protect the country, from all enemies, foreign and domestic. It's not a role he revels in by any stretch of the imagination but one that is necessary to get the job done.

He grabs the long bough he found and drags it into the clearing. It's about as thick as his wrist with dozens of wiry twigs sticking out. Derek draws his survival knife and starts working the blade along the length of the limb, shearing the smaller offshoots until he has a long, bare log. He drags it to the right side of the men and lets it drop. The branch reaches from the last of them to the first.

Sheathing his knife, Derek walks back and grabs his bag. He drops it next to Thomas, the last man in the line, then roots around inside until he finds what he was looking for, and wraps it around the man's neck.

"Is that a damn dog collar?"

"It sure is."

"I ain't wearing no—"

The sound that comes from Derek's open-hand slap across Thomas's face causes other heads to turn toward them.

"You're less than a dog, you piece of shit. You're worthless to everyone here and to everyone in camp."

"Fuck you."

This time, Derek backhands him. A trickle of blood runs from Thomas's nostril into his mouth.

"Anything else?"

Thomas remains silent. Derek goes back to the task at hand. One by one, he moves down the row, affixing dog collars to each man's neck. Brian doesn't say anything, but his eyes bore into Derek like lasers. Before moving on to the next man, Derek pokes Brian in the eyes, eliciting yelps of pain.

Finished with the collars, Derek grabs a handful of unused zip ties. He lifts the branch and drapes it roughly onto the right shoulder of each man. Leaning on the limb with his knee, he threads the zip tie through Thomas's collar and around the branch and then cinches it down. Derek repeats the process with Gerry at the front of the line. With the tree limb held in place at the two anchors, Derek secures the rest of them to the branch. His preparations complete, he looks over the group.

"All right, simpletons. On your feet."

Surprisingly, they manage to get up without falling over, but standing now takes on a new challenge. Most cry out in either an exclamation of pain or profanity or both. The shorter men yell out to the taller to stoop down because of the strain their height is putting on their necks. Derek watches with his arms folded until they sort themselves out.

With most of the grumbling done, he grabs another item out of the bag. Slinging his rifle and putting the pack over his shoulders, Derek moves to the head of the line. He clips a dog leash onto Gerry's collar and starts walking. A hefty yank gets the men stepping along. More curses and demands that he fuck himself are hurled his way. Derek goes through the path between the buildings and brings them into the woods.

He drags them along through the terrain. The collars and the branch work to limit what they are able to see. Trips and stumbles at a minimum cause pain to the entire group and at a maximum forces them to the ground. Each time, he leaves them to stand up on their own. The sun creeps up and shines yellow gold through the trees.

They scream and curse, but Derek pays them no mind, waiting for the eventual to happen.

After yet another spill, Brian screams at Jimmy, "You giant idiot! Will you stop standing so high? You're stretching our goddamn necks!"

Jimmy, trying to regain some of his lost reputation, twists his head as far back as he can. "Kiss my ass! Don't put this shit on me!"

"Both of you shut your goddamn mouths!"

"Don't act like you ain't been dragging your feet, Gerry! You old bastard!"

The hills and rising temperature start to add up. Two and a half hours in, the men are panting and sweating, too tired to throw insults at him or one another. Sebastian vomits again, throwing up all over the neck of the man in front of him.

Derek walks them all morning. Through heavy brush. Muddy bogs. Over rocky terrain and up a steep incline. At the top, Derek turns, unhooks the leash from Gerry, and then sweeps his legs out from under him. The entire group gets pulled with him, and as a whole they bounce and smack their way down the hill.

As they come to rest at the bottom, Derek shouts, "Get up! Get your asses back up here now!"

A tirade of profanity comes his way, but again shifts to one another as they scramble to untangle their twisted legs and stand. Derek smiles, but then it quickly fades. He remembers the time his father made him haul his pack to the top of a hill not unlike the one he stands on. No matter how many times he fell back down it. No matter how many times he begged. Through tears and gritting teeth, Derek had finally clawed his way to the top on his belly. It showed him what determination could overcome. It also taught him to pack light and that his dad was a real son of a bitch.

The men's tantrum continues as they trudge back up the incline, and Derek interrupts them, shouting, "Yeah. Just keep tearing into one another. How are you ever going to protect an entire village when you can't even work together?"

The security team stops. Their ragged, dirty faces stare blankly while they pant and try to catch their breath.

"The first challenge you meet and you all turn on one another? Is that how this is gonna go? If it is, let me know. I'll tell Marshal he's screwed and you're all worthless. But if you're serious about this, then maybe, just maybe, you should, I don't know, try communicating with one another? Work together? Maybe one of you could actually step up? Take command? Organize this gaggle?" Derek shrugs. "Just a suggestion."

Gil glares at him and spits off to the side.

The men look on in silence. Derek doesn't reattach the leash. Instead, he turns and walks. After a moment, he hears them start to shuffle forward and follow. Gil speaks low to the group.

"Gerry, be our eyes up there. Call out the terrain.

Tell us when and where to step. Jimmy, crouch as best you can. Tell us when you need to straighten a bit. Brian, see if you can't sing us a cadence or something. Get us all in step. If we're on the same foot, we might be able to react and walk better."

Derek keeps them going for hours, bringing them through challenging landscapes, but affording them the opportunity to work through each one as a unit. It isn't until the sun is high overhead that he turns them in the direction of the pens. Almost ninety minutes later, they come upon them.

Stepping over soft ground and breaking through the tree line, Derek eyes a bog covered in pond scum at the bottom of a small knoll. A trickle of a stream flows down the decline; the only indication of running water is a minuscule ripple where it meets the bog. Between him and the water is level ground about ten yards wide. Off to his right sits a large cage made of eight-foot-tall logs as thick as a man's thigh. Another sits in the water on the left side of the bog, submerged to half its height. A small walkway of similar logs leads from the shore to the pen in the swamp.

Derek reaches back and grabs the branch they're attached to. Sprinting forward, he rushes down the hill and gives the limb a hefty yank. The group cries out, lurches, and then spills down the embankment. They land in another tangled mess, slick with the putrid mud, flies and gnats buzzing around them. Heat and humidity has settled in the area, trapped by the canopy above in nature's own sauna.

"Damn it! Why'd you have to—"

He silences Bo by stepping on his head and pressing his face into the mud. As Bo shakes the sludge off his face, Derek walks to the end of the planks and opens the top of the pen in the water. He then crosses over and opens the cage on land. Coming back to the group, he draws his knife and cuts the first two loose from the limb, then steps away. Derek assumes a low, ready posture. The stock of his rifle tucked tightly against his shoulder. The muzzle just a precarious flick of the wrist from coming to bear.

"Up. One of you to each. I don't care which, but you'd better make it fast."

The two eye each other and then quickly scramble. The man behind Gerry is up first. He rushes to the dry cage. Gerry reluctantly turns around, trotting down the planks. He hesitates at the end.

"Get in."

"How we know this pond ain't full of snapping—"

Derek starts walking toward Gerry. Gerry thinks better of it and jumps through the opening in the cage. A loud splash goes up as he breaks through the water. Gerry bobs up a second later, coughing and hacking. The smell and taste of the stagnant pool, like wet, hot garbage on a July New York City street corner, forces him to gag and puke. The combined stenches of vomited bile and swamp decay wafts over the area. As if in confirmation, a small water snake dashes out from the grass overhang near the pen and skirts across the pond to the other side.

Derek repeats the process, two at a time. The carpenters did the job right. Each pen is only large enough to hold four or maybe five men comfortably, and he forces six into each. Slamming the lid down on the water cage, Derek begins to walk away when Sebastian starts screaming.

"You gotta let me out of here! I can't be in this!" The man jumps and flails despite his cuffed hands.

The churning water splashes into the other men's mouths and eyes. Sebastian knocks them against the wooden bars in his frantic state. Some try to calm him while the others berate him.

"Please! Please, this ain't right! I can't! I can't!" the man continues to yell, his voice reaching higher and higher pitches. "Get me out of this shit! I don't want any part of this no more! Please! Please!"

Derek walks back over and stands at the cage door. Sebastian stops screaming. Derek puts his foot through the bars and steps on his head, shoving him underwater. The other men in the cage thrash and yell but are packed so tightly that they can't do much to alleviate the pressure. After thirty seconds or so, he lets off and Sebastian pops back up, coughing up ingested pond water.

"Shut your mouth," Derek says, walking away. The man continues his begging between gasps, whimpering them out as best he can.

Back on the dry ground, Derek leans his rifle against a tree and then drops his bag and plate carrier next to it. Stretching the sweat-soaked shirt free from his chest, he looks back into the tree line. He hefts the limb that tied the men together and wedges it into the crevices of two trees, forming a crossbar between them. A quick venture back up the knoll and he returns with two equal-length limbs and some vines. Laying a limb at each end of the crossbeam, he aligns them to roughly the same angle and then lashes everything together. The frame of his lean-to complete, Derek sets about finding and lashing additional limbs diagonally from the crossbeam before covering it all with large ferns and branches full of leaves.

The men watch him create a serviceable shelter in mere minutes. Sebastian calls out to him every so often, but the rest look on in silence. Derek moves about his business setting up camp, disappearing into the woods to gather resources for stretches at a time. On one trip, he comes back rolling a large stump down into the flat area. On the next, he scouts hare trails and sets snares, then returns with an armload of firewood.

Derek gets a tinder bundle smoking with a strike of the ferro rod integrated in the StatGear survival knife sheath and sparks his fire to life. More trips, more wood. He fills his metal water bottle from the trickle flowing down the hill and then sets it over the fire. By the time he has his bed of pine needles formed underneath the lean-to, the water is boiling. He takes it off the fire to cool and lounges down in his shelter.

The men crowd the bars as he digs out a bag of beef jerky and starts to snack. He can hear their stomachs growling.

"You think you might let us out of this shit and actually start teaching us something?" says Gil with a steely glare.

Derek stares right back. "Start? I've been teaching you all day, Major. You rednecks don't want to pick up on the lessons, that's on you. No worries, though. I got a whole month, and it's only three-quarters through day one."

He takes a long pull on his water, gulping down half its contents. The men watch longingly, their throats parched, their mouths sticky. Sebastian starts yelling again.

"You gotta let me out of this cage, man! I can't be in here! I can't!"

"Shut the fuck up, Sebastian!" Gil calls across the pond, cutting Derek off before he can yell pretty much the same. "We're in his world now, dumbass."

Derek smiles and hoists his bottle to him. "At least one lesson is sinking in." He drinks again as Gil moves to the back of the cage and squats.

14

Early the next morning, Derek makes his way to the edge of the pond, halfway between the water and land cages. He takes a deep breath before speaking out over the clearing.

"Survival, evasion, resistance, and escape. Otherwise known as SERE school. Lucky or unlucky for you gentlemen, depending on how you look at it, this was where I spent the bulk of my instructor time while in the Corps. What already seems unlucky to you is that this is the chosen method your leader has tasked me with. To put you through this training to not only enhance your skills in the field but assess your ability to be part of his security team.

"You're going to hate me. You're going to hate the things done to you, but just know that everything done to you has a purpose behind it. You've already been taught the basics of survival. Here we'll see how you use them. When you're hungry, remember that food may not be a commodity when out on patrol. When you're thirsty, you'll see the importance of water and hydration. When the sleep deprivation hits you—and it *will* hit you—realize that you are being given a new threshold with which to operate.

"I'm going to teach you to avoid the enemy should you get separated from your unit. We're going to practice resisting interrogation in case you do get caught by them. All of this will be done for your benefit and for the benefit of the camp you seek to protect. Because if you can't stay alive, you can't keep them safe.

"You've spent one night in the cages, and undoubtedly, some of you already want to give up. You may not be willing to admit it to your buddies on your left and right, but rest assured I'll sniff you out. One night, gentlemen. Pilots shot down over Vietnam lived in solitary confinement for years. You understand me? Years.

"During the day, you'll be taught. You screw up, you end up in the cage. Talk back, fail to listen or execute my commands, in the cage. If, and I emphasize *if*, I am unable to locate you during our evasion exercises, you may then enact your survival priorities and attempt to sustain yourselves. However, if you're found—"

"Let me guess. In the cage," Brian returns.

"Glad somebody is paying attention. Any other smart-ass comments?"

Catching on quickly, the men think better than Brian and keep their mouths closed.

"No? All right, then. Let's get started."

First donning his plate carrier and slinging his rifle, Derek walks to the water cage and flips the top open. As the men struggle to get themselves out of confinement, Derek opens the door on the land cage and frees the men from their restraints. Cradling his M4 at the low ready, he eyes Gil and Brian warily. The men from the land cage wait for those in the water cage to join them. When no one makes a move to help the others out, Derek fires a round into the dirt. The men jump at the sudden boom.

"Just going to stand there and let them flounder for themselves, huh? Especially when your hands are free and theirs aren't. Guess we already forgot the lesson about teamwork. No worries, land cage. Guess where you'll be tonight?"

Glares are shot his way, but the men move over to help their comrades. When they're all gathered and freed from the zip ties, Derek forces them into a file and marches them out of the bog and into the woods. Once they have gone a good distance and the men are gasping for breath, he halts the troop and begins their training in earnest. Standing among a copse of trees in a small clearing covered in waist-high brush, Derek directs the men into a semicircle around him.

"Evasion begins like everything else: with a positive attitude. You keep that and your wits about you and you can overcome each obstacle as it comes your way. Beyond that, the next-best tools for evading the enemy are patience and flexibility. Always remember that as an evader your primary goal is to avoid detection. If you can do that, your success is almost always assured. Remaining flexible, adapting to the situation instead of trying to force your way through, is the key to evasion."

Derek takes them first through a series of immediate actions, teaching them to seek out a concealed location from which they can assess the situation, take stock of any injuries and supplies, and formulate a plan. He shows them how to sanitize the area of any signs, including hiding equipment that they'll need to leave behind. From there, he goes into a lengthy class on using natural elements to apply camouflage. How to read the terrain to know what pattern to use on their faces so that it blends in with the coniferous trees around them. How to break up their silhouette using leafy boughs and loose grasses, yet doing so without overly disturbing the area around them lest they leave tracks for the enemy to follow.

The men nod and follow along, doing their best to stay awake despite the lack of sleep and their grumbling stomachs. When he's done teaching, Derek has the men go through applying natural camouflage to their faces, necks, ears, and hands. When everyone is sufficiently covered in dirt and grime, Derek launches his next class, this time going into evasive maneuvers.

"So here's the scenario. You've just conducted a raid on your adversary's camp. You're in retrograde, but you get separated from the rest of the team. Or maybe you're out on patrol and you get ambushed. Everyone gets scattered, killed, or captured. Plausible, yes?"

The men, many of whom are fighting to stay awake despite standing around him, look at one another. Gil peers to his left and right, spits on the ground when he realizes that no one is going to answer, and opens his mouth.

"The former more so than the latter. I think you're giving them too much credit. They're not military trained as far as we know."

"Neither is this group. Not yet anyway. But from what I've heard, they got the jump on your hunting party without them realizing it. I get it; those were kids and you're all badasses, right? My point being, those scenarios could happen. Which means that you would have to employ stealth in your movements to make it back to friendly lines.

"This is what evasion is all about. You master this kind of travel and you might be able to mesh it into your actions on contact. Imagine conducting a raid and then everyone splitting off to find their own way back. Instead of one trail to follow, the enemy would have twelve. Advanced stuff from where you are right now, but it could be useful."

The security team's interest is piqued by the notion. More than a few of them look to Gil. The leader of the team just stares back at Derek, his jaw pulsing. Derek takes note of the reaction. That particular tactic seemed appealing to them for some reason.

"To perform a successful evasion, you have to limit your movement."

"That doesn't make any sense," Brian quips.

"Maybe let me finish next time. As I was saying, a moving object is easy to spot. Think of a whitetail crossing through the woods as opposed to bedded down. Same principle. You want to restrict your movements to sporadic intervals. Five to ten paces at the most. Then you get back down. You stop. Look. Listen. Smell."

"You expect us to be able to smell them? What is this, *Commando*?" Gerry asks.

Derek can't help smirking. In the movie, John Matrix smells his assailants just before they attack him at his home. "Believe it or not, it's not as hard as it sounds. We humans stink of artificial, and that scent stands out in the wild. Soaps. Deodorant. Bug spray. Maybe they're chewing gum and you smell the flavor. Or tobacco. Chances are more than a few smoke or dip. They'll reek of that shit if they've done it recently, and you can smell it coming a mile away. Just remember, scent goes in both directions. If you're using that stuff before you go out into the field, the enemy can smell you too.

"When you're actually moving, you want to use the natural cover that's presented to you. This brush behind me is perfect. You could low crawl from one end of this clearing to the other without ever being seen or heard, provided you mask your movement, speed, and noise."

Nods come back to him. The men fixate on Derek. His knowledge seeps into them, and for a few moments, they forget what he put them through the night before with the cages.

"In all aspects, you should restrict your actions to periods of low light, bad weather, wind, or reduced enemy activity. These are the best possible conditions for your travel, as they'll do the most to hide your evasion. Everyone following?"

More nods.

"Good. Then get on your bellies and start crawling. Practice makes perfect, gentlemen."

There are grumbles, but fewer than before. The men get down on all fours and start crawling through the brush, hiding themselves behind bushes, lowering their chests to the dirt and scraping along it in between shrubs. Derek walks among them, making corrections as he goes. Stepping on backs or butts to keep the men pressed down into the concealment.

"You've got to constantly be aware of your profile. Don't stand straight up, especially if you're on a hill with no backdrop. A clear sky behind you will point out your silhouette in a heartbeat."

The men emerge from the brush in the clearing on

the opposite side, panting, sweating, and covered in even more dirt and mud. "Great. Now turn around and do it again. Get used to it, gentlemen. This is what we're learning today."

As the men crawl back and forth through the clearing, Derek adds to the lesson. After a few iterations, he graduates them into moving through the forest, showing them where to step to avoid disturbing the brush so they don't leave a trail for the enemy to follow. How to mask their footfalls in the shadow of vegetation overgrowing their line of travel. He teaches them to avoid breaking branches, leaves, or grass for the same reason. Derek tells them to move over rocks and logs when available to help break up their trail while leaving no tracks behind. At another clearing, he shows them how to cross while in the shadow of nearby trees.

All day, the men traipse through the woods. Derek drills them relentlessly through the different techniques and works the team farther and farther out from the bog. Late in the afternoon, Derek holds his hand up, measuring how much daylight is left by counting the number of fingers between the sun and the horizon. With just over an hour left, he huddles the men up.

"All right, gents. You've had a day to absorb and practice. Now it's time to put your evasion to the test. Our bog is due east of here, so put the sun at your back and you'll have your direction. I'm giving you ten minutes to get ahead of me. Anyone that manages to avoid capture can fall back on the survival skills you've been given to this point and attempt to ride out the night. However, the enemy won't stop hunting you just because the sun goes down. That's the price of your freedom."

"Lemme guess. If we get caught, it's in the cages," Beets asks sarcastically.

"Bingo," Derek replies while holding up his wrist to inspect his watch. After a moment, he lowers his hand. The men just look at him. "Clock's ticking."

It takes them another moment to catch on, but when they do, they scatter like cockroaches when the light is thrown on. Derek watches as they sprint away to the east, no regard for the vegetation they disturb or the tracks they leave. True to his word, he waits ten minutes before starting after them. Even with the dwindling daylight, it isn't hard to pick up their trails. The mad dash into the forest bored a swath in the wood line that a rhinoceros could fit through. Derek picks up a steady jog, following the twists and turns as they present themselves.

It isn't long before he comes upon Gerry, stooped over with his hands on his knees, trying desperately to catch his breath. "I can see you were paying attention."

Gerry jumps at the sound of Derek's voice. "Holy shit! You found me already?"

"Pretty easy to find someone standing out in the open. Let's see those hands," Derek replies as he slings his pack off his shoulders. Withdrawing a pair of looped zip ties from his bag, he re-handcuffs Gerry. "Keep going due east until you hit the bog. When you get there, you sit and wait for the rest of your comrades."

"Roger that," Gerry says before ambling away.

Derek doubles back and reacquires the trail, this time branching off to follow a pair of large boot prints. He finds Jimmy attempting to hide in some brush, but the man's excessive bulk gives him away. Derek cuffs him and sends him on his way.

He wishes that they would pose a fighting challenge for him, but it's as though the training went straight out of their heads the moment he released them into the woods. Just like when he'd first met Gil, nothing is more disappointing than seeing students oblivious to his training. Derek finds half of the men before the sunlight is gone. He ranges his way to the bog to make sure the six arrived there. Upon seeing them, Derek splits the trainees up and sends them into the cages. Then he spins around and runs back into the woods.

Despite the lack of light, the retired Marine quickly gains ground on the rest of the team. All he has to do is listen to find Bibbidi, Bobbidi, and Boo. The trio, having lasted past sundown, assumed they were safe for the night and took the opportunity to bed down for some much-needed catch-up sleep. The sound of their snoring leads Derek right to them.

Thomas gives him pause, only because his trail ends abruptly. Derek searches around the area until finally he looks up, seeing him perched in a tree. Sebastian's body odor gives him away, a mix of sweat, vomit, and stale scotch permeating the air around the small alcove he found at the base of a tree. Derek escorts them back to the bog, where Sebastian begins to beg and plead not to be thrown in the cages again. Derek places him in the land cage this time and then ranges out again.

The remaining few grow more confident with the amount of time elapsed in the exercise. Derek finds Dillon and Parker because they are carrying on a conversation as they work their way through the forest. Gil because he rushed too quickly from one spot to the next, both the noise and his movement giving him away. After they are secured, Derek heads out for the final time of the night to find Brian.

Derek revels in the exercise. There was a Hemingway quote on the wall of one of his TOCs years back. It went something like, "There's no hunting like the hunting of men, and those that have hunted armed men long enough, never cared for anything else." His night of ranging through the woods, the moon and starlit sky above him, casting their oblong shadows while the chorus of the night creatures batters his senses is enough to channel memories. Memories of rock-strewn cliffs and ragged trees clinging to the sides of mountains. Of goat paths and rolling hills. Of forest thick as this one, thousands of miles away, where he had hunted the enemy. Then, it was not to teach but to kill, and in that lesson, he was an expert.

It's close to midnight when Derek catches the flickering through the trees. As he stalks his way forward, the unmistakable smell of woodsmoke fills his nostrils. Nearing the source, Derek can hear the crackle and pop of the fire, can see the embers floating into the air. He steps silently, shouldering his rifle as he slowly edges over the top of a shallow depression.

Brian looks up to see his teacher standing over him. "Shit," is all he can produce.

"This depression isn't nearly deep enough to shelter a fire from observation."

"Yeah," Brian replies. "I kinda figured that. After so much time had gone by, I guessed you were either tied up with the other guys still or done for the night. But hey, at least I got the fire going, right?"

"Congratulations," Derek answers. "You're dead. Noise and light discipline. When you're evading, you have to have both. Otherwise, you might as well just scream, 'Come and get me' into the night."

"Yeah, yeah. Got it."

"On your feet. Stamp that out, and then let's get moving."

Derek cuffs him, and the two make their way back to the bog in relative silence. Upon getting there, Derek promptly puts Brian into the water cage before making his way over to halfway between each cell.

"As you can probably tell by where you're spending the night, today's lesson didn't sink in all that well. Disappointing given the amount of practice you were allotted, but that's okay. This is only day one, and we've got an entire week of SERE school ahead of us. You'll get it. I'm going to make certain of that. But for now . . . let's shift gears to something else."

15

Derek moves swiftly to the water cage and flips open the lid. "All right, Jimmy. Out."

The blood vanishes from the man's face. He looks around at his compatriots. The largest of them all, he tries his best to shrink back from the opening, but his bulk and the tightness of the confines won't let him. "Why?" he asks frantically. "What do you want with me?"

"I'm asking the questions tonight, Jimmy. Now either you get out on your own or we spend the next twenty minutes with me dunking you under the water. You know how many iterations I can get done in twenty minutes?"

"Why don't you just leave him alone, tough guy," Brian replies.

Derek just looks at Brian flatly for a moment and then reaches over and grabs him by the hair. He dunks him under the surface and holds him there for thirty seconds while Brian thrashes about.

As soon as Derek lets go, Brian's head pops up,

coughing, gasping for air, and spewing out the funk of the bog. "You fuck!"

"Sucks, doesn't it? You think that's bad, try being waterboarded. What do you say, Jimmy, want to give that a shot?"

The large man's face remains placid, but Derek sees the faintest trembling of his lower lip. Sticking his shackled hands up through the cage opening, Jimmy pulls at the top to get some leverage. Derek grabs him by the back of the shirt and helps haul him up. When they're both standing again, he gestures to the wood line with the muzzle of his rifle.

"Start walking."

"Where . . . where are we going?" Jimmy asks as he follows the command. He does his best to keep his voice from cracking.

"I'll let you know when we get there. Now keep your mouth shut and move out. You're a prisoner, re-member?"

They walk south into the moonlit forest. Every so often, Jimmy half turns around, begging to be told where they are headed. Derek silences him with a nudge of the flash suppressor on the end of his rifle, turning the big man back in the direction of travel. They move steadily through the woods for fifteen minutes when Derek calls a halt next to a large spruce. "All right. Back up against the tree."

"Why? What are you gonna—"

"Jimmy, you ask one more question and I'll drag you back there and dunk you all night. Now do as you're told."

Jimmy complies.

"Good. Stand still."

Derek lets his rifle rest against his plate carrier and shrugs out of his assault pack. Withdrawing one hundred feet of figure-eight-bound five-fifty cord, he begins unraveling the parachute rope. When Derek has enough, he ties a single loop around the tree and Jimmy together, then proceeds to wrap the cord around Jimmy's torso a half dozen times. Cutting the length and knotting it off, Derek repeats the process across Jimmy's shins just above his boots. When Jimmy is sufficiently restrained, Derek replaces the bundle and slips his pack back on.

"Okay, then. Sweet dreams."

As Derek goes to move off, Jimmy blurts out, "Wait! What are you doing?"

Derek stops and looks at him through the pale darkness.

"You can't just leave me here!"

"Why not?"

"Are you serious? There're bears in these woods. Coyotes too."

"This far north, I bet you get a lot of lynx as well. Hope it works out for you. If you're still here in the morning, I'll bring you back for class."

"Wait. Wait! Derek, don't go! You can't leave me out here!" Jimmy screams at the top of his lungs while Derek heads back toward the bog. The farther away he gets, the more frantic Jimmy's screams become. "Help me! Someone help me! Help!"

Derek is happy to see that the screams reach all the way back to the cages. Genuine fear sits in the men's eyes as he makes his way to the water cage again. "Okay, Brian. Your turn."

"Fuck off. If you think I'm going anywhere—"

His voice cuts off as Derek steps on his head and

dunks him under the water. Letting him up after a few moments, Derek just smiles. Brian spits out more pond scum.

"Bastard," he adds but then proceeds to climb out of the cage.

After returning from lashing Brian to his tree to the east of the bog, Derek gathers up Gil. Jimmy's screams come out more like ragged cries now. Gil merely walks forward, not saying a word. Derek ties him to his tree and goes to step away.

"You know this ain't gonna break me, D," the man says. "I been through too much to be afraid of the dark."

"What about the lions and tigers and bears?"

"They're liable to get Jimmy the way he's hollering before they ever get to me. I might lose out on a few hours of z's, but I'll be none the worse for wear. You'll see."

Stepping a little closer, Derek looks him square in the eyes. "Maybe you will. Maybe you won't. But can you say the same thing for your men? What will they be willing to give up for a little more water? More food? Some real sleep?" Derek pauses to let the point settle in. "Guess we'll find out in the morning, won't we?"

Derek can sleep through the persistent cries Jimmy emits throughout the remainder of the night, but he's certain the other men cannot. Between having to listen to Jimmy and being restrained and caged, the security team succumbs to another sleepless night. Derek awakens and takes his time going through his morning routine. He boils water and eats some more rations. Ranges out for firewood and checks his traps. By the time he returns, the sun is well up over the horizon.

Leaving the men again, Derek heads south toward Jimmy. The consistent bellowing had turned to ragged whimpering the longer the night went on. Now approaching the spruce, Derek can hear the large man sobbing to himself. As Derek steps around the tree, Jimmy's head lifts, fresh tears falling from his eyes.

"Have a nice night?"

"Please . . . please let me go. I can't feel my legs. I'm so tired. I can't do this anymore."

"You want out, Jimmy?"

The big man vigorously nods.

"Then you're going to have to answer some of my questions."

A look of reservation passes over Jimmy's face, but with it, he wrestles with his longing for freedom. "What kind of questions?"

"Tell me about your boss, for starters."

Jimmy's lips compress into a thin line. "You know I can't say nothing about Marshal."

"Suit yourself," Derek replies as he starts to leave. "You can spend all day and night out here for all I care. Until you're ready to talk, you'll stay tied to that tree."

"No, wait!" the big man calls out.

Derek freezes in front of him. "Well? Which one is it going to be, Jimmy? Isolation is a key component of being a prisoner. I'm perfectly content with leaving your ass here if you don't start talking."

Jimmy's eyes shift back and forth with Derek's. "He hates the government. He blames them for everything."

"Nice try. I already knew that. See you later."

"No, wait!" Jimmy hesitates, and to Derek, it appears that he is making a calculation. Weighing the options that are available to him. Derek sees the strain on Jimmy's face before he finally relents and blurts out, "The banks foreclosed on his grandfather. When he started logging here, they declared it state land and took over the operation for themselves. They ruined him. Put Marshal's family out in the street."

Jimmy goes on frantically, the floodgates opened to try to avoid more isolation. "He had to join up at sixteen just to get some money. His best friend went with him and was killed over there! His daughter OD'd on heroin! His wife! His wife died of something terminal a couple of years back! Please don't leave me here any longer!"

Derek shifts to further intelligence gathering. "The men out there hunting this group. How many of them are there?"

"What . . . I . . . I don't kn—"

"Don't give me that shit, big man. You want out or not? Better start talking."

"I'm telling you, I don't know anything."

"Numbers? Weapons? Which direction do they approach from? Which way do they leave? It's called *ingress* and *egress*, you worthless lump."

"I . . . The east. They always come from the east. A dozen of them. Maybe more. It's dark out when they do."

Jimmy's shifting gaze and facial twitch tell Derek that he is lying. He hasn't the first clue about what is supposedly out there harassing them. Interesting for a group of men being assembled to counter that exact purpose.

Untying the knots, Derek sets Jimmy free and escorts the whimpering man back to the bog. Jimmy regains some of his previous composure, but the sleepless night and lack of food and water clearly have taken their toll. He can't help keeping his eyes down-cast from the others as he's returned to the cage.

He finds Brian delirious with lack of sleep, and as such, the man doesn't offer much save for a few halfhearted expletives. Derek deposits him just like he did with Jimmy before and then keeps on to the west, finally linking up with Gil late in the morning. Gil smirks as Derek makes his way around the tree.

"Mornin', D."

Standing in front of him while cradling his rifle, Derek regards Gil with a blank face. "I take it you had a pleasant evening?"

The smirk widens. "I told you this was nothin' to me, D. Easy as pie."

"I don't suppose you'd like to share any info with me? You know, as compensation for cutting you loose."

To this, Gil throws his head back against the bark and roars with laughter. Derek smiles and lets him have his moment. When Gil has calmed down, he looks back at Derek.

"Ain't that a hoot! You really think I'm going to roll over that easy? Marshal might as well be my kin. No way you get anything on him from me."

Shrugging, Derek slowly takes a seat on a nearby fallen log. "Yeah, you're probably right. You're too stubborn to talk. Hell, you might even be intelligent. But can you say that for the rest of your boys?"

The smirk shrinks. A smile ticks at the corner of Derek's mouth. He goes on.

"Oh yeah. I got the whole skinny. The foreclosure on Grandpa. Korea. His daughter. His wife. Quite the horror story of a life, if I'm being honest."

Gil spits to the side as the smirk vanishes completely. "What of it? So you found out some shit that happened ages ago. Chances are you were going to learn some eventually."

"You don't seem to get it, Gil," Derek says, standing up and walking back around the tree. He talks while he unties the knots to Gil's bindings. "It's not about whether I learn the information on you people or not. I couldn't give a shit about your pasts. What you should be concerned about is that after two nights of hardship, your so-called security team started singing like canaries.

"What's gonna happen if these men get taken? They going to give away critical info about your camp? Armament? Supplies? Where the lookouts are posted?"

Free from his bonds, Gil comes around the tree, a scowl plastered across his face. "Who sang, D? You let me know right now."

Derek shakes his head. "My job is to assess you and the rest of the men for Marshal. I'll present him with my findings."

"You know I'm gonna find out anyway."

"Maybe you will," he replies, "but until then, the information stays with me. Besides, that was just the first night of isolation and interrogation. Who knows how many more might spill their guts the longer this goes on?"

Fuming, his face beet red, Gil stomps his way forward, brushing past Derek and continuing toward the bog. Derek smiles and follows him. Back at the cages, he secures Gil and then pulls Thomas out of the water cage. When they get to dry land, Derek cuts him free from his cuffs. Pointing at the buckets, he says, "Go fill those up from the stream and set them on the fire."

At first, Thomas looks confused, but then he quickly does as he's told. When the buckets are in place, Derek puts him in the land cage. Stoking the fire first, he then leaves to gather more firewood. Coming back, he finds the buckets boiling and takes them off to cool. Derek begins the slow process of freeing the men from the cages and then their flex cuffs. Once they are done, he tells them to get a drink. Completely parched, the men scramble to the buckets and start spooning handfuls into their mouths, jostling for position and shoving one another until Gil screams at them all and establishes some order. After that, they take turns gulping from the buckets until both are empty.

"Everyone enjoy breakfast? Good. Class is back in session. On your feet. We're hiking out to the clearing we were in yesterday to work on evasion again since you all did such a shit job with it last night. If you can show some progress this morning, we'll get into water and food procurement. Then it'll be up to you how much you eat and drink while out of the cages. Sound good?"

A smattering of murmurs come back to him. Displeased as they are with the need to crawl through the mud again, the promise of some actual food gives them a modicum of motivation to hang on to. Derek marches them out and drills them into the afternoon.

For the next three days, he follows the same routines. Classes during the day. Isolation of three at a time at night, followed by periods of questioning at first light. Each man gets his turn. For the most part, the security team keeps their composure in the face of their deteriorating conditions, and Derek learns little more beyond what he already found out from Jimmy. Even Sebastian manages to hold his tongue, despite the offer of freedom from the cages.

On the morning of their fifth day at the bog, Derek drags each one out of their pens and places them on their knees. They're exhausted and filthy. Hungry and dejected. A few raise their eyes to him but quickly drop them back down when he looks their way, even Brian the dissenter. Sebastian breathes rapidly, on the verge of hyperventilating, relieved to be out of the cages.

Derek barks out commands as he did a few days earlier. The men turn and sit. They wait patiently as he breaks down his shelter and places the beam across their shoulders. Derek straps them to it, and they begin another hike. He pushes them hard, forcing them through thick brush and steep inclines.

Even with the exertion, the men's spirits begin to perk up with the assumption that they are moving into a new phase of training. Late in the afternoon, the combined effects of their exhaustion overcome their exuberance. The group stumbles and falls often. Their eyes droop and heads nod despite dragging their feet through the hike.

Long shadows stretch through the trees. The daylight diminishes. They don't notice as the ground gets soft under their feet and the water soaks through their boots. As they come through the trees, the men are brought back to the present by Sebastian's screams.

"No! No! I can't go back in! No!"

Their heads snap up and look around. The pond ripples slightly as frogs and snakes scurry away. The cages await them, their doors open like the maws of starving jackals.

"Settle in, ladies," Derek says.

The men groan. Sebastian screams unintelligibly even as Derek shoves his head under the water.

The interrogations continue.

16

The next morning, Derek pulls every man out of the pens and sits them in a line next to one another. If they looked dejected before, they are absolutely submissive now. Filthy, their eyes barely able to stay open, and with signs of weight loss already visible in many of them, Derek feels the time is right. He picks up the handheld and calls down to base camp. Sitting on the stump as buckets of water boil, Derek stares at the security team. No one looks back.

Half an hour later, the sound of a Gator's engine chopping through the trail carries to them. Some of the men lift their heads ever so slightly at the noise. Others are kicked awake by it. Derek waits until Marshal and his escort come into the clearing before standing up and going to his bag. He comes out with a pair of zip ties that he threads through each other to form loops. Derek puts his arms behind his back.

"Marshal? Will you do the honors?"

A confused look passes over the old man's face. Several of the men in the QRF pick their heads up, sharing in the puzzlement. Derek holds the makeshift cuffs out until Marshal steps forward and cinches them down. Hands restrained behind his back, Derek sits down in front of them. He waits until he has full attention from the group.

"If your captors allow you to keep your boots on, you have a chance to escape from zip tie restraints. You'll have to do this right after capture or while in transit. After you get to whatever facility you're going to be held in, you'll be strip-searched and your footwear removed, so the window for this is short."

The men look at one another and then at Marshal.

Derek flops to his side, pulling their gazes back. "To defeat zip tie cuffs, first get your hands in front of you." He scrunches into a ball and pulls his knees up to his chest. He works his hands down across the backs of his thighs until he gets them over his ankles and in front of his body, then sits up.

"If you were in a single cuff, you could try to pop it." He mimes the movements as he describes them. "You would raise them above your head, and then pull them violently down toward your gut. At the same time, you want to flare your elbows out to the side while pinching your shoulder blades together. The pressure should bust the plastic, but the movement draws a lot of attention to yourself. Plus, if the tie is too thick, it may not break, even with multiple attempts."

A few of them begin to perk up, the realization that they're being taught tradecraft cutting through their exhaustion.

Derek continues, "To stay under the radar, use the friction method. With your hands in front of you, untie your shoelaces. Thread one through the cuffs, and then knot it with a lace from your other foot.

Once your knot is pulled tight, pump your legs back and forth in an alternating motion. The friction saws through the plastic, and the ties pop off." Derek gives a few more kicks, and then his cuffs break.

The men stare at him.

"Do it."

He stands. A few of them exchange glances, doubtful.

"This isn't a trick. Do it."

Slowly but surely, the men start to flop over and work their hands around their bodies. After they've all managed the first part, Derek walks up and down the line while they begin to fumble with their laces.

"If you have to, wedge a lace into your boot top to help hold it in place. Leave two inches or so of slack, and then scoop the lace with the cuff," he says. "Once you have the thread through, you can just pull it the rest of the way."

Gerry pops his cuffs. A few moments later, Thomas pops his. Derek walks to his shelter and grabs another item from his bag. By the time he gets back, the last of the cuffs is broken. The men rub at their wrists and stare at him. Derek draws his sidearm and sits on the stump.

"That spark you're feeling? That's a bit of adrenaline coming from your first taste of freedom. Don't let it go to your heads. You may think you can rush me. Get retribution for all the shit I did to you the last few days. Truth is, you're well beyond your normal physical limits. Even if you did try something so incredibly stupid, you'd all get light-headed from jumping up too quickly."

Turning his pistol over in his hand, Derek eyes the weapon and then stares down the men. "There's a ten-round magazine in this. One in the pipe. Meaning even though I can't get all of you the first go-around, I'm more than confident that I can reload and handle the rest, given your state. You picking up what I'm saying?"

Gil's gaze shifts to Marshal. Derek can practically read his thoughts. He's the only one sharp enough to realize that the escort with his long rifle could tip the scales, but that would require Marshal to allow it. The curt shake of the old man's head tells Gil everything he needs to know. Derek still has Marshal's favor.

"Now the chain on regular handcuffs," Derek says, slapping a pair on his wrists while still clutching his pistol, "despite urban legend, is not easily broken. To get out of these, you'll need a bobby pin or something close to it."

"We ain't exactly puttin' our hair up lately," Brian says, the slightest bit of edge returning to his voice.

Derek reaches into his boot and feels along the inside. A moment later, he pulls out a bobby pin. "A small incision in the rim of your boot top, and then you sew it back up with the same color thread. In a time of need, you pull the thread loose and get the pin out. I carry one with me all the time.

"The bobby pin is roughly the perfect width and strength you need to work the inner mechanism. Insert it into the keyhole and work it around until you feel a lever. Give it a quick lift, and . . ." The handcuff pops open. Derek flicks his wrist until the single strand comes free, then repeats the process with the second cuff. He stands up and walks over, cuffing Jimmy and then handing him the bobby pin. "Each of you take a turn getting out and then pass it down the line. When it gets to the end, do it a second time and then send them back to Jimmy."

The big man gets to work while Derek sits back down on the stump. "In the two weeks when we first trained together, I observed each one of you. I learned who was in charge. Who the influencers are. Who cuts corners and on what. Brian has a temper. Dillon is a jokester. Beets falls asleep first. Gerry wakes up early. I figured out who gets nervous. Excited. Overzealous. The whole time, I was taking stock of my surroundings. Have any of you done any of that? Can anyone tell me what my routine was?"

The men are content to keep their heads down. The realization that they hadn't taken note of any useful detail creeps into their minds.

"At least three times a day, I left you. Checked my traps. Gathered resources. Hunted. If you were watching, you would have noticed. That would have been the time to coordinate your efforts and attempt an escape. Granted, Marshal told you to do as I say, and that might have taken the initiative from you. But we train as we fight."

Jimmy pops the lever, and his first cuff comes off. A few seconds later, he manages to get the second one off. He passes them to the next in line.

"There's a tenet in dealing with enemy prisoners of war. An acronym to remember it by. Military Police officer, tell me what it is."

Gil looks up. Anger clear on his face. At himself or Derek is the question. Probably both. "Search, silence, segregate, safeguard, and speed to the collection point."

Derek nods. "The five *s*'s. If I did any of those, it

was the last two, and poorly at that. No gags. No separation. Left you alone for hours at a time. Those bars in the land cage. Those are rough-hewn logs. There are knobs on them. Knobs you could have worked your cuffs against and used to break them."

A few heads pick up and look at him, accompanied by nods of understanding.

"You see?" Derek continues. "It's a mindset. Always. In survival. In interrogation. Training aside, if this had been a real situation, you let one man dictate the terms of your capture. I created the mindset of dominance, and you bought into it the moment I took your loudmouth, your linebacker, and your leader out of the game. You need to be able to overcome that, because I promise you the experts won't make mistakes. Even in isolation, you need to be working on the internal victories. The observations. The formulation of plans. Those victories. Those goals. They are the fuel for your resistance and eventually your escape and evasion."

Brian gets the second cuff to fall off his wrist. The asshole actually smiles when it does so. He looks up at Derek, who has all their attention now.

"What you experienced this past week. What I put you through. It serves a purpose. Despite what you may think of me or my intentions. Put that shit out of your head. Easier said than done, I know, but you won't learn anything if you're hell-bent on getting back at me.

"The truth is, you've all been given a threshold. You've learned just how much further you can be pushed. What you can endure. Your eyes have also been opened to a major truth. Everyone breaks. No one can endure forever."

The cuffs freeze in the middle of the line. The men stare at him. A few swallow.

"Keep them moving," Derek says, waving his free hand. "I say all this because it should reinforce the biggest lesson thus far. The best way to avoid being interrogated is to not be caught at all."

Nods meet him at this conclusion.

"Now. Right here at this point. This is where you need to learn. Starved. Exhausted. Beaten down mentally and physically. This is what you're going to have to fight through. To push yourself beyond to avoid pursuit and capture. To live off the land with nothing but the clothes on your back and your bare hands.

"Make no mistake, gentlemen. SERE is about survival, yes, but it's more about getting back to friendly lines. This isn't 'set up a shelter and go fishing at high tide.' This is 'cowering in a naturally occurring hovel while a patrol passes you by.' Reading the terrain and maximizing camouflage to blend in to your surroundings. Using streams to wash your scent. Sprinting through rain because it cancels out the footprints you leave behind. All the things that you've been taught to this point."

Jimmy pops his cuffs off a second time. He looks up at Derek, the last set of eyes to do so.

Derek looks at them all in turn, stands, and holsters his sidearm. "Let's get going."

As the men stand, Derek suppresses the bile creeping up his throat. If he's right and these men are running guns or drugs, the knowledge he has imparted on them will make them more formidable in the field. At the same time, he knows that the only way to get to the confirmation he needs is by gaining their trust. He can't do that by sandbagging the curriculum. An accusation that he's holding back or dragging his feet would only serve to sabotage his intelligence collection by placing him under further scrutiny or getting him kicked out altogether. Like it or not, Derek has no choice but to forge ahead until the evidence mounts. Still, there are other ways to diminish the group's capacity.

17

The trees and trails begin to look familiar. A distinctive rock formation here. A fallen pine there. Gil thinks he can smell something cooking. The slightest hint of smoked meat. At the very least firewood burning.

It's enough to set his imagination running wild. His stomach gurgles, and his mouth waters in response. The perceived notion of a meal just a few hills ahead helps him to ignore the chafing of the shoulder straps against his neck. To look past the fact that he'd only eaten roots and oozing grubs last week.

What the scent, real or imagined, can't make him ignore is his burning hatred for the man walking at the head of the column.

Bringing up the rear of their march, Gil can see the other eleven members of the security team lined up ahead of him. Laden with their packs that had somehow been brought out to the bog, the men had been marching today for hours.

Gil spits and glares. A final test. The goddamn Army loved to tack a goddamn road march onto the end of everything. Gut check time. Let's see that intestinal fortitude. Can you persevere? Can you endure, even when the chips are down?

Get bent, he thinks. *I really shouldn't be so surprised that the Marines would do the same stupid shit.*

He hopes that this is the end and not another one of D's mind tricks. When he brought them back to the pens after the first round of interrogations, it had crushed morale. Hell, it had nearly broken Seb. That poor bastard howled day and night after he was thrown back in the cages. The man had his issues—who among them didn't?—but claustrophobia? Who knew?

Up at the head of the column, a few of the men laugh. Derek, walking to the right of the group on the trail's edge, says something that Gil can't quite make out. The men burst out into hysterics. Derek joins in the laughter.

Gil scowls at them. Don't they realize what's going on? How can they be joking around right now? The man is literally walking with his muzzle pointed in their direction. His finger is poised over the trigger well, Gil is certain of that. Yet these idiots are laughing with him.

Don't they see? D had flipped them over and turned them inside out. Names. Personal histories. He knows each of them through and through. This man is now very, very dangerous to their group. And the fact that he'd done it so effortlessly. Like the way he'd gotten them to turn on Thomas after all D used him for was chores around the camp the first few days while the rest of them were tied to trees. It fuels Gil's rage even more.

The team crests another hill and starts to make its way down the other side. Gil thinks he knows the trail for certain now, even if he'd only been on it a few times himself. Their land is so damn massive, and this far north into it, not even the tourists or hikers come around.

D had ranged them out farther and farther from the pens. He hadn't lied about pushing them. They crawled through mud and brambles and bush so thick it tore at their skin. Sleep was a luxury that came minutes at a time, not hours, if it came at all. It was hard to sleep when you were crouched under a pricker bush or chest-deep in a muddy bog.

The man knows his stuff, Gil has to give him that. Not just his HUMINT. It seems like D can walk into the woods with nothing and not only disappear but live for years. He is a master at foraging, stalking, evasion, and bushcraft. Probably why the others have started to take to him so much. Even in light of their pain and hunger, no one can deny the skills. If they continue to perfect them—and Gil has every intention of making sure that they do—the men will be a formidable group to go up against in these woods. Once they get the tactical component, of course. According to D, that is still weeks away.

What he has to make sure of is that this tilt D's way doesn't become permanent. Gil can't let the infatuation with D get to the point where the men question his orders. Or Marshal's, for that matter. Especially Marshal's. D isn't a part of their group. The guy doesn't even bother to hide his disdain for them. But given the amount of credibility he gained with the men in such short order, he could cause serious problems if left unchecked.

It is something to keep an eye on for sure and work against the moment they get back to camp. Still, there are other issues. More pressing ones that the training has revealed. They will need to be dealt with. Quickly.

The men laugh again. Gil spits. Fucking officers. They're all the same. Even Warrants. All they ever do is swoop in and take the credit. Never get their hands dirty. Never do any of the heavy lifting. Just ride the people below them until they get their big payout or their big promotion. Gil is the one who painstakingly put this team together. Who brought them into Marshal's fold. How quickly the group is forgetting that in the face of D and his fancy Special Operations title.

Gil swallows hard and frowns, looking off to the side of the trail and letting the rhythm of the march propel him forward. That self-righteous rat bastard D. Leaving him tied to a tree like that. All alone with nothing but his thoughts and memories.

It had triggered Gil, and suddenly he was there again. Upside down in their vehicle, covered in blood and limbs from the men who moments earlier had been his crewmates. All four of them, blown to shreds by the IED that flipped their Humvee as easily as if it were a pancake on Sunday morning. The forensics later said that his seat in the right rear, along with their bodies accepting the blast, had been what spared his life.

He wished it hadn't. Trembling and trying to get out of the mangled wreckage of the truck, Gil had to listen as the rest of his platoon fought off the ambush. Cocksucking hajji had set off three IEDs daisy-chained together so that the first, second, and fourth vehicles all got disabled. The remaining truck had to not only repel the blistering wave of incoming bullets and RPGs but also tend to three other trucks' worth of wounded.

Eventually, someone got hold of battalion, and a quick reaction force was sent. Gil was told, much later after the shock had worn off, that two Apaches had screamed overhead and put the nail in the coffin with a couple of rockets. But in those minutes, those long, disgusting minutes, Gil heard it all.

He listened while men openly wept and screamed for their mothers. He heard the animalistic, unintelligible cries of human beings dying in excruciating pain. He smelled the fuel leaking. Felt it soak into his uniform. He lived in absolute fear, knowing that a single spark from the firefight going on around them would burn him alive. Gil vividly remembers pissing himself when that realization hit. When they finally got him out, all he could see was body parts. Body parts of soldiers. Everywhere. Discarded like Popsicle sticks. And blood. So much blood it had softened the hard-packed earth.

And what had it all been for? The lieutenant had told their captain. Protested, even. The farmland was too open. The gullies and wadis were perfect cover. The intel reports had said that IED activity had been extremely high in the region lately, and there hadn't been enough reconnaissance resources to go around. The enemy had been scouting, and planning, and digging with practical impunity. And their commander sent them up that road anyway.

Because he was going to get promoted. No matter what it took to do so. Maybe not the very next rank. Major was somewhat automatic, from what Gil understood. But your service record had to be impeccable and filled with overachievement if you ever wanted a star. That's what their captain was chasing. He had stars in his eyes. All officers did, whether they admitted it or not.

And that's why Gil had smashed that arrogant prick's skull in. Had the men in the CP not gotten hold of him when they had, Gil would have dashed his brains against the wall. His only regret was using the pry bar instead of the pickax. He would've driven the spike into that bastard's worthless brain.

They round a bend in the trail. Gil knows exactly where they are now. Unless D is going to let them see the camp and then force them to about-face, they will be home soon. *That would be so fucked up,* Gil has to admit. If that is to go down, he'll have to put up a fight.

The notion dawns on him that he is going to have to anyway. D can't be allowed to blow them all up. Not with the information that he has. Not with his desecration of loyalties. Gil won't let him. They've come too far to let another officer in power somehow throw their lives away with what he thinks he knows. Gil will make sure of it. Hopefully with Marshal's blessing, but if not . . .

As they slide down a saddle from one trail to another, the banter among the men picks up. They realize now what Gil just picked up on a moment ago. This is the main trail, somewhere between the outbuildings and the camp proper. Elation and adrenaline partially washing away their fatigue, the security team picks up their pace while laughing and joking all the more.

As they continue down the hill toward the camp, the smell of lunch stew fills their noses while a voice carries through the air. It's Marshal, annunciating with vigor and panache. Gil catches a glimpse through the trees. The whole camp is gathered in a large semicircle around the man in the clearing. A row of children sit while their parents stand behind.

"And so, my children, it is what the good Lord has told us. The promise that He has made! 'Bring the full tithe into the storehouse, that there may be food in my house. And thereby put me to the test, says the Lord of hosts.' Have we not brought our tithe in?" Many in the crowd nod in agreement. "Have we not given? I know we have, my children! All of us. Each and every one of us has given. More so than most!"

"Yes!" someone in the crowd extols.

The men come farther down the hill. Marshal's voice becomes clearer.

"But the Lord has promised us! In that very same passage, He gives us proof that our sacrifice is not in vain. That all we have given, all that we have been put through, is for the greater good! 'I will rebuke the devourer for you, so that it will not destroy the fruits of your soil, and your vine in the field shall not fail to bear, says the Lord of hosts. Then all nations will call you blessed, for you will be a land of delight, says the Lord of hosts.' Malachi, chapter three, verses ten and eleven.

"You see? You see, my children? Our time is nearly at hand! The time to rebuke our devourers! We shall be called blessed, and after our rebuke, we will inherit the land of delight!"

The security team comes to the bottom of the hill. Many of the faces in the crowd, only a moment earlier hanging on their leader's every word, take notice and light up. Marshal spins around. His face beams. He spins back to the group.

"Behold! Our deliverers! Remember, my children. Remember verse twelve! 'And all nations shall call you blessed, for ye shall be a delightsome land.' Remember! We shall reclaim our nation! Our nation will see the error of its ways after our message has been delivered! Now go! Go and rejoice and welcome your sons home!"

The camp lets out a tremendous cheer and rushes forward. The QRF breaks formation and runs into the clearing. Families reunite. Hugs and handshakes. Gil notices more than a few looks of shock on the family members' faces at the sight of their dismal condition. These quickly turn to scowls aimed at Derek. D walks through it all unabashed. He meets up with Marshal, and the two talk while the reunions continue.

"Holy shit, Gil. What the hell did he do to you guys?"

Turning, Gil sees Ronald, the camp blacksmith, standing next to him. His arms are outmatched in thickness only by his beard. Like Gil, he's one of many that is unmarried in the group.

Gil turns his attention back toward Marshal and D. "Wasn't no picnic, I can tell you that much."

"Shit, anyone can see that. We've been hearing stories. Did he really tie y'all to trees and lock you in cages?"

Gil gives the man a dismissive glance and looks back. Marshal is nodding thoughtfully. Gil inclines his head toward the two. "When he start preaching again?"

Ronald puts his hands in the small of his back and arches. Gil hears several of his vertebrae pop in quick succession. "Oh, I'd say about three or four days ago now. Each time he comes back from his visits with you boys in the woods, he seems more . . . I don't know. What's the word?"

"Energetic? Invigorated? Enthusiastic?"

"Yeah. Sure. Whichever one you want, that's what he's been."

Over at the discussion, Marshal appears to argue a point only to relent a moment later. The old man goes back to nodding. Gil gets a sinking feeling.

"Excuse me, Ron. I gotta go give my report to Marshal."

"Shit, ain't that what he's doing?" Ronald says, pointing at Derek. "I mean, ain't he in charge of y'all now?"

"No. He ain't," Gil replies as he walks away, his voice dripping with disdain. *Fucking moron. Go sit on your hammer.* As Gil approaches, D squares to face him.

"Zero five tomorrow morning. Lead them through PT. I want them up and down that hill at least three times in an hour."

Gil turns back, looking at the hill they just came down, then turns and gives Marshal a look. The old man returns his gaze expectantly. "What? Running? Man, some of these guys are in their forties. Gerry is pushing fifty-five, I think."

D just shrugs. "These are the ones chosen to protect the camp. They need to be in shape to do so. Breakfast at seven and then the depression to the northwest at zero eight. Full packs, rations, and gear. Weapons too, but no ammo. That'll be brought out later. Make sure they eat well. You'll be doing manual labor most of the day. Marshal will fill you in on the rest." He turns to the old man. "I'll be ready to head into town in about fifteen minutes." He starts to walk away.

"Yes. I'll have your money and driver ready," Marshal calls after him. "If you're available for a meal or a nip later, let me know. I'd very much like to hear about our next steps."

D doesn't acknowledge Marshal's invitation but instead looks directly at Gil. "That reminds me. I don't mind the men taking a drink or two tonight. They've earned it. But it stops at that."

"Listen here, D. We all had to follow your commands out there, but we're back in camp now. You think you're gonna tell me or anyone else that we can't drink, you'd best unfuck that shit right now."

Their stares stay locked and linger. D finally gives a small nod to his left. When Gil turns to look, he sees Sebastian already with a beer and a bottle of scotch in either hand. The man hasn't even taken off his pack yet.

"You want your freedom, Lieutenant? You got it, but now it's on you. As soon as you hit PT tomorrow, you're training again, and that means your asses belong to me." He steps in closer to Gil and lowers his voice so only the three of them can hear. "And mark my words, Gil. You all turn up drunk in the a.m., not only will I drag every last one of you back to the pens, but I'll see to it that you personally experience the ramifications of your inability to lead."

D stalks off without another word. Halfway across the clearing, the kid Bobby runs up alongside him. The two exchange words, and Derek laughs. They talk a bit more, and then the boy dashes out fifteen yards. Bobby throws his football to D, who, carrying his rifle in his left, performs one-arm catches with his right. He curls the ball and pitches it back underhand. The two continue their catch until the man reaches his cabin. D throws the ball and waves to Bobby's parents. They wave back.

Gil looks at Marshal, who raises his eyebrows in response. Gil tries to soften his tone as much as he can for the old man, despite his seething. "You started preaching again, Marshal?"

The old man's face breaks into a smile from ear to ear. "What can I say, Gil? I feel the Lord's message flowing through me! It's as if He's signaling that our time is near. That our cause is just!"

"Yeah," Gil says, loosening the quick-release tabs on his shoulder straps. "About that. You really think it's a good idea and all? Saying such stuff around him? D ain't exactly part of the family, Marshal. You see what he did to us. What he's continuing to do. He hates every bit of being here, and the only reason he's doing this is because of the money you promised him."

"Oh, I don't know," Marshal says, moving around behind the rucksack and helping Gil get it to the ground. "I think Derek might come around. There's so much similarity between him and the others here. Even you. Maybe my preaching now is what will finally open his eyes."

That motherfucker ain't nothing like me. Gil bites the inside of his cheek. "Still, it's an awfully big security risk. The man is a trained intelligence officer. Think of all the information he's been privy to since he got here."

"True, Gil," Marshal says, clapping a hand on his shoulder. "Everything you say is true. But I can't ignore the feelings. It's like the Holy Spirit is confirming that Derek has been sent to us. That he is meant to be here.

Through the Lord's words, spoken by my tongue, I know he will join us."

Gil looks down to hide his grimace. *God didn't send him. I found his ass on YouTube.* Still, he knows when Marshal gets like this, there is little he can say to convince him otherwise. He moves on. "What's this shit about the depression to the northwest?"

Some of the glimmer vanishes from the old man's face. "Derek said he's moving the group into firearms training. He called the lane we use to zero our scopes inadequate for what he has in mind and asked if we had anything resembling a range."

Gil already knows where this is going. "Marshal. There's some decent-size trees in that depression. It'll take us a week to clear that space out and shape it up."

The old man shakes his head vigorously. "Don't worry. I'm rededicating the camp to the task. Once everyone else has had a chance to rotate through chow, they'll head out to help with the clearing. Should only take the day if everyone pitches in."

Something grabs Marshal's attention. Gil twists and sees Sebastian taking a belt from the bottle and then chugging the contents of his beer to chase it. The man crushes the can and throws it down, immediately demanding another from his wife.

"You'd better get a handle on that, Gil. Cut off the head of the snake before it bites you in the morning."

Gil sighs deeply. He leans in to speak in his leader's ear. "Putting D aside for the moment, there are other things that need to be rectified. In the most immediate sense possible." He pulls back out.

The flash. That intensity. The corner of Marshal's lip lifts in the quickest of snarls. From singing with the angels to dancing with the devil. The old man can switch on you in a heartbeat.

"Let's you and I sit down later tonight. I want to hear what you have to say. We'll draw up plans for the now," Marshal looks back at Derek's cabin, "and make contingencies for the later."

Gil nods, feeling his first bit of relief since D tossed tear gas into the outbuilding shacks a week ago. Marshal claps him on the shoulder again, firmly, and then moves off. The old man's face lights up with a smile as he goes to greet Jimmy. Spinning around, Gil stomps over and rips the bottle out of Sebastian's hand, berating him in front of his wife and friends.

18

After handing Derek his keys, the teller swipes his card to the safe-deposit box room. Holding the door open, Derek raises the thick envelope in his hand. "I'll just be a minute. Need to count it first."

"Yeah, okay, but be quick, all right?" replies Brady, the lookout who was on duty the first night of training.

Letting the door close behind him, Derek withdraws his box and places it on the table. The bank manager has been keeping up her part of the investigation. A small stationery organizer is filled to the brim with pens, pads, paper clips, a stapler, and an assortment of rubber stamps phrased with things like "Confidential," and "Past Due."

Pulling out the chair and sitting, Derek unwraps the envelope and then grabs a pad. He scrawls down the information he's committed to memory as quickly as he can while still keeping his handwriting legible. Tearing off the sheet, Derek folds it over twice and then inserts it into a stack of bills. Dropping the bundles into the box with one hand, he pulls his burner phone out with the other.

Derek scrolls to the contact labeled "Kim" and hammers out a text message using their predetermined cipher.

> **Hey there. Still upstate but will try to call in a little bit**

Hitting Send and stuffing the phone back in his pocket, Derek locks and replaces the box. After tidying up the table, he steps out of the room. Brady is ambling about in the pathway that leads to the front doors. His perturbed look doesn't diminish at all upon seeing Derek, who pauses a moment and asks, "You ready?"

"Yeah, man. Let's get out of here."

Derek makes for the door and out into the summer day. Brady heads toward the pickup in the lot across the street.

"Hold up," Derek says, pulling the phone back out. "I gotta call my boy."

"Man, come on. Marshal said there and back."

"And he also said I would have the time each week to talk to my son. There's no reception up there, so this is the only chance I got. You don't like it, take it up with him when we get back."

Brady's mouth compresses into a thin line. He checks his watch but makes no motion to leave.

Derek digs into his pocket. "This is only gonna take a few minutes."

He peels a twenty-dollar bill out of his money clip and hands it over, nodding to the café next door to the bank. "Jump in there and grab us sandwiches, and some decent coffee for a change. My ex may not even let him talk to me. If I don't get through, I'll meet you inside. If I do, by the time you come back out, I'll be done. Ten minutes tops."

Derek is about to give the man credit for not going along with his ploy, but then Brady reaches out and takes the money. "Ten minutes, and you stay in front of the store."

Derek can't help smiling to himself. The draw of a decent meal and cup of coffee is more than any of the hill dwellers can resist, especially the younger ones like Brady. The upscale vacation town of Saranac Lake provides plenty of temptation that Derek could leverage. Pulling out the phone, he sends another text.

> **Got a free minute. Can I call Michael?**

To anyone looking, the messages would seem to be heading to his ex-wife. They had actually gotten a woman to record a voice mail, so even if you dialed the number, someone claiming to be Kim would be on the other end. In reality, the transmissions were being routed through various switches and channels, ultimately sending them to Kelly. Anyone trying to trace the call or the message's path to their recipient would be greeted with a maze of shit.

It feels odd, even guilt-laden, to be using his family this way. The father in him feels like a piece of shit. Pretending to call and text Michael for the sake of OPSEC, when the one thing he desires most is to just talk to his boy. He tries to push it away.

Sparing him from any further contemplation, the phone rings in his hand. "Hey, pal! How are you?" Derek answers with all the enthusiasm he can muster.

"How much time do you have?" Kelly's voice returns.

"I'm sorry, bud, I have to go back to work."

"Got it, and your text. I'll make sure it gets picked up."

"That's great, pal. A home run! Wow."

"You good otherwise?" Kelly says.

"Yeah, the weather up here is still kinda hazy. No thunderstorms or anything yet, though, so that's good."

There's a slight hesitation from the agent on the other end. "Hmmm. All right. I'll check it out. Stay safe, brother."

"Yup, you too. Love you, bud."

"Love you too, buttercup."

The line goes dead. Derek can't help laughing. As he spins around, Brady is walking out of the café. The smile on Derek's face is genuine for a change. It also washes away his earlier angst.

The man hands him a tall cup and a paper sack. "I didn't know how you take it, so there's some sugar and cream in the bag."

"As long as it's hot and wet, I take it any way I can get it."

The younger man rolls his eyes. Apparently, not everyone was enamored with Marine Corps humor.

* * * * *

She was finally getting used to being called *Emily*. After a year in the applicant division and then languishing behind a desk for three months in organized crime, Karen . . . Emily had been more than ready for fieldwork. It wasn't easy being thrust into an undercover assignment with so little prep time, but Emily had never backed down from a challenge. Hell, that was half the reason why she'd joined the FBI in the first place. Not only the challenge of getting in but the challenge of the work once you were there.

The reality of it, however, was another thing entirely. Monotonous days of driving and interviewing, interviewing and driving. Typing up reports of the interviews and then driving and interviewing some more. It was common knowledge that this was how the FBI liked to develop their agents out of the gate. Let them put their academy training into play and refine their technique in what should be a nonthreatening environment before moving on to actual criminal enterprises. It all sounded reasonable, but good lord, was it boring.

Running database searches on would-be goombah gangsters proved just as mind-numbing. So when the offer came to go into the field, Emily jumped at it. After all, it's not like she wasn't a perfect fit for the assignment. She was a wizard when it came to math and had worked as a teller in the summer between her junior and senior years at Hofstra. The parameters were easy enough. Wait for word. Retrieve and transcribe. Even the cover story was simple. A Long Island girl whose parents had just retired upstate. She had moved nearby to be closer to them. Simple enough.

Now in her third week, she'd settled into both the routine of her persona and processing everyday banking transactions. The initial excitement and alleviation over being pulled from the mundane, along with what she'd thought was a jump on her colleagues in terms of career progression, had long since worn off. Being a bank teller in a small town, even a summer vacation town like Saranac Lake, was just as boring as interviewing FBI hopefuls. The highlights were days of apprehension waiting on word and nights spent working through her Netflix list.

She catches herself staring at the clock on the wall when her phone buzzes. Lifting it, a single-word text is sitting on her home screen.

Deposit

The immediate dump of adrenaline makes Emily's legs start shaking. Gathering her composure, she gets up from her station and makes her way over to the manager's office. She knocks gently on the doorjamb.

"Um, Delores. Sorry to bother you, but would tonight be a good night to start showing me the lockup procedures?"

The woman's bespectacled face goes pale, but she manages to contain herself. With a solemn nod, Delores says, "Just let Abigail know she doesn't need to close up."

"Great, thanks, Delores!" Emily says, bounding back to her workstation. The time could not go any more slowly, but eventually, the doors are shut and the other employees' end-of-the-day closeouts are complete. A little before 6:00 p.m., the doors are locked and Delores hands over the keys to the safe-deposit box.

With her Surface Pro in hand, Emily goes into the room and retrieves the box. It only takes her a moment to find the embedded slip of paper and unfold it. Connecting through a remote server and using a secure file exchange, Emily takes a picture of the note and then transposes the contents of the list from the informant's sloppy handwriting.

M4s not ARs w/ ACOGs, EOTechs, PEQ2s
S/N#—LE112124, others are random. Not
from same lot.
Mix of sidearms—Glocks, .45s, Beretta 9 mm
Chevy Silverado L/P#—FYD 2704
Marshal—Korea 1953
Marshal's family cleaned out, inheritance
unlikely
Money must be from weapons or drugs
Possible white supremacist ties / no POC
present
70–80 adults in camp. 10–20 kids
More next week

She hits Send and waits until the transfer confirmation email returns to her in-box. Once it does, Emily seals the handwritten page into a plastic bag for evidence preservation and then packs up the deposit box. When she steps out of the office, Delores practically deflates. Emily suppresses a giggle. The woman probably expected an Eastern European hit team to come barging through the doors. The relief on her face when Emily hands the keys back confirms that this is the most nerve-racking thing Delores has ever done.

Fifteen minutes later, the two part ways. Emily still rides the high of her first official function. She's done it. She's a real agent now, actively part of a developing case.

She can't wait until next week.

*   *   *   *   *

The next morning, the men straggle into the depression a few minutes after eight. Derek knows their look well. That first taste of a hot meal. A soft bed. Maybe a drink and some love. It does a lot to bring the exhaustion crashing down on a man. The PT would have worked to clear out some of the cobwebs, but not all. You can't erase a week of fatigue in a single night.

In fact, the best thing to combat lethargy is to get right back into rhythm. Derek strides forward, finger hovering near the trigger as usual. The grumps and groans persist even as he reaches the group. Derek nods over his right shoulder.

"There's a small nook in the southwest corner behind some bramble bushes. It's big enough to accommodate you all. Go ground your gear and weapons. You can work on your shelters tonight."

"What? We're not going back to camp later?" Thomas asks.

"No. You're not." Another set of grumbles comes back at him. "We are going to stay out here, and you are going to build, and improve, and trap, and honestly do whatever the fuck I tell you to. Now drop your shit, grab an axe, and get to work. We're burning daylight."

The men move off, muttering to themselves but obeying his orders nonetheless. When they get back, they grab axes, saws, and shovels from a pile. Then they look at him for direction.

"Don't stare at me like assholes. This area needs to be made into a firing range. Make it happen."

Derek walks away. Several of the men go off separately or in pairs.

Gil yells out, "Wait up!"

The group stops and looks at him.

"Two teams of axes, two men each. You two, take that one on the east. You two, that monster over there. Two-man saw teams. Stay near the axe groups in case they need your help, but work on the thinner trees and saplings until they do. Shovels, we work in line with one another from the south to the north digging up these bushes. Pile everything at the northern rim of the depression to build up the berm."

"Why the north end, Gil?" Beets asks.

"That's where the targets are going. So we don't fire rounds toward our camp, you dumbass. Now get moving."

The men nod and walk off, their purpose more legitimate. Derek catches Gil's eye and nods. Gil stares back for a second and then turns to get started. The sounds of chopping and hacking soon fill the air, along with the banter of men doing anything to pass the time and take their mind off the labor.

The sun is unrelenting. Even the early-morning hour can't help them with the heat. Within a few minutes, the men are stripped to the waist, drenched in sweat and covered in dirt.

It's an hour later when the first group from the camp begins to arrive. Derek doesn't say anything. He lets Gil form them into teams and integrate them into his plan. More and more people arrive, even Sarah, who gives him her usual glare. She takes the shovel off her shoulder and digs into a particularly stubborn bush.

Derek moves about, keeping his focus on the security team members, but as more from the camp join in, he begins to feel uncomfortable. He's never been one to just sit back and watch while others do the work for him. Gil has caught on to his leadership role, finally, and has a decent plan going, and until the range is up, there is nothing else for Derek to do.

Moving to the east side of the depression where he put his pack, Derek lays his rifle across the bag and drops his plate carrier, keeping his pistol and knives on him. Pulling on a pair of Mechanix gloves, he moves out to one of the working groups and starts giving breaks to each person there. Derek goes on like that, chatting and talking with the people as he helps with whatever task they are set to.

Most are standoffish at first, but inevitably, some-one talks to him, even if it's only to break up the mo-notony of the work or take their mind off the heat. More than a few times, the first words exchanged are *thank you,* which is enough to get the conversation going.

They ask questions too. About him. His back-ground. What he is teaching the men. Many want to know what he did to them last week. Derek assumes that they already know, but they probably think the men of the QRF are embellishing the way others do when a bass is on their hook.

Derek plays up the embellishment angle and guides the conversations back to the people he is working with. It isn't hard. They aren't trained in how to avoid intelligence-gathering techniques, and his experience makes maneuvering them as second nature as breath-ing. Bit by bit, he learns about the people of the camp and the misery that brought them to this place in their lives.

The stories are heartbreaking, but not unusual. Fore-closures. Terminal illnesses. Escaping abusive spouses. The untimely deaths of loved ones. Addiction. Prostitu-tion. One family lost everything in the housing bubble burst. Another had their 401(k)s stolen by an executive at a firm in one of the golden parachute moves.

It isn't long before the theme emerges. Each of them had suffered loss. Tremendous, gut-wrenching loss that can all be tied back to the quote-unquote system that had failed them. The government, or the safeguard, or the policy that should have protected them but didn't do so. Crushed between the cogs of the machine that must perpetually roll on. Slipped through the cracks as the unfortunate of society. They were left destitute as a result.

And in each of those instances, Marshal and his church were there. There to take them in. There to provide a meal. A roof. They didn't know where the funding came from. Most just guessed it was charitable donations.

Slowly but surely, they'd turn to the old man's preaching. The message of the tithe. Of the giving they have done. Of the rewards that are to come because of the sacrifices they have made. Derek smiles falsely while being inwardly dismayed at the way their faces beam when they talk about Marshal.

Derek had done case studies on this back when he was earning his human intelligence designation. These are the nameless faces of Waco. The blanket-covered bodies of Heaven's Gate. The piles of people, like scattered refuse and litter, in Jonestown. They've bought into everything Marshal has said and follow him unquestioningly.

One thing missing was anything about the so-called adversaries that threatened the community. Beyond a basic concept that they existed, no one could pinpoint a specific date that the camp was supposedly infiltrated or their vehicles messed with. Those that did provide passing details invariably had one thing in common; they learned about them from either members of the QRF or the lookouts. Not surprising given that those two groups would be the first to make contact, but the vacuum of knowledge almost universal to the camp sets Derek further on edge.

At noon, a pickup, ATVs, and Gator side by sides arrive with more people from camp, including Darryl and his kitchen staff. They set up folding tables and pass out sandwiches and water. The work carries on into the afternoon. The group manages surprising efficiency, even through a late downpour. As the sun begins to descend and all but the team disembark for the camp, the depression is mostly clear of trees, and a large enough swath of open land runs down the middle of it.

Derek sets the men to building their shelters and then moves off to erect his own. As he works, he tallies up what he learned, cataloging the names and faces. An uneasiness settles along with the information, and he spares a glance for his rifle lying on his bag. The reconciliation of their loyalty combined with their armory. Derek swallows as the image of a Ruby Ridge–esque siege rips through his mind.

He can't quit, not even if he wants to. He doesn't even have enough evidence to prove they are low-level meth dealers out to protect their investment, let alone anything worse. He hasn't spotted a lab or even any paraphernalia. And if they are gunrunners, then where is their stash of firearms? Worse, what if they are something more than he and Kelly suspect? Something is definitely going on, and that he still doesn't have a clue worries him. To leave now will be turning a blind eye when people's lives could be lost. How will that be serving his country?

Tying off a knot with some cordage, the course of action presents itself. In either case, more evidence is needed. He has to double down and discover just what these people are up to. Without knowing for sure, there is no way Kelly will be able to get the leverage to come in here and shut them down.

In the morning, he proceeds to take his anxiety out on the men, leading them through PT, pushing the group at a frenetic pace. As out of shape as he is, Derek knows that he is better conditioned than the men in front of him. He doesn't stop until several of them fall out, dizzy and puking.

In the aftermath of the physical training, the carpenters arrive from camp, bringing materials and ammo crates filled with 5.56. Under Derek's direction, they set up six human-size silhouettes tacked to posts driven into the earth on the north end of the depression. Each one is adorned with shapes painted in different colors. As they do so, he orders the men into their plate carriers and has them load their magazines. Once each has a full complement of rounds, he lines them up two to a post. After a brief class on fundamentals, he starts with the drills.

Derek stands behind the firing line, calling out different combinations. "Purple star! Yellow circle! Green square!"

With each command, the men swing their rifles up, search out the corresponding shape, and fire two rounds into it. Or at least toward it. After several iterations, he makes them stand sideways to the target, forcing them to turn left or right before engaging. After that, it's with their backs to the silhouettes. Then lying prone. From their butts. From their backs. The rounds squeeze off continuously. The reports echo through the surrounding hills like the percussion section of a demented philharmonic.

The men shoot. When they run out of bullets, they go to one of the Gators the carpenters rode in and break out more ammo from the crates. They go back to the line and shoot some more. Spent brass flies through the air and piles at their feet. The drumming goes on.

Marshal rides in with the lunch break, bringing soup, sandwiches, and more ammo with him. He chats lightly with the men, who can taste carbon and gunpowder residue in their venison. The old man stays on while the kitchen staff rides back, sitting on a camp stool and watching as the drills progress into the afternoon.

Derek works in different challenges. Starting on a knee. Dropping to a knee. Magazines loaded with only a few rounds, forcing changes mid-exercise. The men take to the regimen quickly and by the afternoon start to show improvement in their accuracy. Derek isn't surprised. Even the men who hadn't served had been around firearms their whole lives. They are hunters and sportsmen. They know how to acquire a target and put a bullet through it. This is just raising them up to a new level.

As the men retire to take their dinner break, Marshal rides back to camp. Derek gives a class on the proper way to clean an M4 and sets them to the task, not letting any member of the team sleep until he has personally inspected and approved each weapon.

It's after midnight when he gives the final thumbs-up.

19

In the morning, Derek starts integrating movement, training them on proper posture. Carrying at the low ready. Stalking forward in the crouched and stable position of operators, firing as they go. Then the men take turns, each individually working on the tenets taught to them while Derek follows behind, yelling out commands and corrections. They move forward toward the targets, walking with precision as they fire with the same.

The group is standing around him as he reinforces some points from the morning's training when the Gators arrive at the top of the depression. With his back to the ridge, Derek can't see Sarah and Marshal getting out of one of the vehicles together.

She walks in front of the old man down the switchbacks turning every so often to make sure he's managing the decline. Upon both of them reaching the bottom, Sarah leaves him behind and storms into the open field. Derek sees smirks creasing the men's faces and turns around just as the diminutive woman whips up her hand. She slaps a piece of paper against his chest.

"What in the hell is this?" she snaps.

Derek grabs the paper from her hand and looks at it. It's the same piece of loose-leaf he wrote out for Marshal the night before. Sarah's hands are planted on her hips and a vein is popping out of her forehead.

"What?" he says. "It's requisition numbers."

She shakes her head, doing a double take. "I'm sorry, what?"

"Requisitions. An estimate of how much ammo we're going to need moving forward and a solicitation for it to be provided."

Sarah takes a deep breath. "Yes, I know what *requisition* means. What I am asking is why you think you're entitled to so much."

"So much? This is the bare minimum for what we're working on."

Marshal walks up, concern visible on his face.

Sarah continues, not noticing the man's arrival. "A thousand rounds a day?"

Derek nods. "That's right."

"Per man?"

"I mean . . . yeah. We're slightly off that pace from yesterday, but yesterday was also very rudimentary stuff. We're going to be getting into some high-level shit moving forward, and you don't want to run out in the middle of training."

"Are you out of your mind?"

The men chuckle but quickly swallow their laughter.

Marshal snaps an order over his shoulder: "You men go and grab something to eat."

The men break and do as they're told, with sub-dued jokes and quick looks over their shoulders as they move off. When they're out of earshot, Marshal turns back to Derek and Sarah.

"Now, do you think the two of you might address this with a bit more civility?"

Sarah rubs her eyes with one hand, the other on her hip. "Yes. Of course. You're right, Marshal. What I meant to say is that there is no way we can sustain this. You need to dial it back. A lot."

"You brought me out here to train these men, Marshal," Derek says, turning to the old man. "This is what it's going to take. The only way you get better at shooting is if you shoot. When we talked about it last night, you said you could manage."

"Yeah, well, it's my job to say that's not possible," Sarah responds.

Again, they square off. "I didn't think this was go-ing to be a problem. This is what I need to get them up to standard."

Sarah shakes her head. "No. No, it isn't. This is what you want. And I'm telling you you're not gonna get it. Never mind the fact that bullets don't grow on trees, but what the hell do you suppose the neighbors are thinking? A day and a half of nonstop shooting? The ones we're on good relations with are gonna start asking questions. The ones we're not—you know, the bastards that are trying to breach our camp—they're gonna assume we're burning our supply."

Marshal nods. "I have to agree with Sarah there, Derek. We're isolated, but that doesn't stop the ran-dom hiker, or even state trooper, from passing through these parts. All it takes is one complaint and the safe haven we've worked so hard to construct will be lost forever."

She eyes him for a moment before going on. "I'm giving you a daily allotment of twelve hundred rounds. Twelve hundred total."

"That's ridiculous."

"I don't give a shit, Derek."

He tosses up his hands. "How do you suggest we alter the training, then?"

Sarah shrugs. "You're the prized professor making twenty grand. That's for you to figure out."

"Listen. Marshal and I made a deal, and he said you could get the ammo that I need to train them properly."

"All right, cowboy," she says, looking at Derek. "Tell you what. You want more ammo, how about this? For every round I don't put on target, I'll find you another case of bullets. That should bolster your allotment a bit. What do you say?"

Derek looks down at the pistol on her hip and then back at her eyes. His mind flashes back to her with the ledger, walking all over camp with it. *How good could she possibly be?* "Two magazines' worth, and you have to work all of the targets. Do that and you're on."

Sarah smiles at him, then with a twitch to her right, she squares to the targets. Her sidearm is out of the holster in one smooth motion. Sarah stalks forward, fingers wrapped around the grip of her pistol, thumbs atop each other and pressed tightly against the left side of the weapon. She punches her hands forward, squeezing off two rounds into the far left target. They hit dead center in the chest of the silhouette. She adjusts and immediately fires another through the center of the head portion of the target.

Walking toward the targets, she rakes her pistol from left to right, burying a combination of three expertly placed rounds into each before moving on to the next. When she reaches the last target, her slide locks back to the rear, the weapon empty. Sarah brings the pistol up in her right hand, ejecting the magazine with the motion. Holding the smoking firearm in front of her face so as to not take her eyes off the target, she grabs a magazine from her left hip and slams it into the mag well. Grip returned and slide released forward, she resumes her firing. Drilling a head shot into the last target, she works the process in reverse. She could drive nails with her groupings.

When the final shot has finished echoing, she drops the clip and releases the slide. Holstering both her sidearm and the empty magazine, she walks to the east side of the firing line, scoops up her other discarded mag, and turns to face the men.

Derek, Marshal, and the entire security team at the table stand in stunned awe. She looks them over and smiles. Striding toward Derek, she plants herself in front of him. She points the magazine into his chest.

"Get it done, Marine."

Sarah brushes past him. The two men turn and watch her walk away. She swaps out the empty with her last full magazine and replaces it into her pistol, then re-holsters the sidearm. As she moves up the switchbacks, Derek looks at Marshal.

"You're okay with this?"

The old man nods. "It's in the interest of our secrecy and sustainability. Your payment won't be affected by what we decide. You're just going to have to do as the lady says. Besides, a Dev Group veteran like yourself? I'm sure you have all sorts of tricks up your sleeve. You know the old saying better than I, Derek. Adapt and overcome."

The old man walks over to the men finishing up their chow, offering a few more words. The group laughs, and Marshal waves, walking slowly up the switchbacks.

Derek doesn't even wait until Marshal reaches the top.

"Chow's over! On the firing line!"

. . . . .

Derek leads the men back to Sanctuary. They're filthy and tired, but they move with a swagger in their step. He had readjusted, reluctantly, and focused them on tactical formations with a practical live-fire exercise at the end of each day to hammer the lessons home. By the end of the week, the training had the intended effect. The men were improving.

As a reward, Derek decides to bring everyone back in. Besides, they need an overall resupply plus a few nights of hot meals and sleeping in their own beds. And showers. Lots of showers. They all stink to high heaven.

The team is greeted as they arrive, but it isn't the same fanfare as their first return. The men are met with waves and hellos but little else. Derek orders the weapons to the armory and their packs resupplied. He places the same constraints for time in camp as their last return and releases the team to their own devices. Gil immediately steps in and gets the men moving toward the cinder block building.

Inside his cabin, Derek locks his door and drops his gear. Plopping down on a cot, he gives his rifle a cursory cleaning but doesn't go through the full breakdown. Outside of zeroing it, he hasn't shot his own weapon much, instead borrowing from the men when a demonstration was needed. Besides, he doesn't have the motivation for it. Out of the eyes of his employers and trainees, the intense pace he has been keeping to stay ahead of the men settles on him like a warm blanket. Tired and agitated, he sits hunched over, arms draped between his legs.

It isn't long before the bell rings outside the chow tent, beckoning everyone to the evening meal. Derek listens to the banter as clusters of people straggle past. They laugh and joke. They discuss the day. Make note of things that need to be followed up on afterward or tomorrow. If he closes his eyes, he might be listening to the conversations on a sidewalk. Regular people. Just normal, everyday people going about their lives.

Derek looks around the empty cabin. The few nights they were in camp previously, he would just grab a plate and bring it back to his room after the tent had cleared out. After meeting everyone and talking with them, the opportunity would now be present to further his intelligence collection. He jumps up and undoes his lock. Pulling the door open, Derek hesitates. He looks back at the rifle lying across his plate carrier. Taking a step back in, he stops himself and then wheels about. Stepping down the stairs, he crosses the short distance to the chow tent and stands at the end of the line. A few glances and whispers are thrown his way at first. The people directly in front of him turn and exchange pleasantries as the line steadily progresses inside.

When Derek enters the tent a wave of silence courses through it like an electromagnetic pulse. The clinks of silverware and murmur of voices die out as everyone turns to look. He folds his arms and stares straight ahead, but when the conversation doesn't start back up, he looks over the crowd.

The wave of silence hits Marshal's table at the far end of the tent. The old man looks up from his plate and glances around before finding the cause of the sudden mood change. Marshal's face beams with a smile. The old man gets up and begins to wave Derek over just as a child's hysterical screaming erupts into the quiet.

Everyone turns toward the noise even though the canvas blocks their view.

"Help! It's Bobby! Someone help!" another voice cries out.

Derek is out of the entranceway, running toward the cries for help before his mind even registers what is happening. Behind him, he vaguely hears the chaos of people jumping up from their tables. Following the cries, he runs toward the river, darting through the trees until he finds the trail.

Three-quarters of the way to the water, a ten-year-old girl comes running in the opposite direction. She sees Derek and stops, waving her arms frantically. "Bobby's back there. He fell out of his tree stand! His leg is torn open!"

The boy's screams come louder now, the pain, fear, and panic audible in his cries. Derek feels the gut-wrenching pull of a parent as his body kicks into overdrive. He spots the tree stand looming ahead, a jagged branch underneath it, broken off and covered in blood.

Sprinting over, he reaches the tree and finds Bobby rolling on the ground, desperately gripping his leg in an attempt to stop the bleeding. The boy wails uncontrollably as Derek pins him down so he can inspect Bobby's wound. There are multiple punctures and a wide gash high into his groin, just below the hip. Blood streams from the openings. The boy looks at him with terrified, pleading eyes.

They're a different color, but the look is the same that he saw years ago on the other side of the world. The same that haunts his dreams in the deep, black hours of restless nights. Derek had reacted as he was trained to. That boy had only been a little older than Bobby. Twelve, maybe thirteen at the most. Old enough to be a combatant for sure, especially in that part of the world. Not old enough to know the full weight of his actions.

Derek hadn't known any of that as he had spun, alerted to the threat by the plume of the boy's Molotov cocktail, his arm coming up to hurl it against the exhaust vents of the Abrams tank. Should the flames have entered the compartment and the engine caught fire, the whole vehicle would have burned from the inside out, engulfing the men within. The Chief Warrant Officer's shots were true, putting the boy down, the bottle tumbling from his hand.

But as he advanced on the threat, as his team fanned out and took cover, he saw what he had done. Those eyes. The horror and confusion frozen on the boy's face.

"Damn it!" Derek shouts. He reaches under his web belt and undoes the buckle to the belt on his pants. Pulling it free, he lashes it around the boy's upper thigh. Derek cinches the belt down and twists the leather in his hand. The streaming blood lessens to a trickle, and several other puncture wounds stop flowing completely. Even with access to the trauma kit in his assault pack, Derek knows that the boy is in trouble.

More and more people begin reaching the tree. Faces go pale at the sight of all the blood.

"How far to the nearest hospital?"

The onlookers stare at him, some with hands over their mouths.

"How far?" Derek bellows.

"A . . . about an hour? Maybe more with getting out of the woods."

Derek looks down at the boy. Bobby's screams lessen as his face grows white, and he begins to hyperventilate. An hour is too long. Derek searches the faces in the crowd and finds the man he is looking for. "You! Your forge still hot?"

Ronald snaps out of his stupor. "What? Uh . . . yeah."

Scooping Bobby up into his arms, Derek rushes forward. "Make a hole!"

The people part as he charges through the gauntlet.

"Go get the backpack from my cabin!" he shouts at anyone who is listening.

The crowd follows behind as he continues to shout commands.

"Meet me at the forge! Get a van to the clearing, running and ready to go! Find his parents!"

The last order is rendered null and void as he runs by the couple. Bobby's mother catches sight of her son and cries out in hysterics. His father catches her and holds her back from getting in the way. Derek sprints past them. Behind him, a flurry of activity emerges from the panic to accomplish the tasks he set out for them.

Heart thundering in his chest, Derek dashes the final distance to the blacksmith station. Sarah appears next to him, matching him stride for stride. She looks at Bobby and then up at Derek. They dart under the overhang together.

"What can I do?" she asks.

He hands Bobby off to her, placing her hand into the slick tangle of his belt. "Lay him down and keep this as tight as you can."

Derek goes to the forge. Alight and aglow, the orange coals glisten with their ripple of reduced flame. He works the bellow until they are blazing bright. In the flames, he sees the Iraqi boy, blood spreading from his chest and stomach. Begging. Derek dropped his rifle and reached for his med kit as he started to run to the boy.

"No!" Derek screams. *Not again!* He draws his throwing knives and shoves each knifepoint into the coals, and then drops down next to Sarah and the boy.

Onlookers that didn't rush off in other directions now crowd around the entrance to the forge, Bobby's parents at the front. "Please! Please save him! Please!" they both cry out.

Two of the men in the QRF, Gerry and Brian, stand next to them.

"Don't worry," Brian says. "He knows what he's doing."

Ronald pushes past the gathered masses.

Derek points at him and then at the forge. "Tend to the knives. Tell me when the tips are glowing, and then hand them to me when I ask."

Sarah looks up from Bobby's face. "He's short of breath. You think he can handle this?"

"Not much of a choice. We don't close these over, he'll bleed out."

"They're ready!" Ronald calls from behind.

"Jimmy! Get over here and pin his shoulders down! He's going to thrash!"

The big man does as he's told, turning his head and gagging at the sight of the blood. Derek takes the first knife handed to him and presses the point into the gash that was squirting when he first saw it. Smoke rises with the smell of seared flesh. Bobby's eyes go wide as he howls in pain.

Derek hands the knife back and takes another, the blacksmith returning the former to the coals to be reheated. His hands and eyes are methodical as he goes from the largest of the wounds to the smallest. Bobby thrashes and screams with each new application, but as Derek progresses, the boy dives further and further toward catatonic.

"He's going into shock," Sarah says, low enough so that only the three crouched over the boy can hear it.

Derek looks at Bobby's face. His eyes stare vacantly at the ceiling as his breath goes shallow. Derek presses another knife against the last wound, and this time, Bobby doesn't even flinch. A moment after he removes the blade the boy seizes and gasps, his eyes rolling into the back of his head.

"CPR!" Sarah calls out.

Derek places his hands over Bobby's chest and counts out the rhythmic compressions as Sarah shifts from her place, shoving Jimmy out of the way. She tilts the boy's head back and waits until Derek hits thirty before delivering two breaths.

Derek wipes sweat from his eyes as Bobby's chest rises and falls. He spares a glance for the boy's leg, seeing the cauterized flesh holding. He goes back into compressions, his own breath coming raggedly as he counts aloud.

They go through a third and fourth round of CPR. Onlookers are weeping, embracing one another. Holding their own children close. Some hide their faces from the horror. Derek does another thirty compressions. As Sarah leans in to breathe, Bobby suddenly sputters and coughs.

The boy's face flushes with color. His eyes remain shut, but he starts breathing on his own.

"He's breathing!" Sarah yells out, relief clear in her voice.

The crowd cheers. Tears of grief transform into tears of joy. Screams of adulation fill the air.

"A miracle!" Marshal yells above them all. "This is a miracle!"

Derek sits back, mentally exhausted and breathing heavily as Bobby's mother rushes in to cradle her son on her lap. Someone pushes through the crowd with Derek's assault bag. Derek points at Sarah and then the bag.

She nods and goes over to the backpack, finds the kit, and kneels next to Bobby's leg a moment later. Derek moves to get up, but Sarah holds out a hand, stopping him. Over the next several minutes, he watches as she expertly cleans, dresses, and binds the leg. She looks up at him when she's done.

Derek nods to her. "Well done. Now let's get him to the emergency room."

Marshal stands in front of them. "That'll be all right, Derek. You need to take a breather. Sarah can ride with them to the hospital in case he goes under again. Jimmy, carry him to the van."

"It really should be me," Derek protests.

"Sarah is more than capable, as you just witnessed yourself. Your duties lie here with us," Marshal replies and then gestures to Jimmy.

The big man scoops up the boy and moves off with Sarah and the parents in tow. Most of the crowd follows them to the vehicle. Gil walks up to Derek and extends his hand. Derek takes the help and gets to his feet. The men of the security team and those still in the blacksmith station look at him with admiration.

"Do you see now, Gil? Do all of you see? This man was sent to us. Sent to us by the Lord Himself! This is a miracle! You, Derek, are a miracle!"

He catches the sideways glance that Gil gives. "Miracle or not, wouldn't have been cause for anything if the boy hadn't been up in a tree stand in the first place," Derek replies.

Marshal's face goes tight. "Yes. I suppose that's true."

Uncharacteristically, the old man turns and walks away. He passes the group at the van, talking to them briefly, before continuing to his cabin.

The men gather around Derek as he walks out. One hands him a towel, another a warm beer. Derek hesitates at the second but then grabs the can and rips the tab open, chugging it down while the men laugh and pat him on the back.

"You did good, Derek."

"Well done, boss. Well done."

"Holy shit. That was amazing."

Soon, the larger crowd returns following the departure of the van. They also fawn on Derek. Kissing.

Hugging. Shaking hands. Derek smiles and does his best with the heaped-on praise, trying not to become overwhelmed by it, to keep a distance from these people.

After some time, the crowd breaks up. A few move back to the chow tent, but most head off to their cabins. Derek retires to his as well, not even bothering to lock the door behind him. Sitting on a cot, he breathes deeply.

The eyes come back to him. Derek stares into them, as real as the floorboards directly in front of his face. Two sets now. Two frightened, pleading kids. Clinging to life when they should have nothing but years ahead of them. One he had caused and couldn't save. The other he had nothing to do with and might have given the boy a chance.

He digs into a cargo pocket and pulls out his wallet. Taking it out of the plastic bag, Derek flips it open to pictures of Mike, and for a moment, his son's eyes flicker to the terrified expression after Derek had pummeled the dad at the baseball game.

Tears form. He holds one hand over his mouth. Derek notices the blood covering the hand holding his wallet. He drops it to the ground and pulls his other hand from his face. Both are stained a deep red with Bobby's blood. As the tears stream down his cheeks and land on his palms, Derek buries his face in his hands.

20

Sebastian takes a deep breath. He reaches down and feels for the keys in his pocket, the fiftieth time he's done so tonight. Outside, the crickets and other night creatures sing their nocturnal melodies. He looks back over his shoulder. His wife, Sofia, gives him a solemn nod. Her lower lip trembles while her eyes glisten. Sebastian nods back.

Shouldering his pack, he eases the cabin door inch by painful inch, careful not to let it creak the way it does when three-quarters open. Sebastian stands on the steps. He stares out into the blackness of the camp. Waiting. Listening. Nothing moves. The camp is still and asleep in the dead of night.

After what had happened earlier in the day with Bobby, he figured everyone would be emotionally exhausted and out for the count. Now was the time to make their run. They couldn't expect to have a distraction on that level come their way again. With any luck, the camp would still be reeling in the morning over the day's events and not even notice they were gone.

Sebastian holds the door open as Sofia steps down, looking about while she nervously strokes the length of hair she has pulled over her shoulder. He waits until she reaches the bottom step and reverses the process with the door. It slips from his sweaty grip and rattles in the frame. Their hearts freeze as they stare at each other. After a few moments of silence, Sebastian lets out a held breath.

He walks down the steps and starts off to the south. Sofia follows in his footsteps. Each footfall is placed strategically to make the least amount of sound. He was always a good stalker when he went for whitetail, but now with Derek's training, he feels like he's nearly silent. So long as Sofia follows exactly in his path, their noise should be minimal. The squirrels and raccoons skittering through the woods make more clatter than they do.

As the couple bends their way to the east, a figure stands up before them. Sebastian's hand goes to his heart while Sofia's breath catches. The figure emerges from the shadows by stepping into the intermittent moonlight. They relax as Jimmy comes out of the dark. The large man wears a pack of his own and gives them a curt nod.

United, the three make their way through the rest of the camp, sticking to the edges and avoiding other cabins as best they can. They cut across the path that heads up the hill to the outbuildings and move farther along the border. Turning right at the armory, they head east toward the vehicle clearing.

When they've put a few football fields behind them, Sebastian whispers to Jimmy, "Hard part's over. We hustle, we can be outta here in fifteen minutes."

"Let's get after it, then," Jimmy says, eyeing the

woods around them. "The sooner we've got some distance on this place, the better."

Sebastian agrees and looks back at his wife. Sofia tries to smile, but he can tell she's shaking all over. He reaches out and squeezes her hand. Facing forward, the man pushes on, longing and wishing for this to be done. He needs a drink.

Up ahead, a space in the trees appears. Sebastian offers them both a supportive smile. When he turns around, several red dots dance across his chest. He stops short, throwing his arms out to the side. Jimmy halts, a puzzled look on his face. The large man looks down to see three on his own.

"What? What is it?" Sofia says, stepping up between them. She sees the dots and clutches her fists to her mouth. "Oh no! Oh my God!"

"I would think in your situation, Sofia," Marshal says to them from the shadows, "taking the Lord's name in vain would be the last thing you'd want to do."

Crunching twigs and crushed leaves underfoot come from the right and left of the trail. Dark masses begin to take shape, separating from trees and bushes and stalking forward. Marshal comes out onto the path ahead of them. Gil, rifle at the ready and trained on the trio, moves by his side. Sebastian looks from right to left, seeing Brian and Thomas there as well. He can't make out the other three faces, but he's sure they're members of the QRF.

The man swallows. He tries to speak, but no words come out. Sebastian closes his mouth and swallows again. "M-Marshal. We was just—"

Marshal waves a hand and shakes his head. "Please, Sebastian. Don't make this any worse."

"We won't say nothing, boss. Please," Jimmy begs. His voice begins to crack, and tears start falling down his cheeks. "Just let us go back. We can go back to the way it was."

Marshal lets out a deep sigh. "I wish that were the case, Jimmy. Truly, I do. But I can't take that risk."

Marshal's right hand whips up from behind his back. A searing flash accompanied by a sharp pop splits the night, followed immediately by a wet slap. Sofia's mouth falls open as her body topples to the ground.

Sebastian drops next to the corpse of his wife, yelling, "No!" His shout is quickly curtailed when Gil rushes forward and smashes him in the side of the head with the buttstock of his rifle. The man slumps over, cradling his skull in his hands while moaning.

Jimmy holds out his hands before him. "Please, Marshal! Please! Don't kill me! Please!"

Marshal levels his pistol and fires two rounds into Jimmy's chest. Jimmy flies backward and lands hard on the trail. Marshal spares a glance for Sebastian and then walks a few feet away. The old man puts the silencer against Jimmy's head and fires again. He flinches as some of the big man's blood spatters across his face.

Turning back, Marshal clasps his arms behind him as he makes his way to Sebastian, who gets to his knees.

"You bastard," Sebastian mutters. "You cold-hearted bastard. Why'd you have to kill her? Why'd you have to kill any of them?"

Marshal furrows his eyebrows. "Why, Sebastian? You know why. You're a drunk and a liar. Sofia was a weakling, and an enabler at that. She was never one of us. You just brought her along to fetch you another beer or bottle. You think I would let someone like that out of my sight? And Jimmy. Poor Jimmy was a coward. True, I might have let him stay, albeit not as part of the mission, of course. Yet you had to sway him."

"You crusty old shit. You're just a twisted rat fuck living in the woods!" Sebastian finishes the statement by spitting at Marshal.

Another deep sigh. "I harbored you for too long. I can see that now. My mistake was believing you could be something other than what you are. Your mistake was being that person in the first place."

"Go to h—" the man begins to shout, cut off as Marshal puts a bullet through his mouth, blowing his teeth out the back of his skull. As Sebastian crumples on top of his wife, the old man fires another two shots into his torso. He is about to put his gun away when he thinks better of it. Marshal sneers and fires into Sebastian's body until his clip runs dry.

The steady rhythm of the forest night comes back to fill in the silence. Gil is the first to speak. "Men, go and get the Gators from the clearing. Bring them back here so we can get rid of the bodies."

"Right," Brian answers.

Hasty footsteps rush up the trail.

Gil moves closer to Marshal. "You okay, boss?"

"It had to be done, Gil," Marshal says, still staring at the bodies. "My conscience is clean. Proverbs, chapter twenty-six, verse eleven: 'As a dog returneth to his vomit, so a fool returneth to his folly.' They couldn't be allowed to leave. Not after everything we went through with Leland. After how close we came to losing everything back then. I will not echo the mistakes of the past. Tonight solidifies that."

"And Derek?"

Marshal shakes his head. "I still have faith that he will join us, Gil. Do I have to keep repeating this for you? We'll wait and see."

Gil shrugs and moves on. "We're going to need to replace Jimmy on the SAW. He was the only one big enough to haul it and all the ammo."

"Gerry can do it."

"Gerry? He's pushing sixty."

"I'm eighty-one and I'm still climbing these hills at three in the morning. He'll be just fine. Out of all of you, Gerry is the one that is least fazed by change."

Gil looks behind him quickly as the sound of the Gators starting up breaks through the trees. "The men are going to need some encouragement after this. They know what they signed up for and all. Being confronted with it? Another matter altogether."

"They'll be all right. I'll speak with each one tomorrow. They'll understand."

"And the rest of Sanctuary?"

Marshal sighs. "I'll talk to everyone at breakfast. Let them know that these three chose to leave us after the accident, and we sent them on their way. It'll be all right. Now, if you don't mind, Gil, I'd like a few minutes alone to pray, please."

"Of course, boss. Of course."

Gil turns to meet the Gators as Marshal brings his hands in front of him. The old man folds them together and bows his head, pistol still in his grasp.

■ ■ ■ ■ ■

Derek lies awake, sweating. Sleep won't come to him. Not after what happened. Even if it could, he's not sure he would want to. Who knows what form the demons might take tonight?

One thing he is certain of: the boy shouldn't have

been in that tree. The children shouldn't be living like this. More than likely, it's their parents involved in some criminality, although Derek hadn't figured that out to his satisfaction yet. Even so, if he's right about his intel so far, it puts the kids in harm's way, and he just can't stand that. They deserve better.

His mind returns to evidence collection. That's the best way. The only way to ensure that this place gets shut down and kids like Bobby don't get hurt again. Whatever their motives might be, it's clear to Derek that the camp should no longer exist.

A cabin door bangs shut across the clearing. He listens but can't hear anything further. It's probably just someone's run to the outhouse. Still, he gets to his feet and crosses to the window. After a few minutes of nothing, he's about to go back to his bunk when a flicker of movement catches his eye. He stares again. Sure enough, he picks up shadows moving toward the vehicle trail.

Middle of the night or not, he can't let this opportunity slip by. A possibility that, as they head into the tree line, they'll lead him to whatever they've been hiding from him.

Sliding his plate carrier and rifle over his head, Derek slips out of his cabin. He crouches low at the bottom of the steps, looking toward where the sound came from. He starts east, working to gain ground on the figures while remaining silent.

He's a good distance from the camp perimeter, but still well north of the vehicle trail when a sudden crash through the woods comes toward him. Thinking bear or deer at first, Derek freezes. When he sees the human-size silhouette coming through the forest, he raises his rifle.

He trains it on the person as they draw closer. About to flick his safety off, Derek stops himself as he catches a glimpse of auburn in the moonlight. A moment later, Sarah emerges through the foliage. The shorter woman stops and throws her hands up in front of her when she sees his posture. She pulls a pair of night vision goggles off her face.

"Mind putting that shit down?" she whispers.

"How about you tell me what it is you're doing out in the woods in the middle of the night first?"

"I could ask you the same thing."

Derek adjusts his sight, realigning his red dot on her forehead. "I'm not playing games. Start talking."

Sarah lowers her hands. She glances over her left shoulder, then back at him, her face deeply concerned. "Not here. Come on. Follow me."

"Lady, if you think—"

"Derek. Shut. Up. I'm trying to save your life here. Now let's go." She looks toward where the vehicles are stored. Her body language is antsy. For the first time since he met her, Derek thinks she's nervous, and it's not because of his rifle. He glances through the trees at the trail but can no longer see the shadows.

He looks back at the woman. "What's going on?"

Sarah shakes her head. "Like I said. Away from camp." She turns and starts heading to the northeast.

Derek hesitates a moment longer, but then lowers his weapon and starts to follow. Her demeanor and sense of urgency are different. Out of character, even. Quick assessment though it may be, Derek trusts his training and gut.

Sarah moves with speed rather than stealth. Derek crashes after her, cringing at the noise they're making while justifying it against the distance they are gaining. He figures they've gone a thousand meters or so when she dips down into a small gully running between two hills. She looks back at him, panting and sweating.

When she speaks, it's just above a whisper. The bubbling water is louder than her voice. "Okay . . . okay. That should be far enough."

Derek rests his off hand on his hip, catching his breath as well. "Far enough for what?"

That same, I-can't-deal-with-your-stupidity look returns to her face. "You know, for an intel guy, you really are completely oblivious. Do you have any idea how much trouble you've caused me?"

"Why, because you're undercover?"

Sarah's eyes go wide. "How did you—"

"Come on. Really? You shoot like a cop. Your field medicine training. Hell, you're carrying a standard government-issue pistol. With the money flowing through here, I originally thought DEA, but given that I haven't seen anything regarding drugs, and the amount of guns in this camp, I'd guess ATF."

The water churns next to their feet.

She swallows. "All right, maybe not so oblivious, after all. For now, let's just leave it at you don't need to know who I'm working for. But as for you, what the hell are you doing here? What agency are you with? Who sent you?"

"Not happening, Sarah. You want info, you'd better start establishing trust and fast."

She stares at him, tapping her foot, and then opens her mouth. "You're right, okay? I'm ATF."

He searches her face. Not seeing any signs of deception, he relents on his part. "No one sent me," Derek says, shaking his head. "Gil picked me out from my website or YouTube or something."

She cocks her head, measuring his words. "So . . . you're not here to extract me, then? I figured with your background . . ."

"Lady, I had no idea you even existed until we met. Quite frankly, now that I know you're already looking into this, I'd be happy to go home."

"Well, I'm afraid that won't be possible," Sarah says, shaking her head. She visibly deflates as her expectations get shattered. Sarah sits down on a nearby boulder with a heavy sigh.

"And why is that?"

"Because Marshal doesn't let people go. I just stopped you from walking in on what he does to anyone trying to escape his little fiefdom. Had you continued down that path, you'd be dead in a ditch right about now."

"What the hell are you talking about?"

"Sebastian, his wife, and Jimmy. They made a break for it. I was on duty at the shack when I saw them leave. I moved out through the woods to try to stop them, but I was too late. I just watched Marshal gun them down in cold blood."

Derek scratches his beard, shaking his head. "You mean to tell me that the old man just murdered three of his own people? Why didn't you stop them?"

"Do what? Charge out of the woods at half a dozen men in full tactical gear and wave my pistol about screaming, 'Federal Agent!'? I'd be in the ditch with them and you. There's no backup out here. We may as well be in another country."

They stare at each other for a long time. Derek sees the sincerity in her face. That and something else. Not resignation. No, there is still fire in her eyes. But along with it . . . fatigue. Deep-seated exhaustion that permeates not just the entire body but the spirit as well.

Derek sits on a rock formation next to her and leans forward. "I think it's time for you to tell me what the hell is going on here."

Sarah measures him again, but after a moment, she begins to speak. "About a year and a half ago, these guys popped up. Normally, a group like this wouldn't even register on the ATF's radar, but a confidential informant turned us onto them. The guy had a pretty good track record with tips despite being a piece of shit."

"Piece of shit how?"

She shrugs. "Standard stuff. Beat his wife. Peddled some drugs. Degenerate gambler. Whenever he got jammed up, he would roll on people to get bailed out."

"All right," Derek says, waiting for her to continue.

"Anyway, he comes to us looking for protection. Says he's in danger and brings up Marshal and his little troop. Talks about a stash of money and weapons. As you probably noticed, this place operates like a backwoods cult but is geared up more like a militia," she says, holding up the goggles.

"Yeah. I picked up on that."

Sarah's lip twitches. "This guy's always been honest with us when his back was to a wall, so we start looking into them. We're going through the standard workups when the CI disappears. Gone without a trace. The guy was sleaze but not the brightest bulb. No way he could just disappear on his own."

"So, he's dead, then," Derek interrupts.

Sarah nods. "That's what we thought too. Fast-forward a bit. My superiors decide it's worth taking a closer look. I'm from Rochester originally. I know the way people are up here, and I had some undercover work already logged. As you so graciously noted, my bachelor's is in accounting, so . . ."

"You were sent in to pick up on the money trail."

"Bingo," Sarah says sarcastically, pointing a finger at him. "I started with the CI's disappearance. Found out that he had recently come into a big bankroll and blew it all at a casino up in Hogansburg, near the Canadian border. We figure that money belonged to Marshal and decided to work the group on the basis of them needing to keep a closer watch on their cash. I was put into play frequenting the bars that our CI used to hang out at. Word of my cover story got around, and I was introduced to the group eight months ago. When Marshal learned of my background in accounting, he became interested, and I was recruited into the group shortly after."

Derek shakes his head. "Then all that about Marshal knowing your parents? What was that?"

"In a word? Bullshit," Sarah says, waving a dismissive hand. "More than likely, he seized on parts of my cover and made the story his own. The man sees signs in everything and then starts weaving tales like he's writing a novel. They always end up aligning with his intentions. It's fanatical manipulation. How else could he get all these people to live out in the middle of the woods? Granted, they all have their reasons, but this is a pretty big commitment, don't you think?"

"Okay. So you've been investigating him for months now. Why haven't the feds shut this place down yet?"

"Are you shitting me? There's no way to prove he actually killed the CI without the body."

"Well, he just killed three people, and you witnessed it. Let's get in a car and get out of here. Hell, we don't even need a car. Just start walking. I'll get us through the woods."

The woman hesitates. "I can't."

"There's a network behind this. That it?"

Sarah slowly nods. "Marshal has a reach that goes beyond anything I've ever come across. One that I suspect isn't his alone. These assholes have access to funding and government equipment. Something that stretches into the town. The neighboring counties, even. You really think Marshal's the type that will roll if we snatch him up for murder? The whole system would still be active."

His mind flashes to the tavern the old man had him call. The gruff voice that relayed his message to camp. Still, Derek isn't about to divulge his information. "I'm not buying it. These are just a bunch of inbreds in the woods, not some vast rube conspiracy."

Sarah tilts her head and lets out an exasperated sigh. "Think about it. This land adjoins a state park. You fired off thousands of rounds the last few days. Not one state trooper. Not one park ranger. The farms surrounding us. Hell, even parts of the towns. No one says a goddamn thing. That's not just silence being bought, and it has been. Trust me. I do the books. That's power on a grand scale. You don't get that with money alone. You get that with fear."

"Okay," Derek says, getting up and beginning to pace. He works to keep the conversation going now that Sarah is opening up on details, his mind cataloging the data he's being given. "Okay. Not that I believe it, but say you're right about the backwoods network. To what end, huh? What's their objective?"

Sarah stands, brushing off her pants as she does

so. "I don't know. Or more to the point, I haven't been able to find out yet. From what I've observed so far and based on other ops I've worked, this looks like the foundation for a black market distribution site."

"The weapons. You think they're setting up shop?"

She gives a slow nod. "I think what they have here is just for themselves. After your training is complete, they'll bring in their supply and then get the word out. This location gives them perfect cover for meet sites, and your training will give them an advantage against any potential buyers that decide to get cute and try to rip them off. At least, that's the theory I'm working with."

"You don't need women and children present in a camp to run guns. Gil and his crew could handle that once their training is complete. So what the hell are they doing here?"

Sarah shrugs. "That's where it gets muddy. I think they actually believe in Marshal's preaching. That they are part of a new world order or some shit like that. As far as I can tell, they don't know about the larger op at hand. It would explain why the old man goes to such lengths to keep this place secret."

"He wasn't exactly keeping it a secret with recruiting me."

"Calculated risk, Derek. In his eyes, he needs your knowledge. He's probably also hoping that he'll be able to sway you over to his cause."

He stares at her, and she steadily holds his gaze. After long moments, she closes her eyes, runs her hands up to the base of her neck, and arches her back. The stretch pulls her polo shirt tight across her chest.

When she releases, Sarah appears to deflate even more. She rolls her head from side to side, cracking her neck.

"I've had to go deep here, Derek. I haven't been able to get out of camp since they brought me in. I took over shifts in the comms shack just so I could sneak some messages to my handlers, but those have been few and far between. The more I've been entrusted with numbers and logistics, the more Marshal's paranoia has taken hold. I haven't connected with my home office in weeks. But I'm close to something. I know it."

The weight of his ammunition is nothing compared to the reality of the situation being draped across his shoulders. The drug and inheritance theories are blown to hell, but the weapons have just become very real and more extensive than he would have imagined. As dismaying as the information is, duty comes up to meet it head-on. There are questions here that need to be answered and a comrade that needs backup. Allegedly.

"I don't suppose you have a badge or ID that you can show me to put my mind at ease about all this, do you?"

Raising an eyebrow, Sarah gives him a wry smile. "Sorry, cowboy, but if you're hoping for some Hollywood bullshit where I pull a miniature shield out from between my tits, you're gonna be disappointed."

Lifting his head, Derek stares at the canopy above. After a long moment, he exhales, "Fuck me."

Sarah laughs a little, the sound of breaking tension. "Yeah. I know the feeling. How about this, though? Marshal's name is actually Roland Marshal Emeritus.

And Gil? Gil's name is Eugene Gilchrest. That help with my credibility?"

"Yeah. Actually, it does."

"For what it's worth, nice try attempting to bleed them of their ammo. A little aggressive, though, for undercover work, which is why I shut you down, but I can respect the motive."

"We Marines have a bit of a reputation for aggression."

She sniffs. "No shit."

"What do we do now?"

"Best thing for you to do is carry on like nothing has changed. Believe it or not, your arrival has opened doors for me. The mistrust that I've had to negotiate all this time has shifted to you. Of course, that'll probably change now too, given what you did for Bobby today, but it is what it is.

"Stretch the training out. It's no secret that it's very important to Marshal. So we run with that. Buy me the time that I need. Once I've found the links that I'm looking for, we can figure a way out of here."

It's as solid a plan as he can think of for the moment. If Sarah is who she says she is, she would be in a better position to find evidence than he. All of this would need confirmation, but Derek knows he can get that with his next message relay. Either way, the best thing to do is to play along for now until he can get it all sorted out.

"Okay, but up to my last day is all the time you'll get," he says, extending a hand.

Sarah takes it, her grip firm. "We'd better double back and then separate. Enough time has passed that they're probably done hiding the bodies. If they come looking for me in the comms shack and can't find me . . ."

"Yeah, I understand. Let's move."

As he follows her out of the small valley, Derek can't help feeling like the game has just gone into extra innings.

21

ey, guys, I'm gonna take a rain check," says Emily. "Go ahead and take off. I'll close up with Delores."

"You need to get out, girlfriend," says Abigail, another teller. "You've been here a month already, and all you do is go home every night."

"She's right," says Roxie. "You don't know what you're missing at the Party on the Patio nights, Em."

"Exactly. Who knows? You come out, get your drink on with us a little bit. Maybe you won't even have to go home alone," Abigail says with a wink. "You can't be all work all the time. You need to have some fun too."

"Abby!" says Emily, smiling while unsuccessfully trying to stifle her blush. "Maybe next time, guys. I'm sorry. I'm just beat, and I've got a headache. Honestly, the last thing I want to do is sit through a band set."

"All right, pumpkin, suit yourself," Abigail says with a shrug. "Offer is on the table, though. You know where to find us."

Emily sits back down at her station to close out

her remaining items for the day as the other tellers file out. In all honesty, it probably isn't a good idea to keep avoiding socializing with the group. Single women in their midtwenties were expected to go out, especially when they lived in a summer town where all the bars had themed events every night of the week. She'll need to make an appearance or two to keep her cover intact, lest the friendly banter turn into actual suspicion. The last thing Emily needs is to blow her opportunity because she refuses to go to happy hour.

After the doors are locked, Emily retrieves her tablet and heads into the safe-deposit box room. The top lines of the source's transmission take her breath away.

> Undercover female ATF agent in camp.
> Alias = Sarah. Operation under way? Need
> confirmation ASAP. Possible murders. Check
> names—Roland Marshal Emeritus. Eugene
> Gilchrest.

Shaking off her disbelief, she quickly scans the rest of the message. It's filled with more names and abbreviated circumstances next to them. Things like *foreclosure* and *cancer debt*. Toward the bottom, there is a reference to an emergency room visit for a boy named Bobby at the hospital in Massena. The agent returns to the top line, poring over possible explanations.

Emily uploads the transmission through the secure exchange and packs up. She goes to leave the room, but hesitates. She'd been given a number to call in an emergency, but they never specified what constituted an emergency. What if her handler doesn't see

the transfer notification right away? He would want
something like this brought to his attention, wouldn't
he? Wrestling with her decision, she finally pulls out
her phone and hits the Call button.

After a few rings, he picks up. "Scarsboro."

"Sir, it's Emily in Saranac."

There's the briefest of hesitation. "Is everything all
right?"

"Yes, sir, I'm fine. It's just the transmission I sent."

"I received it. Looking at it now."

"Oh, okay. Good. That's why I called, sir. The first
line—"

"That's enough. I said I'm looking at it," Kelly says,
cutting her off.

"All right, I just wanted to be sure. It seemed like
something you would want to be made aware of, so
I—"

"I appreciate the initiative, but stick to your direc-
tives. The fewer established connections, the better.
Retrieve and transmit. File your daily logs. That's it.
I'll let you know when you're done. Understand?"

Cold sweat prickles at the back of her neck. Emily
swallows. "Yes, sir. I follow."

"Emergencies only, Emily. These protocols are for
your safety as much as the others involved. Make sure
you clear this call from your history." The line goes
dead.

It takes her another minute to gather up her pride
from the floor. When she steps out of the room, Emily
jumps.

"Oh my," Delores calls out, hand going to her heart.
"I'm so sorry, dear. I didn't mean to startle you."

"It's all right, Delores."

The woman must read into her demeanor. "Is . . . everything okay?"

Emily plasters her persona back into place. Flashing a bright smile, she works to quickly spin the encounter. "Everything is fine. Nothing to worry about."

"Okay. Okay, that's good." Delores sags with relief. "Are you heading home, then? Or did you want to meet up with the girls? I was planning to go over for a quick drink."

After that embarrassing conversation with her boss, a few drinks sound good.

"You know what? Sure. Let's go."

. . . . .

Amid the clanking of weights, Kelly steps out of the locker room and into the gym proper. He walks past clusters of free weights, scanning the room. Around the corner is a long row of treadmills. The machines offer a view through floor-to-ceiling windows overlooking the East River, the Brooklyn and Manhattan Bridges spanning it into the next borough.

The whir of belts and slapping of sneakers comes from two machines at the far end. Kelly cranes his neck and smiles slightly as he spots the pair he's looking for. Both in their early thirties, the two men look as though they are chiseled from rock. Despite the speed setting of their treadmills, they carry on a full conversation.

Kelly exhales deeply before pulling down the towel draped over his shoulders. He has an objective, and he's sure the only way to get it done is to go straight at these guys. The agents in counterterrorism aren't the type to beat around the bush. Still, he can't put all his cards on the table right away. If he does that, he'll be shooting any chance at a transfer out of the air with a missile of his own launching. Kelly starts forward.

"Hey, Rob. Jason. How goes it?" Kelly says, stepping up onto a machine next to them. He misses the look they share and the eye roll from Jason while he is putting his towel over the handrail.

Rob leans past Jason, who is running in the middle of the trio. "What's up, Kelly? How's Frankie Coffeecake and JoJo the Whale doing?"

Kelly forces out a laugh. At least the references are from *A Bronx Tale*. *The Godfather* lines were played out within the first few weeks of being assigned to his unit. "Well, you know. Runnin' the numbahs and stuff. Fuggedaboutit," he replies, countering with his best *Donnie Brasco*. No self-respecting FBI agent hadn't seen the movie. Even if it is a throwback to the glory days of the organized crime unit, so what? It's still one of the Bureau's greatest victories.

"Just make sure you take it easy on them, okay, Kel?" Jason, a man with a perfectly formed flattop, says in reply. "I've got a dinner at Carmine's coming up, and I don't want a dip in the cooking."

"You guys got all the jokes. You know there ain't shit going on with us. What's new in your neck of the woods?"

They try to be blasé about it, but Kelly notices their tightening, however small it may be. A pinch and a twinge of the jaw from Jason.

Rob shifts his gaze straight ahead before answering, "Evil people trying to do evil things, my man. Always busy in our neck of the woods."

"I bet. Overworked, understaffed, and underpaid, am I right? Seems like you guys are swamped all the time. I'm surprised to even see you in here."

"Gotta keep up with the PT, bro," Jason replies. "Never know when we might have to run out and kick down a door. Can't be ready to do that sitting in a chair all day."

"No. Of course not. I was just pointing out, what with the way it is and all, that you guys could use some help. Maybe an extra set of eyes and ears?"

Rob chuckles. "Yeah. Sure, Kel. Feel free to put in your transfer paperwork, and the SAC will take a look at it. Again."

Jason glances over at his partner and suppresses a laugh.

Kelly ignores the quip while loading up his counter. "What if I've got more than just my résumé this time? What if I had something for you guys? Something on the verge."

The two share a long look before turning back to stare at him.

"The fuck are you talking about, Kelly?" Jason asks, his tone spiked with annoyance.

"Upstate," Kelly begins, trying his best to subdue his excitement. "Near the Canadian border. I've got in on good authority that there's an operation under way. Possibly with those showboats in the ATF already in place. I thought if I brought it to you guys, we could verify the story. Maybe even pull the rug out from underneath them. Interested?"

The sneakers pound on the belts.

"Upstate, you said?" Rob asks after a few moments.

"That's right."

"Near the Canadian border?" Jason adds.

"Uh-huh," Kelly replies. "Up near Potsdam."

Another long exchange. When they look back, Jason reaches over and slaps Kelly's emergency stop button.

"Hey! What the hell?" Kelly exclaims.

The men jump off their machines as he slides off his own.

Rob sticks his finger in Kelly's chest. "I don't know what game you're playing, Kelly, but you lock that shit up right now."

Jason leans in. "What's the matter with you? Running your goddamn mouth like that? Annoying little insect. You really think that's gonna get you into the division?"

Kelly puts his palms up. "What the hell? I'm just trying to give us all a leg up here. I vetted this as far as I can on my own. It's solid. I wouldn't bring it to you if it wasn't legit."

"Listen here, spotlight Ranger," Rob says, "if we need to track down a pizza delivery boy, we'll know who to call. In the meantime, stay out of CT business." The man snatches his towel and storms off toward the locker room.

"Jesus. Jay, I hit a nerve or something?"

Jason shakes his head and grabs his towel. "I get you're bored, Kel, but Rob is right. Don't mess with things you know shit about. People's lives are on the line here. In more ways than you can imagine." He gives Kelly a dismissive look before following his partner.

"Guys, wait. Come on, let's talk about this," Kelly calls after them.

Rob gives him the finger from the doorway to the locker room.

Once they are both out of the gym, Kelly steps back onto his machine. *Well done, Kelly, truly an expert handling of the situation.* He sighs as he starts the treadmill again. What in the hell just happened?

It wasn't his mention of the ATF. It was the border that got them all worked up. Something clearly is going on up there, something that CT is involved in, and now by proxy through Derek, something that he is as well. The way Rob and Jason reacted, though. Could things be out of hand somehow? What was that about people's lives? People's lives are always on the line in law enforcement. What makes this any different? And did they mean upstate, themselves, or both? Either way, what does that mean for his friend?

His mind races along with the belt beneath his feet. He's probably just shot to shit any chance of working with those guys, but they could go scratch. If they don't want to bring him in, he'll run it himself. He has an asset in place. Not just an asset but a trained human and counterintelligence officer who discovered a serious lead with some far-reaching implications. He'll see this through one way or another.

First things first. He needs to get verification of this agent already in play. Kelly thinks of the friends of friends he has in the spiderweb of the federal law enforcement agencies. Who still owes him a favor?

It will have to be done delicately, but if he can locate her case officer, Kelly can tie his friend in with whatever this ATF agent already has. Then it will just be a matter of running Derek to support the ongoing investigation. He begins his backward planning, deriving the intelligence objectives he'll need his friend to obtain. Variables. There are a lot of variables.

Another thought presses on him from the back of his mind, fighting for space in the foreground. This could be it. Finally. Agents fight tooth and nail to get on a joint agency operation. The rare circumstances are a boost to careers. He smiles.

Jason and Rob can eat shit. He went to them first, but now? Now, if he has to, he'll bring it straight to their SAC. Something concrete that gets his foot in the door? That will spring him from organized crime for sure. Hell, it could even be a promotion. How much would that shine on the dynamic duo, Kelly being their new boss?

22

Derek stands on a platform thirty feet high that's hammered into place between two trees. The day is overcast, and a light mist swirls through the air with sudden gusts. Despite being summer, a chill clings to the mountains, a precursor to the plunge in temperatures still a few months away.

He leans over the railing, focused on the shoot house the camp carpenters fabricated. Essentially a roofless log cabin, the house is a wide rectangle running south to north from where he stands. Multiple rooms and connecting hallways form the interior, each with silhouettes propped in corners or paper targets stapled to the walls.

It reminds him of the *Labyrinth* game he used to play as a kid, trying to get a silver ball bearing through the wooden maze using the knobs on the sides. Beside him, sitting on a camp stool, Marshal coughs into his hand and then turns up the collar of his flannel shirt. Derek gives the grizzled old bastard credit. Scaling the planks nailed into the tree as a makeshift ladder was no small feat for a guy a few years removed from ninety.

The morning after the executions, Marshal had given a long-winded sermon on free will and the prodigal son, somehow weaving a tale that both explained the departure of Jimmy, Sebastian, and Sofia to follow their own pursuits as a wondrous event and also reinforced to everyone in the camp that the best thing for their lives was to stay put. No one batted an eyelash at either message.

After the larger group broke up, Derek had whirled about and addressed Gil, ordering the remaining men to full battle rattle and a road march out to the shoot house site. For the last week, he'd been drilling the shit out of them.

Derek dragged it out as best he could. The first three days were filled with lessons on precision movements, checking corners, clearing rooms. Then it went into individual dry runs with each man. During the wait times, he had one of the other nine teach basic survival doctrine to the remaining eight to keep their skills fresh and their minds occupied. After the one-on-ones, it moved into clearing the structure by fire team. Then by squad.

The second half of the week mirrored the first, except the drills were live fires now. All of it had been culminating to this, a final day of full-squad clearing using live ammunition. The stretch had been done well enough, but Derek knew any longer would begin to look suspicious.

It also had the intended effect of buying Sarah a week without Marshal around. The old man had been transfixed by the training and made regular, extended trips to the shoot house to watch the men progress. It was up to Sarah to make the moves she needed to in the old man's absence.

Derek glances down at his wristwatch, the stopwatch function already running. Thirty seconds in. They should be arriving . . .

Two groups of five men in full tactical gear appear out of the woods surrounding the house, one on the south side at what would be the main entrance and another to the east at a side entrance. Just below him, he can hear Gil speaking with a low voice into his radio, communicating with Brian, the team leader on the east side of the house. Both groups stack up outside their respective entrances. Four men to one side of the doorframe. The fifth to the opposite. Gil gives the command. The teams begin their assault.

The fifth man on each team swings into the doorframe, ramming the door with a sledgehammer and bashing it open. As the teams sweep inside, the breachers drop their implements and take up a perimeter patrol, securing the entry points.

Gil's team moves into the central corridor, the man in the lead engaging a target at the far end. As he does so, Gil and the third man in line immediately split off to the left, kicking in a door. Gil engages a target against the wall, the shots ringing out through the hills, and then sweeps his rifle to the right. He fires at close range into the chest of a silhouette propped in the corner as the man behind him enters and engages the target on the wall for the second time. Yelling, "Clear right! Clear left!" to one another, they communicate with the team members securing the hallway and exit back out.

On the east side of the house, Brian's team makes entry into a wide room and engages with surprising speed, already implementing Derek's critiques from the previous day. The first and second men in fire at the target directly in front of them and then immediately swing left and right to engage the silhouettes in the far corners. The third and fourth men step into the room, firing at the forward target and stepping to the left and right of the doorframe. Before they move on, Brian, in the northeast corner, adjusts his stance and fires through the open doorway into the adjoining room, eliminating one of the targets repositioned into a new corner for this iteration.

The teams flow through the rooms of the shoot house. Derek watches intently as the individual members yell out to one another, communicating an intricate choreography to eliminate threats and ensure their own safety. They move with a coiled poise now unleashed and deliver the methodical death of a rattlesnake sprung loose.

As the two groups close in on the center of the structure, Derek watches Gil and Brian keying their respective radios, coordinating efforts to make sure every room is clear and the two teams don't engage each other. Decision made, Brian's team begins to flow back out of the house while Gil's makes one last entry into the northwest rooms. There, the first two in fire at their targets while the second two immediately move to the adjoining wall. Mimicking their initial stack, three go to one side while the fourth kicks in the door and peels away.

The first man in fires but then lets his empty rifle drop against his chest. He immediately goes to his sidearm to continue the engagement. The second and third in sweep to their targets. The group yells clear, and the fourth man they left in the previous room signals the okay. Then, just like Brian's group, the men make a controlled movement into the central corridor. Gil's team proceeds to the exit, making sure they aim into open doors and cover connecting hallways as they do so.

When both teams reach their exits, they shout out to the perimeter security. Receiving the all clear, they exit as fast as they arrived and fade back into the wood line. Derek punches the button on his watch. He looks down and smiles. Fast. Much faster than last time. He holds his wrist out for the old man to see.

Marshal smiles at the time and then up at him. "They're getting good, aren't they?"

Derek nods but doesn't say anything. They are getting good. Very good. He'd seen teams of operators with worse times when they first started out. The men were taking to the training better than he could have ever imagined.

Shaking free of the pride swelling up, Derek reminds himself that this burgeoning expertise could be used to kill innocent people. Especially any law enforcement called in to take the cult down. His only hope is that by focusing on urban combat, he's tipped the scales in favor of the boys in blue. Marshal's group might know the land, but to this point, they hadn't learned shit about fighting in it.

Derek spits the taste of vomit out of his mouth. He straightens and screams, "End ex!" to end the exercise.

The teams stand up from their covered positions behind trees and boulders and amble out of the woods. Rifles slung across their chests, they fist-bump one another as they make their way toward the platform. The friendly chiding is that of men whose confidence in their abilities is skyrocketing.

Once they've all gathered in a loose semicircle under the platform, Derek addresses them from above. "Not bad, gents. Not bad at all. You shaved close to forty-five seconds off your last run. Still, always room for improvement. Dillon. On your second entry, you didn't check behind the door. There wasn't a target in that room, but there could have been.

"Parker, you're still flagging the man in front of you as you enter. Rifle at the low ready, stand offset to him to clear your firing lane, and snap it up to engage. Gerry, on the first movement down the main corridor, you failed to rotate and pull rear security. Someone you missed or someone that was wounded could have come out and fired into the whole team while their backs were turned. You gotta protect against that."

Gerry nods, soaking up the critique. "Noted, boss. Won't happen again." The man hefts the belt-fed squad automatic weapon, reassigned to him now that Jimmy is gone.

"See that it doesn't."

"Yeah, see that it doesn't," Parker retorts sarcastically.

Gerry looks back at him. "Eat shit, Parker. At least with my mistake, it's the enemy shooting us in the back."

The men laugh, and Derek can't help chuckling himself. "All right. Settle down. Thomas, not a good look running dry on your mag, but you made a smooth transition to the pistol to compensate for it. Remember what we talked about, all of you. That tactical pause. Take that half second to assess the situation.

Check the window on the side of your rifle mags before exiting a room. If you see the springs, you're low. Change it out before moving on."

The men nod, their attention focused.

"Okay, last point. Brian."

The second team leader looks directly at him. Derek notices the flash of anticipated rebellion, but the once combative man dismisses it, waiting patiently for his critique.

"Good innovation and initiative engaging the target in the adjoining room from your vantage point in the first one. You would have eliminated a threat, and that makes the transition to the next clear that much easier. Just remember, if you can line up on him, he can do the same to you."

"Okay. Will do," the man replies, sounding surprised.

The others in the group slap him on the shoulder and shove him around a bit while giving him kudos and busting his chops.

Derek lets it go on a little longer and then chimes in. "Listen up. I want the teams to switch entrances. Take five minutes to transition and get set, and then we're going again. Let's get one more run in before chow."

The men move, albeit slowly, as they continue to joke and change places.

After another iteration and critique, Derek and Marshal climb down the ladder from the platform and fall in with them. The group moves down the path, giving one another shit as they progress back to camp.

Derek walks at the rear with Marshal.

"I gotta tell you, Derek, the men are looking fantastic. Just fantastic. What you've been able to do with them in so brief a time is nothing short of remarkable. The Lord truly blessed us with such a guardian. Our security won't be questioned again, that's for sure."

"They are doing well, you're right in that." Derek throws a sideways glance at the old man. "Speaking of security, no reports of those probes or movements in the last few weeks. Any idea why they may have suddenly stopped coming around?"

The old man chuckles. "Probably because of the few thousand rounds being fired off this side of the mountain. Would you go walking into that?" he replies, not skipping a beat.

"No. No, I don't suppose I would." The charisma and charm are almost impenetrable. Marshal has an answer and counter for practically everything. Derek is content to walk the rest of the way in silence. His mind drifts to the pieces of the puzzle that are still obscured, and he hopes that reuniting with Sarah will help to clear them up.

Going back into the camp, Derek is greeted with a warm welcome. Ever since the morning after Bobby's accident, he has been viewed with different eyes. They crowd around, hugging and shaking hands, as if saving Bobby's life has made him fully accepted into their community. That kind of belonging could be leveraged if need be.

At the same time, he recognizes the sincerity in their words and actions. It isn't lost on him that many, maybe even most of the community, are more than likely oblivious to the machinations of Marshal and the plans for his security team. For those not involved, they have truly bought into this way of life and truly accepted Derek as part of that. He knows the inevitable conclusion of his actions will be another heart-break for people already racked with suffering.

Bobby's parents embrace him tightly, begging him to come by their cabin and see the boy as soon as he can. Derek assures them that he will, having to shake hands with the kid's father no fewer than four times. His mind quickly flies south, a silent hope that dinner trays and profanity aren't being hurled about in his own father's room. Derek knows how much stabler the man is when he's around, which is ironic in its own right. Growing up, the man could barely stand to be in the same room with him unless they were talking about their next hunting or fishing trip.

As the welcome begins to break up, he catches sight of Sarah standing at the edge of the celebration, arms crossed tightly under her breasts. The chow bell rings, calling everyone in camp to their evening meal. He stops Gil as the man goes to walk by him.

"Turn in the weapons and gear, then head to chow."

"I think I know the routine by now, D."

"Yeah, I know you do. But I'm making an adjustment. Tell the men to take their time and enjoy their dinner. They have the rest of the night off. And no PT in the morning. Let them sleep in. They deserve it."

Gil's eyes narrow for the briefest of moments, but then soften. "Whatever you say, D." He heads toward the armory, where the rest of the group has already started stowing their gear.

Stalking over, Sarah plants herself in front of him. "Are you hard of hearing or just plain dumb?"

The men standing at the armory twist their heads around. Smiles and laughs abound until Derek looks over her shoulder and they turn away. "Jesus, lady, can I even get my shit off before you jump down my throat?"

"No, you can't. How many times do we have to talk about the ammo you're—"

Rolling his eyes, Derek turns and walks away from her.

"Oh, you son of a bitch. You don't get to walk away from me!" Sarah yells while storming after him.

Once they are inside his cabin, Derek closes the door and secures his lock. Sarah continues the charade for a few more moments while he grounds his gear. Once finished, he sits down on a cot and takes her in. Another time and place, Derek would have been hard-pressed not to entertain pursuing a more social engagement with her. The thought immediately conjures an image of Kim, and with it guilt for having considered Sarah in the same way. She lets her ranting lecture trail off.

"Anything?" he says softly.

Her face goes solemn. "I think so. You remember the night you started all your commotion up on the hill? When you came and got me?"

"You were working with the ledger," Derek replies.

"Exactly. Large portions of the ledger are straight accounting, but intermixed in it are swaths of figures that don't add up. There's nothing to support the transactions and expenditures."

"So . . . what exactly? Money laundering on top of arms sales? The two of those usually go hand in hand. Not exactly earth-shattering news."

She shakes her head. "That's what I thought too at first, but I think it's deeper than that. I think I found a cipher within those sections. Even more so, since I've been working with it for a while now, I think I've figured out the code. Or portions of it, at least."

After a few moments of silence, Derek finally asks, "What does it say?"

"If I'm right, it's a list of their first shipment. Armament nomenclatures plus the number of units ordered for each. Accompanying ammunition. Ancillary equipment. But beyond that, I think I've found something else. The preliminary logistics of an operations order. Possibly coordinates or at the very least some compass headings. As well as a date."

"When?"

Sarah hesitates slightly before answering, "If I'm right, a week after you're gone."

Derek lowers his head and pinches the bridge of his nose. "I'm training them. I'm training them for an op."

"There's more," Sarah says softly. When he doesn't lift his head right away, she raises her voice slightly. "Derek."

He lifts his eyes, hand held out to the side of his face. "What, Sarah? What is it already?"

She takes a deep breath. "Don't freak out on me, okay? Elsewhere in the ledger. There are names thrown in almost at random with other entries. Sometimes tied to a business or an address. Several of them are synonymous with other groups the ATF is watching."

His skin prickles with sweat. "Jesus," he whispers.

Her eyes lock with his. "I'm sorry. I'm sorry you got caught up in this."

"You can keep your apologies," he says, scooping up his rucksack. He starts packing up the items scattered about on the neighboring cot. "I'm out of here. Tonight. You may not be able to leave, but I'm not messing around with this shit show any longer. You tell me who I need to talk to and I'll see that they pull you out, but I'm not about to be responsible for the next Mumbai. I'm stopping this thing before it goes any further." He reaches for his assault pack, but she blocks him.

"Will you stop and think for a minute?" Her voice is ragged. "I don't care what your background is. You really think you can just walk into the ATF and drop this shit? By the time my people sort everything out and validate your story, these bastards will be long gone. We won't have the shipment; we won't have the source of the arms. We need to go about this the right way or else we risk losing the inside track."

Derek clenches his jaw. "Goddamn it. What do you suggest we do, then?"

"We keep going—"

Derek hisses.

"Listen to me. We keep going. I get that we need to move on it. I'm with you on that. But I need a little more time. Just buy me enough to make copies of what I need out of the ledger. It'll coincide with the end of your training, and then we can get out. The most important part of this is making sure I have a full transcription so that we know exactly what we're dealing with."

"I can't do it, Sarah. I was barely able to hold it together around these people before. Now you want me to keep training them at this level knowing full well they might supply a bloodbath?"

She nods. "Yes. That's exactly what I want you to do. It's the only way to keep our cover intact. Don't let up at all. In the meantime, I'll keep digging. I just need you to stick it out a little longer."

Letting the rucksack drop, Derek walks over to the window and peers out. "I've dragged my feet as much as I can. If I take them back into the field, I have to teach them formations. Man traps. Things that could get a SWAT team killed or at least make their job considerably more dangerous."

"Come on now. You, the master instructor?" she says, arching an eyebrow. "You mean to tell me you can't string out some basic-level shit for a few more days?"

Crossing back to his cot, Derek drops onto it and rubs his face with his hands. "I just . . . I don't know if I can."

"Please, Derek. That list? It had things on it like M240s, .50 calibers, claymore mines. Mass-casualty-type equipment, okay? We need to know where it's coming from, and we can't let it get to where it's supposed to go. There is something larger at hand here. Something that goes beyond just gunrunning. The ledger might be the key to that. The revenue being used to support something else. This is no time to lose our nerve, Marine. With your skill set and my cover, we can take these bastards down. I know it, but I . . . I need your help."

"I'm here one more week, Sarah. A week. And then I'm out."

"Okay, then. One week. Now listen, there's one final thing to this. I'm locked in here. I was only able to sneak away the other night because of what was going on. Marshal won't let me go to town for an hour like this arrangement he made for you. I swear the man was desperate for a Special Operations guy."

"He does enjoy watching the training."

"Of course he does. He's a sick, demented old man,

Derek." She sits down across from him. "You're due for a run into Saranac Lake, right?"

"Now that we're back, yeah."

"Okay. I need you to get this info out. If something should happen to either of us, my people at least need to have an idea of where we left off and what they're walking into. But we can't risk it going through normal channels. If there is a leak anywhere along the chain of command, we could both find ourselves in a ditch."

"Fuck!" Derek says at one more problem laid at his feet. "Now you tell me your department could be compromised?"

"Will you keep your voice down? I have nothing to support it, obviously—I've been out in the middle of the wilderness this whole time—but let's face facts. There's got to be government involvement here at some point. Fort Drum is two hours away. It could be a general or a DoD contractor for all we know. My point being, people of influence are making this happen. The same type of people that could silence a whole region. You think they couldn't have a set of eyes and ears in the agencies?"

Standing up, Derek paces across the cabin. The angle is plausible, but Derek sees another. Ambition. Sarah knows that this is a career-making bust, one that she's working to safeguard so that others won't swoop in and steal the glory. It's yet another wrinkle that starts turning his dread to anger.

"This shit just keeps getting better and better."

"Do you have anyone you trust that we can turn to with this?" Sarah says, cutting to the chase. "Anyone that we could get this info to through a back channel? I'm thinking if they can take it up their chain of command high enough, they might be able to leapfrog into the upper echelons and avoid wherever a compromise could be."

Derek stares into her eyes. Resolve. Determination. Fire. Still, despite all of that, he hadn't had a chance to hear back from Kelly yet. "Nothing. I sort of . . . cut loose from that life. Isolated myself. Severed the connection. It was the only way to cope." Though not entirely true, the words still sting with a semblance of reality. It adds another layer of guilt onto an already hefty burden.

"Damn. All right. Well, try to think of someone. We're gonna want that insurance policy." She stands up and heads for the door, stopping just before it and turning back to him. "You good, cowboy?"

"Good as I can be."

Sarah gives him a smile. "Okay, then." Pulling the lock free, she rips open the door and starts yelling again. "I'm not gonna have this conversation again, you understand?" Sarah lets the door slam shut, adding an emphatic "Meathead" as she crosses to the chow tent.

Every part of Derek wants to run. Right now. He could be in the woods in minutes and they'd never find him. A part of him, probably the logical part, wonders why he isn't doing just that. The other part, though, however illogical, drowns it out.

This isn't his fight. It's not what he had signed up for. Sure, they anticipated things being dangerous, but nothing on this level. There's his son to think about. Kim. His father, sitting in assisted living. This group knows all about him. Why is he still here?

You know why. Twenty-two years of service, that's why. Two plus decades of protecting this country to . . .

*what? Turn your back on it now when faced with an-
other threat? That's not how we operate. What is it
the guys at the clinic say? You can take off the uniform, but you never stop serving. Service is for life if
your country needs you.*

Staring at his rifle and then his bags, a final singular
thought blasts through his mind like a freight train.
Unending. The cars just keep rolling by on the tracks.
What am I gonna do?

23

The following morning, Derek riffles through the stacks of money in the safe-deposit box. He flips through each one, searching for what he hopes will be a reply from Kelly. When making his drops, Derek has been putting the notes close to the front and buried two stacks down. It seems like the agent in the bank has taken much greater precaution. With his search taking this long, Derek begins to wonder if there is any response at all.

After breakfast, he gave the QRF their schedule for the day. The men were to spend the morning cleaning their weapons and resetting their supplies and gear. Come early afternoon, Derek would give an introductory class on squad tactics, the foundation for which the next week of training would be focused on. Afterward, Gil and Brian could do layouts and inspections of their men's equipment. Once done, the rest of the time was theirs to spend with their families and friends. A day of reset and regeneration for the team to take a quick breather before their final iteration.

It also gave Derek an opening to get to the bank.

With everything he and Sarah had discussed the night before, he needed to receive word as well as send his own. Finally, he finds the slip in the seventh stack of cash and hurriedly pulls it free and unfolds the paper.

> *Working on confirmation of credentials.*
> *Provided names check out with histories*
> *gathered.*
> *Tie in with agent for now, but be cautious.*
> *Will get back to you ASAP. Call if able.*

Had the wall in front of him not been lined with metal doors, Derek would have put his fist through it. The anger comes over him so suddenly that the only thing halting his reaction is a semiconscious realization that the punch will break his shooting hand. A week. He had given Kelly a week's lead time on this. *No shit, be cautious. Just a pretty monumental detail, confirming whether or not I'm in the middle of an ATF operation. You think you could get an answer on that?*

As he seethes and tries to bring himself back down, the sensible side of him works hard to push explanations to the forefront of his mind. Kelly would have to proceed lightly. It's not exactly like the FBI and ATF go out together on Friday nights. Compounding the issue is the fact that his friend is essentially running him outside of agency guidelines. Granted, Derek is classified as a CI, but still. That's a pretty thin justification if your career is on the line.

Derek pulls himself together. He's with a new escort today. Hunter, another one of the lookouts. The man hadn't made the trip with Derek before and seemed antsy the way Brady was their first time out. Derek had already spent crucial minutes looking for the slip. Without further delay, he rips up the note and pops the scraps into his mouth. While chewing on the paper, Derek goes to the desk and hastily scrawls out a reply.

> *Potential attack in development.*
> *Exfil in 1 week. Be ready to move.*

The rest will have to wait until Derek is on the go, with or without Sarah. He's already over what would be a reasonable amount of time to count money and put it away. Packing up as fast as he can, Derek leaves the room. Hunter ambles around nearby. Hearing the door shut, the man turns.

"Ready?" he asks.

Derek nods. "Let's go. I've got classes to teach this afternoon."

■   ■   ■   ■   ■

Brady crosses the clearing, the sun starting to dip in the west behind him. Near the chow tent, the security team is gathered in front of Derek's cabin as he gives a class on something about which Brady can't be bothered. He's happy to sit in his perch and all, but screwing around with sticks and scraping rocks together? Hard pass.

Striding past the armory, he makes for the vehicle clearing. Within a half hour, he exits the logging roads and, a little over an hour after leaving the woods, pulls into Saranac Lake. Guiding the truck around the back roads of the summer town, he arrives at the apartment that they had rented. Brady jumps out of the pickup and into the shower. The smell acquired during extended periods of time spent in the forest did little to support a civilian lifestyle.

Toweling off, he goes through the closet, selecting an outfit for the evening. Of all nights in particular, tonight, he has to be sure that he blends in. Although they aren't exactly the clothes he used to wear—in truth, back then, he wouldn't have been caught dead in the cargo pants and flannel shirts worn ad nauseam up here—it still feels strange to be wearing anything other than camouflage.

Seven years ago, the furthest political action he had ever taken was protesting with his college buddies. Rallying in Zuccotti Park with hundreds of others during Occupy Wall Street. It was only after meeting Marshal that he saw the truth. No matter how many rallies the masses held, the rich would continue to get richer while the poor withered and died at the wealthy's expense.

It happened to his mother. And then after she was gone, all she left were her medical debts. The net result was being thrown out in the street when they took his mother's house as repayment. Brady sees the truth now. He's shocked at the number of people who still don't. Protesting this government with any hope for remediation is a fool's errand. If you want to change it, you have to overthrow it.

So he traded in the skinny jeans and the suit jacket a size too small. The snarky graphic tee. The fingerless gloves and his favorite scarf. All in exchange for Realtree camo and an assault rifle. Brady chuckles. To think his junior high Boy Scout lessons with a .22 rifle would have resulted in this is morbidly ironic.

Slipping on the best plaid concoction he can find, Brady douses himself with Polo Black cologne and heads out. It's only a short drive from the apartment to the lively downtown area. He parks at Waterhole, across the street and just a stone's throw away from the bank. The bar's Party on the Patio is already jumping. The live band has got the ever-growing crowd amped up. Brady orders a beer and climbs up to the second-story balcony. Finding a perch near the end where he can simultaneously view Main Street and the crowd below, the lookout sips on his brew and bides his time.

It takes over an hour and another pint before he finally spots the four of them coming in from the lot. They disappear inside and come back out with beers and mixed drinks. Brady watches patiently. Now that they're here, he's content to let the night unfold. Close to the bottom of the group's second round, he watches as Abigail heads toward the bar. Brady slides from his railing and proceeds inside as well, quickly negotiating the press of bodies to work his way to the ground level.

He sidles up next to her at the bar, raising his glass in request of a refill. When Brady speaks, he stares straight ahead at the taps. "Took you long enough to show up."

"But we did, didn't we? You can't rush hotties when they want to get dolled up." The woman's voice drips with an attitude that's one short-term-lease apartment removed from a trailer park. "I told you she wasn't gonna skip out tonight. Not for Roxie's birthday, she wasn't."

"Yeah. Great. Just make sure you get her drunk. And that you keep her here."

The bartender arrives with four beers.

Abigail points at them. "What do you think? I'm here filing my taxes?"

Brady throws a sideward glance at the woman.

"Bud Lights ain't gonna cut it. Start doing some shots next round."

"Shit. She ain't gonna do those. Bitch is only drinking light beer—and nursing it at that."

"Do what you have to do. Use the birthday angle to convince her if need be. You want to get paid or not?"

Despite his attempt to not look like he's talking to her, the woman rounds on him and plants a hand on her hip. The other hand waves around in erratic gestures while she speaks. "Rounds cost money, punk. A lot of money. Shots more so than most. You expect that to come out of my end?"

Rolling his eyes, Brady reaches into his pocket, pulls out a wad of bills, and throws a twenty on the bar for the beers, then counts off five more of the same and holds them out. "Just get it done."

She eyes the money before snatching it out of his hand. "That's what I thought," she replies before walking off with the drinks.

Brady returns to the balcony and resumes his overwatch. It isn't long before the entire group is retreating to the bar for their first round of tequila. More rounds lead to more shots. Two and a half hours after they arrived, Abigail looks up at the balcony level and gives him the smallest of nods.

When he makes it to the restrooms, she's already waiting for him outside the doors. She looks around frantically before handing him Emily's keys. Brady grabs them with a beverage napkin in his palm. "You're gonna be quick, right? I don't want her realizing these are missing."

"Twenty minutes. A half hour, tops. Buy another round just to be safe. If she asks questions, start searching the place. Make a show of it. If I can't get them back to you before she realizes they're gone, they'll magically appear in the lost and found at the end of the night."

The woman grimaces but holds out her hand all the same. Brady slips the keys into his pocket while pulling out his money clip. Five crisp Benjamins come off the top and go into her waiting palm.

"There's definitely something about her. Always poking around and whispering with Delores. No one gets access to the safe-deposit room that early."

"Your powers of observation are astounding."

"Why were you asking about the bank anyway?" she says, folding up the bills and stuffing them in her bra.

Brady shoots her a glance. "You want to keep that money and earn any in the future, you don't ask questions, and this never happened. Got it?"

He doesn't wait for her reply.

A couple of minutes later, he's at Emily's apartment. Outside her door, he slips on a pair of latex gloves and then slides the key into the lock. No prints. No forced entry. Just like when he was living on the street, finding any way he could to survive, in the months before Marshal took him in. He'll get to the bottom of this for Gil. If she's a threat, he'll find what he needs to prove it. From there, it'll be up to the security team.

Setting about the task, Brady inches around the apartment, light on his toes and quick with his fingers. It doesn't take long. The compact handgun in the purse she left behind is a good start. Upon further inspection, the purse has an inner compartment sewn into the lining, easily overlooked. He finds a miniature badge inside of it, and his stomach sinks. Brady shoves it back into place.

The rest of his search doesn't go nearly as smoothly. Coming up empty on the obvious places like her closet and dresser, Brady finally finds a small safe hidden behind a smattering of ramen noodle cups and Pringles cans in the pantry. The box is secured with a keyhole. Brady pulls her keys back out of his pocket and searches through them until he finds the one that fits.

The door pops open with a turn. After perusing the contents, Brady takes out his cell phone. The next few moments are spent capturing everything he was sent to find out. Picture after picture. A set of FBI credentials. A full-size Glock 9 mm. Several handwritten notes, preserved in ziplock plastic bags. He reads each one in turn. The last one speeds his already lit fuse toward the powder keg of anger he was keeping in check.

Potential attack in development.
Exfil in 1 week. Be ready to move.

That. Fucking. Bitch.
Returning everything to where it was in the first place, Brady closes the safe door. As he goes to leave, his eyes flirt with the handbag, his mind with the pistol inside.

He could do it so easily. Take her gun. Return her keys and then come back to the apartment and wait for her outside. It would be a simple matter of following her to her door and pulling the trigger. Granted, he had never killed anyone before, but he was more than willing to in order to preserve Marshal's vision.

Still . . . the cause. He was trusted to get this task

accomplished without making selfish, uncalculated moves that would draw unnecessary attention to the group. Against every inclination to do otherwise, Brady walks to the door and leaves, locking it behind him.

Driving back to the bar, he fights the urge not to wrap his hands around the woman's throat the moment he lays eyes on her. Steady. Calm. Follow the mission. The last helps him get through the drive back to Sanctuary.

Brady longs for another shower.

•   •   •   •   •

A low-lying mist blankets Sanctuary, obscuring the clearing and filling in the spaces between the cabins and trees. Derek and the men of the QRF stand at the center of the opening, hefting packs onto shoulders and checking one another's gear. Inspecting star chambers before slapping home magazines and letting their slide releases slam rounds forward.

Slowly but surely, the rest of the camp comes alive. First the blacksmiths to wake their forge, and then with others moving about the daily chores needed to sustain their way of life. The sun breaks through the canopy, and the fog begins to dissipate. Derek orders the security team out to the east. As they begin to road march in file, Brady, looking hungover, in need of a meal, a gallon of water, and a day's worth of sleep, walks toward the camp from the opposite direction.

When the QRF passes by Brady, he waves and calls, "Gil, got a quick second?"

The squad leader stops short and spins toward Derek, looking for approval. "Probably just some lookout rotation nonsense. He's been complaining for weeks. Okay if I straighten his ass out?"

Derek eyes them both before returning a piss-off

glare to Gil. "I'm not holding the rest up. You want to hang back, it's on you to catch up."

The man actually smirks in response. "Would expect nothing less, D. I'll be quick. Promise." As he peels off, the rest of the security team carries on up the vehicle trail.

Gil rushes over to Brady. "What's up?" he asks after ensuring the rest of the team has moved out of earshot.

"We've got a problem." Brady pulls out his cell phone and scrolls through the photos taken the night before.

Gil's smirk quickly vanishes. "Follow me."

Dropping his pack, plate carrier, and rifle, Gil grabs the phone and storms off toward Marshal's cabin. He knocks three times. When beckoned inside, despite the early hour, they find Marshal standing over a bare desk. The old man pours wood oil onto a rag and massages the furniture the way one might their lover. A wide smile creases his face while a distant sparkle illuminates his eyes. The desk glows brilliantly, the deep texture brought out by yet another application. Gil glances at the clock. It's already received its treatment today.

"Yes, Gil? Brady? What is it?" Marshal says, looking up.

He holds up the cell phone. "I'm sorry, boss. He's talking to the feds."

The old man's smile fades away. He places the oil bottle on top of the rag and gingerly moves around behind the desk to the chair. Sitting, Marshal leans back and steeples his fingers. When he looks up, his eyes are alight with fury. "Are we certain?"

"You can see for yourself." Gil moves around the

desk and opens the photos on the phone, flipping through each of them.

"Where were these taken?" Marshal asks after having seen each.

"In the apartment of the woman the feds sent up here. She's working undercover in the bank Derek has been using. We checked it out. She started the week before he arrived. Brady's been on her this whole time and can confirm everything."

"It's true, sir. I saw it with my own eyes," Brady confirms.

Marshal leans forward and puts his elbows on the desktop despite the new oil. He hides his eyes under a roof of interlaced hands.

"We're being played, boss," Gil says.

Long moments go by.

Gil hears Marshal whisper, "Judas. Traitor."

He hurts for the old man, but it had to be done. He had to show him that Derek wasn't the savior Marshal was making him out to be. His self-imposed task finally completed, Gil stands and waits patiently, wrapped in the satisfaction of being proven right.

After a long while, Marshal sits back. His eyes are glassy when he looks up. "All right. Listen. This is what we're going to do."

24

They crest a rise nestled north of the vehicle clearing but south of the swamp training area. The men breathe raggedly, the uphill climb and pace leaving the team winded. As the group doubles over, coughing with hands on knees, Derek fights through his own shortness of breath to launch their next lesson.

"All right, ladies. Can anyone tell me what we're looking at?"

One by one, heads pop up and look past him. Two hills meet in front of the QRF with a barely perceptible game trail running through the ground foliage between them. The hill to the left is steeper with outcroppings of sharp rock. Off to their right, a massive tangle of brush and fallen trees runs away from them, curling up and over the other hill. The upturned roots and earth of a toppled pine sit not more than ten feet away at one end of the natural hedgerow.

The rushing of nearby streams and waterfalls overshadows the insect calls and bird chirps. The ground is more solid than the bog they were in, but it is still soft and damp. Humidity keeps the last remnants of the early-morning mist nipping at their heels, and their already sweat-soaked shirts cling to their bodies. The smell of fresh soil and sickly sweet decay wafts through the air, the two sides of life and death combating and coexisting.

"Game trail in there," Parker offers.

"True, but look closer."

The men fall silent.

Gerry's face lights up. "Choke point."

Derek nods. "Exactly. My guess is that the water you're hearing floods and causes a washout down the hills. Loose branches and debris get pushed with it until it hits these fallen trees and creates this barrier. Game doesn't want to expend energy going up or around, so they've blazed this trail in between. Now, why does that matter to us?"

"We covered this weeks ago," Brian responds. "It's a natural line of drift. During evasion, pursuers would be more apt to follow us along these, which is why we need to move inland and parallel."

"True. All true. But what if I flip the scenario on you?"

Brian squints. "How so?"

"What if this trail isn't an egress route? What if it's an ingress?"

The question lingers over them like the humidity. Derek lets the pause hang there with it.

"I mean, this is really why I'm here, right? Trouble with the neighbors. Who's to say that this isn't one of the routes they've been taking to probe your camp? A trail that could be used for escape could just as easily be used for insertion."

A series of nods comes back in response, perhaps a

little too forced. Derek knows full well that the rival gangs are fiction, and therefore, so are their responses to them, but he can't let on to that fact. Similarly, they need to play along unless they wish to admit that there is something going on besides the supposed enemy.

"Ground your gear. Everyone take a seat or a knee. Any of you nancies start dozing on me, and you can expect to hump down that hill and back up again."

Dropping his pack and sitting down on a rock, Derek lays his M4 across his lap. He singles out Gil. "Field Marshal Montgomery, tell the group about avenues of approach."

Grimacing, Gil wipes his forehead and then rubs his hand on a pant leg. "They're the routes an attacking force uses to get to their objective."

"And what would make for the easiest avenues of approach?"

Gil sighs. "Natural lines of drift."

"Exactly." Derek looks over the rest of the group. "When push comes to shove, men, there's no way that this team can cover three hundred and sixty degrees of terrain around the camp. Let's say half of you are actively patrolling at any given time. The other half is on standby. If something pops off and the QRF is called out to the west, and the patrol is in the east, there's still any number of avenues that these rival groups could get through. That's why we've got to spend time reconning this terrain and identifying the priority approaches. Once we've done so, we can start securing them with noise trip wires and other man traps."

Even though the rest of the group doesn't bat an

eye at the announcement, Brian and Gil immediately glare at each other. Brian turns back to look at Derek.

"Wait, I thought we were going to start learning squad tactics today."

"Yeah, well, I reassessed my plan after yesterday's class, and I think this is more pertinent. We'll get to the active patrolling later in the week. First, I have to ensure that your defensive measures are in place. Set you up for success. If we can lay down a network of listening posts, traps, and defensive positions, your likelihood for successful interdiction will go up drastically."

The two team leaders share another look. Gil seems to signal his counterpart, who grimaces but manages to hold his tongue for once. Derek takes stock of both reactions before continuing. He picks up a two-foot-long branch half as thick as his wrist and draws his survival knife. Working the blade's edge across the top of the stick, he shaves off sections as he rotates it.

"Say what you will about them, but the Viet Cong were absolutely nasty when it came to setting man traps. They would cover the trails they knew our boys would be walking with all sorts of shit. None of them were quite so simple as this." Derek holds the branch up in front of the group, the tip now carved and shaved into the start of a sharp point.

"Punji stick," Henry offers.

"Right. You gather a dozen of these branches and then fashion them like so. On the trails surrounding your camp like the one behind me, you dig holes a foot deeper than the length of the stick so you can create drops. Jam them into the soft ground, points up, and then cover the hole with loose grass and leaves. If your rivals aren't paying attention, they step through the cover, drop a foot into the hole, and the stick punctures right through their boot."

Nods. Derek flips the branch over so the stick is pointing downward. He applies his knife again with two small flicks of the wrist.

"I like to carve notches in mine to make the tips more like broadheads. Small ones, mind you. You don't want to compromise the integrity of the branch. It has to be able to withstand the weight of a two-hundred-plus-pound man. But if you can get that broadhead into or through the foot, it'll be that much harder for them to get it out.

"If you really want to mess them up, harvest some of the camp's shit from the outhouses. Dip each point in feces. If they puncture, it'll add the chance of infection down the line. May not make much difference on the trail, but they'll pay for it later."

Derek looks at them each in turn. "Enough of these traps spread out along your avenues will significantly impede an approaching force. Not only will the guy who steps into the hole start howling, alerting you to their presence, but his team will have to respond. Think of the advantage you've just gained. With that man taken out of the fight, you've delayed their advance. His comrades need to stop to treat his wound. One or two of them might even need to help get him to the rear.

"This is how you even up the odds. The patrol and the QRF can both move in, and if you overtake them before they get away, neutralize the threat." Derek feels his blood beginning to boil. On the surface, he's talking about the supposed rivals, but in his head, all he sees are FBI tactical teams on the trails approaching the camp. He pauses to tamp it back down, can't let his anger get the best of him. "Each of you go into this bramble over here and grab a dozen branches. Then come back and start sharpening them."

The men do as they're told. Derek walks among the group as they work. He keeps his lesson going, discussing more traps and methodologies. A monkey fist created with paracord and incorporating the punji sticks, making it an improvised mace that could be triggered to swing through the air at head level. The tiger trap, another Viet Cong special, where a spiked plank the size of a man swings down from limbs above to impale the unsuspecting.

"Of course, all of these have to be balanced against time and resources. Come the spring, snake traps would be quick to implement and a good enhancement, but keep in mind that they die out eventually."

"Um, I'm sorry, what? A snake trap?" Beets says, scratching his head.

"Yeah, another gift for the GIs back in the day, especially tunnel rats. They used to lash pit vipers to bamboo and place them in the tunnels. The snake couldn't get away, and the tunnel rat would crawl right into a face full of fangs when he got too close. Poor bastard probably didn't even feel the next few bites. Those vipers were known as three-step snakes 'cause that's how long it took for the venom to kill you. Of course, out in the open, the snake ends up starving to death. Once it's natural prey realize it's tied down, they just avoid it."

A sniff comes from behind him. "Might have to skip that one. We're fresh out of Vietnamese bamboo pit vipers here in upstate New York," Brian says, his voice dripping with sarcasm. The rest of the group laughs.

Derek turns to face him. "You may not have them, but you've got timber rattlers. If you can pin one down and lash it to a tree by the trail, you just left your pursuers a big surprise."

The man looks up from his punji stick, his eyebrows furrowed and his lips downturned in a condescending frown. "Not for nothing, but a timber rattler bite ain't exactly three steps and dead."

"Maybe, maybe not. You're completely isolated out here. You think any of these guys looking to screw with the camp are gonna be carrying antivenom with them? Even a moderate bite can be vicious, and it'll have the same effect as that stick in your hand."

"You know what?" Brian replies. He stands up, snaps his punji stick in half, and throws down the pieces. "I've had enough. I'm not buying it."

"Which part?" Derek says, cocking an eyebrow.

"Any of this bullshit. You're telling me that your Mickey Mouse Boy Scout crap is somehow gonna keep these drug dealers off our backs? That somehow sharpening sticks is gonna make all the difference?"

"Why don't you shut your face for once in your life, Brian?" This comes from Thomas, taking everyone by surprise. "The man is just trying to teach what we asked him to."

Brian rounds on him. "We asked him to teach us Vietnam arts and crafts? Hanging planks and maces from trees? What's the matter with you, bro? This is garbage and a waste of our time. We have rifles. Good ones. We just spent a week operating in that shoot house, but now that we're out in the woods, suddenly we're back to the Stone Age? Fuck that shit. We need to be learning how to hunt these bastards down. That's why he's here."

Several of the others look at Derek expectantly. "We're building to that. I told you, we need to put a—"

"That stuff can wait, D," Gil says, jumping up. "We've only got you the rest of this week, but you want to spend that time mapping out our woods? We know this land far better than you ever will. We can recon the trails and put traps into place after you're gone. Right now, we need to focus on making sure this team can function as a cohesive unit. That means formations. Battle drills. Actions on contact. That's why you're here. That's what you're getting paid for. It's time for you to produce."

Just like that, the pendulum has swung back. Derek can see it in the other men's faces. Their leaders, men they knew. Who they had joined with in this venture to live apart in the woods. Those men had just reasserted control.

It forces the moment he has been dreading.

"All right, then. Picture a squad of dealers coming down that game trail. Look at that bramble patch." He turns and points along the length of the washout debris. "That's perfect cover and concealment for an L-shaped ambush. Two men by the upturned roots facing the oncoming procession. Four men interspersed along the length of the downed tree and brush running parallel to the trail. When the point man steps in your punji trap, it freezes the file in place. His screams initiate your attack. Through interlocking fields of fire, you can take out an entire enemy force approaching your camp. I'm not wasting your time. I'm showing you the importance of these traps."

"Duly noted," Gil returns. "Let's get the operating standards down first. Once we're moving like we should be, we can come back to them."

Rivulets of sweat course down Derek's back. "Very well."

For the rest of the week, against every fiber of his being, Derek gives them what they want. He starts small, teaching them the basics of terrain selection. Performing buddy rushes, where one man moves to cover in three-second sprints while the other man provides security. He shows them patrol formations, teaching the security team to move from wedge to file and back to wedge as the land and objectives dictate.

From individual drills, they go to teams, learning how to conduct bounding overwatch maneuvers. Much like the buddy rushes, a whole fire team advances while the other lays down suppressive fire. It's not a far leap from there to actions on contact, the individuals in the lead fire team coming on line with one another to engage the enemy while the other team flanks the adversary.

In truth, the doctrine he teaches is what every mosquito-wings private receives in basic training. Hell, even snot-nosed ROTC cadets drill the same shit during their quest for a butter bar. Gil can't argue against learning such basic material. None of the others had received even a modicum of this knowledge. Derek is well within the scope of starting here and slowly bringing them along to more advanced tactics.

Should Sarah be right, should this group be planning an operation, Derek will have given them the skills they need to pull it off. Not only could they now conduct tactical transport of their caches, but they could evade detection after delivery, surviving in the woods while retreating to whatever rendezvous they set up. With this latest iteration, applied in another context, they could also maneuver against forces coming for their arrests.

He could end it all now. While they're camped for the night. Wipe them all out and disappear into the hills, emerging a week or two later to explain everything that went on. Why he did what he did.

But what if he's wrong? What if Sarah is wrong and her cipher is just nonsensical accounting? Derek will have murdered these men in cold blood. He doesn't fully buy his own rationale. These bastards are up to something, but still. He's not an executioner. He's taken life, but it's been justified. Shooting them while they're lying under their shelters makes him no better than Marshal.

In a moment of self-reflection, Derek realizes he should have done more to investigate the weapons plot himself. Leaving most of the evidence collection up to Sarah has placed the doubt in his mind. Had he ventured out, he could have gotten eyes on and confirmed everything he needed. Now in the field his final week, Derek has no other choice but to hope the agent comes through.

So he pushes on. Keeps up with the classes and drills. React to sniper. Linear ambush. Conduct a reconnaissance. Conduct a raid. He starts rotating the men through the leadership positions, having them take turns commanding a patrol through makeshift scenarios.

Toward the end of the week, he's exhausted his basic skills curriculum and starts implementing maneuvers used by Special Operations. Securing themselves using tight three-sixty formations, the group facing outward to cover their security while being close enough to exchange information and orders. Break contact drills with rolling suppressive fire, where the team uses a continual leapfrogging effect to move men from one end of the line to the other, thus extending their escape in that direction, while laying down a blanket of lead at the enemy.

Through rain and heat, Derek pushes them, giving them what they asked for. The men are trained to the edge of exhaustion, but with every step he teaches, there is a thirst for more.

As the sun rises on his final day with the men, all Derek knows is that a resolution waits for him back in camp. There is hope that Sarah will have somehow discovered what she needed to call in the cavalry. At the very least that she completed copying the cipher, and the two of them can escape and get the intel to codebreakers in Quantico or Langley.

The men strike their shelters and pack up. Days of intense drilling have taken their toll. No one argues heading back in, especially with such a long trek ahead of them. Their training had ventured them farther and farther out. It will take the better part of the day to get back, and Derek fully intends on making them move tactically the whole way.

They start off, Gil and Brian assuming command as they would in real-world operations. Derek walks through the woods with them, the decision made that he will leave with Sarah or without her. The agreed-upon moment has come. He has done his duty and then some. He'll hand off what he knows. Give all the intelligence that he can. Spare no detail, but his role in this insanity is over.

Time for someone else to do the cleanup.

.   .   .   .   .

Dark clouds roll in as the security team reenters Sanctuary. Between them and the wind steadily growing in strength, most of the group has already sought cover. Laughter and conversation can be heard from the chow tent. Still far off to the west, an occasional crash of thunder is loud enough to encroach over the volume of the voices.

Given the aroma of supper and the urge to get out of the weather, the men are all too eager to turn in their weapons and ground their gear. Derek drops his pack and rifle in his cabin as well, hearing the cheers go up as members of the QRF join the chow line. He wishes he had never stopped carrying the rifle with him around camp. To go back to that now, even though more prudent, would invite unwanted attention and questions. He's just grateful he hadn't stripped his leg platforms off too.

Stepping outside, he goes to join evening chow when Sarah pops out from the alleyway between the armory and Marshal's cabin. She signals him from across the clearing, a nod back behind the buildings. Derek circles around his own shack and into the tree line, bending a wide arc toward the east. She meets him two hundred meters north of the communications hub. The shed is barely visible through the forest.

"Let's make this quick," he says, twisting around to see if anyone followed. "We can link up tonight for—" When he turns back, Derek can see she is on the verge of tears. "What is it? What's the matter?"

"He knows, Derek," Sarah replies, her voice trembling. "I swear to God, he knows."

"What? Who? Marshal?"

Sarah nods. She clutches her shaking hands in front of her. "My runner," she starts, but then can't find the words.

"What about your runner, Sarah? Tell me everything. Quick."

Gathering herself, she begins again. "Last night. I was sure he was asleep. I took out my phone and . . ."

The knot in his stomach starts to tighten.

Tears stream down her face. "When I looked up, there he was, staring at me. He saw me, Derek. Saw me copying pages. Taking pictures of them. I tried to pass it off as part of the accounting, but I could tell he wasn't convinced. Then this morning, I saw him talking to Marshal. Oh God, they're going to come for me. I know it."

Behind Sarah, a deepening purple creeps into the eastern sky. "All right. All right. Let's look at this. Has Marshal said anything to you? Made any comment that would make you—"

"Goddamn it, Derek!" Sarah snaps, her voice violent and hushed at the same time. "You think I don't know? You think I could be overreacting? Every day! Every day for the last seven months he's spoken to me. Talked to me. Kissed me on my forehead. Now today, for the first time ever, he avoids me? You didn't see his face this morning, Derek. I did! It was the face of a man betrayed!"

"Okay. Okay, I get it. Just calm down."

"You don't understand. He'll go to Gil. They'll kill me once the camp is bedded down for the night, the same way they did Sebastian, Sofia, and Jimmy. We have to get out of here. Right now."

Derek looks back at the camp. He can't see anyone moving, but people could start coming out of chow any minute. The sky continues to grow dark. He clenches his jaw as his mind works through the problem. A resolution hits him at the same time he remembers that his rifle and vest are back in his cabin.

"Damn it!"

Her eyebrows furrow. "What? What is it?"

"The ledger. Your notes and phone. You still have them, right?"

"What? Yes, of course. I hid them out in the woods. The same spot where we talked last week."

Okay, at least that's working in our favor. "All right. Good. Start making your way there. I'll head back into camp and cause a distraction for us. Once you hear the commotion, make a break for the vehicle clearing. Get in the first truck you see and go."

Her mouth opens, but nothing comes out. A moment or two goes by before she can find her words. "A distraction? What are you gonna do?"

"Something stupid, but it should buy us a little time." Derek hopes that between the confusion and the coming storm, no one will notice their absence. At least not right away.

"We shouldn't separate. Let's just grab my things and go."

Derek shakes his head. "We need to slow them down. If they notice you're missing, they'll know you ran and will be on our ass. Besides, it'll be better if we split up. Greater chance that at least one of us gets out."

"I don't . . . ," she says hesitantly. Her eyes flicker about.

"Listen, I'll be fine. If I can't make it to the clearing, I'll go over land. Lose them in the woods. You just make sure you call it in as soon as you're clear. Let the HRT guys sort it out with these bastards."

"It's too risky to call," she says, shaking her head. "I told you about the potential for eyes and ears. Who knows where it might end up if I phone it in? I have to do this face-to-face, with people I trust."

"Whatever it takes, then, so long as they go down. Now get moving. Hopefully, I'll see you on the other side of this thing."

Her face actually looks relieved and then immediately pained. "I'm sorry, Derek. I'm sorry you're all mixed up in this."

"Yeah, well get me out of it and we'll call it even."

Sarah shakes her head. "Not even close. I'll see to it we do right by you. I promise."

The two turn away from each other, Sarah heading east while Derek jogs back south to the camp. Halfway there, he stoops down, grabbing handfuls of leaves and grass, still mostly dry despite the mist in the air. He packs it all into a bundle as he moves, gathering a pile the size of a softball by the time he comes out of the woods.

Looping back behind the buildings, Derek drops to his knees and draws his survival knife from its scabbard with one hand, his ferro rod with the other, and makes one strong swipe across the spine of the blade. A shower of white-hot sparks rains down onto the tinder bundle. He raises it to his lips and blows gently, puffing through the cascading smoke until the pile bursts into flame. Jumping up, Derek rushes forward to the nearest cabin.

Using the butt of his knife, he punches out a pane of glass. Derek shoves the flaming ball in through the opening and drops it to the ground. At first, the flames stay stationary, and he worries that the bundle will go out before anything else catches. Then they lick at the edge of the matted old rug covering the center of the floor. The flames spread slowly.

When they reach the oil-soaked wood of Marshal's grandfather's desk, it's engulfed in seconds. After that, it's only a few moments before the flames reach the antique clock, with similar results. Fueled by the well-oiled heirlooms, the fire rages, and smoke billows from under the eaves of the roof. Distraction accomplished, Derek smiles as he turns and rushes into the woods.

He's only a hundred yards away when chaos shatters the coming night.

25

Marshal sits on his knees before the fireball that was his home. Head bowed, he mutters gently to himself, the words lost in the roar of the flames rampaging as they envelop the old man's cabin. The cracks and pops of timber. The collapse of the roof that sends a cloud of smoke, ash, and embers into the night sky. All the while, a line of people chain buckets to the building, tossing desperate waves onto the inferno. The buckets come slower now that the shower cisterns are empty and the water has to be drawn from the river.

Even as he yells for them to speed up, Gil knows it's a lost cause. The buckets of water are Band-Aids on a sucking chest wound. The fire that has already consumed one cabin now threatens to overtake everything they built. If it spreads to the comms shack—or worse, the armory—the entire camp might be lost.

"Split the line! Split it!" Faces covered in sweat, soot, and confusion turn to look at him. "Right line, take your buckets to the armory! Get that roof soaked! Left line, head to the comms shack! The cabin is lost!"

When they don't budge, he moves among them, shoving each person in an opposite direction from the last. They finally catch on, and the group splits up the rest of the way. Once finished, he turns to the onlookers, ones who couldn't find a bucket or a place in the chain.

"There are two teams now! Get in there and fill out the lines from the river!" People scatter. He grabs Ronald and Jasper behind their necks and pulls them in close so they can hear him over the shouting. "Each of you, grab some people. Even the kids if you have to. Get some rakes and shovels and clear out the debris around the comms shack and the armory. Use your goddamn hands if need be!"

"Right," Ronald says, and the two men charge off.

Gil spins around frantically. Trying to see the next move. To order something else into action. Instead, he comes face-to-face with Marshal.

The old man's eyes are red and raw. Tears stream through the smoke stains on his cheeks. He stares at Gil but at the same time seems to look beyond him, detached from everything that is going on. His hands are clenched in tight fists, so much so that Gil can see his knuckles turning white.

"Gil," he says, almost too softly amid the crackling flames. "If you would be so kind. Go hunt down that son of a bitch."

Gil freezes at first, but then it clicks into place. In all the confusion, Gil hadn't realized that D was missing. "Now?"

Marshal's face twists with rage. "I said, hunt that motherfucking cocksucker down . . . right . . . now! I want him brought back here alive! I will strip the godless skin from his bones! That soulless bastard is mine! Do you understand me? Mine! You bring him back here or you don't come back at all!"

Time freezes. In the clouds looming overhead, flashes of lightning flicker before low, rumbling peals of thunder. The collapse of a cabin wall crashing down snaps them back to reality.

Gil nods. "All right, boss. You got it."

The lieutenant holds a hand over his head, waving it in tight circles. The members of the security team leave their places with the damage control and converge on Gil as he storms to the cinder block armory. Marjorie, her mouth hanging open, realizes where they are going and hustles to catch up. While she works at the padlock, the men look at Gil.

"Gear up," he says without making eye contact. "Derek is on the run. We're hunting tonight."

The men exchange glances, each silently asking the same question.

Thomas clears his throat. "You mean, we're going out there? After him?"

"That's right."

"Yeah, but . . . ," Henry begins. He pauses and looks at the rest before continuing, "Ain't he, like, the expert?"

"We're going out there to capture that bastard!" Gil suddenly screams, a flinch rippling through the men around him. Again, the camp quiets down. "He's one man! For fuck's sake! This ain't the movies. Gear up and let's move!"

Brian nods as he follows Marjorie into the armory and helps with the distribution. "About time we killed this piece of shit. Let's do it."

"Marge!" Gil yells to the woman.

She pokes her head out.

"Break out the NODs. It's already too dark to see out there."

She gives him a thumbs-up and heads back inside.

"Full operational kit. Gerry, you got the two four nine. Dillon, you carry the spare drum for him. Thomas and Parker, grab the three twenties and ten grenades each. Everyone else, grab two in case they run out."

The patrol force continues to outfit as Brian joins them from the armory, slapping a magazine into his M4 and pulling the charging handle back. He leans in close so that only Gil can hear him. "That's a shit ton of grenades. I thought he was just one man."

Gil stares at the fire. "I'm not stupid, and I'm not taking any chances. If we can take him alive, we will. If he gives us shit, I'm going to launch that arrogant prick straight to hell."

. . . . .

The security team stalks forward as the storm continues to close. Two teams of five advance in loose wedges like spearpoints side by side. Gil walks at the tip of the right wedge while Brian leads his on the left. Spread out with thirty yards between each man, the patrol moves forward. Gingerly. Hungrily.

They try to remember all that they've learned. Where to step. Where to look. Watch your spacing. Check your six. Scan near to far, then far to near. All the while, their hearts race. Sweat courses down their faces and backs with the understanding that they're out to kill a man so lethal it takes ten of them to do the job right.

The streaks of lightning that accompany the approaching storm do little to help. The thunder masks their footfalls, but it also hides his. They see through their night vision goggles, but each bolt momentarily blinds them. For now the hunt continues, their infrared lasers sweeping in long, thin, neon-green lines back and forth, visible only through the NODs.

The security team presses on, and Derek sees them coming.

Derek fixates on shadows moving when they should be stationary. He catches glimpses through the flashes of lightning. He's still far enough away that they can't see him, but he is moving slower than he'd like, to avoid detection. It won't be long before they catch up to him at this pace, and from the angle they are approaching, they've cut him off from the vehicles.

At the very least, he can buy Sarah some more time. After all, he trained them, and it only makes sense that it's his responsibility to stop them.

His hand caresses the grip of the .40 caliber in his holster. He has ten rounds in the clip, one more in the pipe, and another twenty combined in the two magazines on his left leg platform. Even if he lets them get within a better range, he would only expect to take one or two out in this darkness. Facing off against ten men armed to the teeth with only thirty-one rounds won't get him very far. In fact, it'll only get him dead.

Derek looks about as he slides through another hedge, low crawling over the damp ground. His mind races for an advantage. Anything that will let him vanish. If only it weren't so dark! Save for the flashes and an occasional break in the clouds to let in some moonlight, he can barely see five feet in front of his face.

Dipping into the tiniest of depressions made by an uprooted tree, he crouches and waits. The patrol is closing in. Another few minutes and they'll be right on top of him. *This. This will have to do, then.* The fallen tree acting as a bunker. He draws his pistol and slides into the space between the ground and the tree lying on its side. Steadying his breath, Derek looks through the branches and sights in on the man directly in front of him and waits for the unlucky prick to get closer.

A thunderclap erupts like a gunshot overhead, sending his hunters dropping to the ground, exactly as he'd taught them. Derek smirks at the irony. *Gave them training so good that they're gonna kill me with it.*

His thoughts turn to Michael and Kim. Fear and remorse well up inside of him. Missing his son's high school graduation. Never watching another ball game. Or even the little things like playing catch. Of never getting the chance to reconcile with his wife. Derek's heart races, and his mouth goes dry. Tears well up in the corners of his eyes.

He takes a deep breath, and just like that, the focus returns. The operator in him takes over, switching off the emotions that threaten to get him killed in favor of those that will do the killing.

After a brief period, the men hunting him get to their feet and resume their advance. Derek pulls back on his trigger, squeezing it a millimeter at a time. They continue to move in his direction, rifles at the ready. He squints his left eye and aligns his sight picture through a gap in the branches. Derek squeezes just a little tighter, waiting for the pop to surprise him as the gun goes off. Gil steps within ten yards of the tree and freezes, throwing a clenched fist overhead to halt the rest of the team.

He speaks low into his radio mouthpiece and signals to the wedge off to his left that is commanded by

Brian. Keeping that wedge moving forward, Gil then splits his own. Two men to his right branch off and start making their way around the downed tree. The other two follow Gil around the left side of the obstruction. Derek watches as they stalk past his makeshift bunker.

He eases off the trigger and lies perfectly still, even holding his breath as they brush by. As they pass, Derek smiles at the opportunity they've given him by splitting up.

Slipping out from under the fallen tree, he loops to the right flank of their picket line, positioning himself behind them. He moves silently, and the advantage is temporarily his. Adrenaline kicks in. He's not a cornered animal facing a desperate struggle for survival any longer. Now he is a hunter of the night, out for blood.

Derek trails the two men that Gil had diverted off on their own. Dodging from tree to tree, he closes the distance between them. He watches as they work their way back toward the larger group. He finds his spot behind a large boulder with a small section of somewhat level stone on top.

Shifting his left leg platform, Derek reaches into his cargo pocket and pulls out the nylon pouch. In a matter of seconds, he has screwed and strung the slingshot together. Loading a ball bearing, he draws it back, tracking the man he recognizes as Henry on the left of the duo. They separate to move around a large tree, and Derek lets fly, a sudden *thwip* filling the air.

He hears a loud smack as the bearing impacts on the tree. Henry halts while his partner continues moving around the other side, out of Derek's sight. Henry looks around and then eyes the tree. He puts a finger into the perfectly round dent in the bark and then, a moment later, spins and brings his rifle up.

The second ball bearing impacts on the side of his skull. His head ricochets off the tree before he crumples to the ground. His partner stops in his tracks. "Henry? Henry?" Derek recognizes Beets's voice.

Derek is already moving farther out to the right in a large arc. As Beets comes back around, Derek circles him, watching as he crouches to check his friend.

At the sound of breaking brush over the peals of thunder, Beets's head snaps up. Even with the NODs covering his face, Derek recognizes the sudden panic in the man as he frantically works to get his rifle aligned. He whips a throwing knife, and the blade whooshes end over end before sinking deep into Beets's left thigh. Derek is on him before the man can scream, covering Beets's mouth and driving a second knife through his throat so hard that the point pops out of the back of his neck.

Working the blade left and right, Derek waits until Beets goes limp, then lets his body drop. The throwing knife in the neck stuck and the one in his thigh pinned under the body, Derek leaves them and draws his survival knife. Henry's unconscious form is right beside Beets, and Derek presses the man's face into the dirt and rams his knifepoint into his neck. Warm blood splatters like rain on his face and clothes.

Rushing, Derek replaces his knife and strips the body of its plate carrier. Moving with trained, deliberate actions. Slow is smooth. Smooth is fast. At the same time, he feels the heightened senses that combat brings. The energy coursing through his body as his adrenaline takes everything up a notch. The volatile mix of fear and excitement. Somewhere, recessed at the back of his mind, there's a part of him that missed these feelings.

Carrier on, buttstock to his shoulder, he moves on in a crouched posture. He scans the woods with the pilfered NODs as he hurriedly angles toward where the security team should be approaching. Up ahead, a gentle rise stretches before him. Derek rushes up the side and leans against a tree for cover. A quick look reveals Gil and the remnants of his wedge a hundred yards away, moving directly toward him. The other wedge follows fifty yards behind them.

Dropping to a squat, back against the tree, Derek takes a deep breath before rolling out to his left and flopping onto his stomach. He lines his target up with the infrared laser and flicks his selector switch to burst, then squeezes the trigger.

The rounds belch from the muzzle as gunpowder and smoke fill his nostrils. The artificial thunder rivals that of nature's above. As the man he sighted on falls, Derek rakes his fire across the wedge nearest to him and then back in the opposite direction to fire at the wedge beyond. The security team dives for cover. Thirty rounds are gone in an instant. As he changes out his magazine, the men from Gil's wedge return fire.

Rounds smack into the trees while others whiz overhead. Derek slides down behind the small embankment and moves farther to his left before finding another thick tree. When he pops up again, he is at a nearly forty-five-degree angle to the QRF. The farther wedge fires at where Derek just was as they dash forward to join Gil's. The man he shot crawls back for cover. Derek fires at the men of the farther wedge as they already forget their training to avoid extended periods of exposure.

Another man falls, screaming and clutching his arm. The patrol reorients on his muzzle flashes and returns fire while Derek squeezes his trigger again and again. The cacophony of gunfire fills the woods. Tracer rounds exchange in the night, illuminated like meteors in the pale green of the night vision goggles.

His bolt locks to the rear, and Derek sinks down behind cover to reload.

The space around him erupts. Rounds whistle and ricochet as they tear up the terrain. The uninterrupted fire means Gerry has arrived with the SAW, releasing a chain of belt-fed death. Crawling across the ground away from the onslaught, Derek finds new cover behind a medium rock formation.

The ridge off to his right from where he'd just come would be the hardest to assault. If the security team were to follow the drills he'd taught them, they'd assess the terrain and try to flank him to his left, where the tree line is more open and the ground more level. Rising to a crouch, Derek sprints to intercept the likely flanking maneuver. He's gone ten feet when a concussive blast slams into his back and hurls him to the ground, an explosion of dirt, debris, and shattered branches raining down from above.

Ears ringing, Derek rolls onto his back just in time to see a tree disintegrate in a fiery blast as the earth shakes below. Continuing the roll, he covers his head as flaming limbs and hunks of wood shower down, then pushes himself up and stumbles into a run.

Grenades explode all around him, none of them direct hits, but the concussive blasts throw him to the ground again and again. One after another, geysers of earth spray up and trees uproot. Boulders that have stood for millions of years shatter into a spray of jagged shrapnel.

A blast hits off to his right, near enough to send him flying backward, losing his NODs in the process. His eyes well up from a fresh, burning pain. Pinching them shut, he grits his teeth until it becomes manageable. Opening them, Derek sees his right pants leg peppered with a dozen holes and bits of tree embedded in it. He forces himself back to his feet and hobbles off, feeling the wetness of his blood soaking into the tattered remains of his cargo pants.

Two more grenades explode behind him. Another shower of dirt. Limping. Panting. Derek tries desperately to get out of their kill zone. Another explosion erupts behind him, the concussion throwing him into a nearby tree. His world goes dark.

.   .   .   .   .

Gil scans the broken landscape, moving his eyes past any fires that come into view to avoid washing out his night vision. Clusters of them burn among the shattered trees and rocks. A tendril of smoke rises from the muzzle of his rifle. Slowly, the crickets and night creatures pick up their chorus, adding to the wounded groans of pain. A light rain begins to fall as the thunder booms, nearly on top of them now.

After some time, the radio squawks in his ear as Brian keys up. "Think we got him?"

Gil keys back. "Don't know."

"Hard to imagine anyone living through that. Want me to take my guys forward and check it out?"

To his right, Parker works to get a bandage tied around Brandon's wounded leg. "Who's hit from your team?"

"Billy got hit in the forearm. Dillon is patching him up now."

Gil surveys the rest of the area. "All right. Once they're done, have them come to my position and grab Brandon. The two wounded can help each other back to camp while Dillon pulls security for them. The rest of us will check out the impact zone."

"Roger."

"Let me know when you're ready."

A few moments pass while Brian relays the orders to his team. "Ready," the radio crackles.

"We move on line. Go," Gil replies.

The remainder of the security team closes the distance between one another as they enter the killing field. It's a collection of mangled branches, deep craters, and broken stones. They sweep their rifles at every shadow. Every flicker of the burning limbs. They look at every possible cover. Nothing.

Brian sidles up to Gil, letting his rifle drop against his chest. "Either we vaporized that son of a bitch or he ain't here."

"I doubt the first. There'd be body parts," Gil says, his mind flashing back to that day in Iraq.

"Here! I've got him!" Thomas shouts. "Come here quick!"

The rest of the team rushes farther into the trees.

"Over here!"

When they find Thomas, he's standing behind a thick pine with his rifle trained on Derek. Gil moves the rest of the men into a position to cover them and then approaches with Brian. Gil drops to a knee, quickly ripping the rifle away from the unconscious man. Next, he unhooks Derek's web belt and leg platforms, taking away his pistol and knives. Brian helps him get the plate carrier off. Lastly, Gil strips the sling from the rifle and binds Derek's hands in front of him.

Standing up, he keys the radio button on his chest. "Henry. Beets. Sound off." When they don't answer, he repeats the transmission.

"You don't think he got them, do you?"

Grimacing, Gil spits to the side. "We split off earlier. He must have jumped them then."

"You sure? Maybe they're just—"

The team leader points at the plate carrier, specifically the radio button. "We never gave D any of our tactical radios, just the Motorolas. He took this off one of them, and since they both ain't here . . ."

"Motherfucker!" Brian screams, kicking Derek in the gut.

The man groans as he starts to come around.

Gil holds up a hand. "Save it. Marshal wants him back alive and in one piece."

"To hell with that!" Parker says with murder in his eyes.

"Trust me," Gil says. "No one wants to plug this asshole more than I do, but he ain't getting off that easy. He answers to Marshal, sure, but then we'll each get our turn with him. That's when we settle our scores. Understood?"

They answer with nods and murmurs of agreement. Gil turns and unzips his pants, looking down at Derek.

Derek becomes more alert as urine soaks his face and hair. The men of the security team laugh.

Gil zips back up. "Get this piece of shit on his feet."

"Rain's picking up. Think we can leave the fires to it?" Brian asks.

"Yeah, leave 'em. Let's move."

They collect the gear and their prisoner. It doesn't take more than a few minutes of searching before they find Henry's and Beet's bodies. They drag their fallen with them back toward camp, at a certain point catching up to the wounded, arriving just as the skies open in an outright downpour.

Giving orders for Derek to be taken to the cinder block outbuilding, Gil and the rest walk into the clearing. The cabin is still smoking, but otherwise, the fire is out. People mill around, even with the rain, unsure what to do next. When they see the hurt members of the team, several rush over to help. Cries go up at the sight of the two dead men.

Marshal storms over.

"Well?" the old man asks.

Gil smirks. "We got him, boss."

"Dead?"

"Alive. Brian and the others are taking him up to the cinder block building now."

Marshal pulls Gil into a tight embrace. "My boy. Oh, my boy. Thank you. Thank God for you. Bring him here. I'm gonna kill that bastard."

Looking around, Gil takes the old man by his arm and leads him out of earshot. "Boss, you think it might be better to keep him up there? We're against time now. If we're going to stick to the plan, we've got to get the evacuations under way and work all through the night. You really want him seeing all that going on?"

"He won't be able to see anything when I gouge his eyes out."

"You want everyone seeing you torture this bastard out in the open? To hear his screams? We need them to stay focused. We can't give them a reason to doubt you. Let's go up there and do what we need to do while they pack. We can have everyone en route by sunrise."

Some of the tension goes out of the old man. He puts a hand on Gil's shoulder and bows his head. "You're a good man, Gil. And right, of course. Order the evacuation of all nonessential personnel to Pennsylvania. Everyone except the lookouts. Pull them in to replace the losses on the team."

Marshal smiles the false smile of a politician. "Once the main body has gone, we'll bring the matériels down and pack them for shipment. It's taken forever to accumulate even this much. I won't leave it behind."

"Sounds good," Gil replies and then after a moment adds, "You gonna be okay, boss?"

The old man's smile fades, and he sighs. "We are all tested, my boy. This . . . betrayal will be added on to the larger tab. 'And evil will befall you in the latter days; because ye will do evil in the sight of the Lord, to provoke Him to anger through the work of your hands.' Deuteronomy, chapter thirty-one, verse twenty-nine. That son of a bitch is about to have his come down upon him."

26

Kelly sits near the end of the bar, alone as usual. Despite being an FBI agent and a bachelor in the greatest city in the world, he couldn't get a date lately to save his life. Another round of laughter behind him. He throws a glance their way. Professionals out after work. They're a little younger than he is, but not by much. He turns back to his beer and scans the TVs broadcasting baseball and hockey games.

In the mirror behind the bar, he catches a glimpse of one of the women in the group standing up from the table. A moment later, she's next to him. The woman is shorter than he is and wearing a black pantsuit. Her blond hair falls to the middle of her back. As she signals the bartender, Kelly perks up.

"Drinks after work?"

She eyes him warily before giving a polite yet even smile. "Yes, it's one of my coworkers' birthdays."

"Excellent. Happy birthday to them. I'm Kelly," he says, leaning over and extending his hand.

"Brittany," she replies with a quick shake.

"Brittany. Pretty name. Can I buy you that drink?"

"I'm ordering for the table, but thanks anyway."

"That's all right," Kelly replies. "How about the next one?"

"I don't want to be rude, but this is kind of a group thing tonight."

He forces out a tight smile despite the crush of rejection. "Sure. No problem. Nice meeting you."

"You too." And with a flip of her hair, she turns back to her table.

Kelly upends his drink and waves at the bartender.

A moment later, his cell phone buzzes. Kelly digs it out of his pants pocket, a fresh text message on the home screen.

Agent Scarsboro?

Kelly looks around the bar and then back at the screen. His eyebrows furrow as he takes a swig of his drink. Setting it down, Kelly thumbs open his phone. **Who's this?**

We've never met, but we're on the same team. Working on the same thing.

It takes him a second, but then it clicks. **How did you get this number?**

We have a mutual acquaintance. Upstate.

Kelly feels his stomach sink. He still hadn't managed to tie in with the ATF and verify the agent they had in place. No one in that agency knew he was looking for the woman yet, which meant no one there had his number. Two people were in possession of it, and they were both upstate. If it had been passed along . . . I need authentication.

He said to tell you
Designated Hitter.

His immediate apprehension jumps up a few notches. Only Derek, himself, and Emily knew the CI code name, the latter for emergency purposes in case she had to identify herself to Derek. The circumstances with which it ended up in the hands of an unknown could mean any number of conclusions. Highly irregular at best. Catastrophic at worst.

What's going on? he frantically types back.

There's been a development.
I'll fill you in but not over the
phone. I'm coming in. He
said I could trust you. Can
you meet me?

What about DH?

The ellipsis seems to drag on for an eternity. We got separated. Can we meet? I'll explain then.

He takes a hefty swallow from his glass. His plan to pull this operation over to the FBI and ride it all the way to a counterterrorism promotion seems like a fading dream. If he wants to have any chance at making it a reality, he has to see this through. Yes. Where and when?

Central Park. 3 a.m.

Kelly looks at his watch. 11:47 p.m. Why then?

Won't be back until then. At
the earliest.

He sighs, realizing it's going to be a late night. Sure.
Where in the park?

Azalea pond. In the Ramble.
South of the Seventy-Ninth
Street traverse.

Ok. I'll find it.

There is a long pause before she texts again. When
the words come over his screen, the sinking in his
stomach turns into a straight gut punch.

Come alone. Don't
speak to anyone. Bureau
compromised.

He drains the rest of his drink and leaves the bar.
A cab brings him uptown, where he finds an all-night
coffee shop. Ordering breakfast and cup after cup of
black coffee, Kelly sits and contemplates what this
could mean. If the texts are coming from the undercover agent Derek mentioned, then one of dozens of
different variables involves the very real possibility
that Kelly's friend is dead.

And what of the last text? The Bureau being compromised. Which bureau? The ATF? The FBI? Both?
The different scenarios play on repeat while time slows
to a crawl.

More than once, he works through his own con-

tingencies. She had used the CI code name as a veri-
fier, but that didn't ensure she was actually who he'd
be meeting in the park. Even Derek would be the first
to tell Kelly that everyone breaks eventually. Could
his friend have been compromised? And if so, what
would Kelly be walking into as a result?

It wouldn't be difficult to call in backup, even at
this hour, but that would let the cat out of the bag. The
operation would have to go through channels from
then on, out of his control. That meant everyone stepping in. Taking credit for his work.

Worse was if it amounted to nothing. If this whole
thing was a bust, or small fries, the level of professional embarrassment would be insurmountable. In
the end, he comes back to her last message. If this is
as serious as she'd made it out to be, then maybe the
cavalry being called in would be anything but reinforcement. Better to play it straight, see what she has,
and then go from there. It's the only way to cover all
his bases.

At two thirty, he pays his bill and makes his way to
the park. Kelly navigates the twists and turns of the
narrow paths in the section known as the Ramble, a
dense stand of trees north of the lake the Loeb Boat-
house sits on. He finds a bench not far from the water and sits down a few minutes after three. The air
is still, save for the humidity and crickets. He regrets
wearing a sport coat to the bar, even though it makes
concealing his sidearm that much easier.

Waiting impatiently, Kelly looks up and down the
path at the slightest noise. He checks his phone. Then
his watch. Then his phone again. At ten after, he sends
a text: Here. He doesn't get a reply. At twenty-three after, he takes out his phone to text again. That's when

he hears the breaking of brush behind him. Kelly twists to his left.

A woman steps out of the woods dressed in black running pants and a dark, long-sleeve runner's shirt despite the summer heat. A marathoner's belt stretches around her waist, two small water bottles resting in their sleeves on either hip. Her hair is tucked underneath a black baseball cap. She checks the path around her, forward and back, as she makes her way over to the bench.

"Agent Scarsboro?" she says, sitting down at the far end.

"You're Sarah?"

She looks at him and gives the faintest of smiles. "The one and only."

"I need to see credentials."

Sarah holds his gaze for a moment before breaking off and reaching toward the zippered pouch on the front of her belt. "Of course."

Kelly's hand drifts to the edge of his blazer and runs down its length. He stops when his fingers brush his belt underneath. Sarah's eyes flick to his hand and back, so quickly that the movement is nearly imperceptible. A moment later, she produces a leather billfold and hands it over.

Kelly takes it with his off hand and flips it open. An FBI gold shield and identification card greet him. "I thought you were ATF."

Sarah shakes her head while nonchalantly reaching an empty hand back out. "Afraid not. Derek came to that conclusion on his own, and it never seemed necessary to break my cover."

Flipping it closed, Kelly suppresses his dismay. So much for a joint-agency operation. He hands the credentials back. "What's going on? What do you mean, the Bureau is compromised?"

She sighs, returning the billfold to the pouch. "Just what it sounds like. Major players are involved in this thing. It's why I couldn't just go to the office. I don't know who's working for them. Once they know I'm out . . ."

"And Derek?"

"I honestly don't know. Everything happened so fast. I was compromised, and we had to make a run for it. He risked himself to help me get away. We were supposed to link up, but then a gunfight broke out. He had said not to wait for him, so when I heard the shots, I took off."

Swallowing, Kelly feels a wave of guilt wash over him. The man's last message had warned of a potential attack, but without the details, Kelly couldn't move. Now it feels like he should have forgone the operation and pulled them all out.

His mind jumps to Emily. He would need to extract her, but for now, she was an hour away from the campsite. He could get word to her as soon as he had settled things here. "I need more details."

Sarah looks around, then says, "I will, but not now and definitely not here. We gotta move on this. Fast."

Kelly nods. "All right. How do you want to play it?"

"I've got to get out of sight. A safe house. Hotel or something like that. Then we can work on figuring out how to get what I know to the right people. Set up safeguards for me coming in. Officially."

"Yeah. That makes sense. Any idea who you can turn to?"

"A couple, yeah. I doubt they could be mixed up in

this. What about you? You have anyone you know? Anyone you talked to about this already that we could go to?"

"My SAC has cursory knowledge, but no details. He gives me a lot of latitude," Kelly replies, shaking his head. "I was running DH on my own. Kind of a side op. Developing him as a confidential informant. Neither of us expected it to turn into this."

Sarah grimaces. A short-lived, pained expression. He can't imagine what she's been put through. She inches closer and grabs one of his hands in both of hers.

"I need your help to get messages to the right people. Derek said I could trust you. Said you were the one that could act as the intermediary. Someone outside my division might be better positioned to make the connection we need."

"Of course. I can—"

Rapid footfalls crush gravel on the path. Sarah twists and looks up. "Shit! Quick!" she says and then closes the final distance between them, pressing her lips to his. Kelly's eyes go wide, but he catches on just as a jogger comes around the bend. He folds into the kiss, running his hands up and around her back. The jogger trots past them, but even after he's gone, she doesn't pull away.

Instead, she kisses him further, their mouths and tongues working in heated concert with each other. Sarah grabs his jacket collar tightly and pulls him closer. When their mouths separate, she exhales deeply, shuddering as she does so.

"God . . . that was amazing. I haven't been kissed in a year."

Kelly smiles. "Well, you certainly made up for it." She laughs, a breaking of tension. He laughs with her.

"You know, if you want to, you can come back to my place. Stay there while we sort this whole thing out."

She raises an eyebrow at him. "Is that so? It's certainly tempting."

"Let's get you there, then. Make sure you're—" A sharp pinch in his left side is immediately followed by a spreading wetness across his belly. Kelly looks down at his stomach and sees blood soaking into his dress shirt and spilling down onto the bench. The hilt of a blade juts from his stomach, her hand wrapped around the grip.

Kelly looks up. His eyes go wide, and his mouth drops open.

Sarah lurches up onto her knees, left hand grabbing his right wrist to stop him from drawing his sidearm. She pulls the blade out and jams it into his neck. Kelly's hands go to his throat. He coughs and chokes on his own blood, gasps as his eyes cloud over.

He slumps forward.

Sarah catches him by the shoulders and rocks him backward, easing him down to the bench. She turns him onto his side so that his back is to the path and then props his legs up. Kelly's blood drips down onto the leaves and pavement below.

Running into the wood line, Sarah quickly strips off her outer garments, revealing a pair of shorts and a sports bra. She wraps the hat, pants, knife, and ankle scabbard in the shirt and then puts the marathoner belt back on. Moving a little farther down the path through the trees, she pops out and jogs with the bundle underneath her arm to the lake, stopping next to a trash can.

Taking the knife from the bundle, Sarah walks to the edge of the water. She whips the blade out into the center of the lake and then rinses her hands. Back at the trash can, she reaches into the zippered belt pouch and pulls out a lighter. Stuffing the garments into the bin, she draws one of her water bottles and sprays a steady stream of lighter fluid over the contents. Striking the wheel on the lighter, she touches the flame to the clothes, and the fire bursts to life. She drops the lighter in the bin, then jogs off as the flames spread and smoke.

Just a woman on an early-morning run. A drunk sleeping it off on a bench. Some kids setting fire to a trash can. Another summer night in New York City.

．　．　．　．　．

The sound of a car door closing picks Kim's head up from the kitchen sink. Wiping her hands, she glances at the clock on the microwave—7:36 a.m. The doorbell ringing adds to her curiosity. *Who could possibly be here this early?*

Crossing into the foyer, Kim yells up the stairs before answering, "Michael! Make sure you brush your teeth. And you'd better have those shoes on! We're leaving soon."

Opening the door, she finds a woman standing before her wearing a black pantsuit with a white dress shirt underneath. Wide aviator sunglasses cover her face. Her auburn hair is pulled back into a tight bun.

"Can I help you?" Kim asks.

"My apologies for the early hour, ma'am, but I'm afraid this couldn't wait." The woman reaches into her jacket and produces a credential billfold. She flips it over to reveal a badge and an identification card. "Special Agent Kittle, FBI. May I come in?"

Kim puts a hand to her heart. "Oh my God. He's not . . ."

"No. No, I'm sorry. I didn't mean to alarm you. Nothing like that." The woman looks around while she stows her badge.

"Oh." Kim sighs. "Oh, thank God. Please come in." She steps back and then closes the door after the woman enters. "Can I get you some coffee or anything?"

"I appreciate the offer, ma'am, but no, thank you. I've got a bit of a drive after this, and coffee tends to go right through me."

"Right. I know the feeling. So, what can I do for you?"

Pulling off her glasses, the woman stuffs them in a pants pocket before answering, "Is your son still home?"

Kim squints ever so slightly. "Yes. He's upstairs getting ready for school. What does—"

"Can you ask him to come down, please, ma'am? This pertains to both of you."

She tilts her head but then complies with the request. Turning to the stairs, Kim yells out, "Michael, come down, please!" Turning back, Kim says, "I think you should tell me what—"

The agent has her gun drawn and leveled at Kim's chest. In her left hand are a set of handcuffs. She holds them out. "Put them on. Tight."

"What the hell is this?"

Feet on the upstairs floorboards can be heard walking toward the stairs.

"Ma'am, I swear if you don't do exactly as you're told from here on out, the last thing your boy is going to see is me splattering your brains on the wall. Just before I do the same to him. You understand?"

Kim's lower lip trembles as she reaches out with a

shaking hand and takes the cuffs. "Just . . . just don't hurt him," she says as she puts them on.

"Don't give me a reason to."

Michael appears at the top of the stairs and starts to come down.

The agent hides her pistol under her jacket, but keeps it leveled at Kim.

"Mom, it's too early to leave. Who's this?"

"I work with your dad, Michael. I'm going to take you to see him."

The boy starts to smile, but then he sees his mom's face and, a second later, the handcuffs. "Mom? What's going on?"

"Nothing, sweetie. Just listen to what the woman has to say, all right?"

The agent pats Kim down. Pulling Kim's cell phone out of her pocket, the agent sets it and Kim's Apple Watch on the steps, then inclines her head. "Get the door."

Kim does as she's told, pulling the door open with bound hands. A black Lincoln Town Car sits in her driveway, the back door already ajar.

"Get in," the agent commands.

As they approach the car, Michael becomes emotional. "Mommy, where are we going? Mommy? Mommy, I'm scared."

"Just do as the woman says, Michael. It'll be okay. Mommy's here."

He climbs into the car first. Kim follows, immediately noticing that the back seat is sectioned off from the front of the vehicle with a cage. A bucket sits on the floor on Michael's side, and a lunch-pail-size cooler sits on hers. Kim twists around, but the door slams in her face.

Outside the car, the agent holsters her pistol, returns her aviators to her face, and then takes off her jacket. When she gets into the driver's seat, she tosses the jacket onto the passenger side. Turning the engine over, the woman sighs and runs a hand across her brow, then takes a large pull from an iced coffee.

"Here's the deal," says the woman, turning to face them. "I'm only going to say this once. No questions. No complaints. No asking what's going to happen to you and all that. You follow my orders when they're given and do as you're told, you'll be fine. You screw with me, and I'll kill your kid on the side of the road and then do the same to you."

Michael starts to cry. Tears stream from Kim, but she manages to stay resolute.

"We've got a long drive with no stops," the agent continues. "You need to relieve yourselves, use the bucket. You get hungry or thirsty, use the cooler. And keep him quiet."

The agent throws the car into gear, and they pull out of the driveway. Kim reaches for her son, draping her arms over the boy and pulling him in close.

*   *   *   *   *

With the second part of her plan accomplished, Sarah works to bring her heart rate down. The adrenaline is making her nauseous. On the flip side, it's helping her fight off the fatigue from the overnight drive to the city. Between that, the rendezvous in the park, and now this, she is becoming increasingly exhausted, and there's still seven hours of driving ahead of her. She takes another sip of her coffee.

Fucking Gil. That asshole had really made a mess of things this time, and of course, she is the only one who can smooth it back out. The plan had been simple. Once they came back in from the field, Sarah would lure Derek away under the pretense of being compromised. At the vehicle clearing, Brady, Hunter, and the other lookouts were waiting to ambush him. If they could take Derek alive, they would. Then they could interrogate him to confirm everything that he had passed on. If not, they'd kill him and end the whole threat right then and there.

Of course, no one could have anticipated that Derek would go back and try to burn down the entire camp. When she saw the orange glow through the trees and heard the screams, Sarah knew what had happened. The sustained gunfire that later followed told her that the capture portion of her plan was screwed. Hopefully, Gil and his team actually put their training to use and filled that bastard full of holes.

Whatever the end result, she's still the only one who can tie up the loose ends down here. Only Sarah could get the details on who Derek had been working with. Only Sarah could get close enough to Scarsboro to silence him. The men created this mess. They needed a woman to clean it up for them.

Pulling out her cell phone, she calls the bar. This early in the morning, it takes more than twenty rings for the man upstairs to make his way down from the apartment and answer. The gruff greeting tells Sarah he'd probably been asleep for only a few hours.

"It's Sarah," she says. "Tell them I've finished the two tasks on my to-do list. I'm on my way back up, plus two." She hangs up before the man has a chance to reply.

No matter the outcomes, the damage from Derek's infiltration had been done, and the camp had no choice but to evacuate as a result. These measures were buying them time, nothing more. There was no way they could remain at the logging site. Who knows how much information was passed besides the notes? If Marshal and Gil had followed the plan, they would have already started evacuating. That said, the radios would be the last thing they broke down, to keep communication lines open for as long as possible.

Behind her, the boy whimpers, and the mother whispers to him reassuringly. She'd keep them for leverage, ensuring his compliance, but in the end, their fates were sealed.

A twitch of remorse. How many innocent children has this government slaughtered? How many have they dropped bombs on overseas? Sarah knows the answer all too well. She used to be part of making it happen. Now because of Derek's involvement, another innocent child will need to die. Another casualty of war.

Even more egregious is the treatment of the children back here. Letting them starve. Running up school lunch debts while billionaires line their pockets with tax breaks. Cutting food stamps so they go hungry and cry, clutching their bloated bellies. What about locking them in cages? Letting children, who gives a damn where they're from, die cold and alone on concrete floors after being ripped from their parents.

Marshal. The old man was a means to an end. All the speeches and sermons, they were exhausting to her, but at least they brought in the support needed. If the battle were to come, Sarah would need soldiers. Marshal was a recruiter and general all in one. He would light the fuse, but it was she that arranged the explosives in the first place. She and those above her who had connected them. Sarah would see this through, no matter the means necessary. A few sermons were worth the price of retribution. A new order was coming.

With any war, there are casualties. Innocents included. If this is what it takes to show the rest of the country—hell, the rest of the world—that the indigent of America are no longer going to suffer needlessly, then so be it. The tree of liberty must be refreshed from time to time with the blood of patriots and tyrants.

27

Sounds slowly come back to him. Arbitrary things. Scrapes and bumps. They resolve into muffled notes, like a mute shoved into a trombone. Notes become voices. A sensation of swaying washes over him. Derek feels dizzy as his eyes flutter. The voices become clearer. There are more than a few people speaking in the room. He can hear a Zippo lighter flipping open. His vision starts to sharpen.

Crates and boxes hang from the ceiling around him. Two sets of boots stand off by a door, defying gravity. His view shifts a little to the left, then slowly back to the right. Creaking wood synchronizes with his drifting gaze. The room is musty and smells like compost. Large lights on stands, the kind you might use when working in your garage at night, burn bright and cast misshapen shadows. Judging by the crickets outside and absence of thunder, he estimates at least an hour or two has passed since the gunfight. Maybe more.

Another pair of boots walks right past his face, the body stretching away from him in the wrong direction. His knuckles scrape the roof. Derek stretches to look at his hands. Tight around his wrists are a pair of handcuffs. The ceiling looks like floorboards.

Everything clicks. Derek pulls his chin to his chest and sees his legs stretching upward. A thick chain is wrapped around his boots, the other end around the rafters that he's hanging from. The sight of his tattered pants reminds his body of the pain, the dozen shrapnel holes crying out all at once. After the initial wave, it helps to clear his head. The room rights itself as he looks about.

Derek's head drops back down. The boots clomp their way over. Two sets move off to either side of him while the third grabs a wooden folding chair and drags it across the floor. He begins to sway faster, drifting farther to each side as the men shove him back and forth. His head throbs. The rocking works to make him even more nauseous than he already is. Gil's face finally pops into view—upside down, as it were—as the man sits in the chair.

"Well, did you have a good rest, big guy?" The sarcasm is thick in Gil's voice. Others in the room laugh, including voices behind him that Derek hadn't seen.

"Go fuck yourself," he responds.

A chorus of mocking jeers comes back at him.

Gil laughs along with them. "See, that's what I like about you, D. You're surrounded and swinging from the ceiling, but still being hard and shit. The ultimate badass, right, boys? No way we redneck yokels could ever live up to this walking legend."

"That's right. We're just good for bar fights and banging meth heads," a voice adds. Derek's pretty sure it's Dillon.

Gil keeps laughing. "Right! Right! Not like John

Rambo here. Come on, Rambo, tell us how insignificant we are again."

Sighing, Derek begins preparing himself for what's to come. Brick after brick starts to fall in place. "You know, if we're going to do a John comparison, I was always more partial to Clark than Rambo." he says, swinging slightly.

"Cute, D. Real cute. Now—"

"You know who else was pretty good? John McClane. Nakatomi Plaza, am I right?"

"All right," Gil says, gritting his teeth.

"Wait! I forgot about John Wick. That boy can shoot. How about him? Think I match up?"

The men in the room laugh with Derek, not at him.

Gil flashes a scathing glare, and they cease immediately. "You think you got jokes, motherfucker, but the joke's on you. What? You really think we're not gonna check out the bank that you want to drop your money in? You stupid son of a bitch. You think we're that dumb? That we're gonna just let you waltz right into our world?"

Gil leans over the chairback, staring down into Derek's eyes. "This up here is our country. Our people. Ain't it convenient that a week before you arrive, a new girl starts as a teller there? We were on her since her first day. Hell, Brady's been following her for weeks now.

"After we went to work on her, she sold you out quick. Not only you but your boy downstate. Gave us your code name so we could authenticate. We got people on the way to him right now, asshole."

Derek manages to keep his face calm, but inwardly, panic begins to rise. If they had figured out Emily's cover, not only was she more than likely dead, but the threat to Kelly was genuine as well.

Leaning back, Gil pulls out a can of dip and puts a plug in his lower lip. Spitting to the side, he folds his arms over the top of the chair and rests his chin on them. "Let me tell you something you probably already know, D. You're dead. Ain't no way you're walking out of here. We've already got a ditch picked out for you."

"Yeah, it's the trench under the outhouse." This comes from Brian. A few men quickly chuckle, but the tone has shifted in the room.

"The manner in which you die," Gil goes on, "well, that's up to you. I won't lie and say this is gonna be easy. You killed two of us. Shot two more. You've got to atone for how you did Beets and Henry. But if you work with me, tell me what I want to know, I'll see to it we put you out before throwing you in that trench. You give me the runaround, and I swear on everything that's holy I will personally drown you in our shit."

Derek takes in a deep, cleansing breath. The wall steadily rises, nearly in place now. He slowly exhales. "I say again, go fuck yourself."

Their eyes lock momentarily, and Derek can see a viciousness in the other man's stare. Gil gets up and stalks over to the opposite side of the room. Derek can hear him rustling about in a container before the man returns. He crouches down in front of Derek's face.

"You're not gonna talk."

"That's what I'm telling you. You can do whatever you want. You ain't getting shit outta me."

Gil shakes his head. "Nah, you don't understand,

D. I wasn't asking that time. I was telling you." In a flash, Gil digs the plug out from under his lip. He forces the wad of chewing tobacco into Derek's mouth. Before Derek can spit it out, the man wraps duct tape around his skull. Once done, Gil tosses the tape aside and then rams his fist into Derek's stomach. The other men join in, taking turns punching him in the back, the chest, the kidneys. At a certain point, the rope keeping him suspended slackens. Kicks and stomps rain down the moment after he crashes to the floor.

Someone throws on a radio that blasts death metal as high as the volume will go. Periods of intermittent violence combined with varying degrees of lucidity continue over the next several hours. Through it all, Derek stands behind the mental wall, his back pressed against it, pushing with all his might to keep his separation from tumbling over. After the beating, the men leave him crumpled on the floorboards, sweating and bleeding, gasping for air. He can hear them laughing at low points in the songs. The smell of scotch fills his nostrils.

Soon he detects it on their breaths as well. They rip the tape off his head—Derek had long since swallowed the plug of tobacco—and cover it with a sack. Laying him over a crate, the security team pins down his arms and legs. As the water starts to flow, they scream obscenities at him. Rail against his murder of their friends. Demand what he reported to the FBI. Derek throws up, water and the tobacco spilling out of him. They roll him over and let him get it all out, only to put him right back in place for another round.

Behind his wall, he finds other places to put his mind. People from times of happiness. His honeymoon with Kim. Holding Michael in the maternity ward. After another bucket, he recalls the first time he was waterboarded in SERE school. The instructors then had been impressed with his endurance. His ability to separate from both the physical and psychological interrogation. That natural talent had led to his eventual return. Once the student, now the teacher.

Derek smiles as a thought of his dad pops to the forefront. The old bastard's abuse is what taught Derek to separate in the first place. He can't help but laugh at the irony. *Thanks, Dad.* The reaction enrages the men around him even more.

He can't say for how long or how many iterations they continue. Derek goes in and out of consciousness a few times. On some of those occasions, they bring him back. At others, they seem content to take their breaks. At least once, they string him back up and douse him with more buckets of water. A car battery with jumper cables attached is applied, giving him fits of shocks.

"*Lethal Weapon*!" he can hear Gil scream. "I love that movie!"

When he is awake, Derek does his best to detach himself. To find his wall and stay behind it. He doesn't fight. There's no point to fighting. With every groan. Every scream. Every blistering flare of pain, Derek works to get back to that removal. His tolerance is higher than most, but he knows more than anyone that the well runs dry eventually.

Lying back on the floor, someone in the room calls out, "Pliers! Get some pliers!" Laughing and cavorting abounds as the men tear apart whatever storeroom they're in to look for the tool.

When they return, Brian delivers a punch to Derek's stomach that curls him into a ball. The wind knocked out of him, he is easily maneuvered back atop a crate.

Gil puts a knee on his chest while the others hold his mouth open. "I'm really going to enjoy this."

Latching the pliers against a tooth, Gil starts yanking back. Derek writhes and screams. The men shout in his face, scotch-laden spittle showering him as the taste of metal and blood swirls in his mouth. When the tooth finally rips free, Gil holds it high. The men cheer and pass it around while Derek rolls off the crate and crashes to the ground. He spits gobs of blood onto the wood.

He's put back on the box. The men are resuming their positions when the door to the room opens. Daylight splays across the floor, backlighting the figure standing in the doorway. The radio cuts off. Slowly, the man comes forward. The tension on Derek eases up. He's lifted and placed upright in a chair. His head hangs heavily, his face bruised and streaked with blood. The position sends shivers of pain through his body, every inch of him battered and worn. Another chair is placed before him.

Marshal sits down.

For a long time, he just stares at Derek. His face is still covered in soot, save for the lines where tears have streaked through it. The old man's eyes are bloodshot, the bags underneath them puffy and purple. Yet they are alive with barely contained rage.

When he speaks, his tone is disturbingly soft and level. "'You are of your father, the devil, and your will is to do your father's desires. He was a murderer from the beginning, and has nothing to do with the truth, because there is no truth in him. When he lies, he speaks out of his own character, for he is a liar and the father of lies.' John, chapter eight, verse forty-four."

The old man leans forward. "A liar and a murderer, Derek. Not even a tool of the devil. His spawn. That's what you are. That you would come in here. Accept our welcome. Our hospitality. Take the money that we could use to feed and clothe ourselves while selling us out to the very demons we wish to be liberated from." He pauses for a long time. "Deceiver," he says and then spits in Derek's face.

Reaching back behind him, the old man produces Derek's survival knife. He holds the blade up in a trembling hand. "I want nothing more than to carve you up. To string you up and disembowel you so that you can die smelling your own guts as they dangle around your face. You've smelled gut wounds before, right? Horrible stench. My friend Eric died that way. Artillery shrapnel ripped him in half. And when the sphincter releases? Absolutely putrid."

Marshal points the knife at Derek's chest. "I can think of no other end quite so fitting for a wretch like yourself than choking on the foul stench of your own being. That will be your fate, Derek. I will see to it, but for now, we're going to wait. You see, I just got word on the radio. Your friend Kelly is dead. And your wife and son are on their way."

Derek's eyes go wide. His head snaps up. "You son of a bitch."

The old man smiles. "You will watch them die, Derek, slowly, if you don't tell us what we need to know. I can promise you that. I will chop your son's fingers from his little hands one by one and stuff them in your mouth. And while he screams, you and your wife can watch."

Chest thundering, Derek starts gasping for breath. He adjusts in his seat, but Brian clamps a heavy hand on his shoulder to hold him in place. Derek fixates on the image of his son's face contorted in pain and confusion, begging for his father to save him. Of Kim screaming in hysterics at the side of the room. He begins to shake, cold sweat breaking over his body.

He gives over the only thing he has left. "I'll talk. I'll tell you everything you want to know. Just let them go, Marshal. Turn them around and tell them to forget what happened. You can have whatever you want after that. Do whatever you want. Please."

A small tic of the lips jerks Marshal's head back. "Oh yes, you will beg, Derek. Before the end, you will beg. However, I'm going to deny your request." The old man stands up and starts making for the door. "You see, who's to say that you don't renege after I've let them go? You've already proven to be a liar. A snake. A false prophet. Your wife and your child will guarantee you speak the truth this time."

"Goddamn you, Marshal!"

Twisting, the old man's eyebrows furrow. "Damn God? My son, I think you should seriously contemplate repentance. Your end is near." He turns to Gil. "Keep him under guard, but lay off him. I want him awake and aware of everything that happens once his family arrives. We could use a few more bodies to help with breaking down the camp. Leave four here and bring the rest."

"Marshal! Marshal!" Derek is still screaming as the door closes.

Brian walks up next to him and delivers a haymaker

to the side of his face, knocking Derek from the chair to the floor. He lies there in a heap as they stand over him.

"We'll head down to help Marjorie get the armory situated," Gil says. "I want to be sure none of our equipment gets jacked up in transit. Dillon, Parker. You two stay here with Thomas and Bo. I want at least three of you in here at all times. If tough guy here even twitches the wrong way, you stomp a new mudhole in him, understand?"

Murmurs of acknowledgment are immediately followed by boots on the floorboards. Brian spits on him as he walks by. Derek is content to lie there for the moment. To absorb the pain and take stock of his injuries. Clear his head and gather his thoughts. The men left behind are alert immediately following the departure of their counterparts, but eventually, they all settle down on crates and camp chairs. The bottles of scotch start to circulate again.

Shoving down the panic and fear, Derek lets his operational mind take over and backward plan from the obvious need for escape. He starts by assessing the room. It's a storehouse of some kind, filled with crates and boxes. Stacks of lumber and hardware. Garden tools. Old furniture and cots are piled up to his right. To the left is a pallet with bags of fertilizer on it, stacked two rows high. Coiled-up spools of chain-link fencing are piled on top and around the pallet, while bundles of fence posts lean up against it.

He glances at the men. None of them are paying much attention. Derek makes his movements small and short, coming back to his fetal position again and again. To anyone passively looking, it would seem he was readjusting from the pain. The amount that he's in makes it believable, but part of pushing past that pain is bending it to his advantage. With each shift, Derek takes another look around the room.

One such glance between two columns of boxes reveals cinder block walls. Having only seen two such structures his entire time at the camp, and this one lacking copious amounts of firearms, Derek resolves that he's at the outbuildings. Having approximated his location, he next considers his timeline. It was daylight when Marshal came in. Working out the hours between when they got back to camp the night before and then balancing them against the number of hours needed for a round trip from Long Island, worst-case scenario, he has a very tight window to get out of here.

Derek turns his attention to the men. Already their banter is trailing off. He goes perfectly still, feigning sleep when any of them get up to check on him. It isn't long before their eyes begin to droop. Their heads begin to nod. Gingerly, he tests their attentiveness by tearing a piece of his shirt and wadding it into the space where his tooth used to be. No one notices.

It's what he's been hoping for. On top of being awake for the last twenty-four hours, the men had spent the previous week in the field. Compounding that exertion were the massive swings of adrenaline. These men had never been in a gunfight before. The surges brought on by the near-death experience took hours to work their way out of a person's system, and they hadn't let themselves come down for most of the night. Instead, they had stayed awake. Partying. Torturing. Drinking.

A pendulum moving in one direction comes back the same distance when it swings the opposite way. From the highest of highs to the lowest of lows. The men are bottoming out, crashing. Hard. Derek feels the exhaustion as well, but he has decades of conditioning just for this.

Then they string him back up by his feet.

Swaying, Derek silently curses himself. *I should have fought.* Yet at the same time, he knows that four on one in his state wouldn't be possible. Through the slits of his eyes, a glimmer of hope appears as Dillon and Parker leave the shed. Thomas and Bo sit back down, and it isn't long before they're both nodding off again.

Twenty minutes later, Thomas jolts awake. He looks at Derek and then stands up. He comes over and looks closely at Derek. Satisfied, he crosses back and lightly slaps Bo on the cheeks to wake him up.

The younger man points toward their captive. "I gotta take a shit. Won't be more than ten minutes. Stay awake."

"Hurry up, man. Supposed to be four of us in here," Bo mutters back.

"He's asleep or out cold and swinging upside down from the rafters. You'll be fine." Thomas leaves, and Bo's head dips even before the door is shut.

Derek smiles at their biggest mistake now compounding a series of smaller ones: they never put his hands behind his back.

With a burst of hope-inspired energy, he performs a series of sit-ups, each time working himself farther from the floor. He suppresses a groan and grits his teeth against the pain as his body cries out in protest. Reaching his boot, he shoves a finger inside the lip, searching for his hidden bobby pin. After a minute, the realization hits him. Gone. Taken.

Letting himself fall back, Derek feels his spark dwindling but pushes through the demoralizing setback. Adapt and overcome.

Derek stretches his arms down to the floor and extends his fingers. He is just able to touch the floorboards, but it's enough. Derek begins pushing himself from side to side. As he gains momentum, he starts shifting his body with each push, adding his weight to the swing. In short order, Derek manages to get himself close enough that he can shove off some boxes.

Derek swings in the opposite direction and comes back, each time shoving a little harder against the crates. Within reach is the pallet of fertilizer and fencing. So close now. Derek stretches his hands out for the pallet, inwardly wincing at the creak of the chain. But there's no other choice, and so he swings, praying that Bo keeps snoring.

His fingers scratch at the wood pallet. Derek swings back and gives a hefty shove off the crates, enough so that the boxes shift against one another. In his ears, the noise is as loud as a howitzer, but still his guard doesn't budge. Derek soars back across the room. He grabs hold of the pallet and strains against the pull of his reverse momentum, only to lose his grip and swing again. Silently cursing, Derek shoves back. This time, he catches the pallet and manages to hold on long enough to steady himself.

He throws a look at Bo. Dead to the world. Straining against the length of his tether, Derek tips a bundle of stakes toward himself. He catches the bundle with his free hand and lets go of the crate, cradling the stakes against his chest. As he swings back and forth, he makes as little movement as possible until the rope stills in the center of the room.

Placing the bundle on the floorboards just below his head, Derek works against the twist in the wire holding the stakes together, unraveling it and pulling the length free. He straightens one end of the freed wire and inserts it into the handcuffs, shifting it around until he finds the mechanism and lifts the lever. The left cuff clicks open. Derek repeats the process with the right cuff and then places them down quietly on the floor next to the stakes.

Again, he does a series of sit-ups, lifting his torso high enough that he can grab on to the chain and pull himself up the rest of the way. He eyes the padlock securing the chain wrapped around his ankles. He snaps his wire in half. Inserting the two pieces into the padlock, he works it around for a few moments before he feels the tumblers catch. A quick twist and pull and the lock snaps open.

He removes the padlock and hooks it into his mouth. Unraveling the chain from around his legs, he rights himself and slowly works his way down the length while clutching the slack to his chest. As his boots touch the floor, he crouches, placing the chain and padlock down without a sound.

Searching frantically, he skirts to the lumber for something he noticed earlier. Reaching into one from the collection of boxes, he pulls out a five-and-a-half-inch framing nail. He places the head between the first two knuckles of his right hand. Crouching low, he rotates on his heels and silently stalks forward.

Bo's head is tilted back as it leans against the crates stacked up behind him. Derek eyes the rifle clutched loosely in his hands, the pistol strapped against his leg. The man wears a Night Ranger bayonet on the left shoulder of his plate carrier, the Army's dick-measuring version of the traditional Marine Corps Ka-Bar knife.

Slapping his hand over the man's mouth, Derek punches the nail down, driving the full length through Bo's eye socket. The man begins to twitch and thrash. Letting go of the nail, Derek draws the bayonet free and slashes it across Bo's throat.

Once Bo is still, Derek pulls the rifle and vest free. He undoes the leg platform and attaches the rig to his own belt and thigh. Returning the knife to the sheath, Derek pulls on the plate carrier and then loops the single-point sling attached to the M4 over his shoulder.

He slips out of the door just as Thomas rounds the corner of the shack adjacent to him. The younger man jolts with surprise, the reaction costing him the valuable half second that he could have spent raising his weapon. He makes up for the error by diving back behind the hut just as Derek lets loose with a burst of three rounds from his newly acquired rifle.

With the camp likely alerted to his escape, he wastes no further time on stealth and fires the remainder of his magazine, raking his rifle from right to left, sending a hail of bullets through the shacks as he had on the first day of training. Except this time, he fires through the centers of the buildings versus aiming at the rooftops. With any luck, he will have killed one or two more of the bastards.

Bolt locking to the rear, smoke curling into the air, Derek drops the clip and spins. While he rushes into the woods, he winces at the pain in his leg as he slaps a new magazine home. Within moments, he fades into the tree line. His first objective is complete. Now comes phase two.

He has to save his family.

28

"What the hell was that?" Gil screams into his radio as reports from the gunfire echo through the hills. The rest of the security team, save for Brandon with his leg, charges after him as he barrels toward a pickup.

Thomas's voice crackles back over the net. "Derek got out! He's got Bo's rifle!"

"Damn it!" Gil screams as the truck races up the hill. When the road begins to level out, they see Dillon waving them down. The men leap from the flatbed and fan out as the pickup comes to a stop, weapons at the ready, while they form a perimeter and inspect the forest around them.

"How the fuck did he get away from you four?" Gil yells as he storms down the center lane between the shacks. Thomas, Parker, and Dillon can't meet his eyes.

"We strung him back up, Gil. We was gonna work in shifts. Two on, two off," Parker says.

"You were asleep?" Brian says, incredulous.

"Not all of us. Thomas and Bo were watching him."

Rounding on Thomas, Gil holds his arms out to the side.

"I only left for fifteen minutes, Gil, I swear. Twenty, tops. I had to take a shit."

"Idiots!" Gil screams. "Where's Bo?"

The men look down and away.

Gil walks over to the entrance of the storehouse and peers in, seeing the body lying in a pool of its own blood. "Get him out of there," he says flatly.

The three he had left on guard rush in to remove their fallen.

As they're carrying the body out, Brian comes over. "What now? Head after him?"

Gil spits. "Nah. As busted up as he might be, I don't want to go at him out there in the daylight. We've still got his wife and kid on the way. We'll make him come to us."

"Gil. Gil! What's going on up there?" Marshal says over the radio.

Keying back up, Gil replies, "The area's secure. We're coming back down with the matériel. I'll explain then." He turns a knob on his radio, cutting off any possible response. "Spread the word to switch to channel four, but do it quietly. We need to neutralize Bo's radio. Then let's grab the sacks and get back down there. We still need to get our transport vehicles to camp and the gear stowed before we can fully head out."

"The old man ain't gonna like that we didn't go after him," Brian replies.

"Let me worry about Marshal. You just get these assholes moving."

As the truck rolls back into the camp clearing, Marshal is waiting. "Well?"

Gil pulls him aside and explains the situation.

"What are you doing here, then?" Marshal explodes. "Get your team together and get out there! Now!"

"Boss. Don't you see what he did to us? We were already down two with Jimmy and Sebastian. Now he's killed two more. He took out Henry with a slingshot. A slingshot! Bo is up there with a nail driven into his brain. I've got six men left, and two of them are wounded. If I go out there in broad daylight with the other four, he's likely to kill more of us. Think of what's at stake here."

"What do you propose then, Gil?"

"I say we focus on our efforts here while Sarah makes her way back. We keep all our bodies, my team and the lookouts, pulling security while we load up. We'll use the trucks to shoot into town and pick up our vans. He's in no condition to go chasing after a four-by-four on foot. Then when his family gets here, we make him come to us."

Slowly, a grin spreads on Marshal's face. His gaze lingers a little longer. Marshal's stare is not at Gil but at something Gil, and probably no one else in camp, can see. The expression is unnerving, even to a man that has witnessed what Gil has.

"Yes. Yes, we will do just that. See to it, Gil. And be ready."

■   ■   ■   ■   ■

Derek drinks deeply from fresh puddles he finds scattered about. He can feel the water coursing through his system, a parched sponge soaking up whatever it can find. No doubt his headache is as much from dehydration as it is from the beating he took.

After rushing into the woods, he made a slow circle to the east to get a vantage on the comings and goings of any vehicles to see when his family arrives. His mind races as his battered body lags. He needs to formulate a plan, but with the odds so tilted, it's hard to come up with anything beyond a headlong charge, tantamount to suicide.

As an alternative, he focuses on the minor objectives that need to be accomplished. Vantage point. Reconnaissance. First aid. Rest, if possible, to assuage the injuries and exhaustion. As logical as the last is, knowing full well what lies ahead of him, Derek doubts that's possible. Not while his family is in danger.

It takes the better part of an hour to work his way through the woods and find a suitable position. Derek sets up on a small outcropping of flat rock atop a hill nestled in between the trails that lead to the vehicle clearing and the outbuildings. He gets into a prone position and raises his new rifle. Bo had affixed an ACOG sight to it. The magnification optic allows him to look down into the camp through a break in the tree line, just enough to see a good portion of the main clearing.

Activity is continuous, but he can tell that there are far fewer people in the camp than there were last night. Men from the security team and the lookouts stand with weapons at the ready while others pull bags of fertilizer from the bed of a pickup and stack them on the ground. More people move back and forth from the armory, lining up weapons and ammo near the sacks.

When the staging is complete, a few of the group load into the trucks and take off at speed toward the vehicle clearing. He observes through the scope, watching Gil bark orders into the radio. With nothing coming through on his end, he realizes that his battery is dead. He pulls the earpiece out of his ear.

As the work output dwindles to a lull, he focuses on his injuries, assessing the holes in his right leg, pleased to find that they are superficial. He picks out pieces of debris that are still embedded as best he can and staunches the minor bleeds with pressure and time. For his swollen left eye and sore ribs, there is little that can be done. He settles into the acceptance that he's going to hurt all over for the foreseeable future.

Morning turns to afternoon. He struggles with the pain racking his body, trying desperately to relax, until he settles into a mode of silent observation, the way snipers might lie in the field for days on end. Alert, yet relaxed. A plan starts to formulate. The group isn't paying much attention to the west. If he can skirt the river, he might be able to come up behind them . . .

His anxiety spikes as three vehicles make their way into the camp. The first two are large work vans, white and nondescript. Trailing them is one of the pickup trucks. The two vans pull in and then do three-point turns to reverse direction and face to the east, their rear doors stopping just short of the cache of weapons, ammo, and fertilizer. The truck pulls alongside them, the three vehicles now lined up in a neat row.

The members of Sanctuary who had left earlier in the pickups spill out of the vans. Derek's stomach sinks as the driver of the truck steps out of the vehicle. She's dressed in a white button-down and black suit pants, pistol and magazines on opposite hips.

Derek stares in shock, the realizations coming

to him. All along. All along she had maneuvered him. She hadn't been trying to stop Jimmy and Sebastian or witness Marshal in the act the night of the murders. She had been their lookout. Her prods at who he was working for. To whom they could relay information. It wasn't to safeguard the operation, it was to plug a leak. It was a game of chess with blindfolds on, and Sarah had kicked the shit out of him.

When Kim and Michael step out of the truck cab, his panic goes into overdrive. Kim clutches their son to her hip, her face one of absolute terror. The boy trembles while he clings to her.

He needs to move. He needs to act. *Think, goddamn it, think!*

. . . . .

Marshal approaches the clearing, pointing at the smoldering ashes of his cabin behind him. "Did you know about this? Did you let this happen?"

"Did I know about—" Sarah stops short. Her hands fly up and cover her mouth. "Oh no. Oh, Marshal. I'm so sorry."

"Did you know?" the old man shouts, red in the face.

Sarah regards him flatly. "Of course I didn't know. He said he would make a distraction. How could I possibly know that would mean burning down your cabin? Speaking of which, where is that bastard? Is he dead, or do we have him stowed somewhere?"

The old man just glares at her. Gil, standing nearby, spits on the ground before answering.

"We had him, but he managed to escape. He knows we got his wife and kid, though. He's out there somewhere."

Sarah turns and eyes Gil. "He . . . escaped?" She

sniffs and looks back at Marshal. "How surprising," she adds sarcastically.

"Listen, bitch, if you think—"

"Bitch? You're the idiot that's managed to bring an FBI informant in here not once but twice. Leland was your contact too, remember?"

Gil grits his teeth and flips her off. "You always gotta dig up old shit. If it weren't for me, we never would've known about the girl in Saranac. It was my crew that beat the code name out of her. Where would we be without that, huh?"

"Sure," Sarah replies, squinting, her lips compressing into a dismissive line. "Your boys did a hell of a job slapping around an unarmed, restrained, twentysomething year-old that was so scared out of her mind she would have told you who shot Kennedy if she knew. Big props, bro. Really. Bang-up job."

"I'm gonna—" Gil says as he takes a step toward her.

"You're gonna do what?" Sarah replies as she strides forward to cut him off, bringing them nose to nose. She points at him, the tip of her finger hovering just at the edge of his eye. "You got a code name. You think that was the end of it? No, asshole, I fixed this. Do you have access to FBI databases? Were you the one that located the confidential informant file? Did you link Derek's CI designator to Scarsboro?"

Gil quivers with anger, but he holds his tongue.

"I'm the undercover agent, remember? My credentials are what got me next to her handler. They're what put us in a position to salvage this thing, not your redneck goon squad." She looks him up and down, disdain obvious on her face. "I'm the one who's always cleaning up your mess."

"Enough! Both of you!" the old man shouts. He looks at Sarah. "It's done, then?"

She nods. "I plugged the hole downstate, but we still don't know how much communication Scarsboro had with the upper echelons. I'm not sure how much time we have before the Bureau looks at his caseload. Eventually, they'll reach out to Emily to bring her in, and when she doesn't respond, they'll start looking for her up here. We bought ourselves a couple of days. We need to move. Once we tie up the remaining loose ends, of course." She looks straight at Gil with the last statement.

When she looks back at the old man, his eyes are fixated on Derek's family. Veins bulge in his neck. Marshal looks at Gil.

"Make sure the men are ready, and get me the bullhorn out of the armory."

Gil throws a sideways glance at Sarah but then turns and jogs toward the arms room, waving Brian over to follow.

"What's the plan?" Sarah asks.

Marshal offers a creepy smile. Brian returns and hands Marshal the bullhorn. The old man nods over his shoulder.

"Take these two and throw them in Derek's cabin. Then grab one of the ATV gas cans and stand by. Wait until I give you the word."

Brian sneers and nods. He grabs Kim by her hair, the boy by the scruff of his neck. They scream as he drags them to the cabin. They're still screaming when he throws them inside.

The old man waits until Brian has retrieved the gas can. Marshal clicks on the power to the bullhorn and grabs the hand microphone attachment. The apparatus screeches with feedback.

Marshal looks at Gil as he returns to the clearing. "Be ready. I want no surprises when he comes out."

■   ■   ■   ■   ■

In the instant he realizes where Brian is taking his family, Derek is up and sprinting through the woods. His body screams in protest. His legs burn with lactic acid exertion, but his mind pushes it all back into a deep recess. There is a singular focus now. A sliver of a chance.

"Can you hear me, Derek?" Marshal's voice booms through the woods, amplified by a bullhorn. "Of course you can. We know you're still here. Sarah saw to that, didn't she?"

Derek runs, glad for the man's amplified voice that covers his approach.

"We have your family, Derek. Show yourself! Throw down your weapons and walk into camp, and I promise no harm will come to them. But if you don't, if you try to stop us, I will burn them alive! I swear it to you. You took my two most cherished possessions. It's only fitting that I take yours in the same manner!"

Marshal looks at the surrounding woods. Only insects and birdcalls greet him back. He keys up again. "Do you really think you can stop us, Derek? Do you really think you can stop the Lord's plans? This is only the beginning.

"Every autumn, Derek. With every harvest, we will give our ten percent. But we will not yield in treasure. No, we will give of our pain. Only a fraction, mind you, but it will be enough. Ten percent of a lifetime of pain. We will inflict it on these so-called righteous so that they too can feel our loss. Every year, we will remind this country of what it does to its citizens. They will know what it means to suffer. Their sorrow will not be the loss of a child to hunger or to the termination of the unborn. Nor the loss of a wife to preexisting conditions. No, Derek. Their loss will be that of destruction by the Lord's hand. A reign of His holy fire until they turn from their wicked ways!"

Seeing the burned-out remains of Marshal's cabin from his position in the tree line, Derek stops and mops his face free of sweat. Taking several deep breaths to steady himself, he pushes on. So close. He is so close.

Marshal waits again, long moments dragging by with no response. "Show yourself!" he screams into the bullhorn. "Don't think I won't do it, Derek. I will start the Lord's offering here and now! It will begin with your family unless you show yourself!"

Derek creeps within ten yards of the back of his cabin. Ducking behind a boulder, he props his rifle against it and pulls off his plate carrier. *A little bit more. Rant on just a little bit more, you sick bastard.*

29

Going to his stomach, Derek inches out from behind the boulder. He pulls himself along, the Beretta 9mm taken from Bo gripped in his right hand as the old man continues to shout. He slides under the cabin. Brian's feet are visible off to his right, the man standing in front of the steps. Derek moves farther to the left and gingerly tests the floorboards with the muzzle of his pistol. When one pushes upward, he props himself up as best he can and slowly lifts the boards out of place.

"We're ready, Derek. With or without you revealing yourself, we will unleash our tithe. First your family, then this country. How does it feel? How does it feel knowing that you've trained God's very own soldiers to wage holy war against this nation of sinners? How does it feel to turn your back on Him? You are the second coming of Judas! Judas!" Marshal screams.

Derek puts his head up through the makeshift trapdoor and looks out from under the bunk covering it. Kim and Michael sit with their backs to him on the next rack. His wife holds tightly on to his boy, gently rocking him and reciting, "It'll be okay," over and over.

"Psst," Derek whispers. When Kim doesn't turn around, he tries again louder. "Psst."

This time, his wife hears and looks over. Her face lights up, but Derek quickly holds a finger to his lips. When she nods, Derek mimics cupping his hands over his mouth and then points to Michael. Kim nods again and then covers their child's mouth. Derek waves them over, and Kim dutifully follows the commands. Michael tries to break free of her grip when he sees his father, but Derek reinforces the quiet with his finger again.

"I won't wait much longer!" Marshal bellows outside. "You have two minutes. Two minutes before your family burns. 'And when you go to war in your land against the adversary who oppresses you, then you shall sound an alarm with the trumpets, that you may be remembered before the Lord your God, and you shall be saved from your enemies.' Numbers, chapter ten, verse nine."

Derek helps them down through the opening in the floor. He points to the boulder beyond the cabin, then looks at his wife. Placing his mouth directly against her ear so he'll be heard over the bullhorn-enhanced ravings, Derek whispers, "When you get clear of the cabin, run toward that boulder and then keep going. Do you understand? No matter what happens. No matter what you hear, you keep running."

She nods in affirmation, a tear shaking loose and landing on his cheek.

"One minute, Derek!" Marshal bellows. He rants about Numbers.

Derek kisses Michael on the forehead and Kim on the lips. "You two are my everything. I love you. Now go!"

They shuffle to the edge of the cabin. Popping out and standing upright, they start to run. Marshal's voice continues to boom. Derek turns back around, watching Brian's boots. The man doesn't move.

"You coward! Only a true traitor would be so unworthy! Watch, then! Watch your family die in agony! Brian, burn them!"

Derek looks on as Brian bends down and picks up a gas can. There is the sloshing of gasoline, rivers of it raining down all over the stairs, and then he hears the flip of Brian's Zippo. Derek takes a deep breath and steadies his grip. Aligning front sight with rear, he pulls back on the trigger.

At this close of a range, the shot blows Brian's right leg apart. He crumples to his side, the gas can landing in front of him. Derek sees the red plastic looming through his sights. He remembers the boy he shot. The way he burned. Derek had acted in the defense of his brothers in arms and lived with the guilt of it every day since.

With Brian, there is no such consideration. He falls, and as he hits the ground, his eyes go wide as they come upon Derek.

Derek fires, the bullet punching through the plastic and slamming into Brian's right shoulder. The gasoline ignites, and the can explodes, a cloud of flame engulfing him. Derek scurries backward out from under the cabin.

Those on the clearing duck at the sound of the shots and then watch in horror as Brian bursts into flames. Gil stands beside Marshal, Gerry right next to him.

"Open fire on that cabin!" the old man yells.

Gerry unleashes a streaming torrent of hot lead from his belt-fed machine gun. The others join in, pouring hundreds of rounds into the cabin.

A screaming human torch, Brian tries to climb to his feet. The bullets instantly tear into him, and his body slumps forward against the cabin. In moments, the gasoline-soaked wooden steps catch fire. The flames rush up the doorjamb and begin to swallow the rest of the structure.

Bullets rip through the wooden walls and surrounding trees, showering Derek with debris as he low crawls back to the boulder. Leaves and shattered branches rain around and upon him. A ricochet bounces off the dirt and grazes his left buttock. Derek grits his teeth and groans against the pain as he pulls himself around the cover. He grabs his ass and looks, dismayed, at his red palm. Wiping the blood on his shirt, Derek puts the plate carrier back on. As he slams his pistol into his holster, rounds impact on the large rock, sending splinters of stone into the air. He clutches his rifle to his chest and throws the sling over his shoulder.

Gerry's ammo drum runs dry, smoke curling up from the muzzle. At the sudden stop of the continuous fire, Gil waves his hand in the air and shouts for a cease-fire among the rest of those still shooting. Little by little, the rifles fall silent as his command gets echoed across the camp.

"Where is he? Did you see him?" Marshal yells, his pistol empty. Next to him, Sarah drops a magazine and reloads her sidearm.

Gil reloads as well, answering, "I saw his muzzle flashes from under the cabin."

Next to him, Gerry drops to a knee and pulls his spare drum out of its pouch on his plate carrier. "Marjorie! Get me another ammo drum! Quick!"

The large woman nods and bustles her way into the armory.

Marshal leans close to Gil. "Flank him. Make sure he's dead. And his family. I don't want any loose ends."

Gil turns and sends out hand signals to the security team. Dillon and Parker nod and break into a trot, running behind the armory and circling around the perimeter to approach the cabin from the east. Gil wheels about, sending signals to the wounded Billy and Brandon to stay with the vehicles. He points to Thomas and directs him to head toward the blacksmith station and approach from the west. Gesturing to Hunter and Brady, he sends the two lookouts with the man from the security team. To the remaining lookouts, Gil signals for them to stand fast by the vehicles.

"The four of us advance. Base of fire on the cabin. Keep him pinned down while they move into position."

Sarah drops back. "Go. I've got to get my body armor and a rifle. I'll catch up."

She runs to the truck before Gil can raise an objection. Next to him, Gerry slaps the cover down on a freshly loaded belt.

"You ready?" Gil asks.

"Ready," the man answers. They start walking forward.

From behind the boulder, rage wells up inside of Derek, a cascade of internal fire, but this time there is no need to suppress it. No danger in what will happen

if he releases the anger. The realization channels his
fury the way a flamethrower does as it spits a column
of fire at the enemy.

They need to be stopped. They need to pay.

They all deserve to die.

He wheels to his right from behind the rock, heading east and coming out from behind a neighboring
cabin. He sees Gerry starting to walk forward. He
shoulders his rifle and aligns the ACOG in one smooth
motion, then fires three bursts into the clearing.

The bullets rake through Gerry's body, striking him
in the legs, groin, chest, and neck. He gushes blood as
he collapses. Gil and Marshal drop into a prone position next to their fallen comrade.

Off to Derek's left, the woods explode with rifle
fire. He drops behind a nearby tree and engages the
muzzle flashes of his new assailants, trading bullets
through the air. He sends bursts to his left and right
until his rifle runs empty, then quickly reloads.

Crawling over to Gerry, Gil frees the M249. He releases the bipod from under the handguard assem-
bly and sets up behind the machine gun. Aiming into
the space where the trail runs to the shoot house, Gil
pulls and holds down on the trigger, releasing an end-
less stream of death. He rakes the weapon back and
forth in the tight area.

The blistering fire explodes all around Derek, coming now from both the south and east. He turns and
sprints back toward the boulder, firing burst after
burst into the clearing as he moves. The snake of
machine-gun bullets follows at his heels and begins to
dance in front of him. Derek knows he can't outrun
it. He dives to the ground and rolls to his right, dipping down into the tiniest of gullies.

"He's pinned down!" Dillon screams into his radio. "Shift fire left, and we'll assault!"

The machine gun obliges. Derek hears the rounds impacting on the boulder, still ten yards to the west of his position. Bullets begin to kick up all around him, sending small splashes of water and mud into the air.

His assailants are close enough now that he can see them. Parker pops up to his right and fires while Dillon advances on his left. Timing their rushes, Derek sights his weapon opposite of their synchronization.

The next time Parker jumps up to lay down covering fire, Derek weathers the onslaught and watches for Dillon. As the man begins his rush, Derek locks on to him and squeezes off a three round burst. The bullets spin him around, and he sprays blood into the air like a lawn sprinkler.

In a fit of fury, Parker screams and charges forward, rifle raised and firing at the gully. Rounds split the trees apart. A flying section of bark scrapes across the right side of Derek's face, throwing him onto his back. Squinting through the pain, he sees Parker is closing in on him fast.

Derek raises his rifle and fires, but after one burst, the weapon runs dry. He throws the M4 across his chest and goes to his leg holster. As Parker barrels down on his position, Derek fires from his back with his pistol held between his legs. Two of the rounds hit the man in the left arm, separating it at the elbow, while a third slams into his stomach. Parker screams in agony as he stumbles forward and falls to the ground, landing close to Derek's position. Parker grabs at his severed limb, desperately trying to stay his blood loss with his other hand.

Another break in the machine-gun fire lets Derek

rush over to Parker. He puts a round through the top of the man's skull and then strips him of his remaining magazines. Stuffing them into the empty pouches on his plate carrier, Derek quickly reloads both weapons while scrambling back to the boulder. When gunshots don't instantly resume, he takes off to the west.

Through the trees, Gil sees the direction that Derek is running. He shifts his position and sights in on the gap between the burning cabin and the mess tent. Gil opens up again and works the machine gun from right to left. Derek sprints past the makeshift chow hall as the bullets tear through the fabric. The rounds kick up dirt and bounce off the trees just behind him. He can feel them getting closer as he charges through the brush. In the forest ahead, three silhouettes move toward him.

Marjorie comes out of the armory, an M249 slung across her back, holding an ammo drum in each hand. She throws one toward Gerry and then realizes that it's Gil behind the machine gun. Her eyes go wide. Marjorie drops the other drum as she sees the older man's body lying next to Gil in a puddle of blood. With a cry of rage, she spins her weapon around.

Holding it by the carrying handle in her left and the grip in her right, Marjorie presses the buttstock of the machine gun against her hip. She spies the direction Gil is shooting and screams again, mashing down on the trigger and raking her weapon from left to right, opposite of the other chain of fire. The rounds rip through the cabins to the right of the blacksmith's shed and continue on.

In the woods just beyond the perimeter, Thomas, Hunter, and Brady continue to circle to the west. They dart from tree to tree with their weapons at the low ready. Derek barrels toward them, pursued by the gunfire. Thomas ducks out from behind a tree and squeezes off bursts that send Derek diving to the ground.

Hunter steps out from behind his own tree and raises his rifle, smiling as he goes to squeeze the trigger. A whip of machine-gun fire cuts him in half. Thomas, Brady, and Derek alike cover themselves as the two streams of bullets intersect.

Thomas screams into his radio, "Cease fire! Cease fire! You just wasted Hunter!"

In the clearing, Gil lays off his trigger, only to hear the rapid report of chained fire continuing behind him. He rolls onto his side and waves at the woman. "Marjorie! Cease fire! Cease fire, goddamn it!"

She doesn't hear him, or chooses not to. She works the weapon through the shower stalls. The cisterns blow apart behind them. Her firing continues into the mess tent. She reaches the end and then rips the weapon back to the left, covering the same ground she'd just engaged.

"Cease fire!" Gil screams at her. "Cease—"

The woman's chest explodes as four rounds impact in quick succession. She flops backward, stumbling over the steps leading into the armory. Her corpse comes to rest just inside the doorway, where more bullets tear into her. When they finally stop, Gil turns and sees Marshal holding his .45 out at arm's length. The slide is locked to the rear, the barrel protruding and smoking. The two men lock eyes until Marshal turns away and starts to reload. Gil sights in and resumes firing into the tree line, but after five shots, he runs out of ammunition. He looks around and scrambles for the spare drum Marjorie had thrown toward Gerry.

Brady jumps to his knees, looking first at his dead friend and then toward their enemy. His skull explodes from a three-round burst. The lookout's body slumps over, settling awkwardly against a nearby tree.

Derek quickly lifts his head and drops it back down. When the machine gun doesn't resume, he jumps to his feet and dashes forward. Aligning his sight on the tree Thomas is huddled behind, Derek fires on the run. The bullets smack into the tree, keeping Thomas pinned. Just when Derek is about to get a clear shot, the rifle clicks empty.

Thomas jumps out from behind the tree. Derek doubles down and sprints for him, now only feet away. His hand reaches for his 9mm as Thomas fires a burst. One of the rounds rips across the outside of Derek's right bicep. The impact partially spins his body. Derek's momentum keeps him moving forward. With a final push, he leaps for Thomas.

The two crash into each other, a tangle of limbs and weapons rolling end over end. They separate, Thomas rising to his knees first. He drills Derek across the face with a haymaker that knocks him down to his hands and knees. Derek rips his bayonet from its scabbard with his right hand, inverts the blade, and drives it into the man's side.

Thomas gasps as Derek pulls the knife free, flips it again, and rams it upward, entering Thomas's head beneath his jaw, then driving the knife to its hilt, burying the entire blade. Thomas's eyes roll back, and he slumps to the ground, body spasming.

Ripping the knife free, Derek flops onto his back,

gasping for breath. For a moment, the air is completely still. Even the birds are silent. Derek winces in pain, lifting his arm up to inspect the wound. He rotates his bicep, taking note of the deep gash, then lets his arm fall limply next to him. He paws at the ground with his left hand and packs dirt into the wound, his teeth grinding with each successive application.

His arm addressed for the moment, he sheaths his knife and goes to reload his rifle. After slapping a magazine into the M4, he rolls over and starts searching Thomas for any spares. His hand freezes, and he can't help laughing.

Gil sits in the stillness, his weapon trained on the western wood line. The men at the vans reload their rifles during the pause in action. The security team leader keys into his mic.

"Thomas. Come back." Nothing. Silence. "Dillon. Parker. Sound off."

Again, the radio crackles with emptiness.

Marshal looks back at him. "What are you waiting for? Get in there and make sure he's dead this time!"

"They're all dead, Marshal. They're gone. We don't pull back now, we won't have anyone left."

"I don't give a damn! You're all sheep! I am your shepherd, and I want that bastard dead!"

Staring at Marshal, Gil has had enough. "This ain't about your fucking clock. We all got debts to settle. I'm gonna make sure I live long enough to see mine through. You do what you want." He turns back to the vans, absently noting that the truck is no longer parked alongside them. Gil yells to the men there, "Get the vans loaded and get inside! Everyone else keep a sharp lookout. We're leaving! Now!"

Derek hears the engines turn over. He stumbles to

his feet. Light-headed and dizzy, he drops back down after a few steps, fighting against his clouding vision. He pushes himself up with his left arm, his right hanging loosely by his side.

Staggering toward the cluster of cabins in front of him, he makes his way between two of them. On the opposite side of the clearing, the remaining men scramble to get weapons loaded into the vehicles. Derek pops out from between the structures. He eyes the stack of fertilizer and ammunition boxes.

Gil freezes halfway to the vans. He raises his M249. Derek raises Thomas's grenade launcher.

A stark *thoomp* sounds out, followed immediately by a massive explosion. A miniature mushroom cloud erupts, throwing vehicles and bodies through the air, the concussion of the blast leveling everything in its path. The weathered camp structures fold over like houses of cards. Trees nearest to the blast uproot and topple. The mess tent pulls free of its tethers and flies away like a lost kite. The flames on the burning cabin extinguish.

The wave flings Gil and Marshal across the clearing. It slams into Derek, a typhoon of power barreling him backward. Timber, debris, and body parts begin to rain down across the camp.

In the aftermath, there isn't just stillness. There is absolute silence.

Derek opens his eyes to a landscape covered in the gray smoke and ash of the explosion now settled down upon the camp, obscuring everything. He hacks and coughs it out of his lungs. The dust turns the blood seeping out of a score of his wounds into a black paste.

His ears ring. All sound is reduced to that of a far-off echo. Getting to his feet, Derek stumbles forward unsteadily, cradling his right arm with his left. Distant sounds of cracking tree limbs perforate the void. Somewhere off to his left, a thunderous crash occurs as a tree falls to the earth.

All that is left of the cabins is torn and jumbled together, the structures having collapsed on themselves. As Derek nears the clearing, he notices flickers of dulled orange light. Dozens of small fires burn in every direction.

He slumps against a tree, one of the few ancient monoliths still standing after the blast. Across from him, he can see the massive crater that the explosion carved out.

Slowly, the buzz in his head recedes. He searches about for his rifle and quickly finds that both it and the grenade launcher were ripped away in the blast. He feels for his pistol and is relieved to find it still locked in his holster. Pushing through the pain, he draws the weapon with his right hand and then transfers the gun to his left. A low groan up ahead catches his attention. He picks himself up off the tree and moves forward into the ghostly terrain.

It's eerie, like the setting of a horror movie. The protagonist walking through a foggy graveyard on Halloween. The sounds of zombies rising from their graves. Except the person groaning isn't a zombie. Derek stops a few feet away and watches as Gil slowly pulls himself along the ground.

"Get up," Derek says.

Gil's head turns toward the sound.

"I said get up!" Derek shouts.

This time, Gil pays attention. He rolls over onto his back, propping himself up on his right elbow. He bleeds from his gut, and his left arm is contorted in multiple directions. He smiles at Derek, blood seeping out of his mouth to streak through the dusty hair on his chin. "Hey there, D." Gil laughs a little.

Derek cranks the hammer back on his Beretta.

Gil holds up his right hand in a halting motion and leaves it in the air as he works himself up to his feet. "All right now, D. Just hang on a second." Gil coughs and spits out more blood. "Why don't you put the gun down and fight like a man." He reaches down to his leg and pulls a tactical Bowie knife from its sheath, then holds the blade out in front of him. A pained smirk returns. "Come on. You're such a badass Marine, you don't need the gun. Edged-weapon instructor, right? Come on, bitch, show me what—"

Derek shoots Gil three times in the chest. The knife topples out of Gil's hand as he falls onto his back. His eyes are wide. His mouth works open and closed. He stares at Derek.

"This ain't the movies, you son of a bitch." Derek stands over Gil and puts a round through his forehead.

Another shot rings out. It snaps as it sails just over his head. Derek dives to the ground as a second shot cracks off. Grabbing Gil's body, he rolls to his right and pulls the corpse up as a shield. Two more shots go off, and then all falls still again.

Derek can hear cursing off to his left. He lets Gil's body sag back down and stands up, walking in the direction of the muttering voice. Marshal's shape materializes out of the smoke. The old man is slumped over on his side, his legs lifeless. He leans on his right elbow, his hands desperately working to get another magazine into his pistol. Derek shoots him in the elbow joint, leveling Marshal to the ground and knocking the weapon free.

Marshal groans through his teeth. "You piece of shit. You fucking traitor. You'll burn in hell for this."

Stopping before the man, Derek shakes his head. "No, old man. Not for this. Maybe some other things. But this? Nah."

"You've stopped nothing, you know. We're everywhere. My death will only spur our cause further. The Lord's work will be done."

Derek spits. "Marshal, if God thought you were so righteous, why'd he let someone like me take you down? Makes you think."

The old man's mouth opens to deliver an answer.

Derek empties his gun into Marshal.

Off in the distance, he hears sirens. He ambles to the north, calling out, "Kim! Michael!"

All around him, the ash continues to fall, gray snowflakes on a dreary Christmas morning. Passing by the remnants of what used to be his cabin, now nothing more than a smoldering heap of burned timber, he continues to call out. He has to lean against the boulder that provided him cover just minutes earlier, resting from the fatigue and battering he'd sustained throughout the last few days. He yells again before walking on. The next time he stops, he thinks he hears the crackling of brush underfoot.

"Kim?"

Like something out of a dream, their silhouettes materialize through the smoke. Michael is by her side, but breaks from it the moment he sees him.

"Daddy!" the boy cries out.

Sinking to his knees, Derek embraces his son with

his good arm, wincing at the pain of his child's tight embrace, reveling in it at the same time. He breaks down, crying uncontrollably as his boy does the same.

Kim is there a moment later, also crying, falling to her knees as she throws her arms around them both.

"You're okay," Derek says. "Thank God you're okay."

"Are you?" Kim replies between sobs. "You're hurt. My God, Derek, you're shot!"

"I'm all right. You hear that?" He pauses to let the sound of the ever-approaching sirens draw nearer. "They'll be here soon. We're safe now."

Derek reaches up a hand and caresses her cheek. She takes his hand in both of hers and kisses it gently. Derek pulls her face toward his, and their lips find each other.

As they break apart, Kim nuzzles her nose into his neck the way she used to in their tender moments. Derek holds his family as tightly as his broken body will allow.

EPILOGUE

Jason and Rob leave the executive-level conference room and close the polished wood doors behind them. Neither says a word to each other. Instead, they make for the small museum at the entrance to the floor. There, among the displays of past Bureau achievement and innovation, they finally stop and let out overly long-held breaths.

Rob reaches up and pulls his collar open, loosening his tie. Jason takes his jacket and tie off altogether. Deep pockets of sweat radiate out from under his arms. He uncuffs his sleeves and begins rolling them up to the elbows.

"Jesus. If we get any more brass jumping down our throats, we'll be shitting shell casings."

Rob gives him a flat, perturbed stare.

"What?" Jason says. "You don't agree?"

"Of course I do, man. It's just that I'm trying to figure a way out of this mess."

Jason shakes his head. "That ship has sailed, bro. A long time ago. Like months ago. We screwed up. Big-time. The only way we're getting out of this mess is by dusting off our résumés. I wouldn't be surprised if I'm selling insurance by the end of the month. Your ass will probably be in an armored car, doing ATM drops."

Rob pulls his cell phone out of his jacket pocket and then takes the coat off, slinging it over one arm while he thumbs open the device. "Nah, man. I can't have that. This is where I want to be. Where I need to be."

"Shit, so do I. That doesn't change the fact that the op turned into a clusterfuck and we were at the head of it. This whole 'administrative leave' nonsense is probably just protocol while they get the lawyers in a row. Those suits already have their minds made up. Guaranteed."

Rob doesn't respond. Instead, he opens an email.

Subject: Almost done?

Hey, you guys have an idea of when you'll be back down here? I've fed him and poured him all the coffee he's gonna drink. The guy's getting really antsy, and I'm running out of excuses.

He looks up at his partner.

Jason cocks his head. "I know that look. What are you up to?"

"Hail Mary time," Rob says as he turns and heads for the elevator. "Come on. Let's discuss it on the way down."

. . . . .

Derek sits in a tight gray room. The walls are gray. The carpet. The cushions on the chairs that surround the small conference table. Even the day outside the windows. A bleak, gray, rainy New York City day.

Once the state and local police had made it to the camp, Derek, Kim, and Michael were rushed to Massena Hospital. Kim and Michael were checked and cleared, but Derek was admitted for treatment to his various wounds and to be kept under observation. It was during that time that Derek exercised his right to remain silent, save for speaking with Special Agent Kelly Scarsboro. The next day, the Special Agent in Charge of the FBI's New York field office organized crime unit arrived with two other agents in tow and confirmed the news to him. Shortly thereafter, Derek was discharged, and they were all flown by helicopter to New York City.

Now, sitting in this room, he drums the fingers of his left hand on the tabletop next to an empty Styrofoam cup of coffee. An agent popped in to ask if he needed it refreshed every ten minutes or so. He stopped coming by as often after Derek's last response. Sitting back in his chair sends jolts of pain through his body.

Derek tries to readjust the sling cradling his right arm for the hundredth time. The hospital polo they gave him is two sizes too big, and it keeps bunching up around the straps of the apparatus.

The door opens, and the two agents that accompanied him from upstate walk back in. Rob looks like he's just seen a ghost, and Jason, looks like he was on an all-night bender and is just now straggling back home to face the wife.

He sized them up three minutes after meeting them and knows their type all too well. Former frontline guys that are living the good life now, but still trying to keep a toe in the water. A job that lets them tear up terrorism in the name of Uncle Sam while still getting to have barbecues with the neighbors every weekend. They don't look too happy with their chosen profession at the moment.

Welcome to the club. Derek isn't too happy either. "You said it would be twenty minutes. It's been three hours," he says.

Rob pulls one of the chairs out and sits, draping his jacket over the arm. Jason tosses his over the back of another and then leans against the wall. The man stuffs his hands in his pockets.

"Yeah, sorry about that," Rob replies. "We were held up with the command element. You know how it is."

"Sounds like a personal problem. Where's my family? Why the hell couldn't they stay with me?"

Jason perks up a bit. "Oh, I made a call and checked on them while we were coming back down. They're fine. They're at the day care in the lobby. Michael was coloring."

It isn't lost on Derek that Jason doesn't answer his second question. Long moments drag by. "All right. Is someone going to tell me what's going on?"

Jason laughs. "Sure. Why not?" The man shrugs. "What would you like to know?"

"Maybe start with how in the hell the ATF missed this?"

Rob shakes his head. "I think we all know that we didn't 'miss' anything. We were actively working this group."

"You mean the ATF was."

Jason puts a hand behind his neck and stretches it to one side. He doesn't even open his eyes while replying, "That's just it, Chief. Sarah isn't ATF. She's been FBI the whole time."

The revelation gives Derek pause, but only for a moment. After everything else that transpired, he isn't surprised that more of the story ended up being false. "What about the gun-running operation? The source point from Fort Drum? That all a lie too?"

Rob shakes his head while his lips compress. "We're looking into those leads, of course, but from our preliminary findings, there's nothing to support either of them. No caches. No sign of this ledger you mentioned."

Derek is incredulous, and another point clicks.

He looks back and forth between them and then sniffs. "Okay, let me rephrase. How did you miss that your FBI undercover who was actively working this group was actually a double agent?"

Each of them grimaces.

Rob answers first. "As far as we can tell, she wasn't one."

"You'll excuse me if I call bullshit on that."

Jason gets up off the wall. "No, really. Not from the outset anyway. There's nothing in her background that indicates any ties to the group or the individuals prior to making contact with them through this case. Other than the fact that she's originally from Rochester, it's clean. She didn't infiltrate the Bureau."

"Her real name is Hanna Kittle," Rob chimes in. "Soccer and track star in high school. Dual majors in accounting and IT at Syracuse. Then 9/11 happens. She joins the Air Force through an accelerated commissioning program and ends up as a Special Investigations Officer. While she's deployed, she gets her master's in criminal psychology with a concentration in behavioral analytics. After she gets out, the Bureau recruiters scoop her right up."

"She's the perfect poster girl," Jason adds, walking over and sitting down. "Young. Pretty. Already accomplished. Seasoned veteran in the field. Degrees in the right areas. Practically everything the FBI could want in the war against terror. Almost immediately out of the academy, she goes into undercover work."

Rob picks up. "She takes down some cells from here and there. Small things. Assholes that are all about jihad videos on YouTube but haven't actually got a clue. But she shows an aptitude for it. A knack for the skill set. With each victory comes higher-level training. More skill sets. Bigger assignments. Before long, Hanna is the rising star in the Bureau's undercover counterterrorism initiatives."

"So, what then?" Derek says. "You're thinking Patty Hearst?"

They nod.

"Somewhere along the line, she went rogue." Jason shrugs. "Kept up communications just enough to string the Bureau along, but all the while, she was working for them."

"I mean, you said it yourself in your statement," Rob says, reaching out over the table. "This guy Marshal. You said he was running a cult. That he had convinced people to live in the woods and wipe their asses with leaves and shit like that."

"You just said she was a trained counterterrorism agent. That she studied the criminal mind. Doesn't that blow your brainwashing theory to pieces?" Derek points out.

Jason looks down at the table, shaking his head. "Maybe, but it's what we've got for now. Marshal was the charismatic leader, but Hanna . . . Hanna was the linchpin for everything else. Her government clearances and undercover contacts were the perfect conduit to facilitate the group. If it hadn't been for you, they probably would have succeeded in what they were planning."

"Which of course we're grateful for, Chief," Rob says, "but unfortunately, there's still the larger problem at hand."

"You mean what she was originally sent in to investigate. The funds and matériel."

Rob nods. "She was supposed to discover who was funneling all this shit to them. That's the bigger fish. Lost in this mess is the fact that we may never know who that entity is, and that's a big hole to have. Hanna might have been able to facilitate, but in no way was she in a position to doctor shipping manifests and redirect funding. That takes senior-level clearances."

"How senior?"

Rob shrugs. "Top tier of the government."

"Incredible," Derek says with resignation. The point isn't lost on him. Intel school had taught him the same things that it had taught Sarah. The best lies were the ones based in truth. By shrouding the reality of the group's ploy in the weapons initiative, she had come across as genuine and established credibility. All the while, she had been maneuvering him to reveal his true purpose. Not to mention providing false leads that would throw him off the group's scent.

The surprise is how ineffective he had been picking up on it.

Another long pause.

Jason lets out an exasperated groan. "Man, this

ain't good. Hey, Derek, let me ask you something. You said that when you saw her pull up with your wife and kid that she was driving a pickup truck. Not a Town Car, right?"

"Yeah. Why?"

The agents share a glance. Rob's voice is grave. "We found a Bureau vehicle in the town just outside of camp. And there's no pickup among the wreckage from the blast."

Derek's heart begins to race. "How can that be? I saw her. Sarah . . . Hanna, whoever you say she is. She was out on the clearing. Right at the start of the firefight."

They both shake their heads. "No truck. No sign of her body either," Jason confirms.

"Then there's the matter of the hard drive," Rob adds.

Derek leans forward, putting his left elbow on the table and rubbing his eyes. "Fellas. It's been a pretty rough couple of days. An even worse month. Want to just cut to the chase? What is it you're trying to tell me here? What hard drive?"

Jason says, "A site exploitation team found the safe you said was in Marshal's cabin. Inside was an external hard drive. Our tech boys cracked it pretty easily. The only thing on it was a manifesto written by the old man. The operation they were planning looked like it was targeting Albany. We think they were going to deliver the message after their first attack. It was supposed to be a Mumbai plus Oklahoma City. Multiple teams in the different government center buildings shooting them up at the same time."

"And when the first responders and mass-casualty collection points were all established after the chaos, detonate vans laden with explosives right in the middle of it all," Rob says.

Derek swallows. "Jesus."

"They call themselves Autumn's Tithe. Marshal planned on having these operations recur every fall. Alluded to other cells in his writings. Other sites across the country. Other preparations already under way." Jason lets the last statement linger.

When Derek doesn't respond, Rob steps in. "So, there's a senior-level government connection. There are multiple sites preparing similar attacks. And their key facilitator is still out there."

"Yeah, I'd say that's a big problem, all right," Derek says, sitting back in his chair.

The men continue to watch him. Their eyes take on a hint of something. Through his exhaustion, he doesn't pick up on it at first, but then it snaps into place. Pleading.

"Don't even try, because it ain't happening," Derek says.

"Chief, hear us out for a minute."

Derek jumps out of his seat, swearing at the pain. "No way in hell." He points at both of them. "I just got out of the hornet's nest, and you want me to go back in? Pound sand, you assholes. Where are my wife and kid? I want out of this shit show."

"Will you just sit down for a minute. Please?" Rob says. When Derek doesn't move, Rob just goes on. "No one is asking you to do what you did up there again, but you can't deny how uniquely qualified you are for this. These cells are going to be in the most remote wilderness this country has. The manifesto is clear on that. Some Bible shit about Matthew, chapter four. Who better to track them down than a special ops counterintelligence Warrant Officer who happens to be a wilderness survival instructor?"

"Anybody else. That's who. I couldn't even infiltrate if I wanted to, which you can be certain I don't. I told you most of the camp had emptied out by the time I escaped. Who's to say those people aren't in the next location? I'd get made right away."

Jason folds his hands on top of the table. "We're not talking about infiltration, Chief. At least not in the sense you mean. We're talking about hunting. Track them down. Find their camps and do some reconnaissance. You hit your GPS. Brief the choppers on the way in. HRT does the rest."

"You'll have the full support of the Bureau. Satellite coverage. Drones. You'd be the tip of the spear for us."

Rob smiles.

Jason smiles.

"Yeah. Eat shit." Derek moves for the door.

The agents pop to their feet. "Hold on a second. It's not that simple. We didn't want it to come to this, but you're not making it any easier," Jason says.

He stops and eyes them. "The hell are you talking about?"

Jason bars the path to the door. "You wanted to know why you couldn't see your family. Why would we let a suspect near a woman and her child?"

Derek flushes in anger. "Did you just say *suspect*?"

"Let's face it," Rob says. "There are a number of dead in this thing, including two federal agents."

"Don't you lay that at my feet! Kelly was my friend. This was all because of your turncoat, and you know it!"

"Hold on a second," Jason interrupts. "Let's make

something clear. Kelly is dead because he decided to slap together some half-assed parallel op. He played it fast and loose by sending in a nobody and a junior agent that had zero business being there in the first place. That's why we pulled her body out of a ditch. He put his career ahead of her and you, so forgive me if I don't buy the martyr routine. If he was really your friend, he wouldn't have put you in this position to begin with."

"I see. Shift the Bureau's blame to the dead guy and me, the unsanctioned participant, is that it? You've got some pair."

"Relax. Both of you." Rob shakes his head. "We're not trying to drop this on you, but look at the facts. You're the sole survivor of a botched counterterrorism op that killed a lot of people. You think there wouldn't be repercussions?"

"You were specifically training their team to be more proficient killers," Jason adds. "How could we not treat you as a suspect?"

"Yeah, and I also killed every last one of them. I think that puts me on the right side of things."

"So you say," Rob replies.

Derek glares, but then he suddenly gets it. "Sarah was your undercover, wasn't she? This was your operation. You two screwed the pooch, and now you're trying to get me to pull you out of the graves you dug for yourselves. Nah, fellas. I'm done. I'm out." He goes to leave.

Rob holds a hand up in front of him. "You're implicated in a terrorist plot against the United States. You're in the middle of a custody battle. There's a restraining order against you. Your ex and son got kidnapped by the same group you were allegedly informing on. You really think you're gonna just go downstairs and the three of you drive back to your lives on Long Island? That you're gonna scoop that money out of the safe-deposit box upstate and be good to go? That shit is gone, bro. It never belonged to you in the first place. That's government money."

"It didn't end well for the last guys that tried to use my family against me," Derek growls.

"And now we'll add threatening a federal agent to the list," Jason glibly remarks.

Derek shifts his attention and balls his left hand into a fist. The veins in his neck bulge out. "Are you gonna get out of my way? Because I'm about to add assaulting an agent to the list."

"All right, everyone," Rob says. "Deep breath, okay? Let's take it down a notch."

Derek makes his way to the windows and looks out. Jason and Rob exchange a glance, the former raising his eyebrows. Rob shakes his head at him and then walks back to the table.

"All we're saying is this isn't cut-and-dry, Derek. Of course, we don't think you're involved, but in light of having an agent go rogue on us, can you really blame the Bureau for wanting to take a closer look at you?"

When Derek doesn't respond, Rob continues, "Now, we can help with this shit. I mean really. You cooperate and we'll see to it that any inquiry into you is wiped clean like that." He snaps his fingers. "Those assault charges from your kid's game. We can help there too."

"That's right," Jason chimes in. "You know how many former agents are now high-priced lawyers on the outside? Hell, some are even judges. All it would take is a phone call, and we can get that all ironed out."

Derek picks his head up and turns around. "If I go to work for you."

Rob spreads his hands out before him. "It's that or you can face the full weight of the federal government while never getting to see your kid again."

"Also, while your dad rots away in a forgotten wing of a VA hospital, since you won't be able to keep paying for his care at the place he's in now," Jason adds.

Derek dips and shakes his head. "Vultures," he mutters under his breath. For long moments, the only sound in the room is rain drumming against the glass.

Rob lets the moment linger on until he speaks, softly but firmly. "Derek."

When Derek doesn't respond, the agent waits a moment, then repeats himself. This time, Derek slowly lifts his head.

"We could help with protecting them too," Rob says.

"Go on."

"Like it or not, Kim is in this thing now. So is your boy. We know it's not your fault, but it's the truth. If they came for them once, they'll definitely come for them again given the chance. We could relocate them for you. Witness protection program. Put you nearby so that you can keep an eye on them."

Derek sniffs, shaking his head. "Clearly, you've never had an extended conversation with my wife. If you think she'll let me anywhere near Michael after this, you're dumber than you look."

"Actually, we just did," Rob says. "She's not exactly happy about it, but she trusts you far more than she trusts us. We think she'd go along with it if it comes from you."

"Yeah. I don't believe it."

Jason picks up where his partner left off. "You forget, big guy. You saved them. If it weren't for you, they'd be goners right now. That's got to count for something in her eyes."

"If it weren't for me, they would have never been taken in the first place."

"Be that as it may," Rob says, jumping back in, "she understands the gravity of the situation she's in. She's a smart lady. She realizes she's better off with the FBI than without us. In short, she's already briefed on the plan, Derek. Say yes and we'll get you all to safety by this afternoon."

The raindrops against the plate glass burst like so many thoughts riffling through his mind. Through the multitude, Derek can see a path forming. A break in the weather, as it were. It may not be much, but it's more than he has now. The glimmer of hope for sunny skies ahead is enough to make him take that first step.

"I'll need other concessions to make this happen."

Rob does his best to suppress the tic of a smile at the corner of his mouth. Derek wishes he could play poker with Jason.

"Let's hear them," Rob says.

"I want a house in a good neighborhood. With good schools. Somewhere out in the middle of nowhere, where they won't look for them. Nebraska or Idaho or wherever. I want my boy to have a normal life. Whatever happens between my wife and me, that much has to happen."

"What else?"

Derek walks back to his side of the table. "I need to be nearby. Dad comes too, obviously, but we can't put him in a home. That would be too easy to track down. So, wherever I end up, he needs to be there as well. That includes round-the-clock healthcare support for him."

Jason walks over to the chair that his jacket is on. He takes out a pad and starts writing.

Derek waits for him to look up.

The man waves at him with his pen. "Keep going."

"I want a team sitting on their house at all times. No agents. Your Bureau is compromised. Contractors. Former operators. Retirees, maybe. Get a husband and wife if you want. Call them her parents and put them across the street from Kim. Anytime I'm in the field and unable to look in on my family, they're attached at the hip."

"That might take some doing," Rob admits.

"Then we're done here."

"Geez, no need to get so dramatic," Jason says as he scribbles. "Anything else?"

Derek sighs. "This is all predicated on my talking to Kim first and hearing it from her that she's okay with all of it. I won't force her into anything. Beyond that, I don't make a move until I know they're protected. And you'll forgive me if I want everything we've discussed in writing and signed off on by the director."

Jason finishes writing. "I got it all."

Rob claps his hands together. "So . . . we've got a deal, then?"

Derek sighs. "Yeah, as long as you come through on your end. We got a deal."

Rob plants himself in front of Derek and extends his hand.

"Welcome to the FBI."

ACKNOWLEDGMENTS

A friend in the know once told me, "It takes a village to raise a writer." She could not have been more correct. The journey for this particular novel started in 2018, and since then there have been countless individuals that have helped, supported, and encouraged me along the way. I've done my absolute best to keep track of all of them across the years, but here is my blanket acknowledgment (and apology) if you contributed and I failed to mention you by name. Please know that your efforts were appreciated, and that my memory just isn't what it used to be.

First and foremost, I owe a tremendous amount of gratitude to my agent, Barbara Poelle. From the outset she saw what this book could be and challenged me to unlock its full potential. I will always be grateful for her taking a chance on me. Beyond that, I am so thankful for her steadfast efforts on my behalf, her friendship, and the doubled-over laughing fits I get from her brilliant hilarity.

While we're on the subject, a huge thank-you to my fellow Poelleans, Nick Petrie, Don Bentley, and

Bill Schweigart who immediately took me under their wing and have been providing expert guidance, mentoring, and friendship ever since. Their work paved the way for this fledgling, first-time thriller writer, and I am grateful for their example.

Many thanks go to my editor, Robert Davis, who continually worked with me to refine and enhance *The Instructor* to become that which it is today. I couldn't have done it without his efforts, and all the efforts of the team behind the curtain at Forge, Tor Publishing Group, and Macmillan. In particular I'd like to thank Julia Bergen, Ashley Spruill, Jeff LaSala, Sara Ensey, Heather Saunders, Peter Lutjen, Rafal Gibek, Katy Robitzski, and Jacqueline Huber-Rodriguez. I'd also like to recognize Colin Anderson for his stunning cover art. He took the vision I had in my head, made it a reality, and enhanced it beyond belief.

A debt of gratitude goes to the absolute titans of the thriller genre who provided their blurbs for my novel. I was, and remain, stunned that such excellent authors could offer such praise for my own work, and I will be forever grateful for their sentiments about *The Instructor*.

A special shout-out goes to Rob K12 for the bullshit session we held one day in 2018 that helped spark the idea that would eventually become this novel. On top of that, Rob provided subject-matter expertise and guidance on much of the wilderness survival techniques employed by Derek, adding the authenticity I so desperately craved to the text. Rob's enthusiasm has never wavered throughout the entire evolution of the book, and I am grateful for his continued friendship.

It takes no smaller than a platoon-size element to

develop a story line that isn't fractured, unrealistic, and, quite frankly, boring to the point of tears. In that regard, no amount of thanks can be spared for the beta readers I had on this novel. In no particular order, thank you to Sarah Ewald, Michael Alliksen, Christopher Smith, Kevin Warmhold, Ray Lopez, Bob (Rob K12's father), author Alexia (A.C.) Anderson, author E. H. Knight, and Erik Hendrickson.

Special recognition for beta reading goes to: Megan Hallquest, the princess of the Post-It notes; Kim Kaye, the ever-encouraging, country-song-singing, pixie ninja survivor that everyone needs in their life; Manny Mosquera, the most well-read man I know in the thriller genre; and last but certainly not least, Stacy Mallia. Stacy was attracted to this manuscript like a magnet, and she helped me peel back the depths of these characters like the layers of an onion. Thank you Stacy for everything you contributed to this project.

The religious aspect of *The Instructor* is meant as an example of what depravity and lengths a person can go to in the name of faith-based zealotry, regardless of which doctrine they follow. In this regard, Catholicism and the King James Bible were merely the vehicle for this point. I apologize if the way in which the religious text was utilized offends anyone. I remain grateful to God for all that He has given to me, especially the second chance at life to see this goal and dream come to fruition.

The FBI takes it on the chin in this novel, but I am in constant awe and admiration for the work of not only their agency, but all of the federal agencies, as well as that of law enforcement and military personnel across the country and the globe, for standing on the front lines to keep this nation safe. Though it may feel at times that they are unrecognized, please know that your efforts are truly appreciated.

To my fellow veterans. The segments of PTSD that Derek experiences are largely based on my own symptoms and episodes that have persisted all these years, nearly two decades now since I was first commissioned. In that time I have dealt with the tremendous peaks and valleys that come with wrestling those demons. What I will say to you is this. If you are suffering, you are not alone. There are resources and people who have dedicated their lives to helping you cope. Please, I implore you to seek out that help. Do not suffer needlessly for years as I did. You're allowed to find balance. You're allowed to be happy. Keep going. Never give up.

Fittingly, to my family, who has never wavered in their support through my tumultuous episodes, thank you. Your love and loyalty has kept me going all this time. I'm sorry for all that I have put you through in the past, and I'm grateful that you have always been there for me. I love you and thank you all.

If you were to ask, I would tell you that I have had three dreams in my life. To be an Army officer. To be a published author. But far surpassing those, my dream was always to be a father. In that, I can never be thankful enough for the gift Mary-Jo has given me. Thank you for our beautiful girls, and for making me a dad. There is no greater gift that I can ever receive.

And finally, to those amazing, beautiful girls that I am proud and fortunate to call my daughters. Michaela and Charlotte, my KK and Charlie, please always know that my sun rises and sets with you both. I am constantly amazed at all that you do, and who you are growing up to become.

Whenever you are down. Whenever you are doubting yourselves. Whenever you're not sure if you will be able to reach the goals you set, I want you to pull this book down off the shelf, and flip to this page. Let this serve as proof that your dreams can become reality. If you put in the work, if you remain diligent, if you believe in yourselves, you can achieve whatever it is that you set your mind to. I know you both have it in you to become whatever you desire. To accomplish whatever it is that you hope to achieve. I will always be behind you, every step of the way, on both your journeys. I will always believe in you. I will always love you.